The Quest of
Wyndracer
and Fyrehunter

Book 1

DAVID BERGER

The Quest of Wyndracer and Fyrehunter / Written by Da-
vid Berger, Land O Lakes, FL 34638
Summary: Two young boys are charged with stopping a
war of the gods.
ISBN-13: 978-0-578-32867-6 (custom universal)
Printed in the United States of America. Layout by David
Berger. Cover art by Roger Creus Dorico.

DEDICATION

Air and fire—two elements that have a symbiotic relationship. Air helps fire grow, and fire helps air move. Such has been the bond between Scott Bean and me. Ever since we met in December 2014, our friendship has grown into something beyond words. It's as much a universal constant as the two elements that embody who we are. In the world of Avatar: The Last Airbender—a series that we not only both love but also connected over—he is Zuko to my Aang.

As the fire sign of Aries, Scott has the intensity of spirit and confidence. As the air sign of Gemini, I have whimsy and enthusiasm. If this weren't enough, we also found we equally adore The Legend of Korra and Wonder Woman.

One summer morning in 2016, I remembered a vivid, Celtic-themed dream, no doubt fueled by my love of Ireland. Right then, the idea of two friends and the journey they would undertake was born, and I wanted these friends to be based on Scott and me, our very own adventure. He would be Aedan, the Fyrehunter, to my Conall, the Wyndracer.

In the pages of this novel, Aedan and Conall are *anam cara*—soul friends.

To my chosen brother, Scott, your ever-raging fire has inspired me more than you will ever know, and for that reason among others, I dedicate this book to you.

CONTENTS

PRONUNCIATION KEY
(Approximations for Irish)

Odhrain	OR-rin
Gaoth	Gway
Beith Airgid Ghleanna	Beth AIR-gid GLEN-uh
Tine	TIN-uh
Tir na nÓg	CHEER nuh Nohg
Cernunnos	Ker-NOO-nus
Siobhan	Shee-VON
Fionn Mac Cool	Finn Mac Cool
Déaglán	DEC-lan
Daimhain	Dah-VEEN
An Laoich Tairseach	On LAY-kh TAR-shekh
Sídhe	SHEE
Caomhnóir	CAVE-nor
Coah na Shirah	Coh-ah na SHEE-rah
Oisin	O-SHEEN
Fiachra	FEE-cruh
Daithi	Da-HEE
Tuatha Dé Danann	TOO-ah day Dannan
Eagna	AG-nah
Grá	Grah
Eolas	OH-lus
Ciall	Keel
Saoirse	SER-sha
Seamus	SHAY-mus
Sionnain	Shannon
Uaine	WEN-yeh
Dubh	Duv
Dian	DY-an
Dother	DUTH-er
Forisha na Fírinne	FOR-ish-uh na FEER-in
Caorthanach	KWARE-ha-noc
Fomoragh	Foh-MOR-uh
Uaimh na Bronna	OO-av na BRON-na

i

1 | CONALL MAC RINNE

onall's feet pounded the leaf-covered forest floor as he wove through the birch trees of Druid's Wood. Every so often, he would look up through the canopy, his green eyes darting into empty spaces where sky poked through. His leather boots had little traction on the moist leaves, and occasionally he slid, careening off trees. He needed to reach the dolmen in the middle of the meadow beyond. That was his focus, and he'd do everything he could to make it there. His own breath countered his heartbeat, and his legs ached, crying out for rest, but he couldn't. He had to reach that meadow. Shafts of powdery arrows of sunlight shot through the canopy, striking the undergrowth, and making the birch leaves glisten. Conall glanced up when a shrill sound pierced his ears, and he knew it would be close. He had memorized every part of the forest and felt assured he would reach his destination in time.

As he rounded a birch cluster, his left foot slid out from under him on wet leaves, causing his legs to give out, but he reached toward a branch to stop his fall, wrenching his arms in the process. Slowing down for even a few seconds could affect everything. Sweat poured down his temples and trickled down his back. The meadow would be coming into view, he thought, so he had to keep an eye above. That dolmen was his only concern. The stone tomb had been a monument to his people ever since he could remember, and his adoptive father had told him the variety of stories of who might be buried there. It could be a great warrior who had given his life to protect the Gaoth Clan of Beith Airgid Ghleanna — the Silver Birch Glen. Another story told of a druid who had disrespected the woodland spirits and was taken into Tir na nÓg, the Otherworld. The spirits allegedly built the dolmen as a warning. And yet a third story told of a brother and sister lost in the woods, eaten by wolves, and found by a bard who took pity on the mutilated children and gave them a proper burial. Legends also said that when one entered the meadow, whosoever he or she saw there when sunlight struck the dolmen on the summer solstice would be bound to that person for life.

Conall rounded another cluster of birch and a gaping hole lay in his path. Unable to stop to go around, he offered a silent prayer to Cernunnos, his patron god, and leapt forward, somersaulting on the other side. Things like this he would normally investigate, but he was nearing the end of the wood, and this was too important. In his peripheral vision, he caught a glimpse of something above him, higher than the canopy, and he pressed on. Branches thinned out and gave way to the meadow, and he saw his goal. Percussive heartbeats drowned out the forest sounds as he closed the distance. Squawking from above pierced his attention, and he stretched his legs as far as he could. Before he realized it, he had reached the dolmen. Leaning against the weathered stone, he concentrated on catching his breath. He looked up to see something fall from the sky and land on the highest part of the slanted roof of the tomb.

"A valiant attempt, Lann, but I beat you." He wiped his sweaty brow with his sleeve. "You almost had me back there, though."

Conall reached his arm above his head as if to shield his eyes from the midday sun, but the creature flapped a bit and landed on the leather bracer on his left arm.

"Pretty slow for a hawk." Conall chuckled. The raptor squawked. "I jest! You're the fastest hawk I know. Perhaps tomorrow you'll beat me."

Lann's head jerked and snapped, his eyes taking in everything. Soon, he leaped off Conall's arm and flapped toward a looming shape from the forest. Conall heard the grunting first, but then he saw the source: a brown bear. The creature stood up and was easily seven feet tall, its paws the size of Conall's head.

"Lann! Get out of there!"

Beating its wings against the bear, Lann's angry scream combined with his talons striking the bear's head near his eyes. The massive animal lurched forward as if ignoring the hawk's attack, but Lann circled around and continued his assault. After a few more minutes, the bear returned to the forest. Lann climbed higher, circling above, perhaps to make sure the bear had truly left.

"That shouldn't have happened. Bears don't attack that easily. Perhaps someone offended the bear goddess Artio. I'll have to tell the Elders." He looked up and Lann still circled. He remembered the day six years earlier when that hawk came into his life, and since then, they had been inseparable.

—m—

Conall had just turned ten when his adoptive father Rinn started to give him more responsibilities around the farm. Unable to till fields or wield an axe, Conall could easily weed the vegetable patches and carry the baskets into the house his adoptive mother Siobhan filled with produce. When set to a task, he always put his full attention into it, much to the chagrin of his parents when he'd go wandering through the forest alone. If Conall went off to explore, Rinn would actually have to find his son and carry him back. One morning as the sun's rays launched over the horizon, Conall joined Rinn in the garden for their morning chores. On his way back into the house with a basket, Conall heard what sounded like high-pitched squeaks. Something moved by the base of the large oak tree near the lake. Curiosity won out over fear, so he moved closer. Whatever it was flopped around by the roots, making those same noises. He crouched to see that it was a tiny bird, a fledgling eyas. Conall's eyes welled, and he instinctively dumped out the basket and gently put the baby hawk into it.

"Mum, come quick! Hurry!" He moved as fast as his little legs would take him, hoping his mother would hear him.

Siobhan burst through the front door. "Conall? What is it? Where are you?"

He ran around the house toward the front. "Here, Mum! Look! He was flopping around by the oak tree. Help him!"

Siobhan took the basket with one hand while putting her other arm around her son's shoulders and kissing his head. "Let's see what we can do."

After a few minutes, she assessed that the bird had broken its wing. Offering a silent prayer to Brigid, the goddess of healing, she gently wrapped the wing against its tiny body. Conall brought tiny pieces of roasted mutton to feed the eyas, but the bird just squawked. Siobhan could see her son getting frustrated.

"Give it time, Conall. He'll eat when he's ready. Come, sit with me while I offer a prayer to Brigid."

He leaned against her, watching the hawk, and made his prayer to Cernunnos. Later that day, he was able to give the bird some pieces of meat. Without the ability to fly, the hawk would undoubtedly die, his father told him. Hawks need to hunt. Conall placed the basket next to his bedside, watching and feeding the bird, often sacrificing his own sleep. He would repeat his prayers to Cernunnos to heal the bird, sometimes asking Brigid as well since she was his mother's patron goddess.

One night, Conall dreamed a story he had been told dozens of times of a Sídhe, the evil Aillen, who would lull the inhabitants of the Hill of Tara to sleep and then burn them every Samhain. The great hero, Fionn

Mac Cool, was able to defeat him by staying awake. At the moment of Fionn's victory, Conall would wake up. He dreamed this for a week.

The morning after the last dream, he peeked into the basket and saw the hawk was fidgeting.

"Easy there, or you'll hurt yourself." He carefully removed the cloth binding.

The bird shivered and then stretched its wings.

"Feeling better, are ye?"

The hawk squeaked and then flapped wildly. Before Conall knew it, the hawk flew right out of his window. He smiled, knowing that his prayers had been answered, but then he fell back into his bed, realizing he would never see the bird again. The rest of his day weighed upon him, his thoughts scattered. He pulled weeds in different beds, carried baskets of produce, and helped his father move fyrewood into the house — small logs, but he couldn't stop thinking about the hawk. He'd done all he could, he thought, offering prayers and keeping a vigil. Conall spent the following week trudging along, barely aware of himself. Every time he heard a bird chirp or saw one fly past him, his heart lurched a little. His parents had taught him that there was a purpose to everything, and his purpose had been fulfilled by watching over his winged friend.

Each morning, he would wake up with a start and look at his bedside table, hoping to see the basket. A month to the day after the hawk had vanished, Conall awoke to the smell of eggs cooking and fresh bread baking. Rashers of bacon sizzled over the fyre, too, and he inhaled deeply to take it all in. Out the window, a sky free of clouds or any ill omen lay before him as the sun rose. He hadn't woken up this at ease in a while. After breakfast, he joined his father for morning chores, but for some reason, he didn't have a care in the world.

By midday, the sun was beating down to where he had to sit beneath one of the oak trees for a bit. He enjoyed helping his father and mother with the work; it gave him a sense of purpose. Watching the wispy clouds move across the sky, he caught a glimpse of distant birds whirling about, and his thoughts went to the hawk. Daydreams gave way to drowsy eyes, and soon he was fast asleep. Visions of flying above the glen melted into other thoughts. He dreamed he was moving on the wynd itself, more than flying as if he were part of the wind. Moving over the landscape, he could see the rivers, the forests of birch and ash, as well as the other tribes. He heard his own heartbeat with the adrenaline coursing through him, and the idea that he was untethered to the earth brought tears to his eyes. Amid all this joy, a noise interrupted the moment, at first indistinguishable, but then it got louder. It sounded like a screech or a scream. Before he could figure it out, his eyes flew open. He was still beneath the tree, and not much time had passed. He exhaled out of relief, and then he heard the sound again. Looking up, he grinned.

"You came back!"

He jumped up and waved at the little hawk about ten feet above him on a branch. Conall wanted to climb the tree, but he saw no footholds in the bark or low branches. All he could do was grin and giggle to himself. A wynd blew through the tree and, when the sunlight broke through, he held up his arm to shield his eyes. The next thing he knew, something pinched his forearm. Sitting on his sleeve was the hawk. Its head moved in small jolts, taking in Conall. The boy's wide-eyed enthusiasm changed to a wince when he realized the talons were digging into his arm through the fabric. Hawk eyes met human ones, and the bird cocked his head.

"Ow, you're cutting into my arm, you know."

As if he understood Conall, the hawk moved to the root at the base of the oak. Where the talons had poked through the sleeve, small drops of blood showed, but that didn't matter to Conall. His dream state hadn't completely left him. Sitting near the hawk, he pulled his knees up and wrapped his arms around his legs, resting his chin on his knee. The hawk remained on the root, moving its head around.

"Those talons are like little blades. I'll have to wear bracers if you're going to keep doing that. Like little blades." He giggled.

On his walk home, the hawk flew above him, following him. When Conall reached the house, he ran inside and grabbed a leather bracer he had for when he used his bow. This time when he extended his arm, he did so standing tall. A moment later, the hawk landed on his forearm.

"Much better. This is amazing! And I know what I'll call you. Lann."

Blade.

From that day, Conall and Lann were like brothers — inseparable.

Fate had decreed the kinship of Conall and Lann, and even Conall's parents had come to think of the hawk has an adopted son. Rinn had built a treehouse in the oak by the river for his son and Lann that overlooked the glen with an unobstructed view, and Lann had his own perch. Rinn knew his son was nearing the Nascah — the Bridging — that coming of age where Conall would find his spirit guardian, his caomhnóir, and cross into adulthood. He knew that, despite their connection, Lann wasn't Conall's. Everyone in the Gaoth Clan had found a different guardian, and the Elders couldn't foresee what one would meet on that sacred journey. The Nascah was not only a deeply spiritual experience, but it could oftentimes leave the individual emotionally scarred if not completed properly. Most felt they had to pursue their guardian, too, taking great pride in their eager approach, rather than waiting for it appear to them when the moment was correct. The connection between a spiritual guardian and its companion could be contradictory to the child's nature, and that bond would become clearer the longer the two spent time together.

At sunrise, the day before reaching his sixteenth year, Conall went to help Rinn with some morning chores. The man was already tilling the soil. Normally, he waited for his son to arrive, and they would begin together.

"Couldn't wait to start, could ye?" Conall chuckled as he caught up to Rinn.

Something about Rinn's face gave him a chill.

"What's wrong, Da? You look like you've seen a ghost."

Rinn continued, but then Conall jumped in front of the tiller, his arms spread.

"Da!"

As he came to a halt, Rinn snapped out of his distraction.

"Conall? You daft? I could've cut your leg off!"

"I tried to get your attention, but you didn't respond."

"My thoughts were elsewhere, I guess. I woke with a start before dawn, so I started to till without you."

"Da..." Conall crossed his arms. "You've never not waited for me."

Rinn's face sank with his son's scowl. Normally, when Conall took this stance, Rinn could laugh it off because he knew Conall was trying too hard to be angry. This time, he couldn't laugh. He could barely smile.

"We need to talk, son."

With an arm around Conall's shoulders, Rinn brought his son to the bench on the side of the house. Once he sat, he leaned forward, elbows on his knees, and laced his fingers.

"Da, is this about—"

"Conall." It was just two syllables, but they were heavy with paternal anguish. "You were brought to our doorstep sixteen years ago wrapped in a blanket by an elderly woman, during a storm that only the gods could have brought. She said little except that you had been born hours earlier and that your name was Conall, but her eyes spoke of betrayal and rage. I don't know how I saw that within her, but I do remember how her silent story touched your mother's heart. We knew we had to care for you. I offered the woman lodging and food, but she returned to the storm after placing you in your mother's arms. I tried to find her but couldn't."

Conall stared off. His chest barely expanded, but Rinn could see he was breathing. He also knew his son well enough that Conall needed some time to take this revelation in. The silence before Conall spoke was iron on Rinn's heart.

"Why..."

"On the eve of your Nascah, I wanted you to know the truth." He put a hand on Conall's shoulder and squeezed. "Your mother and I have taught you how to hunt small game and forage the forest for food. We've even shown you how to make a shelter. We have tried to prepare you for this journey you're about to take. Your caomhnóir will reveal things to you, even protect you, and I didn't want you to learn this without being able to ask questions."

Conall stormed off to the house in silence, and Siobhan had just opened the front door when he brushed past her, headed for his room. She was taking the laundry to the washbasin by the lake. Rinn, his hands in his pockets, walked up and leaned against the tree.

"What's wrong with Conall? He didn't say a word as he went to his room." She doused some garments in the basin, rubbing them together.

When she looked up, Rinn was staring off across the lake.

"You told him, didn't you?"

He sighed. "Yes. He had to know, Siobhan."

"But his Nascah —"

"Will still happen. But now he'll know."

"And now he'll hate us."

Rinn put his hands up in the air. "Our son needed to know. Don't you remember your Nascah? Your mother pulled you aside and told you about your family line, didn't she? She would have had to tell the story of your clan from the maternal side."

"I'm not daft, Rinn. I do remember." Siobhan rubbed two shirts together. "You should have just told him your own lineage. It —"

"It would have been a lie!" His voice echoed across the lake.

"Don't you *dare* raise your voice to me, Rinn Mac Durmaid!" She pointed toward the house. "That child of ours came to us only hours old, and we've raised him with love for the past sixteen years. Your father, and your father's father... They're *his* family, too. You've instilled within him the values and lessons learned from them as I have from mine. Conall is as much our child as if he had come from my womb."

She threw the clothes down into the basin and jumped up.

"Where are you going?"

With fyre in her eyes, she swung around, her long red hair following.

"I'm going to see if *our* son is all right."

"Siobhan!" Rinn huffed. He knew better than to follow her.

She found Conall lying on his bed, his arms behind his head, staring at the thatched ceiling. On a branch near the window, Lann watched over him. Siobhan sat on the edge of the bed, and he turned away. She put her hand on his arm.

"What do you want?"

At any other time, she'd scold him for being rude to her, but this time, a gentler touch was needed.

"Look at me, Conall." Her voice quivered. "Please."

He stiffened a bit, but then, exhaling, turned only his head. She reached up and brushed hair off his forehead, cradling his cheek.

"Listen to me very carefully. You are, and you always will be, my son. I wish I'd been there when your father told you."

The way he looked at her, his eyes glossy, made her clamp her own eyes shut, tears trickling down.

"I knew we had to tell you. I just didn't know when. When your father spoke to me about your upcoming Nascah, I had a feeling he might say something. Conall, he loves you so much."

"But, why now? Why couldn't he have waited until after I found my caomhnóir? I've been looking forward to this for so long, and now... I don't know. I'll be gone for a few weeks, maybe longer, and now..."

She sat up straighter. "There's a part of the rite, something we didn't tell you about, where a parent recounts his or her lineage as a way to honor the past. For sons, it's their father. For daughters, their mother. He believed he'd be lying to you if he did this."

"Doesn't he think that I wouldn't have known it was a lie? I've always thought of his father Durmaid as my grandfather. Isn't it more important what I've learned from each of them?"

The tears that Siobhan shed came from a deep place where a paradox of emotions existed: she felt both regret and pride. For the first time, she realized just how mature Conall had become. She was so worried about how he would take finding out the truth, but that's not what upset him. Conall sat up and embraced his mother, tightening his arms around her.

Siobhan pulled back, cupping his cheeks, touching her forehead to his. "I love you so much. You are just like your father."

A few minutes passed before they heard a tapping on the door frame. Rinn's massive body filled the doorway.

"I'm going to finish the clothes." Siobhan kissed her son again on his forehead. She smiled at her husband as she left the room.

"May I come in?"

Conall swung his legs over the side of the bed.

"Of course, Da. It's okay."

Rinn sat next to his son, but he couldn't look at him.

"I wanted to apologize. I owe you an explanation."

"Look, Da. I don't like that you and Mum lied to me. I don't like it at all. I have a lot of questions, too. I'm fifteen, almost sixteen. You should have trusted me."

Rinn realized right then that he'd taught his son better than he thought he had. The voice that came out of Conall's mouth was that of a young man, one ready to find his path and his caomhnóir. On the eve of the boy's Nascah, his expression, a soft smile, showed pride.

"I'll forgive you, Da, on one condition."

Rinn raised an eyebrow.

"I want you to tell me about *my* history. I'm Conall Mac Rinne, and I'm quite proud of that."

Later that night, under the constellations and a waxing crescent moon, while Rinn Mac Durmaid entertained his son with the epic tales of the Gaoth Clan: the battles they'd lost and won as well as the journeys they'd made, the fyre in the ring—bright crimson and gold—did a warrior's dance. At dawn, Conall would begin his journey.

Siobhan found her son praying at the edge of the lake. The sun hadn't risen, and Conall used the tattered remnants of night to fuel his words. She waited until he was finished before she joined him at the water's edge, tousling the hair on the back of his head.

"Did you make prayers to Rhiannon for your travels?"

"Yes, Mum." He rolled his eyes and smirked.

"Brigid?"

"Yes."

He looked back at her, his eyebrows raised in insistence.

"All right, all right. Let's get you packed so you can make your way before sunrise."

"I'm already done."

Siobhan smirked and cocked her head, but Conall strode back to the house with a confident grin.

Rinn was finishing his breakfast when they went back inside. He had told Conall he would start the morning chores later. While Conall and his father said their goodbyes, Siobhan checked her son's pack.

"Mum, enough already. I have what I need."

"One can never be too careful." She tied the leather thongs.

"Conall, remember that your Nascah begins the moment you walk out that door. When you return, we fully expect you to have found your ca-omhnóir."

"Yes, Da." He wrapped his arms around his father who kissed him on the head.

His mother came up behind them, sandwiching Conall between them.

"I have to go. You're both crazy. You know that?"

Conall threw his pack over his shoulder and reached for the door, but then they heard three knocks. In the doorway was a man in his sixties wearing a gray wool cloak cinched around his neck by a tree-shaped brooch pin.

"Good, you haven't left yet." The man was out of breath.

"What's wrong, Elder Mac Maírtín?"

"Rinn, you and your family have been summoned to the Elder Circle. I'm afraid Conall's Nascah will have to wait."

"Today's his birthday, Elder." Rinn crossed his arms. "His journey-"

"Will have to wait, Rinn." The man's tone darkened. "Come with me. Now."

Rinn nodded at Siobhan and Conall.

"To put off such an important ritual... Well, this had better be important."

"I assure you it is, Rinn. We need to go. The others are waiting."

Siobhan quickened her pace to keep up with the Elder.

"With due respect, what could be more important than a child's rite of passage?"

Elder Mac Maírtín stopped. "The Coah na Shirah."

Rinn stopped. "The War of the Eternals. Elder, what does this have to do with my son?"

"All will be explained once we reach the Elder Circle."

2 | AEDAN MAC ODHRAIN

Seven-year-old Oisin Mac Cavan tore through the meadow away from Tierney's farm as if a hornet's nest were after him, but it might as well have been. A quarter of a mile behind him were the farmer's three sons, rampaging across the land. For such a wee lad, Oisin ran like a deer from a hunter, whimpering, looking back every few steps to see the Tierney boys closing the distance. At ten, eleven, and thirteen, the boys had age and longer strides as an advantage, but Oisin had fear, and that kept him in motion. By the time he reached the edge of town, the morning market was active with merchants bartering with townsfolk over the price of a melon or a pound of fish. Little Oisin managed to elude the boys in the labyrinth of tents and tables that lined the dusty roads, but he continued to move through striving for home.

Turning corners and meandering around passersby, he reached the other side of the marketplace and the north road that led to the mountains. The youngest Tierney boy, Riordan, jumped out from the side of the tavern, right in Oisin's path. Oisin shrieked, running through Riordan's legs, and continued his escape toward the forest at the base of Oak Mountain. If he could make it through the birch forest and to Brigid's sanctuary by the cliffs, he was sure he'd be safe. They wouldn't dare offend her. He didn't see the boys behind him, but he knew better than to stop, and his legs had started to cramp.

"We're coming for you, Oisin, you thief! You can't steal from my da's fields!" Riordan had managed to catch up, despite Oisin's vigilance.

"Can you catch him?" Padraig, the middle brother, reached Riordan, trailed by the eldest, Kieran, whose bear-like body slowed him down.

Just past the trees, the thunderous footsteps of the other three boys along with their breathing urged Oisin on — they were too close. The sanctuary was in view, and not even the boys would dare to hurt him in Brigid's sacred place. Twenty feet from the cliff, a rogue rock got in Oisin's way, causing him to land face-first on the grass. The fall knocked the wind out of him, and the seven-year-old's face contorted as he cried out. The Tierney boys were only footsteps away, and Oisin hadn't reached the sanctuary. His expression soured, but then a voice intervened, and someone appeared behind him.

"Leave him be, Kieran."

Standing between the three boys and their intended victim was a tall fifteen-year-old boy wearing hunter's garb.

"This isn't your business, Aedan. Back off yourself!" Kieran had clenched his fists and stood in front of his brothers.

"You all right?" Aedan's words were meant for the boy behind him, still heaving and crying. Oisin rocked back and forth while he held his knee.

"I'll give him a reason to cry like a baby. Give it back, Oisin!"

"Padraig, just take your brothers and go. Whatever Oisin took can't be worth all this."

"I-I didn't take anything." Oisin's voice cracked a little.

"My brother said he saw you steal food and run."

Aedan took a step forward. Riordan and Padraig flanked Kieran, and each stepped back a little.

"Oisin, did you take food from Tierney's farm?"

The boy hid behind Aedan, poking his head around. "N-No."

"He says he didn't take anything, boys. Hurry back home to your Mum. There's nothing to see here."

"As far as I can tell, it's just you against the three of us, Aedan. You going to take all of us?"

Aedan whistled. From below the cliff, a roar bellowed, and then a massive form rose above the ledge. With red and gold scales shimmering in the early morning sun, the winged creature loomed over them, grunting, and wisps of smoke curled from its mouth.

"Not exactly. Gentlemen, meet Fiachra."

"It's-It's a bloody dragon!" Kieran put his arms out in front of his brothers and stepped back a bit.

"Yes. Yes, it certainly is." Aedan crossed his arms and smirked.

Fiachra, an adolescent gold dragon, flapped his leathery wings enough to keep him aloft and in the sights of the Tierney boys. For being the eldest brother, Padraig was holding himself together the least, as evidenced by the stain on the front of his pants. Kieran noticed his brother blubbering as well as the mark of shame.

"Really, Padraig? Glad to know you're so fearless. Come on, boys. Aedan, enjoy your victory for now. I hope you're going to keep a keen eye on Little Oisin."

Kieran and his brothers made a hasty retreat, always knowing where the dragon was as they left. As soon as they were gone, Aedan signaled Fiachra to go and crouched before Oisin.

"Okay, now tell me. What did you take? They wouldn't have chased you here for nothing."

At first, the boy shied away, pushing his hands under his shirt, but Aedan cleared his throat and pointed to his palm.

Unable to make eye contact, Oisin slowly pulled his hands out. Aedan was focusing on the boy's tear-filled face and didn't see what was deposited in his hand. As soon as he did, he laughed out loud.

"A doll? You mean, you didn't have any food from their farm?"

Oisin shook his head, still unable to look Aedan in the eye. Aedan shook his head and rolled his eyes. He examined the doll.

"Why didn't you just stop and show this to them?"

Sitting with his knees pulled up and his arms wrapped around them, Oisin started to cough out a few sighs and whimper. Aedan sat next to him and leaned closer.

"A little piece of advice? The truth will always be best. Even if you're not sure it'll work out in the end. Just remember the truth."

Oisin, still trembling, gave what looked like a nod.

"Why don't you head on home. I'll keep watch just in case they come back." He touched his fist to the boy's shoulder.

Fiachra headed back toward the horizon. Aedan smirked before heading home, hands shoved in his pockets. He had just reached the village when he saw Riordan, arms folded, leaning up against a tree. A quick look revealed no other brothers, and Aedan knew he'd probably hear or smell Kieran before he'd see him due to his burly body and a lack of hygiene.

"That was pretty clever of you, bringing your dragon. Didn't think you could handle us all on your own?"

Aedan laughed. "On the contrary, oh bright one. You three aren't worth me getting my hands dirty. Do you know what little Oisin had under his shirt?"

"Probably some of my da's—"

"A doll, Riordan. He had a doll. Had you thought to ask him," Aedan tapped his temple, "he'd have told you, but you and your brothers jumped to a conclusion and scared that boy half out of his wits. Pathetic."

"Who are you calling pathetic? I still say without your dragon you're nothing but a, but a…"

Aedan chortled as he walked off. "Leave the boy be, Riordan. He's under my eye now. If you're not careful, you'll end up on the toasty end of Fiachra's breath."

As he walked off, he heard Riordan rattle off a list of expletives he didn't think the boy could spell let alone define. The Tierney boys had been his adversaries since they were toddlers. Even Old Man Tierney shook his head when the three of them got caught pulling their shenanigans. Aedan knew that Riordan would go back to his brothers and tell them how he'd made Aedan cower or how he'd taught him a lesson not to mess with the brothers Tierney. It didn't matter to him, though. Aedan would keep his word and watch over Oisin, at least until the brothers had their next target. He smiled when he remembered the look on their faces when Fiachra rose from beyond the cliff, especially when he saw Kieran's dampened pants. The day he and the gold dragon came together five years earlier was a memory he'd always hold dear.

A thunderstorm the likes of which Oak Mountain hadn't seen in decades had disappeared with the sunrise, and Aedan, his older cousin Seamus, and his father Odhran, went to see how the farmland at the base of the mountain and its livestock had fared. The sheep had wandered through gaps in the stone walls caused by the storm, and their bleating revealed they had found a patch of grassland less than a mile from their enclosure. While Odhran and Seamus worked to gather the sheep, Aedan wandered up the mountain to check on the goats he knew lived near the crags. At ten years old, he had already mastered how to climb the moss-laden rocks and use the shrubs for handholds. He wasn't concerned at how far he'd gone until he looked behind him at one point to notice his father's farm was but a speck of gray on a sea of green, cross-hatched with stone walls that demarcated various animal folds.

He hadn't seen any goats, but they could have found shelter in one of the many small caves along the mountainside or perhaps had ventured to the other side to avoid the tempest. Aedan was just about to head back when he heard a sound he'd never heard before coming from higher up the mountain. Right then, he also heard his father, who had seen him, calling for him to return. That awkward squawking came again, and Aedan waved to his father before continuing his climb.

After meandering his way farther up, a tree growing sideways out from the mountain blocked his path and resting on the branches was a nest the size of a cow. The closer he went, the louder that noise came, and his breathing quickened. Mossy rocks made his climb more of a challenge, but he kept moving. His tongue poked out of his mouth slightly, something his father had told him was the way he always knew Aedan was on a mission. He couldn't worry about disobeying his father at this moment—the fyres of his curiosity blazed. As he reached the sideways tree, the noise had taken on the mewling of a kitten combined with that of an eaglet. He pulled himself onto the tree and shimmied across the trunk to the nest. The sight of what made the noise almost made him lose his balance.

Sitting among the shattered remains of eagle eggs was a gold and red creature whose wings had barely spread but had a soft, leathery appearance.

"A golden dragon," Aedan muttered. "But why are you in an eagle's nest?"

He craned his head around to see if the mother were nearby, wondering how a giant dragon could have used this nest for its offspring. Eagles weren't known for stealing eggs of other creatures, he thought, and he knew that an eagle's talons would have cracked the shell open if it tried to take hold. That would have to wait—this baby dragon was shrieking in pain for some reason, and Aedan saw why. A rock the size of his fist had fallen into the nest and had pinned down one of the dragon's wings, immobilizing it. The poor hatchling didn't have the strength to move. Using soft tones, Aedan reassured the little one that he meant no harm while he gently removed the rock. Shards of dragon shell had been crushed into the wing, but before he would attempt to remedy that, he felt the first thing he needed to do was take the dragon to safety. If it had been abandoned, it would die.

Aedan's feet slid down toward the bottom of the mountain path to find his father and Seamus managing the last few sheep back into their folds. Once they filled the gaps in the stone wall, Odhran began berating his son for wandering off until he saw he had something in his hands.

"Da, look! A golden dragon. I heard it squawk and had to rescue it before—"

"How many times have I..." He saw his son's eyes quivering and knew that scolding him wasn't going to change anything. "Okay, okay. Calm down. What did you find?"

"Look." Aedan opened his hands a little to reveal the tiny dragon no larger than both his hands, one wing hanging by its side. "We have to help it, Da. It could die."

"Where did you find it?" Seamus leaned over Odhran's shoulder. "A golden dragon? Really?"

Aedan covered it again, instinctively wanting to protect it. He knew Seamus was just curious, but he didn't want anyone poking at the little dragon. "An eagle's nest, of all places. Da, I thought eagles didn't steal eggs?"

"Hmm. They don't. We'll have to figure out that mystery later. Let's bring it home and see if we can't help removing those shards of shell. Seamus, go fetch your aunt Saoirse."

Father and son went to the barn, and Aedan placed the dragon on a wooden table covered in sheepskin.

"Aedan, you keep it calm, and I'll tend to the shards."

The boy stared at the dragon, stroking the back of its tiny head, and he wondered at the small golden and red scales. Normally, or at least from what he had heard, golden dragons were pure gold, but this one had vibrant dark red scales speckling its body, with some taking on a darker hue. Under Aedan's care, the tiny creature calmed down and didn't flinch much when Odhran removed the shell pieces. Saoirse came in with Seamus, and she held her hands to her mouth.

"By Brigid's fyre… It's so tiny. Careful, Odhran…"

Odhran scowled. "It's just fine, Saoirse. I'm not hurting it."

"Aedan, are you okay? Seamus told me you'd climbed Oak Mountain all the way to the tree."

The tree? Aedan thought. She referred to it as if it were a certain tree.

"Did you know about the nest, Mum? Have you seen it?"

Saoirse looked at Odhran. Glancing at his wife, he nodded once and returned his attention to the dragon. Aedan caught the exchange.

"Mum? Da?"

"Son… it's really nothing. Just an old legend from the village. The Elders used to speak of a dragon, a golden dragon, who would leave its eggs in an eagle's nest just after it was born. This fledgling is gold and red, so it must mean something. If we have a chance, we'll ask the Elders." Odhran continued to remove the shards.

Aedan rubbed under the scaled chin of the dragon which made it purr. The tiny head rubbed against his hand as a cat would. A few seconds later, the dragon hiccupped, and a wisp of smoke escaped his nostrils.

"Did you see that, Aedan?" Saoirse leaned in closer. "If I'm not mistaken, I think this little one is a fyrebreather. That's not so common anymore."

Within a half hour, Odhran had removed all the pieces and lightly dragged a piece of wool down the wing, looking to see if it caught on any remaining pieces of eggshell. The dragon stretched out the wing to where it shook a little and then squealed. At first, Odhran thought it was in pain, but it stretched both wings and flapped them, rubbing its head against Aedan's hand again.

"I think you've made a friend." Odhran patted the back of Aedan's head. "We'll have to keep an eye on this little one for a few days, but then I'm afraid he'll have to go back to the nest. We can't take care of him here. Plus, neighbors are nosy, and they'll want to see or touch him."

"But, Da…" Aedan cupped the dragon in both hands and headed toward his bedroom in the back of the stone farmhouse.

Saoirse started after her son, but Odhran touched her arm.

"Leave him be for now. He'll come to understand what the right thing to do is. If not, it'll be a long night. Where's Seamus?"

"Leaning up against the plow, writing. He said he was inspired by Aedan finding the dragon. If only my sister could see her son now. He's becoming quite the young bard." She leaned against Odhran.

"Last winter was hard for all of us, Saoirse. Praise Brigid that Roisin didn't suffer long before she passed. And, yes, she would be proud of her son. Let's leave Aedan for now. Come help me with the cows."

While Aedan's parents tried to bring order to bovine chaos, wrangling the rest of the cows into their folds, the young boy lay on his side tending to the dragonling that cooed next to him. Aedan had used a shirt to create a small nest-like spot for his little friend. Just like any newly born creature, after it had settled in from its stressful morning, it curled up and fell asleep. Stroking the back of its head with his fingernails, Aedan smiled.

"Fiachra. That's what I'm calling you." *Hunter*.

It didn't take long for both to be sound asleep, and Fiachra occasionally hiccupped, tiny curls of smoke puffing through his nostrils. A few hours passed, and Saoirse poked her head into her son's room. She peered over her slumbering son to see that the dragon had curled into a gold and red ball. If the legends were true, then Aedan was truly blessed: those who found a multicolored dragon had an enviable fate. Saoirse worried, however, that this fate would take her son from her, and along with Odhran, he was all she had.

Reaching the age of the Nascah had weight for any teenager, although Aedan didn't get as excited as his parents did — well, one parent, anyway. Aedan had just arrived home shortly before sunset after helping little Oisin when his father came into the cottage, his arms filled with wood to chop.

"Where've you been, Aedan? I could've used your help getting this wood and some peat. You off chasing Fiachra again?" Odhran crouched to put the logs down. "I need you to pack your rucksack —"

"Da… not the Nascah again. I've told you that I really don't —"

Aedan's father shot up, grabbing his son by the shoulders.

"So help me, Aedan, I won't talk about this anymore. Your mother and I had planned for this day ever since you were born. You'll not deny us."

Pulling free from his father's grip, Aedan pushed his way through the doorway outside. When Odhran followed, he saw Aedan kicking the dirt and muttering to himself.

"Aedan Mac Odhrain, get back inside. Now." The man didn't have to raise his voice to convey how he felt. His voice did drop a level to where it sounded like a growling wolf.

Huffing, the boy stomped back into the cottage. He knew how his father felt about open displays of aggression, especially when neighbors already doubted that Odhran could raise his son on his own. The man re-entered the cottage and saw his son, arms crossed, sitting by the kitchen table. Odhran pulled out the chair next to Aedan and straddled it. He put his hand on Aedan's arm, but the boy pulled away.

Leaning forward, and in the softest voice he could muster, Odhran addressed his son.

"I miss her, too. Your mother, the spitfyre that she was, loved you more than the day is long. Like a mother bear protecting her cub, she'd have stood up to anything to protect you. The one thing she couldn't fight was her illness, though, but Brigid knows, she sure did try. From the day you came into this world, her greatest hope for you was your Nascah. She knew how important that day would be for you, for us."

He paused, patted his son on the arm, and went to the front yard. A short time later, the dull thud of the axe against wood snapped Aedan from his thoughts. He could hear his father's grief in each strike as if the metal was a whip and the wood was Odhran, taking the emotional beating he felt he deserved for letting his wife die. He knew in his heart that he could have done nothing to help her, but he had sworn a vow on their wedding day to protect her from the ravages of the world. As he had said many times, he would spend the rest of his life punishing himself for something he had no control over. He'd chopped about a dozen logs before Aedan peeked his head outside.

"Da. I'm... sorry." He pulled himself away from the door and closed it, using his sleeve to wipe the beginnings of tears.

By the time Odhran returned, Aedan was seated by the fyre, poking the wood with a stick, staring into the flames. Father and son said nothing for about an hour, at which point Aedan joined Odhran at the table. In the man's hands was a brooch that Saoirse used to wear on her cloak — a circle of gold with a flame over it. She said it was the fyre of her family that kept her warm on cold, harsh nights.

"Her grandmother gave this to her." He stared at the brooch. "She told your mother that the Fonn gave it to *her* mother, your great-grandmother."

He brushed his thumb over the flame embellishment and then pressed it to his lips. Odhran handed it to Aedan.

"I think I remember Mum talking about the Fonn once, when I was little." He examined the brooch from all sides as if it were a puzzle needing a solution.

"The Fonn were also known as The Keen Ones. They go way back, before the Tuatha Dé Danann. No one knows much about them anymore. I remember hearing about Eagna, Grá, Eolas, and… who was it… Ciall, I believe."

Aedan handed his father the brooch, but Odhran put up his hand.

"No, son, it's yours. Your mother wanted you to have it." He closed the boy's fingers around it. "She wanted you to have so much…"

For a man with the stature of an oak, Odhran had no shame in showing how he felt. All of Oak Mountain knew how much he loved his family, and when Saoirse passed from the world, the entire community mourned almost as long as he did. While some families needed to hire mourners to keen at the procession, Saoirse had no shortage of bereaved, all of them genuine and equally heartbroken. Her family dated back to the founding of Silver Birch Glen, their tribal home, and no one had an unkind thing to say about her, nor would they dare.

Where Odhran and Saoirse engaged with the community and opened their hearts, Aedan retracted from society, only involving himself when absolutely necessary. His interaction with the Mac Cavan boys and Oisin was a prime example of that—he did have a big heart, though, and he couldn't watch someone without the means to defend himself be bullied or mistreated. Most times, though, he preferred his solitude and generally disliked most people, except perhaps his cousin Seamus.

"Da… Why is it so important that I complete the Nascah? I mean, I know what it is, but why does it matter so much to you and Mum?"

Odhran didn't hear the common snarly nature to the question as he had been accustomed to hearing from his teenage son; instead, he heard a genuine inquiry from someone who needed a truly meaningful response. That, in and of itself, was a rarity and required a response worthy of Aedan's intelligence.

"Aedan, you're a lucky young man. As far as I know, you're the only one in the whole of Oak Mountain who has bonded with an animal to the extent that you have with Fiachra. It's quite remarkable actually. And I know he feels for you as you feel for him. I can feel it. The thing is, he's a playmate. A companion. He's not one whose purpose is to guide your spirit. I know how important your connection to the gods is to you, as it was for your mother."

The young boy's sigh would usually signal resistance to Odhran, and he just watched Aedan turn the brooch in his fingers, anticipating an antagonistic rebuttal. Silence followed, though, as Saoirse's son pondered his father's words.

"You're right."

The words hit Odhran's ears, and Aedan caught his father's wide-eyed expression and faint smile.

The boy chuckled. "Don't let that go to your head, Da. You *are* right sometimes. But I agree. I love Fiachra like the brother I never had, and we entertain each other, but... I know he's not my spirit guide."

Odhran nodded. "I understand your fear. You think that, when you do find it, it will replace Fiachra. I wish I could tell you that won't happen, but that's entirely up to you. Your caomhnóir has a purpose. It bonds with you in a way nothing else can. It provides you with balance, a sense of self that offers guidance and reassurance when you need it, and pushes you when you think you don't. The energy comes from a different place than love or friendship. A caomhnóir isn't really a friend. Rather, it's a loyal guardian of your spirit. Someday, Fiachra will pass from this world, or you will, but your guide will remain with you, including into the afterlife. It's your link to the divine."

"What's yours? And Mum's?

A pall fell on Odhran's face, and his shoulders slumped.

"Your mother's was a cow." He looked to see if Aedan might laugh, but he didn't.

"I think I understand why. Mum's patron was Brigid. 'One who nurtures.' A cow provides that for her calves as well as for us since we drink her milk. It explains why I'd usually find her in the pasture, leaning up against the fence, watching the cows graze." He paused, cringing. "Was one of our cows her caomhnóir?"

Odhran's laughter shook the cottage. It provided as much warmth as the fyre did.

"No." He continued to chuckle. "The spirit guide is a spirit, in the shape of an animal. It has no tangible form."

"What about you?"

That question soured his father's expression.

"I... I don't have one."

"But, why? You completed your Nascah, didn't you?"

The man leaned back in his chair and crossed his arms, trying to convey what he wanted to say with his eyes so he wouldn't have to voice it. His son's eyebrows lifted almost to the middle of his forehead.

"Da?"

Exhaling loudly, the man shook his head. He moved his eyes away.

"I didn't know how to tell you. If you knew, I was afraid you'd decide not to do it, and I couldn't let that happen. I made a promise to your mother—"

"To lie to me? Da, we've always been honest with each other. Always. How could you keep this from me, especially... especially after Mum left us?" Aedan pounded his fists on the table. "All this time. All this time I've heard about this great tradition that I need to follow. Ever since I was little, you've told me about this important journey everyone takes to find his connection to the spirit world. I heard my friends' parents talk about it every so often, and they all talked about it with so much respect. And the one person in the whole world who I trust has been lying to me."

Odhran sat up and placed his hands on his knees, still unable to look at his son.

"I know. I'm sorry. I'm sorry, Aedan."

He lurched from his chair and left the cottage. Aedan seethed, his eyes locked on the door. In almost sixteen years, his father had never lied to him. He had seen the man as a rock, someone who had done what he needed to do to keep the family happy. When he heard his father talk to the village elders with what could best be described as a regal bearing, or when Odhran would go out of his way to help the villagers, knowing it might put him in harm's way, Aedan had it in his heart to be just like him. He saw his father as a man of honor. When his cousin Seamus fell ill for a time, his father sold family keepsakes to afford the medicine since he knew that Seamus' parents couldn't afford it on their own. This was the man Aedan wanted to be. Not anymore, he thought, not until he knew the entire truth.

When the rooster crowed, Aedan jumped up from the kitchen chair where he'd fallen asleep, not realizing for a moment where he was. Sunbeams bled into the dark purple of the night sky, diffusing the darkness. He checked outside, but his father wasn't there; nor was he in the cottage. It wasn't like his father not to return when he went outside to walk off whatever rage plagued him, especially if it were a rage against himself. Something gnawed at Aedan's gut. He couldn't talk to his father. Not now. He needed time to think. Looking at the brooch of his mother's, he packed his rucksack with everything he needed for his Nascah. Kissing the brooch, he dropped it into the leather pouch.

A short time later, Odhran returned. He checked Aedan's room and found that the bed was made—whether it had been made since the day before or Aedan had done it that morning, Odhran couldn't tell. Back by the table, he saw a piece of folded parchment and a chill made his arm hair bristle. He unfolded it without looking so he wouldn't catch a random word or phrase, but then he read it.

"I've left for my Nascah. I don't know when I will be back. What I do now, I do for Mum."

It took a moment, but as soon as the words sank in, he collapsed into the chair. With his elbows on the table, he put his head in his hands and years of shame and regret poured out of him.

3 | PROPHECY OF THE DRAGONHAWK

Aedan walked for about two hours when hooves behind him made him turn, and a man in a grey wool cloak sat atop a black mare.

"Aedan Mac Odhrain, you're to come with me. Hop on."

The boy's first instinct was always to have a clever retort or snappy barb, but as soon as he saw the man's cloak, he thought better of it.

"Elder... What's wrong? Why do I need to go with you? Is something-Is it my father?"

The man repeated his original request but finished with one word. "Now."

"Not until I know why. I'm starting my Nascah today, and if it's all the same to you—"

The elder reached down, and with strength Aedan didn't know the elderly man had, he lifted the boy onto the horse. He let out a "Hyah!" and they began their journey down a different road. Aedan knew he wouldn't survive if he jumped off the horse, not moving as quickly as it was. Raising his fingers to his lips, he whistled, hoping the summons would be heard. As he expected, from the corner of his eye, he saw Fiachra moving like the wynd to his location, but then something intriguing happened. As soon as the dragon was right above them, the elder looked up, and his eyes flashed orange for a moment. Before Aedan knew what was going on, Fiachra turned and flew off toward the burgeoning sunrise. For the rest of the ride, the boy wondered what he had done to have warranted capture by an Elder. Plus, he wanted to know what happened with Fiachra. Those questions he hoped would be answered soon enough when a cottage came into view.

With the grace of a horseman, the elder dismounted, with Aedan following more clumsily. Before they entered the cottage, Aedan pulled the elder back.

"What's happening? Who are you? What did you do to my dragon?"

Expecting to be shoved inside, Aedan stood his ground. The man removed his hood, exposing an aged man with a mark on his brow.

"My apologies for this, son of Odhran. I am Elder Mac Brannain. The High Elder told me to bring you here. All will be revealed, but fear not, your dragon is unharmed. I simply told him you were under my protection."

"You-You speak with dragons?"

"I do many things, Aedan. Now, come inside."

Before the elder opened the door, white sage and cedar assaulted the air. Aedan stepped inside, and that heady scent surrounded him. He did what a good hunter did and took in his surroundings, noticing the panel of elders who sat at a wooden table before him. Other people — a man, a woman, and a boy — stood off to the side, but he couldn't see them clearly through the haze. Another elder spoke.

"Aedan Mac Odhrain, you have been summoned before the Elder Circle because a matter of grave importance, the Coah na Shirah, is nigh."

"With due respect, Elder, I'm about to start my Nascah."

The Elders at the table muttered among themselves, but it was another voice that caught Aedan's ear.

"Aedan? Is that you?"

Siobhan moved closer to the boy, scrutinizing his face. He leaned back a little.

"By Brigid's fyre, it *is* you!" She pulled him into a tight embrace, and Aedan didn't respond. "Conall, come here!"

Her son approached, squinting in the haze. As soon as he was near the boy, his mother started to cry. Conall cocked his head a little, as soon as the realization hit, he smiled.

"Is that really you, Aedan? It's been a long time."

Aedan looked back and forth from Siobhan to Conall, his face contorted, but then his eyebrows shot up.

"Conall... Mac Rinne?"

Siobhan, grinning and with tears trickling down her cheeks, spoke with the Elders for a moment and returned.

"The Elders are giving you a little time to get reacquainted." She touched Aedan's face. "I was so, so sorry to hear of your mother's passing." She returned to her husband.

The boys stepped into a corner of the cottage, each sizing up the other.

"So… how have you been?" Conall stammered but didn't wait for an answer. "It's so weird seeing you now. Well, not *weird*, but I mean I was just starting my Nascah when the Elder brought us here."

Aedan chuckled, scratching the back of his head. "I'm good. I forgot we had the same birthday. I'm beginning my Nascah as well. It's been, what, six years?" He paused. "Ever since our tribe split…"

They each rocked back and forth on their heels, hands shoved into pockets. Conall glanced over to his mother who gestured he should keep talking.

"I remember. That was a hard time for all of us. I don't even recall why we split, do you?"

"My da told me it was a conflict with the tribal leaders. To be honest, I never really asked. You and I were ten, I think, when our group left Silver Birch Glen to settle near Oak Mountain." Aedan's eyes moved around. "I remember hearing from my da how the Gaoth and Tine clans joined so long ago. He'd said, 'Wynd and Fyre. Air feeds fyre, and fyre moves air. They each help one another.'"

Conall nodded as Aedan spoke but didn't say anything. After a few minutes of silence, Conall laughed to himself.

"Do you remember when we stole all the eggs from the hen house? I could barely hold mine…"

"And our parents found us because we'd left a trail of broken eggs." Aedan also laughed. "Who knew two scrappy little five-year-olds could get into so much trouble?"

"I'm starting to remember." Conall smirked and shook his head. "We also hid behind the woodpile eating mulberries to avoid helping our fathers in the field."

Aedan snickered. "Until they found us fast asleep, our faces all purple from berry juice."

The boys' laughter caught the ear of Siobhan and Rinn.

"It's good to see them getting along well after not seeing each other all this time. I feel bad that we've never kept in touch with Odhran. Once the tribe split…" Siobhan sighed.

Rinn watched the boys. "It takes both sides. We had to hear about Saoirse's passing from Seamus. Still, I give Odhran a lot of credit for rearing Aedan alone."

"I'm sure the village helps. We always did take care of those in need. Look how Aedan's grown. He has his father's dark brown hair, but he keeps it shorter. Also has his mother's green eyes."

"I'll go to Oak Mountain and check on his father. See if we can help out." He squeezed his wife around the shoulders and kissed her on the head.

"But, but, do you remember how mad Seamus was when we hid his quill?" Conall doubled over in laughter. "He... He almost killed us."

Aedan leaned against the wall, his arms wrapped around his sides. "It was your idea, but I hid it in the washbasin. When he pulled it out, the feather drooped."

In due course, their raucousness died down, but their chatter didn't. One of the Elders walked from the table, but Rinn put out his arm, asking for a little more time. It had been many years since the boys had seen each other and, surely, they could have a few more minutes. The Elder nodded and stepped back.

"Right after we settled at Oak Mountain, I heard my parents talking about us. They were carrying on about how we were almost like brothers. Later, she told me she thought we were bonded, like—"

"Anam cara. How funny!" Conall slapped his leg. "My da said the same thing. He told me he was jealous that I'd found a soul friend. Linked forever, he'd say. Strange, isn't it?"

Aedan nodded and sighed. "That we're supposed to be soul friends yet we haven't even seen each other in six years. Since we started talking, I've remembered a lot. I can't think of a time when we *weren't* together back then, you know?" He just looked at Conall. "It's really good to see you again."

Smiling, Conall shoved his hands in his pockets. "Maybe we should see what the Elders want. We've been talking for quite some time."

Aedan glanced over to see the Elders talking amongst themselves.

"We can make them wait a little longer." He winked.

Their voices continued for a while, and then, of their own accord, they approached the table. Rinn and Siobhan stood behind their son. A woman's voice pierced the grassy haze, summoning both boys to the table. Thirteen elders each wore the same grey wool cloak around the wooden half-moon. Beeswax candles burned in dishes across the table, and they made the elders' eyes twinkle. The aged man who sat in the center, dividing the arc in half, stood and removed his hood. A long white braid fell behind his head, and in the candlelight, the mark on his forehead seemed to glow. His eyes, sunken with age, were heterochromic—one was a pale green while the other was a cobalt blue—the colors of the earth and sky.

"The Ársa and the Fonn seek to do battle in our world, and with that conflict comes dark times for our peoples. Many among us have had dreams foretelling the same thing, and each time, we have seen something—"

Aedan crossed his arms. "Just what does this have to do with me? And my friend?" He nodded at Conall.

The High Elder's voice pierced through Aedan's indignance. "Son of Odhran, we have seen the dragonhawk."

"The what?" Aedan huffed.

Conall looked at the High Elder and then at Aedan. "Aedan, I think this prophecy has to do with you and me. Elder Mac Maírtín explained it to me on the way here."

"I think he's been filling your head with fairy dreams, Conall. I've never even heard of or seen a dragonhawk before."

"Listen, Aedan. Years ago, I found an injured hawk and nursed it back to health. It's become like a brother to me. Lann is his name. Elder Mac Maírtín told me that he knew of a boy who had a dragon companion, someone from the Tine Clan on Oak Mountain."

"You mean... Fiachra? What does that have to do with a... a dragonhawk?"

Conall sighed, smiling. "Aedan, it's a prophecy. It's some sort of symbol. I think it has to do with both of us. Somehow, *we* are tied to this. Elder Mac Gavin was just about to explain when you arrived."

Aedan looked hard at the elders assembled, raising his eyebrow when he reached the High Elder whose green and blue eyes emanated something, a different kind of power. The silence lay heavy upon all in the cottage, and Aedan then returned to face his childhood friend.

"Do *you* believe in this, Conall?"

Conall nodded slightly. "I think I do. I've been having strange dreams."

After a few moments, Aedan faced Elder Mac Gavin once more.

"Tell me about this... dragonhawk." He folded his arms and raised an eyebrow.

"In the dreams, this creature has the body of a dragon, but the head and the wings of a hawk. From all accounts, depending on the dreamer, it has either gold and red scales, or gold and red plumage. In its talons are thirteen branches. In the distance, storm clouds gather, and in the clouds, faces can be seen. These are the faces of the Ársa and the Fonn."

Aedan grew pallid. "My father was telling me about the Fonn last night." He pulled his mother's brooch from his rucksack. "He said that this belonged to my great-grandmother, given to her by the Fonn."

He handed it to Elder Mac Gavin. The man's aged hands held it as if it were a newborn, and he brushed his fingers over the fyre symbol. In the candlelight, the brooch seemed to shimmer as if it were alive.

"By Danu's crown..." His eyes welled. "Then, the prophecy speaks true. You, Aedan Mac Odhrain, are of the Fonn."

He handed the brooch back to Aedan and turned his eyes to Conall, who stepped forward. Elder Mac Gavin took Conall's hands and squeezed. Without taking his eyes from the boy, he summoned Rinn.

"You said that an elderly woman brought Conall to you. Do you remember anything about her?"

Rinn shook his head. "No, I don't—"

"Anything. *Think*, Rinn."

The elder's face lowered when Rinn joined his wife, but then Siobhan perked up.

"I-I remember something, Elder." She approached the table, holding her hands together. "A thunderstorm raged in the skies the night when Conall came to us. Rinn answered the door, so I didn't see the woman right away. But when she handed the baby to him, I saw what I think was a chain around her waist. I'm not certain, but I think there was something hanging on it."

"You never mentioned anything before." Rinn stepped forward.

"I just remembered. Just now."

Elder Mac Gavin extended his hands to her. "Come closer, child. Give me your hands."

She looked back at Rinn who nodded. As soon as the elder took her hands, her body shivered for a moment.

"What do you see?" The elder's voice was barely above a whisper. "Just relax. Let the memory surface."

Siobhan's eyes closed. She moved her head as if she were seeing something, and then squinted.

"I see… I see Rinn opening the door, and it is raining outside. There is a thunder flash, and I see the chain. It's silver…"

"Is there anything hanging on it?" The elder's eyes glowed blue and green.

Siobhan didn't answer immediately. She moved her head again and parted her lips.

"She's turning to go, but another flash of lightning, and I can see… a feather. Yes, it's a feather hanging from the chain. She's gone now."

She opened her eyes, and the elder released her hands.

"Siobhan." Elder Mac Gavin smiled. "The crone that brought Conall to you that night was an embodiment of Aer Mór, one of the four Ársa. She took a great risk in finding you."

"But, why us? Why bring Conall to us?"

"Conall is of the Ársa." Elder Mac Gavin sat. "I see now why you both were chosen, Aedan and Conall. Siobhan, you lost a child years ago, before Conall arrived. The Ársa felt you were worthy because you are both with loving and compassionate hearts. Son of Rinn and Siobhan, it is your destiny to prevent the Coah na Shirah."

Rinn stamped up to the table. "Elders, my son is to embark on his Nascah. He is of age. We've planned for this for many years. Is there no way to—"

Elder Mac Maírtín rose. "Rinn Mac Durmaid, you would put your son's destiny before that of the world?"

"How do you even know that he, that *they*, are truly destined for such things? They're boys, not elders, druids, or seasoned warriors. What you're talking about is sending them to fight a battle they're not prepared for!"

"You will lower your tone, or you will be escorted out!" Elder Mac Brannain slammed his hands on the table. "The prophecy speaks of the dragonhawk, and the Council knows this involves your son and the son of Odhran. That Conall and Aedan each have creature companions that match both animals cannot be overlooked."

"Consider, too, that we have determined that Aedan is of the Fonn and Conall is of the Ársa. What more do you need to see that our fate is in their hands?" Elder Nic Ruori, a short, stout woman, rose from her chair. Removing her hood, her red braid fell down her back. Her right eye had a silver patch.

Siobhan pointed a finger at Elder Mac Brannain, "Do *you* have children? Would you send them into harm's way? You said this war would bring dark times. Look at them!" — she pointed at the boys — "Do you think they're ready to stop such a thing?"

Elder Mac Brannain rose and, outstretching his arms, caused a wynd that blew open the door. Swirls of air surrounded Rinn and Siobhan, moving them outside, and then the door slammed shut. Both Aedan and Conall tried to open the door, but they couldn't make it budge. Rinn and Siobhan pounded on it from the other side, calling out for the boys. Aedan slammed his fist on the table.

"Open the door!"

Elder Nic Ruori shuffled to Aedan, her hands clasped within her sleeves. Aedan huffed and yelled at her to let his parents in. Again, he tried to open the door, and grunting, kicked it, only hurting his own foot. He hobbled back to the table where the elder was.

"If you would listen, we will explain. When we have said all we need to, the door will no longer keep your parents out." Her voice had a grandmotherly tone.

"Fine." Aedan crossed his arms.

Conall had remained a few steps back but moved closer to his friend.

—⚙—

When the door finally creaked open, Elder Nic Ruori invited Rinn and Siobhan back inside. Rinn rushed over to his son who communicated he was fine as was Aedan. Before Rinn could say anything, Elder Mac Gavin invited them all to sit.

"I apologize for Elder Mac Brannain's behavior earlier. He can get a little… hot-tempered. However, we explained to the boys that this is new for us as well. Normally, such a task would be granted to a warrior, or one at least seasoned a bit more in the ways of battle. Trust me when I say that we do not *want* to send two young boys on such a quest."

Siobhan was about to speak when the elder put up a finger.

"But, we have scryed using whatever power that has been given to us, and we have seen no other individual, man or woman, who is attached to this prophecy."

"And if we refuse to allow our son to do this?" Rinn leaned forward.

Elder Mac Gavin shrugged. "Then… we let the Ársa and Fonn wage war when the time comes and hope that the days that follow are not as dark as we think they will be." He leaned back and interlaced his fingers against his chest.

"So, you're saying that we have no choice." Siobhan put her hand on Rinn's arm.

The elder shook his head. "There is always *choice*. But there are also consequences. If you decide to keep Conall from this, that is your choice to make. As the elders who govern Silver Birch Glen, Oak Mountain, and all of this island of Inis Crainnshir, we have to consider what is best for all who live here. We do not take that responsibility lightly."

Siobhan turned toward her son and Aedan.

"What else did they tell you? How are you with all of this?" She caressed a cheek on both of their faces.

"Mum, they would send an elder with us, someone to keep watch. He or she would know how to fight, too. I don't know what *we're* supposed to do exactly?" Conall looked at Elder Nic Ruori.

The elder put a small earthen bowl filled with water before him and dropped something into it. Her lips moved, but her words were indistinct. Covering her eyes with her fingertips, she continued to mutter in some ancient tongue. From the surface of the water rose elongated forms, like sticks, that formed a circle. As she pulled her fingers from her eyes, he gasped.

"Look…" She stared at the image as it hovered over the table. "The way to prevent the Coah na Shirah, it seems, is with the thirteen Wands of Danu, the Slata Danann, but they have been lost to the world for quite some time. Not even the Elder Circle knows where to look for them."

Siobhan gripped her son by his shoulders. "What matters most to your father and me is your safety. We take the risk with the Nascah because it's part of our heritage. We've taught you ways to protect yourself. But to send two boys to find something most sacred would put you in more danger than a mother can allow." She turned toward the elders. "I am sorry, but I simply cannot –"

"Mum, the elders would send an elder with us. To keep us safe." Conall attempted a smile.

"Is this true?" Siobhan put an arm around her son. "Just how much danger would they be in? A war... I can't even imagine —"

"Siobhan, be at peace. Remember that the great hero, Fionn Mac Cool, was no older than these boys when he ate of the Great Salmon of Knowledge. Who is to say that this is not part of their Nascah?"

"Elder Nic Ruori, that may be true, but to see my child, my only child thrown into a war of the ancients..."

The old woman went to the weeping wife of Rinn. The elder was a good head shorter, but she reached up and rested her hands on the sides of Siobhan's face. Using her thumbs, she wiped away the woman's tears. This time, her voice had the lilt of a new spring breeze.

"I was a mother once upon a time, so I understand the pull of your heart. I firmly believe that the power of the world set before us a path, one that we can follow with the right guidance. You have reared Conall with strength and wisdom, love and compassion, things that armor his soul against the darkness of the world. In the same way, the son of Odhran has become emboldened by the loss of his mother, and the guidance of his father. If they do not take up this quest, two ancient and powerful forces will do battle here, and they have no regard for mortal concerns. I prefer to put my hope in Conall and Aedan than await the destruction of the world."

Siobhan took the woman's hands from her face and brought them to her lips.

"Yes," she nodded, "I would rather put my hope in them as well."

Elder Nic Ruori reached up once more and pulled the woman's forehead to her lips. "May you and Rinn be blessed."

"Rinn," began Elder Mac Gavin, "you have remained silent. Do you feel reluctance as well?"

A man with the imposing figure of an oak tree took his wife in his arms.

"I would be lying if I said no. But... I have faith in my son. If Conall feels he can do this, with Aedan, then I will allow it. These two were close as brothers once. If they are of the ancients, as you say, then I must believe they will succeed. What other choice do I have? The gods saw fit to bring us a son, and now it seems that they need him to do their will."

Elder Mac Gavin asked the boys their thoughts, especially since they had learned so much in this short visit with the Elders. Conall turned toward his parents.

"Mum. Da. For as long as I can remember, I knew I was different. Now that I know I am of the Ársa, those feelings make sense. I was born with something inside me. This war scares me. I'm not sure what to do. But I think Aedan and I can do it."

He then addressed the Elders.

"Can you tell us how dangerous this is? I mean…" — he contorted his face — "Will there be monsters to fight?"

Elder Nic Ruori had a soft smile that made her cheeks puff up. "I wish I knew, child. You will meet others along the path, that much I know, who will guide you both."

"Beyond your tribal homes lay challenges, to be sure," added Elder Mac Gavin. "Keep an eye on one another and be cautious. We have faith."

Aedan looked for encouragement in his friend's eyes. "I like a challenge. And I think Conall and I can do it. I mean, you said things will happen if we do it or not. We should try, right?"

Conall extended his arm toward his friend, and they gripped forearms.

"We *should*."

Rinn stepped forward.

"Are you sure, son? Say the word, and we'll take you home."

"Da, I have to do my Nascah. You know that. If I start it, things might happen anyway. I think Aedan and I should help each other find our caomhnóiri."

Siobhan pulled Rinn into a tight embrace, and she clenched her eyes shut. Conall reached for her but his father put up his hand that he should wait. Aedan ignored that and walked up to them.

"I give you my word that I will look out for Conall. I know we haven't seen each other in a while, but we're still friends."

Rinn put a hand on Aedan's shoulder and, bearing a slight smile, nodded his thanks. Siobhan released her husband and hugged Aedan.

"I am trusting you with my only son," she whispered, her tears staining his shirt. "What other choice do I have?"

Elder Mac Gavin introduced Elder Mac Conohar, a man of six feet with a sturdier build than the older members of the Circle. He would accompany the boys, and he had been trained not only to use a quarterstaff but also with some hand-to-hand combat skills. His hood, like a cowl, covered his face, showing only a short, dark beard. Siobhan stood taller and got right up to him. He removed his hood to show heterochromatic eyes, one blue and one green.

"Take care of my son and his friend." Her words came out like a command.

Elder Mac Conohar nodded once and replaced his hood.

"Does he speak?" Aedan sized up the elder.

Elder Nic Ruori replied, "Only when needed."

Elder Mac Maírtín summoned the boys to him.

"Upon leaving this cottage, you must head west toward the island Dún Ancróga, the Fort of the Brave. According to legend, a druid who protects the fort will tell you much more than we can, but we do know a little about the wands. Thirteen wooded areas lay scattered around Inis Crainnshir, and each brought forth a wand of immeasurable power. At the heart of each wood lies a sacred shrine guarded by an animal."

Elder Mac Maírtín nodded to a darkened corner of the cottage, and a slight man edged toward the table. He looked younger than the others, almost as young as the boys. He positioned himself in front of the Circle and softly sang. The melody touched a part of the assembled that recognized the ancient and sacred:

"Of Brigid's dancing fyre came those to guard three sacred wands:
For the *Fearnslat*, a fox in the Alder,
For the *Tineslat*, a stallion in the Holly,
And for the *Ruisslat*, a hawk in the Elder.

Born of Dagda's waters came those to guard three sacred wands:
For the *Nionslat*, an adder in the Ash,
For the *Duirslat*, a wren in the Oak,
And for the *Ngetalslat*, a wolf in the Reeds.

From the airy Sídhe came those to guard four sacred wands:
For the *Luisslat*, a cat in the Rowan,
For the *Huathslat*, a seahorse in the Hawthorn,
For the *Muinslat*, a swan in the Vines,
And for the *Gortslat*, a butterfly in the Ivy.

From Anu's earthen grace came those to guard three sacred wands:
For the *Beitheslat*, a stag in the Birch,
For the *Sailslat*, a bull in the Willow,
For the *Collslat*, a salmon in the Hazel."

The youthful elder continued in a soft voice.

"Be warned. The guardians do not give up their wands easily, and you will encounter others seeking them, but we will leave that for the druid to tell you."

Aedan and Conall laughed to themselves. Rinn held his wife whose eyes were lost in thought. He waved his son over and placed his hand on Conall's shoulder.

"You have always made us proud, Conall. I know you and Aedan will succeed. Go with our blessings and our love."

"Da… Mum… I won't let you down. I promise."

Rinn's arm brought Conall into an embrace with Siobhan. Rinn looked up and waved Aedan over.

"You were always a good friend to my son when you were lads, and I know you will look out for him as he will for you."

Aedan lowered his head. "I left without seeing my father. I just—"

"I will tell him. I've known your father for a long time. Aedan, that man loves you more than life. He's proud of you."

Elder Mac Gavin told Rinn and Siobhan to bid farewell to their son. The boys remained with the Elder Circle while the elders spoke quietly among themselves. Aedan and Conall couldn't hear what they were saying even though they were in the same room.

"It's Sídhe magic. That's why we can't hear them." Aedan squinted, trying to read the lips of the elders. He turned back to Conall. "Our ten-year-old selves never thought we'd be going on *this* kind of adventure, eh?"

"It's better than raiding the hen house, for sure. I'm glad we're doing this together. The journey will give us time to catch up proper."

The Elders summoned the boys.

"You each represent the forces that seek to do battle among us, and while they have not approached you to take sides, we believe they will. Keep faith, not only in yourselves and each other, but also in those who love you. That will be your greatest shield against those seeking to do you harm. Head for Dún Ancróga. The druid will guide you further, but he asks a price."

"What kind?"

"Conall, we know not. None of us has ever seen him, and those who have ventured for him have never returned."

Aedan huffed. "Well, that doesn't make me feel very good."

"I am not afraid, my friend. We will find this druid, and together, we're going to find the wands." Conall crossed his arms and pushed out his lower lip.

The Elders gathered around the two and, in an ancient tongue, invoked Rhiannon to bless their journey. The boys gathered their belongings and left the cottage, noticing that time had not passed while they were with the elders. The sun should have risen much higher, but it was still just before sunrise.

"Brigid can bless our journey as the sun rises." Aedan lowered his head and whispered. "Watch over my father and bring him peace."

Patting Aedan on the shoulder, Conall stepped onto the westward path that remained in shadow, and for the first mile or so, silence stood between them. Elder Mac Conohar stayed ten paces behind. Among the wrens and willow warblers, the only other sound was the crunch of the earth beneath their boots. Every so often, each exhaled loud enough to be heard. Gentle hills of grass and lavender wove through patches of slate that looked like the earth had been worn down by the elements. Scattered along the route, cairns — piled stone markers — rose up, with each unique arrangement sending a message to those along the path. Some of these cairns were of one kind of stone, and other times, the motley hues of random rocks and slate gave a painted appearance. Conall slowed by a cairn of white stone, a conical tower that was about five feet tall.

"What do you think it means?" Aedan walked around it, careful not to disturb it.

"I'm not sure. My father used to tell me that cairns can be warnings or glimpses of what's to come down the path."

"Did he ever talk about a white cairn?"

"It means 'adventure lies ahead'." Conall smirked. "Let's go find it."

Once the boys left the cottage, Elders Mac Gavin, Mac Brannain, and Nic Ruori convened in a corner. Elder Mac Gavin's face was pale.

"We didn't tell them everything. Not even Conall's and Aedan's parents know."

Elder Nic Ruori put a hand on his arm. "We don't know how it will affect things."

"But if they find out that —"

"They cannot!" Elder Mac Brannain cut off Elder Mac Gavin and immediately lowered his voice. "Conall and Aedan must never learn that their tribe split because of the prophecy. They must never know that the Gaoth and Tine clans were kept apart to save them all."

Elder Nic Ruori looked back at her brethren at the table. "We underestimated the bond these boys share, their anam cara. And when I heard Siobhan say she had heard about Saoirse's death from Aedan's cousin, that is what weakened the magic keeping both tribes hidden from one another. We —"

"We couldn't have found a way around the prophecy." Elder Mac Gavin shook his head. "This was inevitable. Instead of preparing these boys from childhood for this task, we lost sixteen years. The sacred bond between them will strengthen. They might learn everything we know."

"Then," Elder Mac Brannain, "they learn. We can do nothing else but wait."

"No other clans can help the boys?" Elder Mac Gavin asked.

Elder Nic Ruori shook her head. "They are not part of the prophecy, so no."

4 | FINN MAC COOL

Tints of the early morning bled across the sky like swirls of paint in a cup of water. Gray melted into the morning blues and yellows while touches of orange blossomed as the sun rose behind the mountains that lay behind the boys. It had only been an hour since they left the elders. The countryside brightened, and the greens sparkled as the sun's rays touched the morning dew. Conall stopped by a brook to fill his water pouch. Crouching, he splashed some fresh water on his face. He gestured for Aedan to pass him his pouch and turned to ask Elder Mac Conohar for his.

"He's gone."

Aedan swung his head around, narrowing his brows. "Maybe he went to get water somewhere else?"

"He's supposed to look out for us, isn't he?" Conall rolled his eyes. "I'm sure he'll be back."

"You know, the one thing we didn't ask the elders for?" Aedan stood on his toes as he looked down the road.

"What?"

"A map. I have no idea where we are. Do you?"

Conall laughed. "No, but we have to find a village at some point. Someone built that cairn, and they would have traveled this way. I could be wrong, though. Here." He plugged the pouch with the cork and tossed it back.

"Look, there." Aedan pointed, squinting. "Beyond that hill. Do you see smoke? Could be a village, no?"

Adjusting his rucksack, Conall joined his friend. "That could be. It's a ways off, though. A few hours on foot. We'll need to get some food too.

Breakfast has just about worn off. The first village we see, we should get some supplies."

"Including a map."

A few minutes into their walk, that inescapable silence settled upon them like a bird of prey.

"Aedan. I can tell you're thinking about your da. Don't worry about him. I'm sure he'll be okay. My da said he would talk to him."

All Aedan could do was nod. This was the first time they'd spent time together in almost six years. They had quite a journey ahead of them, and Aedan's silence made Conall slow his pace.

"You know what's funny? After you left, I don't remember thinking about you. My da and mum never mentioned you or your da. But how could I forget you?" He cocked his head, his eyes moving around in thought. "What about you?"

At first, Aedan didn't reply. Conall muttered that now Aedan would think he didn't really consider him a friend if he hadn't thought about him in six years. This whole journey together would now be strained.

"You're right." Aedan stopped. "It wasn't until I saw you in the Elder Circle that I remembered you. Hmm." He glanced over. "You think it was some sort of druid magic? I mean, how could we just forget each other?"

Aedan shrugged. "Maybe the druids did do something." He wiggled his fingers. "Did they not want us to meet again? Then, why bring us together? Maybe they're connected to this Coah na Shirah."

"We're still doing this then?"

"Conall, something tells me we really didn't have a choice. I have a feeling that we'd be doing this whether we realized it or not."

Conall pushed out his lower lip and narrowed his brows. "Yeah, you're probably right. As long as our priority is the Nascah. And we still haven't seen Elder Mac Conohar. Some protector."

"Should we go back and look for him?"

"It's been a while. I'm afraid if we start looking for him, it'll take up too much time. He'll probably show up later."

The dirt road rose and fell, meandering around, and for a short while they were left to their own thoughts. Every so often, each one looked to the skies for their winged friend. They each whistled, but neither companion arrived. This kept their silence in place a bit longer, at least until they stopped to eat.

"So, how's your cousin Seamus?"

"Doing well. Writing his poems and his stories. He helps my da as a farmhand." Aedan saw that Conall was smiling, and his cheeks turned pink. "Are you blushing? Do you like Seamus?"

Conall, still smiling, turned away slightly.

"Well, I'll be. You fancy him." Aedan grinned.

"Used to. It's been a while since I've seen him. Remember, he was seven when I was five."

Aedan shook his head and laughed. "You'd hardly recognize him now. He's taller than both of us. We'll have to pay him a visit when we go back." He winked.

"We don't have to. I was just curious. Besides, I don't think he likes me very much."

"Why do you say that?"

"When we were kids, he would never play with me. I tried to toss him a ball once, and he turned away to go be by himself in the woods. He always had some parchment and quill. I don't know what he wrote when he was so young, but he sure spent a lot of time doing it."

"He hasn't changed much. Are you sure he wasn't just being a seven-year-old? Seamus always did keep to himself more than he played with anyone."

"It really doesn't matter, Aedan. We don't know how long we'll be gone, and I have a feeling he fancies girls. It's all well and good." He cleared his throat. "So, how about you? Someone caught your eye?"

Aedan had that look on his face like someone who had a load of secrets and would share for the right price. He brushed his short brown hair back with his fingers.

"Well? Surely someone in the Tine Clan has worked his way into your heart." Conall nudged him with his foot.

"Every now and then. I prefer to keep my options open."

"You dog! Tell me. Come on. We have some time to kill."

The chuckle that came from Aedan had that giddiness one saw in new love, a playful laugh.

"There *was* the son of Turlough, the blacksmith. His name is Niall. He's the most recent."

"When we were little, you always kept your feelings to yourself, but as soon you said Niall's name, your eyes jumped. You said *was*?"

Aedan kicked the ground as he walked and pulled on the straps of his rucksack. His smile softened a little, but it was still present.

"His da wasn't too keen on me. Niall would sneak out at dawn before his parents woke up so we could sit by the river. In the end, he got caught. Turlough then said I was a rascal, someone not worthy of his son. But there were others before Niall. I can honestly tell you that my virtue's intact. I've only ever *kissed* a lad."

Conall raised an eyebrow and smirked.

"As Brigid's my witness, I swear it." Aedan held up his hands and laughed. "How about you?"

"Well, we've already talked about Seamus —"

"I mean someone who would fancy *you* as well." Aedan had a smug look.

Lowering his head, Conall slumped as he walked, saying nothing. Aedan, turning away, walked on. No more than ten steps later, Conall admitted that he'd never paid much attention to the boys in the Glen. He was much more interested in helping his da and mum. But he had always had a dream where he walks hand in hand with someone who has the sharpest eyes and a smile that could stop the wynd. Being in love was something he saw as unreachable yet entirely desirable. He laughed a little, adding that he hadn't told that to anyone before.

The well-trodden road rose and fell, passing through the occasional birch forest or grassy mead, and the morning sun neared its midday zenith. With the passing of the hours, the boys shared stories on many topics, including Aedan's mother's passing, and the truth about Conall's birth. It was then that Conall realized something, and he scanned the skies.

"What's wrong?"

"I've not seen Lann since we left. That's not like him."

Aedan raised his eyebrows and shrugged.

"Sorry. My hawk. We've been together for years. He's usually somewhere where I can see him. But it's odd... Ever since we left the elders, he's not been around." He shielded his eyes from the sun.

"I'm sure he's okay. Maybe he and Fiachra are playing tag. Fiachra's my dragon. Come to think of it, I haven't seen him, either. I guess he'll show up at some point. He's a mind of his own."

Crossing the next hill, they saw the source of the smoke — a hamlet nestled in the dale between the hills. They picked up their pace, as neither had eaten anything since before he left his home. At about a half-mile from the hamlet's entry, they heard shouting coming from one of the thatched cottages. Two men emerged, barely able to stand and whose clothing was soiled and unkempt. One looked like a bear wearing clothes, and the other a pole bean. Toward the tavern came a young couple, hands clasped, not realizing they were about to walk toward the two drunkards meandering through the street. One of the two men stepped in front of the couple, and all Conall and Aedan could see was an agitated man, gesticulating, and the poor girl cowering behind her companion. The other man joined, and they circled the couple like raptors before the kill. Aedan started to run toward them, but Conall stopped him.

"Wait! Look!"

Another man, at least two heads taller than the inebriated men, took one step outside the tavern and picked up both men by the throat, one in each massive hand, and tossed them onto the road as if they were dolls. Bald with a blond chinstrap beard and goatee, he wore only a great kilt with a silver brooch and fur-lined leather boots; with a look, he directed the couple to go home. Then, cross-armed, he waited for the two men to get on their feet to see if they would continue their foolishness. Conall and Aedan had stopped just short of the tavern and hid behind a cart. They saw the brawny man put the tip of his thumb in his mouth as if he were thinking. The lanky one of the pair picked up a log, brandishing it like a club. His companion drew a dagger from his boot, and they both circled the bearded man. Shaking his bald head and laughing to himself, he waited for the attack. He looked as if he weren't really taking the threat seriously, but then his hand flew up, stopping the log just as came crashing down. The other heavier man, staggering behind, tossed his dagger from hand to hand. He lurched forward to bury the blade in the bald man's back when the log knocked the dagger to the ground.

"Have you had your fun, Colum? Sean? Now, why don't you go sleep off your ale before you get hurt." To make his point, he snapped the log in two as if it were a twig.

Sean and Colum grumbled something in reply and glared at the bald man who simply smirked and tossed the log halves to the side of the road.

Aedan came out from behind the cart and headed toward the tavern with Conall close behind. Inside, they found a rickety table by the wall and saw that the bald man had returned to his own table, downing his tankard.

"Torin! Another, if you please."

On the other side of the tavern, Aedan leaned over to Conall.

"I'm going to get us some ciders and whatever food I can."

After Aedan told Torin what he wanted at the bar, he looked over at the bald man who took a swig of his ale and wiped his mouth with the back of his hand. The tavern keeper put two wooden tankards of cider and a plate of roasted meat in front of Aedan.

"Tell me, who is that man over there?" Without turning back to Torin, he handed him a few coins.

"That? That, m'lad is one of the finest men I've ever known. You wouldn't know it from his own mouth. Humble he is. But that's Fionn Mac Cool."

"Fionn Mac Cool? The hero? By Brigid's fyre…"

Aedan grabbed the ciders in one hand and the plate with the other, nodding at Conall, who looked confused, to join him. When they both approached Fionn's table, the man looked up.

"I hope you don't mind, but the tavern keeper told me who you were. May we sit with you? If you mind, we –"

Conall started to tug on Aedan's sleeve when Fionn slapped his hands on the table. "By all means, lads. You look a bit road weary. Sit and enjoy your food."

Aedan looked over at Conall. "*This* is Fionn Mac Cool." He smiled and nodded.

With wide eyes, Conall held out his hand. "I've heard a lot about you. You're a famous hero."

Fionn gripped Conall's forearm. "People like to tell stories. I'm just glad they tell the good ones. So, what brings you both to Rowandale?"

The boys said they were on their Nascah, but said nothing of their other task. The hero nodded, moving his eyes from Conall to Aedan as each one spoke. If he weren't amused or interested, it wasn't obvious by his slight smile and head nods. When one of the boys was speaking, the other was shoving food in his mouth. Fionn shot a look to Torin who then brought over a plate of fresh brown bread and cheese. Aedan and Conall looked at each other, mouths agape.

"You have a long journey ahead of you. Surely, you should fill your stomachs."

"So… what's it like, being a hero?" Aedan shoved a piece of meat into his mouth.

Fionn laughed deeply. "I do what I do, lad. I don't think about it the way others might. I live my life to do right by my fellow man, or woman, and I let the results speak for themselves. When you start thinking you're a hero, you forget your place in the world. You become entitled. Arrogant. That's no way to act."

Hours crept past them, and then Fionn wiped his mouth. He asked which way the boys were headed, and as soon as Conall mentioned Dún Ancróga, Fionn had a scant smile.

"A piece of advice, young ones. When you arrive, bring an offering for the druid. He won't ask about it, but it'll ensure you're regarded with respect. He might help you without it, but with it, you're almost guaranteed more information. There's a merchant just before you leave town. "

At the road, Fionn clasped each boy's forearm.

"I'm heading in the other direction, but may your path be free of obstacles, and may your journey be fruitful. Until we meet again, lads."

"One question, before you go."

"Of course, Aedan."

"When you were fighting those men earlier, you didn't act like you were in a brawl. I'm not used to seeing someone so calm in a fight."

Fionn grinned and patted Aedan's shoulder. "That's the difference between leaping into thought, and leaping into action. The first gives you a plan, the other can get you killed. No one ever died leaping into thought. Fare thee well, lads. I am sure we'll meet again. Best of luck on your Nascah!"

The boys continued their westward path, sharing how each couldn't help but notice the size of Fionn's arms or that he was handsome, for being older. Starting on this leg of their journey, they opened up a bit more, sharing stories that seemed to come from nowhere but resonated with each other—a full belly and good company can do wonders for one's mood. Moving away from Rowandale, the landscape gradually lost its sylvan charm and became more slate mixed with rough, short grasses. The skies, too, lost their colorful presence and shades of gray mixed with the slightest pale purple. Even the wynd rose, and it brought a chill that the boys hadn't experienced yet. It seemed as if time had moved forward toward a winter climate, but it was the middle of summer. Flatter land lay ahead, and in the distance, crows circled around like leaves in a breeze. Eventually, the path melded into patches of gray slate, and the only way they knew which way to go was marked by a circle of stones in the distance. Conall stopped and looked around.

"Do you hear that?" He scanned the landscape. "What is it?"

"I don't know what you're talking about. I don't hear anything."

"I'm telling you. I hear something, like a flute." Conall resumed his approach to the stones. "You mean to tell me you can't hear that?"

Aedan laughed. "That's exactly what I'm saying. Your mind is playing tricks. Let's keep moving. We'll need to make camp soon anyway.

Aedan continued on, but Conall would stop every few footsteps and turn his head. Once the stones were in full view, they both saw something moving around the circle. About a quarter of a mile from the stones, Aedan stopped and put up his hand.

"Wait. I hear it. You say it sounds like a flute? That's what I hear all right. Come on."

By the time they reached the ring of stones, the sun had started its descent toward the western horizon. They walked into the circle and saw a small stone fyre ring in the middle. Conall kept turning around and looking everywhere while Aedan dropped his rucksack by the fyre ring.

"Look at this place. It's incredible. I've never seen anything like it. This isn't Dún Ancróga, though. I wonder where we are."

"Well, the Elders did say that we'd find a druid, so perhaps this is where he or she is." Aedan picked up two small stones. "I'm going to build a fyre. It's gotten quite cold here."

Distracted by the massiveness of the stones, Conall didn't hear Aedan's last comment, but when he saw his friend about to strike two stones together to start the fyre, he leaped forward.

"Aedan! Don't! You don't know what—"

A spark from the stones touched the old wood, and it burst into a pillar of fyre. From behind one of the stones came someone cloaked in white.

"—you'll summon!"

Conall joined his friend by the fyre, and he couldn't take his eyes off the white figure making its way toward them.

"What do you mean, 'summon'? It's a fyre pit. We're cold, and —"

"*Look*, Aedan!" Conall turned his friend so he could see the approaching figure, too.

A cold wynd picked up while the fyre burned brighter and hotter. Whoever approached did so slowly, using a gnarled staff to walk over uneven ground. As he or she made the way around the fyre pit, Aedan took a defensive posture, putting a foot in front of Conall. Conall stepped away from his friend, and his facial expression showed he didn't need protecting.

"I-I am Conall Mac Rinne, this is Aedan Mac Odhrain. We're supposed to meet a druid at Dún Ancróga. Are you the druid? What is this place?" His voice trembled even though he tried to stand tall.

With a gesture, the cloaked figure lowered the fyre until it was at a more normal level and removed the hood. An older man, whose long, hoary beard was braided, bowed his head.

"Aye. I have been expecting ye. You have entered An Laoich Tairseach and lit the sacred fyre. Only those who are worthy can do so. I am… impressed."

"The Hero's Portal?" Conall stared at the druid's heterochromic eyes, like some of the Elders: one blue and one green. "What would have happened if we weren't worthy?"

The druid smiled. "You simply wouldn't have been able to light the fyre. My name is Déaglán, and I have guarded An Laoich Tairseach since the day I was born. You have found your way to holy ground, and it is by Brigid's grace that you enter."

The last words made Aedan perk up, and he removed a satchel from his rucksack.

"Since the day you were born? How long —"

Conall hit him with his elbow.

"Here." — Aedan shot Conall a look — "This is a gift. From both of us."

The druid opened both palms together and gently closed them around the bundle.

"May the blessings of the Tuatha Dé Danann be upon you." Déaglán placed the bundle in a pocket of his cloak.

"Are you not going to look at it? You know, to make sure it's a worthy gift?"

"Son of Odhrain, a stone from the river Sionainn with the emblem of a salmon is a most worthy gift."

The druid explained that the megalithic stones themselves were portals to other places, some mortal and some divine. He also told them that knowing the proper dríochta, or magical incantation, could open mystical portals to some of the most mysterious places in the world. Not all who enter the circle have been worthy, and those who sought passage without the knowledge could become the Idir, those trapped "between" places. Then, Déaglán placed a palm on Conall and Aedan's foreheads and closed his eyes. Mumbling in an ancient tongue, he opened his eyes, and each pupil swirled with light and magic. His mutterings became louder and more emphatic.

"You have received an omen, young ones, a most favorable one, indeed. From Rowandale you have come where you encountered a man of great renown. Your gift confirms it."

"You *know* that? You know we met Fionn Mac Cool? That's incredible. What else do you know?" Aedan looked at Conall and shrugged. "Our gift? What does that have to do with Fionn?"

"I know as much as I don't know. My path is always one for learning. I also know that you are tied to a winged prophecy, one that has brought you here."

Conall stepped forward. "Wait. I know what the gift has to do with Fionn. When I was little, my da would tell me all about Fionn's adventures. His birth name was Deimne, and he was the son of Cool, the leader of the Fianna. He studied with Finegas, a druid. When Finegas caught the salmon of knowledge, Deimne cooked it for him, but he burned his thumb and stuck it in his mouth. From that, he gained the wisdom of the salmon. That stone we gave you had the salmon carved into it."

"Well told, young son of Rinn. Later, when his hair turned blond, he was given the name Fionn."

Aedan laughed. "Well, when we saw him, he was bald. But his beard was fair."

Night took over the sky, and the stars emerged like eyes to another world. Déaglán instructed the boys where they could build their tent inside the circle. Within the confines of the stones, no animals would harm them while they slept. Conall wanted to know why he hadn't seen Lann since his journey started, and all Déaglán could tell him was that they would meet again soon. It wasn't destined that they follow the same path yet. The same was true for Fiachra. This put Aedan's mind at rest especially. Ever since Elder **Mac Brannain had dismissed the dragon, Aedan hadn't seen him at all. The druid walked them around the inside of the stone circle, stopping at certain monoliths.**

"This one, with the right dríochta, could take you to Avalon, an idyllic place of the Sídhe, one where kings are made."

Two stones farther, Déaglán pointed with his staff.

"Here, a doorway to Connla's Well lies. It was here where Fionn Mac Cool gained his wisdom from the salmon. And this one" — he tapped the rough stone — "is a gateway to Tir na nÓg, the Otherworld. Not even I know the correct dríochta to open that portal."

Conall's eyes remained wide as he learned what he assumed was privileged information. While Déaglán moved around the circle, Conall lifted his head toward the heavens, and the stars twinkled all around. A memory surfaced from his childhood when he and his father had lain back on a hilltop and watched the parade of constellations. Rinn would point to a cluster of stars and tell stories. Sometimes, if the heavens permitted, other figures appeared, the planets. Conall recalled how his father referred to them as "the Lords that wander." In the summers, he also saw what Rinn called "the Humble Ones" or shooting stars. Legends told that when a star felt too distant from his mortal cousins, he or she would fall to Earth and live among mankind as An Umhal. These people walked, shrouded, and had the power to heal. They would live as long as they wished, returning to the stars when they felt it was time. On certain nights, clusters of stars would shine brighter than usual, and it was said they were welcoming their wayward brother or sister home. Nights like that were supposed to be lucky for childbearing or taking a journey.

"Conall, are you listening?" Aedan leaned into his friend's ear.

"I am, Aedan. To the stars."

"We just passed the doorway to Carn Slánú, a mountain sacred to Belenus, the sun god. Déaglán says that anyone who climbs the mountain to its summit would be cured of all ailments." His voice lilted in wonder.

The druid called their attention to the last stone. Etched into it was the phrase: Níl ach an cróga dul isteach—Only the Brave May Enter. As if it were a sign, in the ebony sky above, a waxing crescent moon sat as if perched atop the megalith, a shining jewel in a celestial crown.

"So, are we going to Dún Ancróga? This is the door?"

"Be at ease, son of Odhran. Journeys such as these must be made at the sliver of sunrise when the birth of the day is imminent. To go now would avail you nothing. We must travel together."

After setting up camp, Conall approached the druid by the fyre. Déaglán was reciting unintelligible words in the softest voice. His lips moved around the sounds with a rhythm that felt like a heartbeat to Conall. It took the boy a few moments to muster the courage to interrupt.

"If you can answer it, I have a question."

The druid continued his mutterings but gave no indication that Conall shouldn't continue.

"You said earlier that you knew of the prophecy. Can you tell me if Fionn Mac Cool is in any way tied to it? It seems funny that we should meet him, that he should know we should bring a gift, and that, unknown to Aedan and myself, the gift should relate to him."

Déaglán's words slowed until his mouth moved into a slight smile. His eyes remained on the fyre. Conall looked back to see Aedan returning with some peat, as instructed by the druid. Peat burned slower than wood, so it would last the night.

"Son of Rinn, some of your questions will be answered when we reach our destination. As for Fionn, I do see that your paths cross a few times, so he will most assuredly reappear at some point on your journey. When and where, I do not know. You should both get some rest. We need to be ready to travel just before sunrise."

Aedan was lying back on his blanket with an arm behind his head when Conall returned. In the twinkling fyrelight, Conall could see Aedan's eyes were glossy and staring off.

"You all right?"

Aedan nodded slightly. Conall bunched up his rucksack into a make-shift pillow and lay facing away from his friend. He could still see the druid at the fyre and wondered what Déaglán would tell them at the fort that he couldn't tell them in this circle of stones. His thoughts then went to his parents. It had been less than a full day since he had left them, but it felt like much longer.

"Conall?" Aedan's voice was barely above a whisper.

"Yeah?"

"When Déaglán mentioned Carn Slánú, I was thinking I wished I could have brought my mum there. You know, so she could have gotten better. That's why I was quiet just now."

Conall didn't reply right away. He wasn't entirely sure what to say. Even though Siobhan was his adoptive mother, she had always acted as though he had emerged from her womb. He missed her this night. She would want to make sure he was warm enough or had had enough to eat. Rather than say something just for the sake of responding, he pretended to have fallen asleep. Slumber came soon enough for both, and the fyre remained alive, dancing for the stars.

Aedan's eyes opened first, and the first thing he saw was the purple-black sky adorned with its diadem of stars, the same ones that Conall had watched the night before. The air was crisp, and on it traveled the scent of pine from across the plain. Morning birds punctuated the silence with their whistles, giving a placid tone to a morning that would bring forth a new chapter in their lives. Embers of peat glowed in the ring, and the shadow of the druid emerged. Aedan tapped Conall awake who exhaled heavily through his lips.

"It can't be morning already."

"Afraid so." Aedan packed his rucksack. "It'll be dawn soon, and I know the druid wants to leave at 'the sliver of sunrise'." His voice mocked Déaglán's earlier tone.

Conall's eyebrow raised at a new vibrance that came through Aedan's voice, an anticipation or even a sense of eagerness. Stretching and yawning, he saw Aedan pack his rucksack with more intent than he had seen since their departure from the Elders.

"You're awfully energetic this morning." He ran his fingers through his blond hair and rubbed his face to try to wake up.

"We have a new adventure ahead of us. Why shouldn't I be?" He threw a rolled blanket at his friend, hitting him in the face. "Come on. I'm sure the druid is ready to go."

As they walked over to the stone where Déaglán waited, Conall muttered, "Who are you, and what have you done with Aedan?"

All Aedan could do was smile. "Hmph."

At the horizon, the Tyrian purple yielded to a pale lavender as the sun prepared to break open a new day. A sharper pine scent rode the morning breeze. Déaglán, blue and green eyes twinkling with the first light of dawn, held his hands up to the stone.

"Be ready, young ones. Once we reach Dún Ancróga, your first trials begin."

Conall and Aedan's faces paled at the word 'trials'. As they looked back at the stone, the druid had started the dríochta to open the portal. Archaic glyphs and symbols they didn't recognize glowed white, and icovellavna, Celtic knot designs, appeared as if drawn by a divine hand. Some of the shapes, like triskeles and spirals, seemed familiar to the two boys, but other shapes challenged their mind so that they blinked a few times and looked away. The white lines outlined a rectangular shape that traveled the edges of the stone, and just as the white light receded, Déaglán whispered a few words and touched the center. Shimmering like water, the rough surface gave way to an image of another place, one by the sea, where a stone fort stood as evidence of a departed age, one of stronger magics than even the druid could comprehend.

"Step through but be on your guard. Remember your courage."

5 | DUN ANCROGA

eyond the magical portal, Conall and Aedan barely had a moment to get their bearings when phantasms of warriors swarmed before them, setting up a barrier between them and the entry to the fort. A dozen ethereal men and women brandished swords, spears, and maces. Where their eyes should be were dark, smoldering openings. Aedan again took a protective stance before Conall, but Conall moved aside, shooting him a look of disapproval. Déaglán stood behind them in silence.

Leaning in toward the throng of spirits, Aedan squinted to make the ghostly beings crisper. "Are they just going to stand there? What do they want?"

Conall tugged on his arm. "Maybe we should step back. They don't seem like they're here to welcome us. Déaglán, what do you know about them?"

The druid drifted back.

"Fine, then. Don't help." Conall took steps back since there was nowhere to hide.

"You brought us here, and you don't tell us what we're here to do. You're a druid. Aren't you supposed to be able to talk to spirits?" Aedan growled.

Déaglán removed his hood. "Perhaps, Aedan, but they're not here to speak to *me*."

Holding his ground, Aedan clenched his fists. Narrowing his eyes, he took in as much of the multitude as he could before he swallowed hard. Sweat trickled down the back of his neck and his temples. His thoughts traveled back to Oisin and the brothers who bullied him, and then he took a step forward.

As a unit, the warriors moved toward him, their collective footsteps silent where the crunching of earth should be. He clenched and unclenched his fists.

"What are you doing?" Conall hadn't moved. "We need to get out of here."

Aedan didn't answer right away, shaking his head rapidly. "No, Conall. Stand here with me." His eyes didn't leave the approaching spirits.

Conall looked at Aedan and then at the warriors who were inching closer, weapons at the ready. He searched for Déaglán, but the druid was gone.

"Conall..." He turned to his friend. "Trust me."

Something in his Aedan's eyes struck him. It was the same expression he had seen when they were children before they attempted to climb the old oak in the center of the glen, the one they had been warned against climbing. In that single moment, though, he remembered the outcome of that day and felt his heart become more at ease. He didn't know why, but he took a step forward. Then another. And a third, until he was standing next to Aedan. Seeing his friend holding his position, Conall took a deep breath and mimicked the stance. Warrior spirits edged closer, their dark eyes showing no emotion.

In a soft voice, Aedan spoke. "Whatever you do, don't move. Stay strong."

No breath came from the warriors. No heartbeats punctuated their closeness. They towered over the boys. Conall blinked as the sweat trickled into his eyes, and his breathing quickened. His pulse echoed like the beat on a bodhran, deep and rhythmic. Turning his head just a little, he saw Aedan glaring at them. *Why isn't he afraid*, Conall thought. *Why am I?*

A second later, a screeching war cry echoed everywhere, and the spirits melted into the mist. The boys looked at each other and laughed, the involuntary laugh when you've stared down death and won. An icy wynd swept through and took the remaining mists, leaving two quarterstaffs in their wake. The same wynd draped the stone fort in fog. The boys couldn't see the druid anywhere.

Conall turned away from his friend and hung his head.

"What's wrong?" Aedan placed a hand on Conall's shoulder. "Hey?"

"I-I was afraid. Like a little child. But you... you weren't. You faced them. You should go on with Déaglán. I'm not worthy of being here."

Aedan turned his friend toward him, both hands on the boy's shoulders.

"Look at me, Conall. You think I wasn't afraid? I was terrified. I had no more of an idea of what those spirits would do than you did."

"But, how —"

"Do you know where I found the strength to face them?"

Conall, his shoulders slumped, had barely lifted his head to look at Aedan.

"Your da? Cernunnos?"

Aedan poked Conall's chest. "*You*. I got it from you. While I stood here, expecting to be run over, I had a flash of when we were lads. Even at six, *you* were the explorer, always charging ahead. *You* wanted to climb trees or look under rocks. *You* took the risks. I knew you were next to me."

"I didn't do anything. I cowered."

Aedan smiled. "But you didn't *run*. You stood with me. That's what counts. You know what else? The longer we're away from home, the more I remember of your past together. We were inseparable, like brothers. Also, neither one of us is Fionn Mac Cool. We're both going to have our moments. Let's find Déaglán."

"Where'd he go? Tell me he didn't just leave us here. Why are druids so odd?"

"I wouldn't insult him, Conall. He still has to help us get back to where we were. Who knows? Maybe he's with Elder Mac Conohar."

Conall looked around. "It couldn't be that easy," he whispered to himself.

He crouched by the staffs, running his fingers along faint carvings of both, but on one of them, the glyphs illuminated for a moment. He tossed the other to Aedan.

"Why would the spirits leave these for us? If they'd intended for us to use them, they wouldn't have left."

"I don't know." Aedan scanned for the druid.

Conall lingered on the symbols. "There's something familiar about this writing. I think this is ancient Ogham for a... hawk? How can that be? How would I know that?"

"This..." Aedan brought the staff close to his eye. "This looks like the Ogham for dragon. Wait. How can I read Ogham? I've never learned it. My father told me it was an alphabet only the elders, druids, and the Ancient Ones knew."

"The Elders did say we're connected to the Ársa and the Fonn." Conall shrugged.

Spinning the staff, he pretended to spar, his moves awkward and abrupt. He quickened his swings and maneuvers, ending up hitting himself in the head.

"Do you even know what you're doing? You look like a blind man trying to swat a fly."

"When I touched this staff, the letters went white for a moment. I think it was trying to tell me something." Conall swung the staff, smacking his knee from behind.

"Before you accidentally knock yourself out, let's figure out what we're supposed to do next." Aedan had both hands on the staff, moving it in slow motion, his eyebrow raised.

"We're supposed to fight those spirits. That's why we have the staffs. You don't think they're really gone, do you? Two boys stared down a group of ghostly warriors?"

Aedan huffed and shrugged, enrapt with his new staff. He had all the grace of a wounded heron.

Bringing the staff around, Conall smacked his against Aedan's hard enough to get his friend's attention. Aedan returned the maneuver, and their activity turned into a rough sort of sparring. Laughter rose from them, until they turned their ineptness into a game, each trying to outdo the other. From out of the mists emerged Déaglán, and Conall noticed.

"Druid, tell me something." Conall crashed his staff down toward Aedan who moved out of the way. "Why would these warrior spirits leave staffs for two people who have never used them before?"

Their mock melee continued a little while longer with the druid remaining silent. In the midst of a fog-shrouded landscape, the two boys engaged in clacking their respective weapons against each other, or whatever body part happened to be in the way. Since the beginning of their journey, they had been so focused on their next steps that they had ignored the deep-seated need to vent pent-up frustrations. Their play fighting provided the means.

"Okay, enough." Aedan leaned over, breathing deeply. "It's clear that we'd surely be killed in a real battle." His laugh sounded like a little boy's—innocent and eager.

"Ha! So you yield! I knew you'd give up." Conall giggled.

"Hardly. I saw you were tiring, so I thought I'd—"

A shriek cut through the fog.

"That sounded like a banshee." Aedan took up his staff in both hands. "Do you see anything?"

Conall pulled his staff close to him. "No. Maybe it was only a bird? It sounded like a hawk or an eagle."

The piercing noise returned, this time louder, and it lingered, clinging to the air as if with talons. A chill swept through, although the fog didn't move. Aedan stepped back until his back touched Conall's. Once more that sound surrounded them, growing in volume and tenacity. Shapes rose from the earth, forming bodies that took on human form. The warriors returned, and their eyes glowed dark orange this time. For a moment, the boys stared at their ethereal adversaries until the ghostly horde let out a battle cry and leaped forward. A hundred feet stood between them. Conall and Aedan, staffs in hand, backed up slowly. The throng of battle mongers closed the distance.

Conall stopped, as did Aedan.

"This feels different. The warriors look more real. Is this what they wanted, to give us weapons to fight?"

"I don't know, Conall. This time, we're both just going to be ready for whatever comes. Yes?"

"Y-Yes."

Eighty feet.

"You trust me. I trust you. We can *do* this."

Sixty feet.

Conall flashed to a day during their childhood when they ran through the glen together, chasing rabbits. Another memory, one of them climbing trees, where they pretended they were birds perched above, came into focus. A third flash came: the day before Aedan's family left the glen, when Aedan and he cried together behind the woodpile.

Forty feet.

"Yes. I trust you." Conall moved from one foot to the other. "I *have* to."

"Good. Then, let's stand our ground."

They planted their feet, gripping their quarterstaffs until their knuckles turned white. Fiery eyes of the oncoming band sliced through the fog, giving them a beastly cast.

Twenty feet.

Conall started to move a foot back, and then Aedan's hand squeezed his arm.

Ten feet.

Conall clamped his eyes shut, his body shaking, and braced to be bludgeoned by a mace or to feel cold steel slice into his body. His heartbeat was a battle drum in his head, and he opened his eyes when the mass of ghostly bodies, shouting their war cries, was only a few feet from him. In those last seconds, he thought of Aedan standing beside him, thought of his parents, and he stood taller, held fast to the staff, and locked his legs. He expected there to be such a force to knock him off his feet—but the warriors vanished an inch from his face. Again. At that exact moment, that shrieking came through once more, right above him, and Conall recognized it. With tears running down his cheeks and his chest heaving, he held out his arm to welcome his old friend.

"You're back!" Conall fell back and leaned against a boulder.

Lann squawked.

Aedan, catching his breath, put a hand on Conall's shoulder and smiled. "I'm proud of us. So, this is your hawk, eh?" He sat back against the same boulder. "Might want to ask him where he's been."

He caught Conall looking at him with concern.

"I'm fine, Conall. Truly. How about you?"

The son of Rinn smiled and nodded once. "Put up your arm."

Aedan didn't understand at first, but he did it. Conall pushed his arm with Lann next to it and spoke to the hawk.

"It's okay."

Squawking once, the raptor flapped a little and moved onto Aedan's arm.

"If his talons get too much, just scold him a little. I'll be right back."

Lann cocked his head back and forth, never taking an eye off Conall who headed for Déaglán. Aedan smirked, noticing how attentive the hawk was, and then lifted a hand slowly toward him. When Lann didn't protest, Aedan softly stroked Lann's back. He looked back at his friend, smiling, but his words were for the hawk.

"Anam cara."

The druid had remained unmoved during the entire skirmish, and even at this moment, he kept still and hooded. Conall strode up to him.

"What now, Déaglán? Have to say I wasn't prepared for that. Anything else you see fit to share with us? Will we be facing the Mórrígan next?" — He waved his arms — "You tell us we need to go to Dún Ancróga, so we come here and face a mad band of ghost warriors. What next?"

Déaglán's hood slid back from his face, and he was smiling. His eyes sparkled.

"Have you finished?" He walked toward the fort entrance. "Follow me."

Conall whistled, and Lann settled on his arm. Aedan trotted up to them.

"What did you say to the druid?"

"I gave him a piece of my mind. Look. We're going inside."

Aedan laughed to himself, following. "Conall, you might have a strong heart, but you could no more intimidate a druid any more than you could scare a child."

No door barred their entry, simply an opening in the dry stone wall, one where no mortar bound the small stones. Littering the ground around them, remnants of weapons lay strewn, a testament to battles won or lost, to warriors on both sides. When Conall asked Déaglán how the walls remained so strong, the druid simply replied,

"Never deny the ingenuity of man."

Beyond the wall, the fog had settled, and the air grew cooler. The druid put his arm before them.

"We cannot pass. Not yet. *Ceocháin, imigh!*"

Like a receding tide, the fog lifted.

Aedan leaned over to Conall. "That's all he has to say? 'Mists, go!' No special enchantment? When I speak the ancient tongue, I sound like an old man, but when he speaks it, the mists actually move?"

Conall raised an eyebrow.

"I know, I know… 'He's a druid, that's why.'"

Before them lay a sight that neither boy had ever seen: caltrops — knee-high vertical rocks like jagged teeth — spread out like grass. Beyond, another stone wall, about twenty feet ahead.

"What is this?" Conall crouched to touch one, but the druid knocked his hand back.

"No! You mustn't touch them. They look like normal stone, but they are of the Sídhe. Their surface has poison, one that eats flesh."

Conall's mouth fell agape. "Why?"

"They protect what lies within. If the warrior spirits do not scare off trespassers or those unworthy, this field prevents them from advancing. The fog hides these teeth, waiting for the unwary or ignorant."

"What lies beyond that is worth such protection?" Aedan craned his neck to see, but the opening in the wall beyond was shrouded in fog.

"You will see soon enough, assuming you can get past this."

Conall stared out at the rocks. "Déaglán, have I told you lately how much I hate puzzles?"

"You said that the poison on the stones eats flesh. What *isn't* harmed by touching them?" Aedan crossed his arms, smirking at Conall.

"Water, stone, and wood."

The druid backed away toward the main entry, and when Conall turned, the man had vanished.

"We're on our own. Again. First, Elder Mac Conohar, and now Déaglán."

"Conall, I know we're supposed to follow some sort of prophecy, but—"

"No, Aedan. We've come this far. I'm not quite ready to give up just yet."

"Well, how do you suppose we get across the stones? I don't know how water would help us, and I didn't see any around here. The only stones I see are the walls themselves and the teeth before us. I've also not seen any forests or trees of any kind, so wood can't help."

"It's a shame Fiachra's not with us. Your dragon would certainly come in handy about now."

"True. I don't know where he went. But yes, a flying dragon would make this easier. Something tells me that it's not supposed to be easy." Aedan sighed.

The morning dragged while the boys thought about how to get farther into the fort, and Aedan had scouted for anything that he thought could help. He came back with a handful of rocks and pieces of shields. Aedan sat against the wall, manipulating what he'd found mostly out of boredom. A short while later, Conall glanced over to see that Aedan had stacked some rocks into miniature cairns, and on two of the rocks, he'd placed the shield shards, creating a small tower. He smirked but continued to look at it. His smirk became a smile, and he jumped up.

"I think I know how we can get across. It'll be risky, but I think it'll work."

Aedan replied through a yawn, "Ya? What's this brilliant plan?"

Holding a piece of the shield, Conall turned it a few ways.

"This is wood. Weathered by the elements and time. How many pieces did you bring back?"

Aedan made a pile of a handful of fragments.

"Give me the cord from your vest."

Conall took his own cord out and tied a piece of the shield to the bottom of his foot. He did the same with Aedan's cord on the other foot. He stood up, and then adjusting the knots to make sure the shard stayed in place.

"What are you doing?"

Walking around, Conall bounced a little on the shield pieces.

"Watch." Conall, using his staff to support him, stepped on one of the stone teeth, then he pulled up his other foot, using the staff to balance. Gradually, he walked on the teeth, stopping after each step to assure his balance. Six steps later, he had crossed the poisoned caltrops. He whistled, and Lann flew to him. "Take these to Aedan."

The hawk obeyed, grasping the cording in his talons, and dropping them into Aedan's waiting hands. Once Aedan crossed, he handed Conall back his cord.

"That was pretty clever, using the wooden shield pieces like shoes."

Conall winked at his friend. "It was your idea, actually."

The boys walked through the other doorway to find Déaglán standing in the center of a grassy area. A moist ocean breeze blew from behind him, bringing the salty air. Behind the druid was the horizon and a cliff's edge. Conall walked a few steps and leaned forward, careful not to get too close. The distant roar of the waves crashing against the cliff sounded like it was up close.

"Do you want to ask him or should I?" Aedan whispered.

Conall patted his friend on the back. "Déaglán, what are we doing? There's nothing here. We just braved poisoned teeth for this."

The druid didn't answer but moved a smudge stick of sage all around the boys—a cleansing ritual upon entering a sacred space. The sweet smoke moved as if it were alive, and the wisps twirled in on themselves.

"Conall Mac Rinne. Aedan Mac Odhrain. You have entered this sacred space willingly and with pure intentions. You have shown bravery to the ancient spirits who guard this fort, and they have blessed you with enchantments. The staffs you now carry bear your mark, the hawk and the dragon. Created for you alone from part of your soul, the staffs can be tools of peace or weapons of conflict. Use them as you see fit."

Déaglán turned toward the horizon and raised his arms, speaking in a jumble of sounds. Like stampeding horses summoned, dark clouds rolled toward the fort, bringing with them thunder and tendrils of lightning that struck the sea beyond. When the clouds were overhead, the heavens opened, sending warm rain.

"Blessed Danu brings her cleansing waters to you, as you must be pure within and pure without to continue this quest."

Both Conall and Aedan held up their arms to the sky, their eyes closed, knowing that to disrespect Danu would bring misfortune. Peals of thunder shook the ground while the rains drove down upon them. When they opened their eyes, the clouds had receded, leaving traces of electricity all around them.

"The grass at our feet is a bright green…" Conall crouched to touch it. "I can still feel the power of the storm in it."

The sun returned warming the air, bringing with it Lann who perched himself on the wall.

Déaglán turned toward the horizon. "Your training will now begin."

Before the boys could say a word, they heard a deep voice from behind them and felt a hand on their shoulder.

"I told you both we'd meet again."

Conall grinned. "Fionn! How did you get here?"

Fionn patted the boy's shoulder. "Ah, I go where I'm needed."

Unlike his friend, Aedan was silent, but smirked and shook his head. He cast a quick look at the druid.

"The path that lies beyond the fort," Déaglán began, "holds many adventures for you both, and who better to train you than one of my own pupils."

"I see you've passed the test of bravery, and the spirit warriors saw fit to give you your tools." Fionn nodded toward the staff in each boy's hand. "That, my young friends, will be one of the paths *we* walk down together. I know of your destiny." His smile diminished. "You will need certain skills to retrieve the wands. Those who protect the wands have been charged to guard them because they can do just that. You will have to earn them."

"Earn them?" Aedan took a few steps closer to Fionn. "If it's our destiny, if we tell them that, why won't they just give them to us?"

The hero's laughter shook the air around them. "My young friend, others seek the wands as well, and they are keen on deception. That is one reason why you're here. Within these walls, you're protected from the darker magics that seek the same things you do. While the prophecy is known to many, your identity is not. If they were to learn too early of your existence, they would do everything possible to stop you from attaining the wands. They don't follow the same code of honor." Fionn stepped closer to Conall and Aedan. "Your lives will be in danger the moment you leave this fort. That is why I'm here. I have much to teach you."

"Just how much danger?"

The druid's eyes sparkled in the sunlight. "Aedan, heed Fionn. If anyone can prepare you for what lies ahead, it is he. I am here to answer the questions he cannot."

"You didn't think you would acquire the wands as easily as going the marketplace, did you?" Fionn sat cross-legged on the grass. "Join me. There are things you must know."

Conall and Aedan no longer had the smiles they'd had when Fionn first arrived. Once they were seated, Fionn held out his hands, palm up. The boys didn't know how to respond, but then Conall took hold of Fionn's forearm. The hero gripped Conall's in return — a sign of trust. Aedan then did the same.

"This," Fionn shook their connected arms, "is important." Fionn began. "For us to work together, you must remember that I'm here to help you. From this point forward, I need you to listen to what I say and do exactly what I ask. Am I clear?"

The boys nodded, glancing at one another.

"You do that a lot." Fionn released his charges.

Aedan furrowed his brow. "Do what?"

"When you're not sure of what to do, you look at each other. You trust each other. Never let that falter. Ever. Do you understand? The forces that will work to stop you will try to erode the trust you have for each other. No matter what, have faith in your bond."

Conall uttered. "Anam cara."

Fionn nodded. "That, my young friends, is uncommon. Hold fast to it. Now, before I train your body, I need to train your mind. Ask questions. Don't hold back. An unasked question is an unused key. You never know what it will unlock unless you use it. You will encounter obstacles in your path, some you can overcome together, some as individuals, but you can surpass any obstacle with knowing how.

"One of these obstacles is the Fomoragh, a band of evil whose purpose will be to get the wands before you. Caorthanach, some say the mother of all demons, is a fyre-spitter. Her blood-red coloring has golden scales scattered all over body. Some say that for each hero she has defeated, she grows a new golden scale. Since she mostly strikes at dusk, it's hard to say just how big—"

"Fionn…" Déaglán interrupted. "You will make them afraid—"

"They should be, druid. Only with fear can they understand. Rest assured. I will speak of ways to face the Fomoragh. I have done so, and I still live. If you smell the allure of burning wood, like a campfyre, be wary. She lures travelers with that, especially on colder nights, and when they approach the fyre, she snatches them without a sound."

Conall rubbed his palms together and then wiped them on his pants. "Well, I know I'm ready to go on this quest, eh, Aedan?"

"Easy, lad." Fionn patted Conall's shoulder. "First, I tell you about them. Then, I will give you ways to get past them. The next to watch for is Carman—"

"The witch?"

"Aye, Aedan. The same." Fionn saw the pallor on the boys' faces and smiled. "Listen, it's all right. It's not as if you'll run into the Fomoragh often, and you may not right away. But I think it's best that you be forewarned, just in case. Do you want me to continue?"

The boys shared a look and then gave a brief nod. Fionn then explained Carman, the witch-crone, who had destroyed all the land centuries ago, bringing a blight that prevented farmers' crops from growing for years. Legend said she had come from a land called Hellas to the east, seeking fortune here. With her came her sons: Dubh, 'the shrouded one,' whose magic could bring out the evil in even the most noble; Dother, 'the cruel one', also known as the patient one, who would torture his victims simply for sport, and took his time doing it; and, Dian, 'the violent one', who incited violence in those around him. He would watch others fight to the death, spurred on by his magic.

"Fionn," Aedan wrapped his arms around himself, "What chance do we have against them? We're just a farm boy and a hunter. It's one thing to stand up to the Tierney brothers, but to go up against these… these evils?"

Déaglán put his hand on Fionn's shoulder. "They're just lads, Fionn. Give them some hope. Teach them what they need to know."

The hero nodded. "You're right, druid. I'm getting ahead of myself. We can talk more later." He stood and took a short stick off his leather bracer. It grew to six feet and looked similar to the staffs of Aedan and Conall. "Up you go, lads. I'll make warriors of you yet."

Lann, still perched on the wall, jerked his head in the direction of something way off and took to the skies.

6 | THROUGH WYND AND FYRE

Fionn Mac Cool assessed his students as they stood on the cliff above the sea. Every part of their body and mind had to be honed into a keen weapon, one that could withstand the evils beyond the fort. Part of their training would be to wear down their foolhardy eagerness. Untrained zeal would be their undoing.

"A warrior's stance is key to preparing for battle. Don't lock your knees. Keep them bent just enough to move when you need to. You will never win a battle standing still. Also, keep your feet just wider than shoulder-width apart, with your dominant foot out front."

Testing what the boys would do, he instructed them to attack. Aedan lifted the staff above his head like he was chopping wood.

Fionn put up his hand. "Stop! Conall, what is he doing wrong?"

"Um… I'm not sure."

"You've left yourself open to many possible attacks." Fionn moved his hand in front of Aedan's face down to his midsection. "In this position," Fionn grabbed the staff from behind Aedan's head, taking it with ease. "you have no control over your weapon. No leverage. Someone could disarm you easily, like I just did. If you *want* to do a downward strike, I will show you how. Also…" In slow motion, Fionn moved his staff across, stopping at Aedan's ribs. "you left yourself open for not only broken ribs, but also a pierced heart. Never give your adversary a way to disable you."

Lowering his head, his cheeks flushed, Aedan kicked the ground.

"There's no reason to be embarrassed." Fionn lowered his head to look Aedan in the eye.

"I-I should have known better."

"Really. And how much training have you had with a quarterstaff?"

Aedan turned his head, muttering. "Well, none."

"Eh?" Fionn moved to where Aedan was looking.

Aedan raised his voice slightly. "None."

Fionn put his hand on Aedan's shoulder and was about to reply, but the boy pulled his body away. Knowing how important these lessons were, Fionn held his staff in front of him, both hands about a third of the way on each side. He explained why this technique worked in maintaining control and urged the boys to copy him. Conall complied without hesitation, an eager gleam in his eye, but Aedan took it up more slowly. Additional simple maneuvers followed to give the boys' confidence a chance to grow. A half-hour passed, and Aedan's smile had returned, and he and Conall took to playful sparring, putting into practice some of the moves. At one point, Conall tripped himself with his own staff, taking Aedan down with him. Both boys laughed to where they were rolling on the ground. Déaglán hid his amusement under his hood, but even he smirked watching them. Rolling his eyes and chuckling, Fionn stroked his beard.

"Druid, these two remind me of when I was their age. Was it so long ago that Liath Luachra put me on the path of the warrior? Did the druidess Bodhmall tell you of my early days? Or Fiacail Mac Conchinn?"

"Aye." Déaglán laughed. "You were as much a carefree spirit as these two. I seem to recall you were a bit of a practical joker as well. I remember a story where—"

"I think we have reminisced enough." Fionn raised his eyebrows and smiled. "We should eat and resume their training." He dropped a sack next to the boys who had recovered from their fit of laughter.

"Eat up, lads. We need to work on a few more techniques before sunset."

Conall shoved a piece of brown bread in his mouth, his words muffled. "What happens at sunset?"

The druid chimed in. "Magic. You are both tied to the ancient races, so you should learn some simple enchantments. We will work up to others as you become more confident."

Cheese, bread, and dried fish comprised their meal, and the sack somehow had just enough to feed all four of them. Déaglán sat apart from the others, putting small morsels into his mouth. Fionn shoved large chunks into his, washing it down with water from a goatskin pouch. The son of Cool watched the playful banter between Conall and Aedan. Even though the druid sat a good fifteen feet from him, Fionn heard the man's words clearly, although the boys did not.

"They remind you of Crimmal, don't they?"

"My brother and I haven't spoken in years, Déaglán." Fionn chewed some bread. "But, they do indeed remind me of that kinship. These two share anam cara, unlike my brother and me. 'Tis a strange union, one of the Ársa in league with one of the Fonn. The success of this quest depends on their readiness and desire."

"With your aid and mine, they may very well do just that. It's time."

Brushing his palms together, Fionn called to the boys to take their stance. He leapt to his feet, staff in hand, and engaged both in some slow sparring. For every one of Fionn's attacks that Conall blocked, he let two more through.

"Remember, don't lock your knees. Channel the movement through your arms and reposition yourself, never taking your eye off me." Fionn swiveled around to the other side, surprising Aedan.

"You're trying to throw me off." Aedan stopped the strike, preventing it from knocking him down, but the reverberations in his own staff caused him to reposition his hands, and that was when Fionn lunged, knocking the staff from Aedan's grip.

As minutes became an hour, and then two, Fionn quickened and mixed up his movements, challenging the boys to stay alert. When he saw that the two were keeping up, he jumped up and somersaulted over them. Once behind them, he threw off their balance by hitting the back of their knees.

"Anticipate me. Think two or three steps ahead of what I might do. Be creative." Fionn twirled his staff. "Okay, stop for a moment."

Out of breath, Conall leaned on his staff. "What's wrong?"

"First, you're not paying attention as much to each other as you should. You're focusing on your own space, but not the other. Like it or not, you're in this together, so you best start thinking about working with rather than working next to."

"So, on top of keeping up our guard, thinking creatively, and overcoming our blind spots, we need to watch each other, too?"

"Aedan, now you're thinking like a warrior."

Sunset approached before they knew it. The druid looked out over the sea and performed a silent ritual, his arms moving in calculated ways. When he turned back to them, early moonlight caught his eyes, and their twinkle became alive, almost electric. Speaking soft archaic words, he placed five rocks in a circle. He repeated the words a few more times, and a fyre ignited inside the circle, gradually growing into a campfyre, but with blue and green hues, just like the colors of his eyes.

"In the heart of the brave, we beseech thee, Danu, Goddess of the Giving Light. Offer us your protection and guidance, your strength and wisdom." He sat in front of the fyre, gesturing to the others. "Join me."

Crisp sea breezes rose over the cliff, bringing the pungent salty air. Déaglán instructed them to breathe deeply and exhale slowly. He reached into a small pouch and tossed some of the contents into the flames, tiny sparks rising soon after. Blending together, the salt in the air with the smoke of Rowan would protect them from harm.

"We sit in a circle, the sacred symbol of unity. Rest assured that, while you are here by this fyre, you are free from those who seek to do you harm. As Fionn told you earlier, strong powers of darkness want to find the Wands of Danu for themselves. If you are lucky, you will find a map that shows where these thirteen wands are, but you must also rely on your instincts and your beliefs to guide you. Once you leave this fort, we can no longer protect you. For this night, and the five that follow, Fionn and I will teach you all we know."

Conall played with a small twig, rolling it in between his fingers. "Déaglán, I think I speak for Aedan when I say that we appreciate all you have done, and will do, for us. But what about our Nascah? I mean… That's what we were setting off to do when the Elders found us."

The flickering of the fyre and the sea breeze filled the silence for a moment, before Fionn replied.

"Nothing is more important to a young lad or lass than the quest for the caomhnóir. Your spirit guide will be invaluable in your life's journey, as well as in this quest for the wands. It is, however, the one thing we cannot help you with since it's such a personal path. I had embarked on my Nascah when I was a little younger than you, and it was always part of me, no matter what I did. My caomhnóir remains with me, as it should. There's nothing that says that this quest and your Nascah cannot overlap."

The druid sprinkled more Rowan dust into the fyre. "The ancient sages tell us that we can be mindful and act by our own will, or we can spiritual and act because something beyond us prompts us to. You will both find your guide when your spirit is ready, not when your mind is."

"What kind of magic will you be teaching us?" Aedan rubbed his palms together.

"It takes years of training to be a full-fledged mage. I will show you both a few rituals to keep you safe. You may be of divine lineage, but your ability to manage magic is untested. If you try too hard, you can endanger yourself or others. Plus, you would disrespect the ancient ones." Déaglán reached into the fyre and cupped some of the flames. "Aedan, you are of the Tine Clan, those who embrace fyre, the most sacred element. It has the power to consume and destroy or elevate and support. It is important to remember, too, that the elements are neither good nor evil. They just *are*. With its ability to destroy, some have viewed fyre as a tool of malice, but in fact, it protects, guides, and inspires wisdom."

The druid blew out the flames, spinning a finger above his palm. A gust of wynd rose from the sea and swirled around them.

"Air, Conall, is your element, as you are of the Gaoth Clan. It has the power to move and change, be but a breath or a gale. Like fyre, it provokes intelligence. Unlike water and earth, both fyre and air help each other. Fyre—"

"Fyre heats the air, making it move, giving it energy." Conall interrupted. "Air feeds fyre, giving it sustenance and strength." He looked over at Aedan and nodded.

Fionn laughed. "Seems the lad knows a little bit, eh, druid?"

Déaglán closed his hand, ceasing the breeze. He explained that all people have a ruling element, but in the case of the boys, since they had divine blood, they actually drew strength from theirs. Part of his exploration included a caveat that, even though they had a mystical connection to their elements, they could not use them to bring harm. The power of the element, too, would augment an already existing natural ability.

"Conall, what would you say is your greatest skill?"

The boy twisted his mouth while he thought about it, shrugging. He replied that he wasn't sure what to say because he had a few different things he thought he was good at.

"Well, put it this way. If you could do any of those things you like more than any other, what would it be?"

'I suppose… I guess it would be running. I've always liked the feeling of running across the meadows and feeling the wynd as I move through it."

The druid turned to Aedan. "And you, lad?"

"That's easy. Hunting. I don't hunt for sport, mind you, just for eating. But there's something about holding a bow in my hand that makes me feel powerful. Not just over the animals, either. Within myself. Sometimes, when I'm not looking for food, I shoot arrows at tree stumps behind my house. My da says I have a keen eye."

Getting on his feet, Déaglán handed Conall and Aedan each a stone on a leather cord.

"What is this?" Aedan rolled the stone around in his hand and held it up to his eye, seeing the moonlight illuminate it.

"It is a fyre opal. Conall, you have a citrine. Wearing them keeps you in touch with your element."

"Déaglán—" Conall rubbed his on his vest before putting the cord around his neck.

"Conall, come here." The druid walked to the cliff's edge, facing the moonlit sky.

The boy complied, looking over at both Aedan and Fionn, who shrugged. Déaglán put his arm around Conall's shoulders and pointed out into the night.

"You are of the air as much as the Ársa. Your heartbeat echoes your running stride, a desire for the journey and experience. In this way, you are the Wyndracer." He walked the boy back to the fyre, extending his hand to Aedan, who took hold. "Born of fyre, like the Fonn, you burn brightly, and your game is knowledge and wisdom. This makes you the Fyrehunter."

The druid continued, explaining how important names were to those on a quest. They could open doors of opportunity as much as they could evoke curiosity. As they traveled throughout the land, the boys would encounter many guardians who protected the wands from those seeking their power for less than honorable intentions. Part of the journey would be the stories told about their adventure, and the bards would need a name to sing about. Plus, now that Déaglán had spoken the names aloud, they would be carried on the wynd to neighboring lands, bringing the whisper of possibility to those in their path. What they started at Dún Ancróga would be like planting a seed, one that would germinate through their experiences and obstacles. The following days would bring more knowledge, but they would need to rest now, since the lessons to follow would build in intensity. The druid instructed Conall and Aedan to sleep by the fyre, as the night would grow much colder so high above the sea. He and Fionn lay a little ways away.

Conall stared up at the starry sky and the bright moon disk, his arm behind his head. He turned toward his friend, his mouth open to speak, but he saw Aedan on his side, sound asleep. Surely, the day's events had worn him out. A yawn overtook Conall, and he, too, succumbed to the restorative power of slumber, the waves crashing against the rocks below. The flapping of wings made his eyes open slightly, but when he saw the silhouette of Lann on the wall, he smiled and closed his eyes. The hawk would keep watch over them until the sun rose.

—⚜—

Smoke forced Aedan's eyes open, and he popped up.

"Conall?" His voice shook and his heart beat against his ribcage.

"Over here. I told Fionn that the fyre would wake you."

Aedan sighed, and his pulse returned to normal. Sunrise had just started, so the skies retained their indigo hue. Aedan found the others at the fyre, and Conall handed him a bowl of porridge. He leaned his face over the bowl and inhaled.

"I haven't had porridge since I was home." He put a spoonful in his mouth, closed his eyes, and moaned. "This tastes so good."

Laughing, Fionn threw another log on the fyre. "Surely, you must be hungry. I've not heard that about my cooking. This is the best way to begin our day. We have much to do."

Even Déaglán sat with them, cross-legged, and ate without speaking. Unlike the boys who shoveled their food, the druid took measured spoonfuls. Everything he did was calculated and reasoned. Neither the boys nor

Fionn knew that he had left his Order to pursue this task of putting Conall and Aedan on their path. Most of the druidic orders had stepped back from intervening in mortal affairs when the prophecy surfaced, especially since the coming battle would provoke conflict between the Orders. There were some who still held loyalty to the Ársa and the Fonn beyond the gods. Déaglán knew these two boys would encounter their share of difficulty, and that was why he needed to give them enough to build on.

Once they finished the morning meal, Fionn took the boys to one side of the grassy area to continue their training with quarterstaffs. He knew he wasn't going to have much time with them, but he, like the druid, needed to give the boys a foundation. Skies once laden with heavy, dark clouds became flecked with orange, red, and purple. Circling high above, Lann squawked his presence. The druid kept Fionn and the boys in his peripheral vision as he prepared pouches filled with medicinal and mystical herbs to keep the boys safe, although not invulnerable. He included bundles of burdock to remove toxins from the body, nettles to stop blood loss, dandelion to aid against infection, willow bark for a tea that would act as a painkiller, spider webs for healing cuts, moss, among others. He would explain how to use these after their evening meal.

Déaglán didn't have a regular childhood, so when he heard Conall and Aedan laugh or argue with Fionn, he smiled to himself, feeling he was part of their experience. When he was a little younger than the boys, he was selected with two others to join the Order of An Domhan, a private sect of druids whose jurisdiction was the protection of the Earth. These men and women knew of the existence of other celestial bodies via a spyglass, and that the Earth was just one of many. Déaglán's childhood involved much of what he was doing for Conall and Aedan: working with herbs, mastering enchantments, and becoming bound to the Earth spiritually through Danu. He, too, had learned how to use a quarterstaff as well as to become an archer. Even though he was banned from taking a life, he could use his abilities to protect himself and others, as well as find food. Teaching others didn't come easily to him, either, and he hadn't left the Order in many years, but the Arch Druid knew that because Déaglán was one of the Marked Ones, he would be perfect for the task. He was one of five druids whose heterochromic eyes gave him insights not even the Arch Druid had, and that caused some friction within the Order. Perhaps that was the true reason he was sent on this mission, he often wondered.

According to the ancient laws, those with different eye colors became An Marcáilte, marked by the gods, and it wasn't always good. Those with blue and green eyes, like Déaglán, had the blessing of Danu — An Lonrach, the Shining Ones. The earliest Orders believed that An Lonrach would become Arch Druids without the trials. Those with both brown and green eyes, the Shadows — An Scáthanna, had an altogether different fate — exile.

These marked ones were said to bring misfortune and shadow to the Order. When Déaglán thought back to his early days in the Order, he knew even as a student that he had a winding path, and when he saw An Scáthanna, he felt sorry for how they were treated. If he spoke out, he would be ejected, forever to wander unaligned with a druidic order.

Hearing his name, the druid snapped out of his reverie.

"Déaglán, we need you." Fionn waved. He was holding cloth to Conall's cheek.

"What happened?" The druid examined the wound. "It's not deep." He pulled nettle leaves from a pouch and stanched the cut.

"It seems Aedan was a bit eager to block a parry, and he struck his friend's face." Fionn chuckled.

Conall barked back, "It's not funny!"

"Hold still, lad." The druid used one hand to hold Conall's head, dabbing the wound with the leaves. "You're a little too young for battle scars." He smirked.

"I think it'd make him look tougher." Aedan leaned over Déaglán's shoulder to see the wound. "Maybe I should try for the other cheek?"

"Would you shut up, Aedan? Déaglán's trying to fix what *you* did." Conall fidgeted in place.

"Ah, it's just a scratch." Aedan crossed his arms, shrugging. "Tell him, Fionn. He'll probably get a few more when we're on our quest."

Fionn shook his head and laughed. "Let's hope not. The idea is *not* to get hurt. Is he fit for battle, druid?"

Déaglán dabbed the last leaf on Conall's cheek. "That he is. Try not to wound each other too much. I don't have enough nettle leaves."

The rest of the day involved various strategies at disarming one's opponent, trying to predict someone's next move, and sparring drills. Aside from the occasional bruise, the boys managed not to hurt each other too badly. Their enthusiasm and understanding of what Fionn was trying to teach them kept them focused, and a few hours later, Conall and Aedan held a mock fight for twenty minutes without hurting or disarming each other. Déaglán leaned over to Fionn.

"It's a small victory, but we should take what we can get, eh?"

The son of Cool grinned. "Indeed. I'm watching them carefully. Even with a few lapses in their stance, they're making strides. Who knew teaching boys of this age could be so taxing? Did Finegas ever comment about me?"

"Your childhood teacher? He did tell me once that you were… headstrong."

"Then he was understating much." Fionn patted the druid's back, laughing. "I was unruly and arrogant. Ultimately, I fell in line, but not without many bruises from battle drills, as well as to my ego."

They broke the stalemate to have their midday meal, and Conall, when he finished, lay back to stare at the clouds, his arms behind his head. Aedan stood at the cliff's edge, close enough to get Déaglán's attention. Brisk breezes crawled up from the sea. Out in the distance, seagulls and osprey soared, searching for their own meal. The boy outstretched his arms and closed his eyes, letting the salty air wash over him. The druid could see him taking deep breaths and exhaling slowly. He was about to go over to him when Lann perched on Aedan's arm.

"What—Oh, it's you." The boy grinned. "Looking out for me, eh? I'm all right. Just missing Fiachra. Don't suppose you know where he is?"

Lann cocked his head around, the perpetual guardian. Aedan brought his arm closer to his face.

"You know that I'd sooner die than let anything happen to Conall, right? Why do you think we were always spending time together as lads? He's a good spirit." He glanced back at his friend. "If anything ever happens to him, you find me. Understand?"

The hawk chirped. Aedan headed toward the druid, and Lann landed on Conall's shoulder. While Conall adjusted his boots, he reached up and put a piece of dried venison in front of Lann who snatched it with his beak. The boy looked up at his friend.

"Keep an eye on him, eh? Should he ever be in trouble, find me."

Another piece of meat found its way into Lann's beak. Fionn called them back for the final lessons of the day, and the hawk took his place on the wall of the fort. Conall and Fionn had their mock fight first, and Aedan had a determined look. They switched roles, with Aedan going up against a man four heads taller. He goaded Fionn, telling him not to go easy, and the man complied, although Déaglán could tell he was holding back a little. These boys couldn't hold their own against the son of Cool unleashed. By nightfall, the druid had prepared the fyre. Before the others could approach, he took a stick and drew a circle in the dirt around the fyre pit, making symbols in various places on the outer edge. He invited the three of them to join him inside the circle and to be careful not to touch the line or the symbols.

"What's this for, Déaglán?" Conall sat, moving as close to the fyre as he could.

The druid's response didn't answer the boy directly. "Four symbols sit on the outer edge, in the ancient Ogham, and combined, they create a ring of protection. It's stronger than the one I showed you last eve. No one who seeks to do you harm can enter the circle, even if he or she hides that intention. This is one of many enchantments that protect."

Fionn added his own knowledge, pointing. "The symbol with two short vertical lines with a horizontal line on top represents *luis*, the Rowan tree. It's for protection. The next is *duir*, the oak. Notice the horizontal line is under the two vertical ones and mirrors *luis*. It stands for vision. The third symbol is *fearn*, the alder, for strength. It has three vertical lines topped by one horizontal one. Last is *nion*, the ash, for perception. It has five vertical lines topped with a horizontal one."

Aedan glanced back and forth between *luis* and *duir*. "So... how do I know which is which? They look the same."

Déaglán held up his palms, facing out. "Look at my hands. Are they the same? Think carefully."

The boy puckered a bit in thought, looking back from one to the other. "No?"

"Are you asking me or telling me?" The druid smirked.

"No, they're not the same. Is that right? I mean... they look alike as reflections of each other, so in that way, they're not the same."

In the dancing fyrelight, Déaglán's eyes twinkled. "If you were to examine your hands, you would see that, despite their similarities, they are in fact quite different. So too are *luis* and *duir*. While they are both trees, the Rowan and the oak embody different powerful energies. Once you understand that, you will truly understand how to determine the difference between these symbols."

He added that two of the wands the boys sought were of these trees and understanding how to approach the guardians of each wand could determine how easily it would be to acquire the thirteen. A light breeze from the sea teased the fyre, and the flames grew for a moment. The druid talked about what protection from the trees meant, too. Each one had connections to the animals. The natural world and that of the gods was intertwined, and to offend a wand guardian could mean actions from a divine being.

Aedan kept looking at his hands. "I thought the gods didn't interact with people much."

"Thoughts like that could get you in trouble." Fionn tore pieces of dried elk and popped them in his mouth. "They may not interact with us in the conventional sense, but you best be wary of thinking that they're not watching your every move."

Staring into the fyre, Conall didn't hear Fionn calling his name until the third time.

"Wha—Sorry. My mind was elsewhere. What did you say?"

The hero shook his head and smiled. "You're getting lost in the fyre. And I thought that was Aedan's element. I asked you what you thought."

"About..."

"He wants to know what you think about what Déaglán said about the gods. You know, whether or not they're watching us." Aedan tossed a stone into the fyre.

Conall returned his eyes to the flames for a moment before responding, his voice a whisper. "I *know* they're there. I can feel them always with me."

The others fell silent. The druid and Fionn sat up. Even the fyre seemed to settle into a low flicker. Aedan, who had been drawing in the dirt with a stick, stopped.

Déaglán leaned in. "Even now? I don't sense anything."

"He's of the Ársa, druid. Tell me, Conall. When did you first sense them?" Fionn looked up. "I have often wondered about their presence in this world."

"Fionn, they have always been there, I suppose. As a child, I would be standing in my room with the window closed and feel the air move. A tingle would go through me, and then it would stop. I had been raised on stories of the Sídhe, but this wasn't like that. As I got older, I'd have similar moments, usually when I was alone or when I was troubled. Here... now... I feel different energies surround me. Now that I think about it, I guess they've been with me since we left the Elder Circle. I hadn't paid much attention to it."

"We can come back to this, and we should." Déaglán held out a hand to Fionn and one to Aedan. "Join hands with me."

All four created a circle around the fyre, their arms stretched as far as they could go. As if to signify a holy moment, the fyre itself climbed, and the wynd increased, both at the same time.

"This circle should protect you from most problems. Just make sure to draw it big enough to encircle your camp. Once the symbols are in the earth, only you can erase them. Should you go up against something more formidable, this chant should reinforce the circle. Repeat this three times. *With Brigid's fyre and Danu's grace, we invoke their power to protect this place.*"

All four recited the words, and at the third utterance, the line and symbols in the earth glowed white, and the air hummed.

"Since you're not full mages, this dríocht won't last longer than a few hours. But the magic should last long enough to keep you safe while you sleep. While you're awake, the circle alone will be enough. Forces in the world can break this circle, but I don't foresee them wanting to attack you. You're too small in their grand scheme."

Conall pulled his knees in close. "Déaglán, I have some questions that have been on my mind for a while now. When I was in the meadow near my home with Lann, a bear came out of the woods in a rage. Since we're talking about the gods, could that have something to do with Artio?"

Déaglán thought for a moment. "And it didn't harm you. Lann did his duty as your protector too. It could be a sign of the disturbance with the Ársa and the Fonn. It might have something to do with Artio, but I am not entirely sure. What was your other question?"

"The Elders sent a druid, Elder Mac Conohar, to protect us on our journey, but he disappeared about an hour after we left the Elder Circle. Did he—"

"He just vanished? Hmm. Elders tasked with protection are quite powerful, both physically and magically. He wouldn't have abandoned you by choice. He may have been summoned back to the Elder Circle, or—"

Conall turned away. "Or he was attacked… or even…"

"Killed, yes. That *is* entirely possible. The Elder Circle's hut is protected, much like this fort, but once going beyond the confines of the protection dríocht, anyone is vulnerable. I am sorry. I wish I knew more."

—ɯ—

The third day together began, as always, at sunrise, and despite Aedan's protests due to being tired, Fionn casually walked past the groggy young man and poured a cup of water on his head. Aedan grunted his disapproval, but when he saw the hero, arms crossed and eyebrow raised, he shook the water from his hair and met up with Conall who had already been awake for a little while and was feeding Lann. Seeing his friend with dripping locks made Conall laugh, but that invoked a glare from Aedan. They reached for their staffs, but Fionn had different plans for them.

"What? We're not sparring? You threw cold water on me, and we're not using our staffs?"

"I didn't say that, Aedan." Fionn grinned. "Today, we learn some hand-to-hand combat. You need to be able to defend yourself without a weapon."

A lesson of the utmost importance that Fionn needed to show them was how to throw a punch, something that Aedan claimed he knew how to do well. When he demonstrated for Fionn, the hero nodded and commended the youth on his skill. Aedan commented that his father had taught him when he was younger how to fight in case he was bullied, and he'd only had to use those skills once or twice. They did leave a lasting impression, he added, laughing.

"Conall, watch how Aedan holds his hands up so as to protect his face. Look at his stance. See how his knees aren't locked? That's important."

Using himself as an example, Fionn took the opposing side to Aedan and, in slow moves, showed Conall what to do and not to do. The hero also added in some blocking moves that Aedan didn't know, and by late morning, Fionn had the boys practicing those maneuvers. It would take several sessions for these techniques to take root, but Fionn felt that Aedan's prior experience would help him be good teacher for his friend.

It would build some of his confidence. After the midday meal, Déaglán spoke to the boys before they resumed their training.

"One thing, above all else, that you need to understand is the idea of honor. You must always fight with honor. Do you know what that means?"

Conall nodded. "That means you don't strike your opponent in the back. You fight face to face, and you never strike an unarmed foe."

"Exactly. Now, there may be a situation where your opponent will show no mercy and bring you, or others, harm. In that instance, if your opponent is unarmed but still able to deliver a fatal blow, you must do everything in your power to stop him or her. Saving a life is paramount."

"Déaglán, but… what if we have to take a life? You said if our opponent can kill us, we have to stop him or her. I-I don't—"

"Conall, if you are faced with the choice of taking a life in order to save those unable to stand up for themselves, or to protect Aedan, do what you must." The druid put more weight on those last four words.

Taking a deep breath, Conall exhaled. "I understand." He turned his head toward Fionn.

The hero lowered his eyes. "Aye. I have. When I have had to end a life, it has come at a great cost to my spirit. Even in battle, my aim is to disable before anything else. Inevitably, lives must be taken to protect the greater good. You may never have to do it, but you should be prepared to do it. And…"—he held up a finger—"you must never, ever take pride in a kill. For now, let's continue your lessons."

An unseen force pressed down upon the tone of the mock fight, making the boys act more cautiously than they had before. The druid noticed how the two would step back too quickly or refuse to make physical contact. Or, if they did, it was like two old men who had lost the will to fight.

"We don't have time for this." Déaglán's eyes flared with blue and green fyre. "Fionn, we need to show them how important this is. Perhaps I should summon back the spirit warriors—"

"No." Fionn's voice seemed to be followed by thunder. "We cannot put them in harm's way now just to prove a point. There is too much at stake. I'll not risk their safety. Not now."

Summoning the boys, Fionn brought them to the edge of the cliff, gesturing for them to sit. He felt their apprehension radiating like heat from a fyre, but they complied, hanging their legs over the edge.

"Don't think. Just answer. Do you trust me?"

In unison, the boys replied. "Yes."

"Good. We're going to sit here for a bit. It's uncomfortable, isn't it, not knowing whether you could fall into the sea. Not knowing whether a gust of wynd could end your life. I, too, feel the same. I don't want to die, either. But I have faith. I know that I can sit here as long as I want until I decide to move. I can't promise you that, if you fell, I could save you. It's all uncertain. Does that mean we stop sitting here because of what *could* happen? No. We know that we have the power over ourselves. This is the same apprehension you feel about taking a life. You hold yourself back, fearing something that has yet to happen, if it even would. You may live out your entire life having never taken a human life. The reason why the druid and I are training you is so that you have options. Otherwise, I would just show you one killing blow after another. We want you to be able to take care of yourselves. But if you hold back now, when you're training, you'll hold back later when it matters. Do you understand?"

Both boys gazed out at the sea, but they each nodded.

"Good. I'd rather you have a few scrapes and bruises now than for one of you to bury the other. Tell me. What happens if the Ársa and the Fonn are not stopped?"

At first, the boys said nothing. After a sigh, Conall stammered out a response.

"The-The destruction of everything. Their war will destroy everything. All that we know of our own lives will be gone."

"Correct. Do you truly understand what that means, though? Have you given thought to what happens when the world, all of it, including your parents, are destroyed by power beyond your understanding?"

Aedan rubbed his hands together. "Well, I know it's been a passing thought. I've tried not to think too much about it. I do know that a lot is riding on our success, though."

"Let me make this perfectly clear for you both: you and only you stand in the way of the Ársa and the Fonn. None of the other Tuatha Dé Danann can do this. Only you. You don't have time to hold back. You don't have time to be apprehensive."

Conall leaned back behind Fionn and turned toward Aedan, nodding ever so slightly.

"I think we're ready to continue. Right, Aedan?"

Throwing himself backward, Aedan flipped his legs over his head and ended up on his feet. Taking hold of Conall's forearm, he yanked his friend up.

"I'll take that as a yes." Fionn put one arm over each of the boys as they returned to the sparring area. "Just so you know, the druid wanted to summon the spirit warriors to convince you to snap out of your fear. You're welcome."

—⟨⟨⟨—

Sunset brought more magic from the druid. He watched as Conall set up the protection circle from the prior lessons, and it might have been the boy's nervousness coupled with his desire for perfection, but he cast it flawlessly. Déaglán handed each boy a branch that had been stripped of its leaves. Aedan reached for the fyre to ignite it, but the druid stopped him.

"Tonight, we work on basic illumination dríocht. The key to conjuring light is sustained concentration, but once you have the flame, the fyre burns on its own. Hold the branch firmly. Repeat after me, focusing on the tip of the branch: *Ó aer, Déanaim iarracht tine*. From air, I seek fyre."

"*Ó aer, Déanaim iarracht tine*." Both Aedan and Conall spoke the words, but nothing happened.

"Remember to concentrate. Find the tip of the branch in your mind. Say it again."

"*Ó aer, Déanaim iarracht tine*." The boys' words again left their mouths, their eyes unblinking.

Conall repeated it to himself, slowing down the words when he saw nothing happening. He tightened his grip on the branch to where his hand shook, and his words became clipped and heavy. When nothing happened, he threw the stick and kicked the ground. Aedan, however, ignited his branch, his voice smooth and controlled. The flame was small, but it soon grew and fed off more of the branch. A moment later, he had a miniature torch, and he grinned.

"Why do *I* have to do this? Isn't air my element?" Conall shoved his hands in his pockets and walked away.

Aedan blew out his fyre and brought his stick to Conall.

"Don't be intimidated. You were just trying too hard. Here. Use my branch."

A sharp look from his friend would have made most people back off, but Aedan wasn't moving. He put the branch in front of Conall.

"Don't be daft." He chuckled. "Just take the stick."

Snatching it from Aedan's hand, Conall turned from his friend and whispered the dríocht again. As before, nothing happened.

"I can't do it!"

"Conall, what are you thinking about when you say the words?" Aedan's voice had softened a bit.

"I don't know. I'm just trying to think about igniting the stick. *You* know… I imagine that—"

"That's your problem. Don't think about yourself lighting the stick. Just light it. Think about the fyre sprouting from the stick like a flower. It grows from inside the stick and comes out a beautiful flower."

Aedan stood next to his friend, putting a hand over Conall's. He reminded his friend to breathe while he thought about the words and the fyre. He leaned closer, his mouth next to Conall's ear.

"I have faith in you. You can do anything you set your mind to, *mo dheartháir*."

Hearing the words 'my brother' made Conall smile a little. Adjusting his stance, he thought about how he and Aedan had been friends since childhood, and how they had become each other's anam cara. Channeling his attention on the branch, he controlled his breathing. He tried the words again. He was just about to drop the branch when he saw a tiny spark. Seconds later, it grew into a bud of a flame, and then it opened up like a rose.

"You did it!" Aedan patted him on the back. "I knew you could."

"I just concentrated on the warmth of your hand."

They giggled at each other, Conall cocked his head back and forth as the flames took hold of the branch. He blew out the flames and tried again, this time without Aedan standing next to him. Aedan asked if he was sure, but Conall put his hand out.

"I can *do* this. I can do this."

Three more times he ignited the branch and extinguished it. Fionn and Déaglán both nodded at each other with Conall's success. The druid mentioned that it did take time to master that skill, so they should practice it from time to time. He wanted to show them one other that they could use should they not have access to branches. Déaglán took each of their hands, turned them palm side up, and elevated them a little.

"This next dríocht will be helpful if you are walking along in the dark and need to see. Aedan, you'll master this a little faster. Close your fist as if you were containing a small flame. As you open your fingers quickly, say the word, *Solas*."

As the druid predicted, Aedan mastered it on the second try, and much to the pleasant surprise of the others, Conall achieved it on the third try. Déaglán told them to close their fingers when they wanted to extinguish the flame, even though it felt hot. Soon, he mentioned, they would be able to do it without speaking the word. The gesture and the thought alone should do it.

"I have one warning, however. Never, under any circumstances, use that fyre to ignite anything. Its purpose is only to illuminate. If it becomes a combustible fyre, it will be almost impossible to contain. Use the other dríocht for campfyres and such. Am I making myself clear?"

Aedan was practicing this most recent skill but acknowledged the druid. Conall, though, stood at the edge of the cliff and hadn't said anything to indicate he had heard the druid. He was too enrapt with this new skill and played with different maneuvers where he could throw in the illumination. Turning around, he lost his footing and fell forward toward the edge. Conall threw his hands out in front of him, his eyes glowed a light blue, and he shouted the words 'Sciathán aeir!'. Lann screeched from atop the wall, and a gust of wynd from the sea shoved Conall backward.

He landed on his back, breath knocked out of him. Fionn rushed to his side, pulling him farther back from the edge.

"By Danu's grace, are you all right?" Déaglán examined the boy for injuries. "How do you know that dríocht? I haven't shown you any air enchantments."

"I-I don't know. When I fell over the edge, I-I just thought about pulling myself back, and the words came out of my mouth."

Déaglán put his hand on Conall's head. "Thank Danu you are unharmed. Are you sure you're fine?"

The boy nodded and saw a hand thrust in front of him. Taking hold of Aedan's wrist, he pulled himself up and brushed off his pants. Back at their supplies, Conall swallowed mouthfuls of water from the goatskin, wiping his mouth. He closed his eyes and took deep breaths, exhaling slowly. A touch on his shoulder made him swing around.

"It's me." Aedan put up his hands. "Are you sure you're all right? You gave us a scare."

"Believe me. I did the same to myself. I-I don't know where that came from. It was like I wasn't me for a moment."

They headed back to Fionn and Déaglán when Aedan stopped walking and turned.

"Hey… Are you sure you want to do this? I mean… do we *have* to? We have been training and learning things that I never thought I would ever know, but I just want to go back to see my father, to know that he's okay."

Cocking his head, Conall smiled. "I thought you were always up for an adventure. Look, I understand. Trust me." He leaned in close. "I've been in touch with the Ársa. They speak to me in dreams."

All Aedan could do was widen his eyes. He saw Fionn and the druid talking, so he gestured to sit.

"What do you mean they've been in touch? Do they know what we're doing? Are they spying on us?" He tried to keep his voice low, but his agitation came through.

Conall adjusted his boot. "I'm fairly certain it's a one-way connection. With everything we've been doing, they don't say anything directly. In my dreams… I see messages or images. I don't know what they mean, and some of them repeat."

"Are you going to tell Déaglán or Fionn? *Should* we?"

With his eyes on his teachers, Conall paused. "I don't know. What I do know is that our quest is much more complicated than we've been told. I just feel it. We need to know more. I want to ask Déaglán to tell us whatever he can about the Ársa and the Fonn. It's time we knew who we were fighting for."

From the distance, they heard Fionn call them to supper. During the meal, the boys ate without speaking, exchanging glances with each other and their teachers. Like a war boot, the silence pressed down on them. Conall tore small pieces of bread and ate them, his mouth barely moving. Fionn had some fyre-roasted rabbit on a branch that he passed around, and each boy put a handful into his bowl. From across the sea-facing meadow, Lann screeched before landing on Conall's outstretched arm. The boy offered his hawk small pieces of rabbit. Déaglán shifted his glance from Fionn to the boys, and Aedan noticed Fionn nod back to the druid.

Conall leaned forward and cleared his throat. "Aedan and I — "

"It's time you learned about the Ársa and the Fonn." Fionn's words erupted forth.

Aedan stopped chewing and looked up, and Conall froze.

"That-That's what I was about to say." Conall offered Lann more rabbit. "How did you know — "

Wiping his hands together and taking a swig from the goatskin, Fionn told them that the druid and he had wanted to talk about this earlier, but they weren't sure when the best time would be.

"I had hoped you both would have asked when you were ready. I guess that time is now, eh, druid?"

His palms pressed together, Déaglán tapped them against his lips. "Yes. It is now. But first, I want Aedan to set up a protection circle around this fyre. Conall, I need to talk with you."

As Aedan complied, Conall shifted closer to the druid. Fionn took the bowls, saying he would return shortly. In the fyrelight, the druid's eyes sparkled, and his mouth formed the slightest hint of a smile.

"Conall, it's important that you understand something." He put his hand on Conall's shoulder. "What you and Aedan do from this point forward lays out the foundation for generations. Times will come when your roots in the Ársa and Aedan's in the Fonn will bring seemingly insurmountable obstacles to your friendship. Remember here" — he tapped Conall's chest — "that you are both anam cara, and that bond will guide you. Trust it, no matter what happens."

Swallowing hard, Conall replied that he understood. Taking his original place around the fyre, he watched the flames dance. Whispering, "Solas," he opened his fist. Fyre burned just above his palm. He closed his fingers as if he were trying to snatch air and looked satisfied. His friend finished the circle and plopped down in his spot. Aedan's eager smile caused him to return the gesture.

"Your circle is well made, son of Odhran." He paused. "The story of the Ársa and the Fonn is as old as the world itself, perhaps older. Listen and understand."

With the fyre growing before them, the druid began his tale.

7 | ARSA AND THE FONN

Of all the stories ever told, of Eiocha, the Great Mare, and later of Danu and her descendants, the Tuatha Dé Danann, the ancient tale of the Ársa and Fonn comes before them all. Two groups of gods existed: the Ársa, made up of the four elements: Mhór Cré, earth, Mhór Tine, fire, Mhór Aer, air, and Mhór Uiscí, water, and the Fonn: Eagna, the wise Eagle, Grá, the Horse, Eolas, the Raven, and Ciall, the Lion.

"The Arsa made the physical world. The Fonn, the animals. They thought they had brought balance, but they were wrong. Darkness had yet to be born, but when it was, it infected humanity with jealousy, greed, hate, selfishness, and anger. Ciall then created compassion, love, and hope. With this, balance existed in the world."

Cracking and popping of the fire, along with the breeze, were all that Aedan, Conall, and Fionn heard when the druid finished speaking. Like fireflies, tiny pieces of kindled ash wafted away, extinguishing into the night. Fionn exhaled, the sound of exhaustion. Conall and Aedan stared at the fire, each blinking from the smoky air. Even Lann, who had perched on Conall's shoulder, made no sound, his head moving to follow the sparks.

"I have never heard that before." Fionn reached behind him and put another log on the fire, sending up more sparks that In time darkened into soot.

Déaglán extended his hand into the flames, pulling one out. His lips moved, but no words came out, and the fire took the form of a dragon and flew into the night sky.

"Many mysteries of the world, son of Cool, remain shrouded. That is but one." The druid's voice was no louder than the breeze.

Aedan stood, groaning as he stretched. "Nature calls. May I leave the circle?" He knew that he had to ask, otherwise the circle's protections would break for all.

Nodding, Déaglán gestured for Conall to move closer.

"I can sense something weighs heavily on you, more than before. What is it?"

Pulling his knees in, the boy wrapped his arms around them and put his head down.

The druid put his hand on the boy's back and leaned in.

"You worry that with forces so powerful, how you and Aedan can hope to succeed in your quest."

"I know that others are looking for the wands, Déaglán. Aside from the Dark Ones. I'm dreaming about a one-eyed man—"

"No harm will come to you here. Dreams may be powerful gateways, but the Fomoragh cannot touch you. Not at Dún Ancróga. I swear it." His gentle voice softened the boy's expression.

"When will you teach us about the Fomoragh?"

Déaglán snapped his fingers, and the fire blazed. "In daylight."

"But—"

Fionn crouched down next to Conall.

"My friend, they may have no power here, but they are always listening. I wouldn't be surprised if they knew we were here training you both. Once you do leave the protection of this fort, you will engage them at some point." He noticed the fear creeping back onto Conall's face. "But," he smiled. "You will be fully prepared when you do. I promise."

"Much better. So, what's happening?" Aedan walked up and patted Conall's shoulders. "You okay? Why do you all look like you've seen the Sídhe?"

Aedan could tell from Déaglán's expression that he should sit. No one spoke. The druid extended his arms as if he were going to embrace the fire and moved his lips without making a sound. Flying up from the fire came a small hawk and dragon, moving as if they were real.

"Aedan. Conall. Do you know why these two have bonded to you? Did you ever wonder?"

Like a puppeteer, the druid moved the miniature hawk and dragon around them with one finger, one chasing the other, and the reverse. Conall noticed a childlike smile on Déaglán's face. When the boys didn't reply, the druid stopped his hand. The small fiery creatures vanished in sparks.

"Conall, when you saved Lann's life, nurtured him back to health, your compassion could be felt for miles. There wasn't anyone who had ties to magic that didn't sense that energy ripple through the world. And you, Aedan. When you found that little golden whelp? The moment you made up your mind to save Fiachra, another wave of compassion moved across the land. Forces of goodness and light found inspiration by your acts, the acts of two little boys. But you are not just two boys."

Aedan sat up. "We're connected to greater powers."

"That's right. Because of that, the positive force of your compassion got the attention of the Fomoragh as well. Banded together through their evil, this group seeks to undo that which Ciall has done in bringing those good qualities into existence. That was when they knew you were in the world."

Aedan wanted to know why the Fomoragh hadn't done anything to them, if they knew that he and Conall were their enemies. Déaglán noticed Fionn linger on Aedan for a moment before turning away.

"They *did*." Fionn whispered, almost as if he hadn't wanted to say anything, but he couldn't help himself.

"What, Fionn? What do you mean?" Aedan's voice shook.

Still the son of Cool wouldn't make eye contact. Aedan saw the druid had turned away as well.

"What? What is it? Someone, tell me." He glowered at them both. "Please!"

"Now is not the time." Fionn walked toward the cliff's edge.

The druid sat there, his eyes glistening in the fire.

It was Conall who, leaning closer to his best friend, said the words that neither Fionn nor Déaglán could utter.

"The Fomoragh killed your mother, Aedan." His voice cracked as he said the words.

"Wha-What? That can't be. She was sick. She died of—"

Jumping up, Aedan was about to leave, but Conall pulled him back.

"The circle!"

Growling, Aedan fell next to his friend.

"I-I watched my mother suffer… and die. How could the Fomoragh—"

The druid nodded, giving the boys permission to leave the protection circle. Conall put his arm around Aedan's back and guided him toward the wall of the fort.

"Listen to me, Aedan." He put his hand on both his friend's shoulders. "This is what cowards do. They destroy the things we love from afar. I-I don't know how they managed to make your mother sick, but I do know that her death was meant to unnerve you… to be your weak spot."

Aedan's face was toward the wall, in darkness. His breathing was fast, and he exhaled through his nose.

He turned Aedan's face by his chin.

"Mark me. They *will* try to use your pain against you. Your love for your mother is a raw nerve, no matter how much you try to conceal it.

They are beings of darkness and deception. They understand disguise well."

Shrugging off his friend's hands, Aedan crossed his arms and leaned against the stone. Now he was entirely in shadow, with only his breathing to show his location.

"Aedan..."

"You mark *me*, Conall Mac Rinne." His voice was like subdued thunder. "When we meet the Fomoragh, I am going to rip out their beating hearts."

"You can't do that. If you do, you become like them."

"So? They ripped out my heart. I'd be returning the favor."

Conall didn't respond right away. He glanced over at Fionn and Déaglán who were involved in their own conversation.

Fionn paced along the edge of the cliff, a moving silhouette against a pale moon. He started to walk toward the boys.

"No, Fionn. This is something they need to work out for themselves. We can't rescue them every time they're in trouble, or they'll never learn."

"I knew I shouldn't have said anything, Déaglán," Fionn huffed.

"He would have found out anyway. At least now he can use that anger in a productive manner while they train."

The hero took a few steps toward his friend and leaned in.

"Would *you* use that anger in a productive manner?"

Déaglán flourished his fingers and the fire blazed brighter. Again, Fionn took steps toward the wall. This time, vines grew from the ground and ensnared his feet, setting him off balance. He glared at the druid.

Déaglán raised his voice. "No. Leave them be. You can't be their protector all the time. Sit with me."

With one hand, Fionn ripped the vines from his ankles.

"The moment you cross that line, Aedan, there's no going back. We can't finish our quest if you become like the Fomoragh."

"What are we doing here, Conall? We're not heroes. Look at us! We're two lads sparring on a cliff's edge with a druid and a man who could be out doing real good in the world instead of babysitting *us*." Aedan started flailing his arms and pacing. "I'm not ready to go off facing the evils of the world. Are you?"

Conall stared at his friend. "I will be. I have to be."

"Right. You *will* be." He tapped Conall's chest. "*You* don't understand how I feel. I just found out that my mother was taken from me. I can't —"

"Stop!" Conall caught Aedan's hand as it was about to tap his chest again. "At least you know your father is yours. I don't know who my birth parents are. Rinn and Siobhan reared me, and I love them, but I'm not theirs. Not really." He released Aedan's hand. "Odhran is your father. Saoirse was your mother. Even if she's not in this world, she is *here*." Conall poked Aedan's chest. "And here." He tapped his friend's head. "She lives inside you."

After hearing that, Aedan's breathing slowed, and he remained in darkness while Conall crossed his arms and kicked at the ground. The breeze came in, whistling through the cracks in the wall, bringing with it the musk of the sea. That was the only sound between them for a short while.

"How did you know that the Fomoragh had killed my mother? You said it like you'd known."

"I... I've been having dreams. Some I can't figure out. Others are... well, they're vivid."

"Did you dream about my mother?"

Conall sighed. "Not exactly. The images aren't always clear, but the feelings are. In one dream, I was with you on a path through the woods, and when we were clear of the trees, I saw an animal lying on the ground. Around it, I saw a gray mist. We moved closer, and the mist moved toward us. We turned to run, but in the corner of my eye, I saw that it was a cow lying on the path. A wave of grief moved through me just before I woke up."

Aedan stepped into the moonlight, and his cheeks glistened. He wiped the tears away.

"A-A cow? You said you saw a cow."

"I did. Do you know what it means?"

Aedan nodded ever so slightly.

"My mother's **caomhnóir** was a cow. That must... That must have been the Fomoragh."

Staring into the night sky, Conall flitted about from constellation to constellation. Out of the corner of his eye, he noticed the fire jump a little as Fionn threw more wood on it, a swarm of sparks fleeing like angry, ashen hornets. Five minutes passed before Conall opened his mouth to say something, but before he could utter a word, Aedan did.

"Let's go back to the fire. I'm tired."

Without saying anything to Fionn or Déaglán, Aedan unfurled his blanket and lay facing away from the fire. Conall followed, putting his palms to the fire, and rubbing his hands together.

"We're both exhausted. See you at sunrise."

After Conall was asleep, Fionn told the druid he was going to find some more wood and fill the water pouches by the stream. As he always did, Déaglán warned him about lingering too long outside of the fort.

"I can handle myself, druid. Be back soon."

Fionn disappeared through the dark portal that led back to the caltrops. Unlike the boys, he could easily somersault over them as he had many times since their arrival. Using only moonlight, he found the path toward the stream. As he crouched to fill the pouches, he heard a twig snap. Then another. His arm hair bristled. Tightening his grip on the water pouch, he swung around, connecting with whatever had caught his attention, sending him or her back about ten feet. Fionn took two strides, expecting to be standing over someone, but no one was there. He listened again for anything that would give away a presence, but all he heard was the thin whistle of the wind. He gathered the water pouches and tied them to his belt. He still needed to get firewood. The landscape was largely desolate, but one stand of blasted trees had provided the wood the past few days. Blasted trees like these usually had been struck by lightning or damaged in a battle. Some new life grew on most of them, but many were arboreal husks no longer tied to the world of the living.

Like earlier, Fionn heard the snapping of wood, but rather than strike, he took a more measured approach and turned around. A figure about his height had its back to the sky, its features obscured. It was unclear whether it was male or female, or even human.

"Foolish hero." A gravelly voice uttered. "You and the druid cannot protect them once they leave Dún Ancróga. Then, they will be like fangless hounds — impotent and vulnerable."

"Until my dying breath will I protect them from the likes of you, witch." Fionn clenched his massive fists. "You have been warned."

The shadowy figure replied with a sinister laugh. "Cool's whelp dares to threaten me? I am simply here to deliver the message. We shall meet again."

Before Fionn could reply, the figure fell apart into black leaves that flew off like bats, squeaking into the night. He waited a few minutes to ensure Carman was gone before resuming his wood gathering. Whether he would at least tell Déaglán about this was questionable, but he would say nothing to the boys. He had been gone half an hour, so the boys were most assuredly asleep, and telling them would only put them on edge even more.

Back at the fort, he lobbed the wood over the caltrops and then leaped back over with the water pouches. As he passed through the arch into the open area, Lann set atop the wall and shuffled his feathers.

"Everything go well?" Fionn muttered as if he expected the hawk to respond.

He set the wood down next to the pouches and saw the druid, his eyes out over the moonlit sea. As soon as he was within earshot of a whisper, he asked if the boys were all right.

"Their slumber has been untroubled." Déaglán paused. "What did Carman want?"

Fionn smirked. "How did you…? Never mind. I don't want to know. She threatened their safety."

"The Fomoragh will be daunting, Fionn. The lads must be ready. We don't have much time with them before we part ways."

Fionn sat cross-legged by the fire. "Why can't we accompany them for a while? What harm will that do?"

"While our paths and theirs will cross from time to time, the beginning of their journey from here must be theirs and theirs alone. The prophecy of the DragonHawk demands it."

At the mention of the prophecy, Fionn nodded. He had learned from experience that prophecies were unavoidable, even if they could be put off for a time. Carman could do nothing to them while they were within the fort, so that gave him some comfort. As he lay back, he wondered what Caer Ibormeith, the goddess of sleep, had in store for them. Her purview was also prophecy, and she controlled who saw what and when. This night, she kept vigil over them, drifting through heavens in her swan-form, giving them only the most comforting of dreams. She, like the other gods, knew the tumult in store of the boys, and she needed for them to be rested before they continued their travels.

Streaks of golden light broke over the horizon at sunrise, and Lann began squawking and circling the camp. All four jumped up, taking a defensive posture, as they had trained. Conall and Aedan had their backs to Fionn, staffs at the ready, and Déaglán watched the fort for any intruder.

"Are we under attack?" Conall blinked, his eyes still adjusting to the morning.

Déaglán observed Lann's maneuvers above them, and then he smiled.

"Stand down, warriors." He chuckled. "Your friend is happy, Conall. Someone's coming, and one of you will know him."

Conall held up his arm, and Lann perched on it, the hawk's head twitching in all directions.

"What is it, boy? Who's coming?" He rubbed the hawk's chest with his finger.

Over the sea, a speck appeared in the midst of the rising glow where the ocean met the sky. A faint roar could be heard, and Aedan ran to the cliff's edge, wearing a wide grin.

"He's coming." He wiped his eyes with his sleeve. "Fiachra's coming!"

Conall joined his friend, squinting out toward the sunrise. The shape of the dragon grew, and the light twinkled off the red and gold scales, giving the creature a magical luminescence. As Fiachra got to the cliffs, he reached his head forward and nuzzled Aedan, sending out a puff of smoke through his nostrils. His wingspan was easily thirty feet, even for an adolescent dragon, and when he set down in the open space of the fort, he landed softer than one would expect for such a large animal. Aedan couldn't contain himself and threw his arms around the dragon's neck. Fiachra rubbed his cheek against the boy's head and then turned toward the others.

"I-I've never seen a dragon this close before." Conall edged toward Fiachra. "Is it all right if I get closer?"

Aedan laughed. "Of course. He won't hurt you. Will you, boy?" He patted the gilded scales.

Fiachra snorted like a horse, blowing wisps of smoke from his nose. Conall pressed his palm against the scaly skin, lightly moving his hand.

"He feels like he's wearing metal armor." Conall traced the curvature of the body with his eyes, landing at the head. "And his eyes... They're like gems."

"You're one lucky lad, Aedan Mac Odhrain." Déaglán sized up the beast. "Golden dragons bond for life."

As Fionn prepared the morning meal with Conall, Aedan leaned against Fiachra who had decided to nap. Lann perched atop the dragon's head, keeping watch over his new friend. Once they had finished eating, Déaglán sat by Fiachra. Asking a dragon to move would be problematic. He called Fionn and Conall over, and he asked Aedan to set up a protection circle. The boy conceded, shrugging at Conall.

"What's happening, Déaglán? Why do we need a protection circle in the morning? Didn't you say that sunlight offered its own protection?"

"That I did, Conall, but what I am about to share with you needs the added protection of magic. Have a seat." He looked over at Fionn who nodded. "We weren't going to say anything about this, but when Fionn was gathering wood, he encountered Carman, a witch from the east. I'm not going to mince words. She threatened you both."

Both Conall and Aedan fidgeted.

"Hear me, both of you." Fionn sat up. "This may be *your* quest, but if that witch or her sons hurt you, that will be the last thing they do. I swear on Danu."

"You mentioned her sons before."

"Aye, Conall." The druid pulled back his hood. "Dubh the Black, Dother the Evil, and Dian the Violent."

He told them about how Dubh works in dark magic and is the favored of Carman. He appears as a young boy which makes him seem less threatening, but he plays on the sympathy of those he is trying to manipulate. The middle brother, Dother, feeds off fear and uses that to take his adversaries off-balance. Dian, the most feared, prefers the physical to the magical and enjoys acts of violence against others. Conall's face lost all color.

"How do we fight that? All four?" His voice began to crack. "I…"

Déaglán put a hand up. "You are not alone in this. Aedan—"

"So, two against four is better odds?" Conall raised his voice. "We're not druids like you or heroes like Fionn. Just how do you expect *us* to defeat *them*?"

"Conall, we can handle this. We just—"

"Just what, Aedan? Just what? We're two sixteen-year-old boys who can barely handle a staff or conjure a protection circle, and we're supposed to hold our own against Carman and her evil offspring? I can see why you wanted to wait until daylight to talk about this, Déaglán."

"Druid, release the circle." Fionn stood. "Conall, I want you to take twenty steps toward the fort."

Conall reluctantly complied. Fionn reached his hand toward Aedan, and the latter handed over his staff. Spinning it in one hand, Fionn flipped the staff under his arm.

"I'm coming for you, son of Rinn. Be ready."

"What? What do you—"

Before Conall could finish that sentence, Fionn leaped forward swinging the staff at him. The boy swung his staff around, fists clenching it, and blocked the attack, although he took a few steps back. Again, the hero brought the weapon around, and Conall, his eyes following the staff, stopped it. From all different angles, the staff came at him, and with each successive attack, Conall blocked or parried it, although he grunted from the brute strength of his adversary. He jumped when Fionn, attempting to take out his legs, swung the staff low. Only once did Fionn catch him off guard, striking his arm, but Conall compensated and shifted his weight, causing the bigger man to fall forward. Seeing an opening, Conall brought his staff up, slamming into the other one, spun around, and turned Fionn's burly mass against him. He gritted his teeth, and his eyes glazed over as if he were channeling a feral creature. His movements became more streamlined. Conall planted the staff in the ground, gripped it with both hands, and swung his legs into a kick aimed at Fionn's chest. The son of Cool fell on his back, the staff flying from his grip.

"Enough!" Déaglán placed himself between them. "That's enough, Conall."

The boy's breath heaved from him and sweat dripped down his temples. He caught a slight smile on Aedan's face, and he returned it, wiping his brow.

"Well," Fionn uttered, rubbing his chest, "you surprised me. Are you all right?"

Conall nodded, taking a large swig from a water pouch.

Aedan patted him on the back, grinning.

"Nicely done! See, I knew you had it in you."

"I'm sure Fionn was holding back."

The hero twisted from side to side, his back cracking. "Not really. I wanted you to let off some steam, but you put some power in those maneuvers."

"That was a physical attack. What about magical ones? I'm no druid."

Déaglán laughed.

"No, Conall, but you're learning to tap into some basic dríochta. Be creative with what you do know. The best druids use the simplest magic but use it in unexpected ways."

The boys talked a bit by themselves, with Conall showing his friend some improvised moves he'd used. Meanwhile, Fionn played with Fiachra with the druid nearby.

"Tell me. Were you holding back?"

Fionn smirked. "You know I was. I did put some force into it, but if I gave him my full strength?"

Déaglán nodded. "Understood. So, you just wanted to let him get it out. Maybe even build him up?"

"Look, they'll be ready." Fionn raised his voice. "Boys, come on over."

Conall's face seemed more at ease. He and Aedan sat by Fiachra, and the dragon put his head back down for another nap. The sun radiated across the heavens as late morning approached.

"We need to finish talking about the Fomoragh while it's still daylight. We've already mentioned Carman and her kin, but there are others." Fionn shared a glance with the druid before he continued. "Another one to watch out for is Balor, the one-eyed god of death. If he wants to, should he look you in the eye, he can take your spirit. Never look at him directly. Next is Bres who once ruled the Tuatha Dé Danann when Nuada lost his arm in battle and could not be king. When Nuada regained his arm, he resumed his kingship. Bres is both charismatic and cruel. He will appeal to you, compliment you, hoping to take you off guard."

Fionn waited to see if the boys had any questions. Their wide-eyed, expressionless faces signaled him to continue.

"Cethlenn is the wife of Balor, a prophetess who will try to tempt you with offerings of the future. She almost tempted *me* once, but I caught onto her wiles and was able to escape. Her honeyed voice holds you in her thrall, but if you chew mugwort leaves, her voice will have no effect. My advice? Always have some leaves in your pocket."

Déaglán took over.

"Cichol used to rule the Fomoragh, and he wields a double-sided axe that shrieks when he swings it. The banshee are downright pleasant compared to that. The wail is meant to unnerve you and whittle away your resolve. Finally, Tethra. His sword, Orna, speaks all the deeds that it has done for him. It is merely a distraction before he takes your head."

"Seems to me," Aedan began, "that the Fomoragh like to do a lot of distracting." He chuckled, but Fionn cleared his throat, and Aedan stopped.

"You're not wrong. While the Fomoragh are formidable, they're not unbeatable. If they gain the advantage, though, it could mean the end of your quest. Be vigilant." The druid clenched his fist at the last word.

"I am curious about something." Conall sat up. "What happened to our Nascah?"

Déaglán cocked his head. "What do you mean?"

"Well, if we're on this quest for the wands, and we have to be vigilant as you say about the Fomoragh, when will we be looking for our ca-omhnóiri?"

"Conall, your spirit guide finds *you*. It's not the other way around. When you're ready, it will appear."

Aedan sighed and leaned against Fiachra, pulling his knees in.

"I just don't know... All of this sounds so unreal to me. It feels like it was just yesterday that I was helping my da in the fields. The more I learn, the more I just want to go back to a normal life at home. Conall, what do *you* think?"

"You're expecting *me* to have answers? Good one." He chuckled. "Fionn. Déaglán. What happens if Aedan and I just walk out of here and not look back? What if we just don't want to do this?"

Lann took to the skies, squawking and circling. The winds picked up from the sea, and at the horizon, thick gray clouds rolled toward them as if alive.

"I'm afraid there's no chance of that." Fionn jumped up. "Quickly, hop on Fiachra and head east until you reach the Twisted Trees, then head north."

"But, what about —"

"Now, Conall! Both of you!"

Déaglán helped Conall to climb on the dragon's back. He leaned over to the boys.

"Go, and don't look back. Fiachra, up!" He slapped the gilded leg of the dragon.

Letting out a cry, Fiachra spread his wings and pushed off, taking the two into the skies. Conall turned back.

"Déaglán!"

The druid watched them fly off and turned to Fionn.

"It seems Carman and her minions can't wait. We'll engage them here to give the boys time to put some distance between them and us."

8 | THE TWISTED TREES

His red and gold wings outstretched, Fiachra crossed a channel whose murky depths hid all sorts of denizens that neither of the boys would want to meet. Shouting so Aedan could hear him, Conall asked if he had known that Dún Ancróga was on an island. Air moved past them so fast that anything Aedan said was swallowed by their movement, so he simply shook his head. He had wrapped his arms around as much of the dragon's neck as he could. Conall tried to look over his shoulder toward the fort, but they were moving so quickly that he couldn't turn that far. He clung to Fiachra and closed his eyes.

When the dragon slowed, he turned toward the shore of the mainland where, somewhere far away, lay the Silver Birch Glen and Oak Mountain. In a clearing atop another cliff that resembled the one on which Déaglán and Fionn were probably fighting for their lives, Fiachra set down. It took the boys a few moments to realize they had stopped moving, and Conall unclenched his eyes. He tried to get down but slid down the scales into the dirt.

"Now what are we going to do?"

Aedan swung his leg over as if dismounting a giant steed and landed on his feet.

"Show off." Conall dusted his pants off. "But, really, Aedan, what're we going to do? How can we help Fionn and the druid?"

"We can't." Aedan ran his hands through his hair and spit out a bug. "I need to remember to cover my mouth when I fly with you." He glared at the dragon who couldn't care less and was grazing on grass.

Conall flung up his hands. "This is just perfect! We're in the middle of gods-know-where, and we have no food and no map!"

Right then, a familiar sound made him instinctively put his arm up. Screeching, Lann landed on Conall's bracer, finally settling down.

"Did you see what happened to Fionn and Déaglán?" He asked, as if the hawk could answer him.

Aedan managed to get his friend to calm down so he could share his thoughts.

"What we *do* have is our healer's pouches that Déaglán taught us to make. I see yours hanging on your belt. We also kind of know how to protect ourselves, thanks to Fionn, and we can conjure some fyre and protection spells, thanks to the druid. So, we're going to be fine, Conall. Stop worrying so much."

"You think one week of training is going to make us heroes?"

"Are you going to be like this the whole time?"

Mumbling under his breath, Conall nudged the hawk back into the air and headed toward a path going left. Aedan still stood by the dragon.

"What're you doing?"

"Trying to figure out which way is north." Aedan went to the cliff's edge and put his hand up to his brow. "We came from the west, eh?"

Huffing, Conall took Aedan by the arm. "Let's go. *This* way is north." He returned to the path. "Some hunter you are," he muttered.

They walked without speaking, and Aedan kept glancing at his friend and smirking. Eventually, Conall noticed and walked faster. For an hour, they said nothing to each other. High above, Lann followed them, and behind him, Fiachra kept pace. Coming into view was a hazy birch forest, distinctive because of its silvery white bark. The path diminished into it, and farther still was fog that lingered, despite the breeze. Meandering through the forest was a brook flanked by boulders and the occasional cluster of lilies.

"Well, this bodes well." Aedan mumbled to himself. "Let's stop here. We should probably fill up our water pouches."

Conall had stopped, but he didn't respond. He was eyeing the surroundings, lingering on clusters of rocks or tree parts on the forest floor. It was untouched by anyone. Fallen leaves and underbrush obscured the edges of the path, one that had been made long ago.

"Hey, fill up your pouch so we can get moving."

Still saying nothing, Conall knelt by the brook.

"Are we not speaking now? Did I do something?" Aedan shrugged.

Sighing, Conall shoved the pouch into the icy water.

"No. You didn't do anything." He tied the pouch closed. "I was really enjoying the time with Fionn and Déaglán. It was the first normal thing I've done in a while. Well, as normal as dríochta and enchanted forts, anyway."

Aedan crouched next to his friend.

"Believe it or not, I understand. As scary as this all is, I just know that you and I can do it. You're not alone in how you feel. I may sound tough, but on the inside, I'm as scared as you are, Conall."

Tying the pouch shut, Conall patted Aedan on the back before heading north. They hadn't gone far when they heard a screech emanating from deep within the fog-ensconced forest. As they had been trained to do, they stood at the ready, staffs in hand, peering toward the source of the sound. Bursting through the fog came a bristly-furred, tusked creature whose thunderous hooves kicked up dirt into clouds. As it closed the distance, the boys stood dumbstruck. Then, a whistle pierced the air, and three arrows struck the animal, sending it tumbling over itself and into a tree. Leaves rained down upon the boar whose back had cracked upon impact. It lay groaning at the base of the tree.

"What do we do?" Conall crept up to it, gripping his staff so tightly his knuckles turned white.

"What I want to know is where those arrows came from. You think maybe Fionn followed us?" Aedan looked around.

A voice they didn't know responded.

"They're *my* arrows."

From out of the forest came a young woman, at least a head taller than the boys, wearing green leather armor with a brown skirt of hide. She drew her dagger, closed her eyes for a silent prayer, and ended the beast's suffering.

"These woods are sacred to Arduinna. If you wish to travel through them, you should make an offering."

Aedan leaned over the animal. "Aren't boars sacred to her? Won't she be angry you killed it?"

She smiled. "I was hunting this one and had already offered prayers to her if you must know. I was chasing him out of the forest where I had a better chance of snaring him when you two came along."

Drawing rope from her belt, she tied the legs together. Using one arm, she lifted the boar on her shoulder. The boys' mouths fell agape.

"Arduinna keeps close watch here. Tread carefully."

She started down the path, with Conall close behind.

"Y-You lifted the boar with *one*—"

The woman continued, not responding.

"Excuse me, but we're new to this land—"

"I couldn't tell." She kept wide strides, and Conall had to trot to keep up.

"Please, slow down."

"I need to field dress this beast before it's no longer edible. Keep pace, if you must, or be on your way."

Conall waved Aedan to join him, and the boys hustled to follow.

"Why are we following her?" Aedan smirked.

"She might know something about where we need to go."

The young woman, even though she was within earshot, said nothing. When they were farther down the road, she stopped, staring ahead at dark gray clouds on the horizon.

"A storm will be here soon. I won't make it back to camp before it hits, and I have no intention of lugging this," she shrugged, "in a downpour. I know a cave not far from here where we can stay dry for a while."

"Why are you helping us?" Aedan leaned over to stretch.

"Do you want to be wet in an unknown land?" She nodded in the direction off the path where they needed to go. "Look at it this way. You'll get a meal out of it."

—⁂—

Over the rough landscape they went, wildflowers growing between slabs of limestone. To the east, the land buckled into hills, and farther on, a mountain. Both boys took in their new surroundings, making sure to keep an eye on the woman as well. Aedan had perfected a certain look that he would give Conall that conveyed caution. Conall, on the other hand, seemed a bit more aloof to that, and his attention moved everywhere. From the north, the storm crept closer to them like a cat about to pounce, and the young woman quickened her pace as they approached some shrubbery at the base of a hill.

"Quickly. Beyond that bush." Her strides lengthened as she spoke.

Laughing to himself, Conall shook his head as he saw this woman, maybe a year older than they were, bearing the weight of the dead boar as if it were an empty sack. She knew exactly where her foot should land between the striations of rock so as to keep her footing, and she even hopped over a boulder at the foot of the hill.

"Have you ever seen anything like that?" Conall whispered to his friend. "It's as if she was carrying nothing at all."

Aedan leaned in close. "My da once told me about the Banfhéinnithe, warrior-hunters. All women. He said they lived in the trees of certain forests, and no men were allowed. They —"

From up ahead, the young woman's voice interrupted.

"In here." She moved beyond the scraggly bush that was taller than she was and disappeared.

When the boys caught up, they ducked to enter the cave. The air inside was thick and cool, and the rocky walls were spongy and wet. As soon as they could stand, they found themselves in a small cutaway chamber. Some sunlight had lit up the front of the cave, but the back was black as night, and then the woman's whisper got their attention.

"Ó aer, Déanaim iarracht tine."

A torch ignited, and she put it in an iron ring on the wall. The spot on the wall behind the torch flame dried, and a glow spread through the space, giving it dimension.

"She knows the druid's dríocht."

The woman lowered the boar, untied its legs, and drew her dagger.

"Of course I do. I'm not a child. I need one of you to help me."

Conall nudged his friend who shot him a look, but Conall raised his brows in insistence.

"What do you need me to do?" Aedan crouched down to her.

"Hold the legs while I make my first cut. I need to remove the innards. Once I make the incision, hold the skin open so I can reach in."

With precision, she drew the blade down the underbelly and then put it back in the sheath. Aedan held open the body while she inserted her hands up to the elbows inside the glistening crimson mass.

"You there." She spoke to Conall. "Take the cloth from my pack and lay it out before me."

Conall did just that, and she placed the glossy intestines on it. Reaching back in, she pulled out more organs, laying them on the heap. When she was done, she instructed him to tie up the corners into a tight parcel.

"We need some peat for the fyre. I'll be back. Don't leave the cave."

She took the bundle of innards and left. Conall went over to her pack and, without touching it, looked inside.

"What are you doing? She'll be back soon."

"Relax, Aedan, I'm looking, not touching. Don't you think it's strange that she appears out of nowhere, can kill a boar the way she did, and then carry it this far? You and I both would have had to carry it."

Aedan laughed. "Yes, and stopping every few feet. So, see anything in there?" He craned his neck.

"No. Look, I don't know if I trust her yet. Let's —"

At seeing her return, Conall jumped back. She put half a dozen peat bricks on the floor, and the smell of moist earth grew stronger.

"You're not from this region. What brings you here?"

Conall jumped in. "We… We've begun our Nascah."

"I remember mine." She used her dagger to cut a leg off the boar, wrapping another cloth around the exposed shoulder on the animal.

Using the torch, she ignited some of the peat. Once it was hot, she went into a darker part of the cave and returned with two thin logs, each with a notch cut into the end. She shoved each one on opposite ends of the smoldering peat, notched side up. An arrow forced through the leg would become a makeshift spit, and she placed it in the notches.

"You've done this before." Conall took a closer look at the spit. "You use this cave often?"

"As often as I need to. Have you had any luck finding your ca-omhnóir?" She blew on the fyre to make the peat glow.

Aedan and Conall exchanged glances.

"Not yet." Aedan sat down next to her. "I'm Aedan. This is Conall."

She had a faint smile. "Daimhain. Are you two…"

Both boys broke out into laughter.

"Only friends. More like brothers, really." Aedan picked up one of Daimhain's arrows on the ground next to him. "So, where did you learn to shoot like that?"

She took her arrow back. "I was trained to shoot as a child. I'm a—"

"Banféinní."

"Something like that. How do you know that, Aedan?"

He explained how his father used to tell him stories as a boy to help him fall asleep, and they were often of the old gods, as well as any who were touched by them. There were tales of the Sídhe and of the heroes who once walked the land. Those last ones he enjoyed the most.

"My people live in a remote place, shrouded from the outside world. We only leave if we need to. But I can't tell you more. Some secrets must be kept at all costs."

Soon, the smell of roasted boar filled the cave, and just when Daim-hain pulled the leg off the fyre, a crack of thunder echoed above them, shaking the walls, followed by a torrent. Like a waterfall, the rains poured in front of the cave, hiding the opening from those who might stumble past. Conall moved back, thinking the water would flow into the cave, but it didn't. Daimhain handed him a chunk of seared meat.

"Worry not. The entrance to the cave sits above the water level, and the hill's slope will prevent us from getting wet."

He closed his eyes when the scent of the meat hit his nose and took a tentative bite.

"It's been a while since I've had anything like this. Thank you for shar-ing it."

"Well, I couldn't have you both go hungry."

Chewing, Aedan responded. "We'd have found something to eat." He took another bite. "Thank you, though."

—✴—

All three cleaned the bone of its meat, and Aedan wanted to continue to gnaw on it. Daimhain crouched by the entrance behind the wall of wa-ter, and she seemed interested in something beyond it. Even though she was in shadow, Conall noticed she appeared concerned.

"Is something wrong?"

"No." She returned to them. "I saw movement, but it turned out to be a stag. Is something wrong with *you*? I heard a shift in your voice."

He shook his head. Aedan had reclined against the cave wall with his arms crossed, and he was fast asleep. Conall poked at the fyre with a small stick, watching the sparks flurry about and then grow dark. With the cave entrance blocked by the flowing rainwater, the smoke had gathered above them, and it was descending the longer the fyre burned. Daimhain, as if knowing his thoughts, stepped on the peat, putting out the fyre. The torch remained lit, sticking out of a hole in the dirt floor.

"You can't see it, but there is a crack in the stone above, and the smoke will sooner or later leave the cave. It won't go much lower. In this storm, no one will be able to find you because of it."

"What makes you think I'm worried about that?" Conall puffed his chest.

"I can read your body language. Plus, you keep looking up at the smoke."

Conall explained that he and Aedan hadn't been this far from home before, and being unfamiliar to the region made them uneasy. When Daimhain pressed him for more details about the journey, Conall gave some story about how they had each left home, not knowing the other had begun the search for his spirit guide and had met up on the path between their respective villages. He then described everything up until their first meeting with Fionn where he changed the narrative to avoid discussing the events that followed. Once the story changed, Daimhain interrupted him.

"You're lying." She cocked her head. "As soon as you started talking about leaving that town, your tone changed. I could feel it."

"What? What are you talking about? I wasn't lying." Conall tried to remain composed.

Daimhain shrugged. "I won't argue about it. If you're not going to be truthful, then I'd rather not hear it. Since the rain isn't letting up, I'm going to take a nap." She moved toward the wall.

Aedan sidled up to his friend.

"What just happened? How did she know that you were changing the story to avoid talking about, well, you know. She seemed offended that you didn't tell the entire truth."

Shrugging, Conall looked back at her. He wanted to say something, but he didn't know what. He leaned into Aedan's ear.

"I didn't want her to know about what we've been doing. I mean, what if she's in league with the Fomoragh? It seemed odd that she came out of nowhere right when we arrived. Don't you think?"

"I know what you mean. But Conall, she fed us. She brought us to safety from the storm."

"It's called *deception*. Maybe she's trying to earn our trust so she can figure out where we're going?"

Aedan laughed. "Conall, *we* don't even know that yet. You're right, though. Being careful isn't a bad thing. Let's see what happens."

The boys decided to take a nap as well, but as Conall lay back, the rain pouring in front of the cave kept him awake. In time, he slept, but his slumber was fitful. When he woke up, Daimhain and Aedan were still fast asleep. The peat embers glowed softly, and, as she had said it would, the smoke had dissipated. The rain had stopped, too, with the late afternoon sun straining through the remaining clouds. He moved to the opening where he could smell the air had changed. The earth had been pummeled by the downpour, and smelled of petrichor, that musky scent just after a storm. To Conall, it reminded him of home. It was in that moment that he thought about his father and wondered what the man was thinking. At this time of day, Rinn would be sitting down to supper after having worked outside in the fields all day, rain or shine. He knew his father didn't talk about how he felt often, so he would keep in how much he missed his son, no matter who asked. His mother, on the other hand, would try her best to pry the emotions out of her husband. It was also possible that Rinn and Siobhan shared their thoughts about his absence, taking comfort in the thought that he would ultimately find his caomhnóir and return home. Conall's detachment from them knotted his gut. His reverie broke as Daimhain sat next to him.

"I apologize about snapping at you earlier. My people embrace truth above all else, so we have developed a finely tuned sense when people aren't being completely honest. You have no reason to trust me, at least with your secrets, so it's understandable that you're holding back."

He smiled at her. "I appreciate that. Aedan and I are on a quest. I wish I could say more, but there's too much at stake. Those who would stop us are skilled in deception, and sometimes those who show the lightest side to you are often hiding their darkness."

"Who told you that piece of wisdom?" Her face softened as she smiled.

"My mum. That's who was I thinking about when you sat down. This is the longest I've been away from my mum and da."

"It's hard to prepare for your Nascah. Some find their spirit guide within a few days, and others it takes much longer. Mine took two months. As for the rest of your journey, that part you're not telling me, if it's that important you have to keep it secret, then I hope you find what you're looking for."

Sticking his head outside, Conall examined the sky, sighing.

"It looks like we're here for the night. It's getting too late to wander down the path. I feel like we wasted the whole day."

"I believe things happen for a reason, Conall. We were meant to meet. This day might seem like a waste, but in truth, it's an opportunity."

"For what?"

She patted him on the shoulder. "We'll just have to see. Let's wake up your friend."

Shaking Aedan's arm caused him to stretch and yawn. As he propped himself up on his elbows, he took in his surroundings.

"I dreamt I was home in bed. I smelled my da's porridge cooking, too. You been awake long?"

"Long enough." Conall looked over at Daimhain who had started another peat fyre. "She's not half bad. She said we were all meant to meet, and that this is an opportunity."

Aedan groaned as he sat up. "For what?"

Conall shrugged and offered to help her. Supper was another leg of boar, but Daimhain wanted to find some herbs and plants. She asked if either of them wanted to join her, and Aedan volunteered. All alone, Conall decided to stand outside the cave to stretch his legs, keeping himself behind the bush. In the distance, he heard Lann's call, and right after, he heard what must have been Fiachra. It seemed as if they had found a way to communicate. They didn't sound distressed, so he could be at ease that, for the moment, the Fomoragh or any other threat hadn't come close to the cave. He held up his arm, and Lann fluttered onto it.

"Everything all right?"

The hawk moved his head around, squawking once.

"I see you and Fiachra are getting along."

Two more squawks.

"Well, keep an eye out. At the first sign of trouble, sound an alarm." He rubbed beneath Lann's beak and then lifted his arm. Lann returned to his perch in the trees.

"I'd like to see Aedan do that with his dragon." He chuckled to himself.

—⟥—

Daimhain and Aedan scouted around the other side of the hill, and she pointed out the plants she wanted. Her knowledge of the area was extensive, and every time he pulled a plant, he wanted to know what it was. He looked up when he heard the faint roar of Fiachra, smiling.

"You seem to know what that sound is." Daimhain handed him some hedgehog mushrooms.

He nodded. "A friend."

"A dragon is your friend? That's a good friend to have. How did you get so lucky?"

"I saved him when he was a wee one. We've been bonded ever since."

"It seems there's much about you and Conall that goes beyond two boys seeking their spirit guides."

A few feet away, she stopped. When Aedan caught up to her, he laughed.

"It's a fairy circle. A ring of mushrooms like that is supposed to mean that the Sídhe protect this hill."

Daimhain crouched down. "I've never seen anything like this, and I've lived here all my life."

"Don't pick any of the mushrooms here. They're not edible, and you'll upset the spirits. That much I learned from my mum. She said a childhood friend of hers broke a circle, and the Sídhe never let the woman have a moment's peace until she died."

"All right, then. Good to know. We won't be picking these."

Before they headed down, Aedan looked out over the meadow before them. The clouds had moved along enough that the late afternoon sun made the rain-covered landscape sparkle like a field of gemstones. Bright greens of the grass and moss mixed with the yellows and pinks of wildflowers. But something else stood out to him more.

"By Brigid's fyre... Would you look at that?"

Daimhain and Aedan saw at least a dozen fairy rings, of varying sizes, strewn across the field. Some rings were of flowers, but most were of mushrooms. Aedan returned to the cave and saw Conall sitting at the entrance, his head raised and his eyes closed.

"Conall! You have to see this!"

As soon as they joined Daimhain, Conall gasped.

"What in the world... Is that...?"

Aedan put his hand across his friend's shoulders.

"That, my friend, is magic. The Sídhe have blessed this place."

Sighing, Conall crouched down, brushing his hand over the wet grass.

"What's wrong?" Daimhain crouched with him.

"Aedan, I think we need to tell her. Too much is happening. So much that I can't keep it in any longer."

Nodding, Aedan held out his arm, and Conall gripped the forearm, pulling himself up. Back in the cave, Daimhain prepared their next meal while the boys told her everything from the moment each left his own house to start his Nascah except their own connection to the Ársa and the Fonn. Conall finished by saying to her that they had to trust her. If she were in league with the Fomoragh, she could easily have killed them while they slept. Daimhain pulled a ceramic pot from a dark corner of the cave and set it on the edge of the fyre. Into it, she put the hedgehog mushrooms, dill, fennel fronds and some water. All that was left was for the meat to roast and the soup to simmer.

"Thank you for telling me. And you're right. If I had been working with the Fomoragh, you'd be dead. My people know of them, mostly of Carman, the witch. Her cruelty knows no limits." She stirred the soup.

"I just hope we'll be ready when we have to face them." Conall shrugged.

He pulled the wooden rod that becomes a staff from his belt and examined it.

"How much have you learned?" Daimhain nodded toward the staff. "I can help you. If you want."

Aedan laughed. "I'm sure that Fionn was holding back. I'll spar with you, but you actually have to fight. I don't want to be coddled like a child."

She grinned. "Not a problem."

—⁓—

A sky painted dark purple with tinges of silver greeted Daimhain and the boys when she brought them outside to spar. Atop the hill, she held up her staff, and like Conall and Aedan's, it was mystical. By force of will, she could make a short wooden rod extend into an oak staff etched with symbols the boys had never seen before.

"Are you ready? Remember, I won't be holding back."

She spun the staff around and took a warrior's stance, nodding once at Conall.

He stepped forward, extended his staff, and watched her carefully. He met her first movements with his own, and she smiled. For each strike she made, he parried, and when he spun around, clacking into her staff, she almost lost her grip.

"Who taught you *that* move?" She walked around him, her eyes bouncing all over to take in any subtle movements.

"Fionn Mac Cool." He smirked. "No more talk. Spar."

She obliged him fully, and her movements reminded him of a dancer as she did spinning leaps and somersaults. With her staff against his, they pushed against one another until she leaped up and flipped herself over him, bringing the staff down to his legs with firmness. He went down on one knee, and she prepared to take out his other one when he rolled onto his back, parried her attack, and lifted his leg, flipping her over him. She landed on her back with a sharp exhale, shook it off, and put herself back into a warrior's stance.

"I'm truly impressed. The hero taught you well. We're not done yet, though."

Their sparring increased its intensity, and she showed him moves he had never seen with a speed he couldn't match. Aedan's mouth fell open as he saw her make decisions on the fly. He mimicked her as best he could from the sidelines, but he knew the only way to learn this was to get into the fray. He jumped into the sparring, and then the three of them played off each other. Both boys took falls every few moves, but they jumped right back into it, sometimes asking her to repeat what she had done. After a while, the three of them were in synchronicity to where, no matter what they did, no one took a fall. It was an hour before Daimhain put up her hand.

"All right. I need some water. A brief break?"

Conall, with a full grin at Aedan, nodded. They playfully knocked staffs together before taking a seat. Daimhain returned from the cave with a goatskin pouch and took a substantial drink before tossing it at the boys.

"I have to hand it to your friend Fionn. He taught you both well. I was giving you my full effort, too."

Aedan wiped his mouth with the back of his hand. "I could tell you were putting your full strength into it. My arms are still vibrating." He chuckled.

"Mine, too. How'd you get to be so good?" Conall shook out his arms.

"Where I am from, we train daily. We must always remain vigilant. Everyone trains, too. Young and old." She drank some water. "Thank you for the sparring. It was fun."

She jumped up and looked around the meadow.

"We should head out today. You have a little ways to go before you reach the Twisted Trees, and you'll want to get there before dark. Now that the sun is rising, the day will seem to move quickly."

They cleaned up the cave, putting it back as they had found it, at least until Daimhain would need to use it again. She had wrapped the remains of the boar in cloth so she could carry it. Aedan and Conall each took a few peat bricks in their leather packs, but she advised them to use them soon or everything they own would smell like peat. Back on the northerly path, the pale sky opened before them, speckled with clouds. Daimhain walked ahead of the boys, her stride a bit wider, but she managed to keep up her part of the conversation.

"It'll be a few hours walk for us, and then you'll be in less explored territory once you move beyond the Trees. Maps are hard to come by, though."

Conall picked up his pace a bit. "I'm sure we'll figure something out. Have you been to where we're going much?"

"A few times. The last was about a year ago. It's not somewhere you linger."

They continued in silence for a while, stopping for a brief respite by a spring to refill their water pouches. The lack of conversation allowed for the natural sounds to envelop them, and in the distance, a dragon and a hawk seemed to be communicating in their own way. Conall looked into the sky for Lann, but even squinting, he couldn't see him.

"He's around. He and the dragon are keeping watch for us."

Conall and Aedan both raised their eyebrows and looked at each other.

"How did you know that, Daimhain?" Conall again picked up his pace to move closer to her.

"I have a way with animals, you might say. A gift, my people call it. I can sense when animals are near, and I can understand some of their languages."

"You speak dragon?" Aedan chuckled.

She giggled. "Dragons don't all speak the same language, but I do understand some. I haven't learned how to speak to them yet. It's not easy to do. I'd have to find a dragan-cainteoir, and my tribe doesn't have one."

"I've never heard of a dragon-talker. I just talk to Fiachra, and he understands me." Aedan shrugged.

Daimhain turned around. "Only someone who has been touched by the gods can do that." She raised an eyebrow.

Conall smirked at Aedan who shrugged.

"Let's keep moving so we can reach the Trees before it gets too late. We don't want to be on this road after sundown."

Resuming the journey, she kept pace ahead of them again.

With the gentle rise and fall of the landscape came the occasional domed druidic cells, constructs of limestone that served as places of meditation for druids, but also for those who needed a respite from the elements. Trees didn't grow as far as the eye could see, but certain types, like holly or blackthorn, could, as well as various types of orchids. The path they were on had been worn into the limestone by centuries of travelers on foot since this terrain was inhospitable to horses and other beasts of burden. Wagons didn't survive the journey, and remnants of wooden wheels lay along the path, with grasses and wildflowers growing between the spokes. Abandoned wagons served as makeshift water troughs, although many functioned as baths for the avian inhabitants of this austere place.

To the west, tall cliffs towered over the sea, nature's guardians to protect this land from those abroad who might seek to do it harm. To the east, more of this scarred countryside, peppered with flora that had been toughened by brisk wynds. To the far north, the impending mountains that stood as guardians of a threshold to a land unseen by most mortals. Their snow-capped tops obscured by cloud and mist, these earthen sentries performed their task admirably. Crunching beneath the boots of the three travelers, the ground could tell many tales if it possessed a tongue and the will to share. Alas, the silent earth would never reveal what it knew, and those time-lost tales would remain unheard for all days.

Either out of reverence for the majesty of what lay before them, or simply because they had nothing to talk about, Conall, Aedan, and Daimhain pressed on without speaking, and only their breathing made any sound. Hours had passed since they left their cave, and fog gradually grew around them, with the wind moving enough of it around so that they could only see glimpses of the path. From nowhere, they heard heavier footfalls behind them mixed with the clip-clop of a horse, and Conall pulled Aedan to the side of the path when a wooden cart covered by thick cloth led by a single horse and driver moved on through. Flanking the cart were two seasoned warriors, evidenced by their tattered, layered furs and bloodstained hoods. As they passed, the men let out a low growl. Conall shivered, tightening his grip on the staff, sidling up to Aedan.

"Who do you think they are?" he whispered.

"Don't know. But they're heading where we're going."

Once the fog had enveloped the cart and its entourage, Daimhain started up again, with Aedan keeping pace.

"Before you ask, I don't know who they were." She smirked. "The fog will get thicker before we reach the Trees."

"Thicker than this? It's like porridge already!"

"The last time I came this way," Daimhain continued, "it took me two days to walk a mile. Just try to keep your bearings on the path. If you're not careful, you'll find yourself at the cliff's edge."

"Hmm." Aedan raised an eyebrow. Then, he let out a series of whistles. It took a minute, but then a familiar sound approached, and Fiachra flew lower to the ground, flapping his scaly wings, dispersing some of the fog. As if answering a challenge, the fog rolled back in, obscuring the path once more.

"An admirable attempt, Aedan. This fog isn't natural." Daimhain took longer strides.

Conall joined his friend, sighing. Since they had nothing to look at, they couldn't assess how far they had gone or if anything was up ahead. Aedan's face froze in a blank expression.

"What's wrong?"

"She-She said the fog was... It's féth fíada." His eyes bounced around, squinting.

"It's what?"

"Féth fiada. The Tuatha Dé Danann use a mystical fog to keep themselves hidden. I don't understand how she's so comfortable with all of this."

"When you're Banféinní, you probably have no fear."

The temperature dropped to where their breath became mist. Aedan gritted his teeth and pressed on while Conall rotated his head in all directions so he would be prepared for whatever would come leaping from the fog. Tight in his grip, his staff stayed at the ready. Taking Daimhain's warning to heart, the boys shuffled their feet a bit as they walked to avoid losing their footing and falling over a cliff. A faint whistling of the wynd over the stark land made Conall scan the skies for Lann. He hadn't seen him in a while, and he just wanted to make sure the hawk was safe. Lifting his left arm, he whistled a sharp note. The flapping came from the west, and the hawk came in to perch. He lowered his arm to where Lann was in front of his face.

"Are you and Fiachra getting along?"

Lann squawked.

Conall smirked. "That's good. Can you see beyond this?"

The bird flapped a bit and squawked once more.

"That's promising, at least."

Aedan started walking backward to see his friend.

"What did he say?"

Bringing his arm close to him, Conall nuzzled with Lann, the hawk's head under his chin.

"He said that, from what he can tell, the mist lets up soon. That doesn't make me feel any better, though." Conall cocked his head. "There *is* something up ahead."

Aedan rolled his eyes and turned around, catching up to Daimhain. She caught him out of the corner of her eye. He asked her what she planned to do once they arrived at the Twisted Trees. Her response made him stop in his tracks.

"You're going to do what?"

"I think you heard me just fine."

He walked backward again. "Conall, you hear this one? When we get to the Twisted Trees, she's going to —"

Daimhain put her hand over his mouth and pulled him against her, putting her mouth near his ear. She held out her other hand to stop Conall.

"Shhh. There's something in the fog," she whispered. "Don't move."

Conall released Lann and clenched a fist around his staff. With her eyes, Daimhain signaled, 'Wait.' She released Aedan, touching his dominant hand. Nodding, he understood and removed his staff. When she had both boys in her sights, she relayed her plan with her eyes. The last signal was almost imperceptible, but once given, all three spun around to where their backs were to each other, forming a closed triangle, each with a staff at the ready. Aside from the crunching of the soil beneath their boots, the only other sound was their shallow breathing. Then, they heard a sound.

"A woman. She's crying…" Conall muttered. He lowered his guard, scanning the fog for the source. The crying became wailing, and he moved toward it, breaking the circle, with the fog gradually covering over him.

"Con—" Aedan started to shout for his friend, but Daimhain clamped her hand over his mouth again. She put a finger to her lips and nodded in the direction Conall went.

There was no mistaking the sobbing of a woman, and Daimhain pulled some clay from a pouch around her waist, giving Aedan a piece. When she put a piece in each ear, he followed suit, knitting his brow. Fog swirled around them. Within a few more steps, they saw Conall, and up ahead, a small, shrouded woman keening. Conall reached out his hand, so Daimhain struck him in the back of the head with her staff, knocking him unconscious. Confused, Aedan caught his friend, and Daimhain pulled Aedan's arm to put as much distance as possible between them and the woman. It was too late, though. The crying ceased, and the shrouded figure lifted her head toward them. A gaunt, skeletal face fell into the hazy light, and the woman opened her mouth. All sound stopped. The woman shrieked, her wail strong enough to part the fog and strip the neighboring trees of their leaves and some branches. Daimhain stumbled to the ground, with Aedan crashing beside her. He had held onto Conall, attempting to keep him from being injured. The scream subsided, and the figure of the woman melted into the fog. Daimhain helped Aedan, still holding Conall, to his feet. She poured some water from her pouch on Conall's face, tousling his hair.

"Wake up, sleepy head."

It took him a few moments, but Conall opened his eyes, reaching for the back of his head.

"Wha-What happened?"

"Daimhain here knocked you out." Aedan laughed.

Conall glared, feeling the bump on his head. "Why in Brigid's name would you do that?"

"That woman was a banshee. Her wail can wreak havoc with the mind." Daimhain adjusted her pack and secured the boar meat. Her voice softened. "It also signals the death of a loved one."

"The death of a…" Aedan's eyes grew glassy. "Does that mean—"

Daimhain put a hand on his shoulder. "We don't know *what* that means. Three of us could have heard it, which means one of our loved ones will die."

Aedan grunted, kicking a stone. Conall pulled him aside.

"Listen. I know you're worried about your da. I'm worried about my mum and da, too. But there's nothing we can do."

"I have to go back." Aedan tightened his pack on his shoulder. "I can't leave things unfinished, Conall. If I don't—"

Grasping both Aedan's shoulders, Conall shook him, leaning in.

"We're not the only ones who stand to lose someone." He looked over at Daimhain who was fiddling with her belongings. "I don't want anything to happen to my parents, either. So, what, we go home? We wait until something happens? Then what? We've come a long way already."

Aedan straightened up, pulling away from Conall's hands.

"I just left him a note, Conall. He doesn't even know about our quest. At least your parents were there with the druids."

"You don't think my mum and da talked to him? Look, they'll take care of each other." He paused, smiling. "Just like we'll take care of each other."

Looking back at Daimhain, Aedan slowly nodded his head and took a deep breath.

"You have nothing to fear with me by your side. We get the wands and stop this war. We go home, Aedan. Right?"

"All right."

Before they resumed their trek, Aedan stopped.

"Conall? Do you think Lann knows how to get home from here?"

"I'm sure he could. He's pretty keen. Why?"

"Well... do you think we could send a message home with him?"

"Hmm. I didn't even think about that."

Daimhain approached. "We need to keep moving before nightfall. We really don't want to be stuck in this fog after sundown. Remember the banshee. Other creatures lurk in the mists. Can you send your message when we get to the Twisted Trees? There's an inn near there where you can lodge for the night."

The boys nodded. As soon as they found the path, Conall sidled up to her and asked if she was worried about losing someone. Her initial silence caused him to slow down, thinking he'd offended her, but then she commented that her people embraced death as just another plane of existence. If one of her tribe traveled to Tir na nÓg, the Otherworld, she would be happy that her sister had found peace. He wanted to know more about her people, but every time he opened his mouth to ask something, he closed it. When he had the words, he knew he would use them. Until then, he stomped along, his thoughts flashing to his parents, especially after their recent encounter. Behind him, Aedan's boots crunched, and the rhythm of the footsteps provided something else to focus on.

"We're close." Daimhain pulled her pack tighter against her back. "Can you smell the air changing?"

Conall took a deep breath. "Um... no? What do you smell?"

"It's not *what* I smell. It's the density of the air itself. The fog should lift soon."

Catching up with his friend, Aedan tried to match his footsteps with Conall's.

"How does she know things like that?"

"Suddenly, I'm an all-knowing druid? She knows things. I'm just used to it." Conall shrugged. "Besides, she did say she'd been there before."

"I have something to tell you later. When we're... alone." He used his eyes to point to Daimhain.

The elevation rose ever so slightly, and then it fell, like subtle waves of earth radiating from a distant source, as if the ground had long ago rippled and solidified. Gradually, light blue sky peeked through the haze. A breeze perfumed with rose snuck into the fog, giving anyone about to leave the hazy confines hope of something. The path rose sharply, forcing travelers to take more conscious, measured steps. Just as the fog released its inhabitants, the road leveled off once more. Both boys gasped as they took their first look at the arboreal portal before them. Daimhain stopped, grinning, putting her hands on her hips.

"Well, boys, we're here. Welcome to the Twisted Trees."

Conall and Aedan joined her.

"On both sides of the trees lies the town Rusdare. The western side of the arch is an elder tree, to the east, an oak." Daimhain gestured for them to follow her.

Flanking the road, which changed from dirt to limestone brick, everything that made up the town — the merchants, inns, and even the smithy — had gnarled roots of each tree growing through it, binding everything to the main trees.

"On this side of the trees, the south side, only one road leads here. Once you reach the north of town, through the arch, many roads lead away. Some say that the number of roads changes depending on the destination of the person."

Aedan turned around while he walked, trying to take in as much as he could.

"You said that the portal can take people to places beyond, magical places."

"Yes, but you need special keys for that. There are some in town who can help you... for a price. Be warned, my friends. Rusdare seems like a quaint place, but like any crossroads, peril hides in plain sight. I have some business to attend to here before I head home, but I do hope we see one another before you continue on your quest."

Daimhain and the boys shook forearms and parted ways. She vanished amongst those milling about, and Conall and Aedan meandered through the bustling town. Aside from produce and textile merchants that lined the square, a pungent, smoke-stained smithy, billows of black smoke rising into the sky, sat in the center near the fountain. Small groups gathered around buskers who sang, danced, juggled, or performed sleight-of-hand.

"So many sounds, Conall. How do people stand this?" Aedan's head moved all around, eyes wide.

"It's almost too much, you know? I miss the peace and quiet of Silver Birch Glen."

Aedan nodded. "What I wouldn't give right now to be back at Oak Mountain."

"We're going to need food."

"And a place to stay," Aedan added. "Depending on how long it takes us to find a map of the region."

They ambled toward The Flying Minstrel, a ramshackle inn looking as if it were held together by old timber and string, but with the enticing aroma of roasted meat to fill the air, and the mellifluous sounds of a harpist to fill the ears. Through the door they went, and a wall of sound, like a phalanx of soldiers, pushed toward them. Aedan meandered toward the taverner, a young man around his age who was pouring a few flagons of ale.

"Can I help ye?" The man placed the flagons in front of some patrons and turned toward Aedan. His sleeves were rolled above his elbows, revealing strong hands and toned arms.

Aedan, distracted by the young man's appearance, couldn't make eye contact, but if he had, he would have seen the man's green eyes flickering with lamplight. He leaned on the bar and turned his head as if he were looking for someone. "M-My friend and I need a room for the night. And... and a hot meal." Aedan pushed some coins on the bar.

The taverner laughed to himself, drying a few ale glasses. He filled them with the frothy beverage and slid them toward Aedan. "I'll bring you both some bowls of stew." He winked.

Almost tripping over the stools, Aedan found Conall at a wooden table made from an old door, its worn metal work still attached. Conall took a healthy sip from the flagon, licking the froth away.

"He'll bring us food." Aedan kept his eyes on the taverner.

Conall snapped his fingers in front of his friend's face. "Hello? Never thought you'd be one to be distracted by a scruffy face."

Leaning back, Aedan put his feet up on the edge of the table, one foot over the other. "Well, wait until you see his eyes." He lifted his flagon toward Conall and then sipped his ale, leaving a mustache of foam.

Conall chuckled. "Hopefully, we'll find a mapmaker or a merchant to get us where we need to go." He wove his eyes all around the tavern. "Have you ever been to a place like this? It's not the same as the tavern back home. Like a beehive." He took a swig.

Aedan unclasped his feet and tried to sit up as the taverner approached with two wooden bowls. Conall chuckled as he watched his friend almost fall backward.

"Enjoy, gentlemen. Let me know if you need anything else." He turned to go.

"Actually," Conall started, "could you tell us where we might find a map to the north. You know, through the trees?"

Crossing his arms and smirking, the taverner put his foot on the bench.

"Let me guess. You're on a quest for some treasure. You heard from some mysterious stranger that chests of gold lie far to the north, and you want to lay your claim to them. Wish I could help you, lads, but —"

"Th-That's not it." Aedan chimed in. Looking around, he gestured for the man to come closer. "We *are* on a quest. But not for treasure. I can't say what for, but trust me when I say it's important…"

"Eoghan." He looked at the straight expressions of both boys. "You're serious. Hmm. Well, I might be able to help you. No promises." Before he left, he winked again at Aedan.

Raising his eyebrows, Conall shoved spoonfuls of venison stew into his mouth. Their hunger kept them in silence, but after they scraped their bowl clean, they people-watched, commenting on the motley array of townsfolk seated around them. This was the first time in a while where both boys weren't on edge about the Fomoragh or their journey. Both food and drink had softened their demeanor to where they could just enjoy the moment. A trio of musicians entered the tavern, greeted by an uproarious welcome, and they set themselves up in a corner. A young woman, around Daimhain's age, her blond hair braided around her head, played the flute. One man carried a bodhran, a drum whose taut goatskin bore the wear and tear of its use, and a third man had no instrument, but it became clear once they started playing that his musical tool was his voice. A song of untold origin filled the tavern, and as the music moved across the room, patron voices were stilled, and all attention was on the convergence of flute, drum, and voice of a gifted bard.

While the boys listened, Eoghan wiped down the bar with a cloth, mouthing the words to the song. Every so often, he looked over at Aedan, watching the young man's eyes twinkle in the lamplight while he sat back against the wall, his arms folded and with a slight smile. As soon as the song ended, Aedan sat up and took a swig of his ale. He spied Eoghan looking at him, brushed his brown hair from his forehead, smiled, then turned away. The taverner chuckled to himself, shaking his head. A new song started, something slower, and Conall leaned forward, elbows on the table, his hands supporting his chin. Aedan signaled that he would be right back.

"Eoghan, is it? I'm Aedan." He leaned against the bar, one eye on the musicians, the other on the taverner. "Did you think about what my friend and I asked you earlier?"

"Indeed I have." Eoghan leaned over the bar. "There's a merchant just down the way who keeps old maps and long forgotten treasures. He might be able to help you…" He hesitated.

Aedan cocked his head. "I sense a 'but' coming…"

"Well, everything has its price." Eoghan filled a flagon of ale for a man at the end of the bar.

Aedan followed him while he delivered it. "What kind of price? I mean, I know we'll have to pay for a map, if that's what you mean."

Eoghan signaled with his eyes that they should talk at the other end. Harumphing his way back, Aedan leaned in closer, catching a closer look at the young man's eyes twinkling in the lamp light. He caught himself staring and turned around, his back to the bar and his elbows resting on it. The taverner hopped up on a stool next to him.

"If you're just traveling the *earthen* road, all you do need is a map. I have a feeling this quest you're on is more than... earthly, and requires other assistance." He raised both eyebrows and leaned forward.

"Um, yes. You're correct. But we do actually need to travel the earthen road, as you put it, before we can deal with other issues. So, what, do we need a key of some sort then?"

"Now you're beginning to get it. Yes. *That* is what comes with a price. The map itself we can get for almost nothing."

Aedan rolled his eyes. "So, what do I have to do to get a straight answer from you? You sound like a druid friend I know."

Across the room, Conall listened to the harmonies and chords, the lyrics and the pauses, and lost himself in the clouds of sound. When it softened, he saw Aedan talking with Eoghan, how close they sat, and he laughed to himself. His head bobbed to the rhythm, and as he panned around, the twinkling of two green eyes beneath a hood, snapped him from his lyrical reverie. He sat up, squinted a little, and drank from his flagon, trying to look inconspicuous. The figure lurked in the shadows with only a gloved hand visible as it lifted a flagon to its mouth, then lowered it slowly. Realizing it had been seen, it leaned back, pulling its shrouded head more into the darkness in the corner of the tavern. When Conall turned back to Aedan, both he and Eoghan had vanished. Conall gathered his and Aedan's belongings and took determined strides out the tavern door into the chill night. He stopped, his breath emerging as serpentine vapor, melting into the air, and his heart pounded in his ears. The silence of the town square overwhelmed him, and he gripped his staff, the carved wooden glyphs pressing into his palm. He secured Aedan's pack to his own and threw them both over his shoulders, freeing both his hands. With a flick of his wrist, the staff extended, and he put all his training to use. His eyes adjusted to the night with the occasional lamp and the moon providing the only illumination. Conall took control of his breathing to help slow his heartbeat. Of all the buildings surrounding the square, only the windows of the tavern shone with life.

His boots crunched on the gravel with each calculated step despite his attempts to make as little noise as possible. When he reached the fountain, he turned in all directions, but the only people he saw were occasional tavern patrons stumbling into the night to head home. No sign of Aedan. Conall's eyes narrowed, and he snarled.

"If he's done anything to Aedan…" he muttered as he moved toward one of the cobblestone side streets.

Only the silver lunar disk shone its light on this street. The sheen on the stones gave Conall some idea of where to go, but he didn't know where to look. Rusdare wasn't a large town, but it was large enough to lose someone in. Row houses lined the street, their rough clay brick exteriors bearing windows with closed wooden shutters and small flower boxes just beneath. His cottage in the Silver Birch Glen seemed almost primitive by comparison, but not by much. With as much traffic as Rusdare saw, due to the Twisted Trees, travelers had probably shared their skills, including carpentry and masonry, for goods and services. On these streets, Conall's movement made no sound. He stopped when he heard voices in the distance, but continued when one of the voices sounded decidedly female. Skulking down the street, he turned to head back toward the tavern. Perhaps Aedan had returned and was looking for him, he thought. At the end of the next street, he looked left, but the curve of the street kept moonlight from making it clearly visible. He couldn't imagine that Aedan would go down there, so he headed back toward the square. Just as he entered the square, he felt something touch his shoulder and swung around, staff poised to attack.

Aedan jumped back, holding his hands up.

"It's me! Conall, it's just me."

Conall struck him in the shoulder.

"What was that for?" Aedan rubbed his shoulder.

"Are you daft, sneaking up on me like that? Where have you been? You disappeared, and I thought that Eoghan—"

"Calm down." Aedan chuckled, holding up his palms. "I'm fine. Eoghan and I went for a walk… to talk."

Retracting his staff, Conall smirked. "Uh huh."

"No, really. He was telling me about getting a map, but it was too noisy in the tavern, so he said he'd show me."

"And? Did he?"

"Yeah. He pointed toward one of the darkened streets. We talked a bit on the way. He—"

Conall waved him closer as he moved toward the fountain. He hopped up on the stone wall.

"Let's talk here. I feel better at least being in the moonlight. What did you and Eoghan talk about?" Conall asked in a sing-songy voice.

At first, Aedan glared, but then he smiled. "He told me about how he was brought here as a child when his parents died. The tavern owner is his uncle, but the man's too old to work, so Eoghan takes care of him and runs the tavern."

Conall returned Aedan's pack to him. The latter continued on about Eoghan, especially his deep brown eyes and how he had given Aedan a room key for a place to sleep for the night, a room above the tavern. When Conall laughed and said Aedan would be closer to Eoghan, Aedan feigned surprise.

"What are you saying? Do you really think I would take advantage of being so close to such a handsome lad?" He lightly slapped Conall on the shoulder.

"Wouldn't you?" Conall smiled out of one side of his mouth.

"He's actually quite the gentleman. After we returned to the tavern, he told me about the room, kissed my cheek, and bid me a good night."

They fell silent and stared up at the blue-black, starry blanket above them, only besmirched by a few wisps of cloud and the moon's luminescence. Soft breezes carried the heady aroma of burning peat mixed with the perfume of night-blooming jasmine. Behind the boys, they heard the gurgling of the fountain. The journey as a whole had been enlightening for them, giving them new friends, challenging their resolve, and giving them new skills.

"So, what castle in the sky are you thinking about?" Conall tapped Aedan's foot with his own.

Aedan lifted an eyebrow.

Conall chuckled. "My mum used to ask me that when I was lost in thought. Don't know why it came to me just now."

"Nothing." He sighed. "Everything. This is the first time we've had in a while to be at ease, you know? First, we had our time at Dún Ancróga, then meeting Daimhain, now this. I look at Rusdare and see a simple, quiet town, a place where someone like Eoghan can grow up without a care. So much happens here. He seems… happy."

"What about Oak Mountain? Surely, you must like your life with your da and the Tine Clan?"

Aedan nodded. "I've been thinking about my da. Maybe that's why I look at this place and see how comfortable it seems. This town is more active than my village is. I live at the base of a mountain, with farmland and livestock. I have friends and family. But… But, haven't you ever wanted more, Conall? Haven't you ever looked for other castles in the sky?"

Conall didn't respond right away. He dipped his hand in the fountain and rubbed it against his other hand. He perked up when a cloaked person left the tavern, someone who was scanning the square.

"Hey, show me where that merchant is so we can find it in the morning."

"Um, sure. It's down that street." He used his head to point the way. "You okay?"

"I'm fine. Just getting tired." Conall adjusted his pack, keeping watch on the individual. In the moonlight, he could tell that it was the same cloaked person he had seen earlier inside, the one with the green eyes. If it had been Déaglán, he would have been shorter, and he would have had one blue eye as well. This man was at least a head taller than the druid who had trained them.

Entering the shadowy street, Conall stayed one step behind Aedan who started telling his friend more about Eoghan and the merchant. Apparently, the man who owned the market had been a soldier in a great war that happened decades earlier in a land to the north. Once the war ended, he moved his wife to Rusdare and opened a business to have a normal life. During his youth, he had loved to travel, coming across ancient artifacts, some of which supposedly imbued with magic from the Sídhe. When the war came, he hid his treasures, hoping to return for them when his duty was done. That time came, and he held onto some, bringing them to Rusdare. Over the years that followed, he became known in certain circles as one who could obtain mystical objects. He would only work with those he felt worthy and honorable, and he never accepted money since taking money for magic was forbidden; the recipient of the artifact would have to prove him or herself worthy.

The boys turned down another street, one darker if that were even possible, and after a few steps in, Conall spun around, staff extended, and sweeping close to the cobblestones. A figure fell back with a grunt.

Conall pointed his staff toward the individual. "*Ó aer, Déanaim iarracht tine!*" The tip of the staff ignited, shedding its light on a bearded man with one brown and one green eye that glinted.

"Who are you, and why are you following us? I saw you at the tavern." Conall pushed the fiery staff toward the man.

"I'd answer him if I were you." Aedan had extended his staff, his other hand in a tight fist.

"I'm-I'm Elder Padraig. I mean you no harm."

Conall and Aedan shared a look, and then Aedan extended a hand to help the Elder up. He brushed himself off and replaced his hood.

"That answers one of my questions."

"My apologies." Elder Padraig nodded. "I was sent to watch you."

"Wait…" Conall began, stepping back. "Aedan, take two steps back."

"Mm?" Aedan moved his staff from hand to hand, not letting Elder Padraig out of his sight.

"Just do it. Quickly."

Aedan complied. "Conall, what —"

"You're one of An Scáthanna. An exile from the Order of Druids."

Elder Padraig pulled his hood down over his eyes. "Yes. As I said, I mean you no harm." His voice barely broke a whisper.

"If that's so, prove it. A druid friend of ours said you are called Shadows. That doesn't sound very trustworthy to me."

Padraig sighed. "I-I cannot. That is left for you to determine."

Lifting an eyebrow, Conall lowered his staff.

"What're you doing?" Aedan held his stance.

"If he were here to harm us, he could have by now. Besides, asking us to determine his trustworthiness isn't something someone evil would do."

Aedan stood taller. "Are you sure? I mean, he could be one of the Fomoragh—"

Drawing a short sword hidden under his cloak, Padraig turned in all directions. "The Fomoragh? Here? We are doomed."

"Not quite yet, Elder." Conall retracted his staff. "For now, we're safe. You didn't hesitate to draw your sword when I mentioned the Fomoragh." Conall put his hand on Elder Padraig's shoulder. "I believe this man isn't here to harm us, Aedan."

"If you say so." Aedan shook his staff. "But I am keeping this available just in case you're wrong."

Elder Padraig told them that, even though An Scáthanna were exiled, they weren't to be feared. The old gods believed that a druid with both brown and green eyes was impure and would be drawn toward evil. The Druidic Order never sought to disprove that, so they sent all of the druids with those color eyes away and branded them as Shadows. He also told them that, since An Scáthanna had no Order of their own, they tended toward solitary pursuits, helping travelers however they could. A few druids had joined together to protect those who would fulfill the DragonHawk prophecy, and once the boys had taken up the task, word got back to these druids to send an emissary to keep watch.

"My task was to follow, not to intervene. I have failed in my mission by making my presence known to you. I used a dríocht to give myself two green eyes in the tavern so that I wouldn't stand out, but that didn't work. I will take my shame and go. I suppose I became too interested in the trappings of the outside world. Going into that tavern was a mistake."

Aedan told him he didn't have to leave, but he insisted. Another druid would undoubtedly be charged with the task, Padraig told them, and he or she would do a better job at remaining in secret. He hoped that even in this brief time together, he had helped them to understand that An Scáthanna do not have ill intentions. He asked that they keep an open mind and share with their druid friend this encounter. The boys agreed. Elder Padraig bid them farewell and headed back for the square. Aedan brought Conall to the market where they would return in the morning and returned to the tavern. The room on the second floor had a creaky wooden floor, a chair in the corner, and a small bed. One square, curtainless window faced out into the square, and moonlight puddled on every flat surface of the room. Aedan took the chair so Conall could have the bed.

Conall lay against the wall, lost in thought. Aedan, who had kicked off his boots, leaned back in the chair.

"What's on your mind? Your eyes are wide open."

Sitting up, Conall crossed his legs.

"I was just thinking about us. The last memories I have are from when we were ten. After the tribes split, my parents never talked about you and your family. Whether that was something the druids did or not, it's just odd. Why shouldn't I remember my best friend? While we walked here, I thought how funny it is that the two people who are supposed to save everyone are two boys who barely know each other." He chuckled.

Aedan straightened up, his lower lip pushed out. "You know, you're right. Everyone keeps telling us that we're anam cara. Sometimes, that sense feels strong. Other times, I feel like I don't know that much about you. So much can happen in six years."

"I do feel that we have a special bond. Maybe it's because of the Ársa and Fonn connection. What's funny is that now that we're not near home, my flashes of memory of us are clearer."

"I noticed that, too." He leaned forward on his knees. "My da didn't say anything about you or your family once we were at Oak Mountain."

Conall moved to the edge of the bed, letting his legs hang over it. He was looking right at Aedan, nodding intently.

"When we were walking here, memories just kept flooding back. Not all complete ones. Sometimes just moments. If... When we survive all this, I have some choice words for the Elder Circle."

"Same here." Aedan nodded.

Falling back hard on the bed and huffing, Conall said, "This is all so strange."

A sudden exuberance came over Aedan.

"So, tell me things. I'm not tired. Neither are you. Fill me in on the last six years." His eyes lit up. "Start with how you and Lann met." He slid to the floor.

Through giggles, Conall became an enthusiastic storyteller, sharing the story of the hawk, but that launched a story of adventures he and Lann had taken, including when Conall climbed a tree to retrieve a kite and accidentally kicked a hornet's nest. Or the day when his father taught him how to fish by the river and got pulled in by a large freshwater bass. With each tale, his hands gestured, creating pictures that Aedan followed with eagerness. He sat up, eyes wide, when he unfolded the story of the race through the village where beat everyone as if the wynd was helping him. Other stories of sadness were peppered throughout, such as the loss of his friend Dina who drowned or when his cat Thistle disappeared. Every so often, he'd stop himself and check Aedan's interest, but he'd get a "Go on!" or a "And what happened next?" Then, it was Aedan's turn.

Like his friend, Aedan had his share of adventures, including finding Fiachra, which Conall insisted on hearing. He had his scuffles with the Tierney boys, especially Kieran, who seemed to hate him from the day they met. Aedan lowered his voice when he spoke about his first love, Brennan, a twelve-year-old who had moved to Oak Mountain. Aedan was eleven, and he was smitten from the moment they met. Conall leaned closer, seemingly intrigued as to why the softer voice, but it soon became clear: this was truly the boy's first love, but also his first heartbreak. The two met when the boy's family moved to Oak Mountain, and the two became fast friends. A few months later, Brennan's father died in a plowing accident. Brennan's mother's grief drove her to take her son and return to her home village. Trying to lift his friend's spirits, Conall asked to hear about what he and Fiachra had done together, but Aedan said he was tired.

It didn't take long for them to succumb to slumber, but a piercing shriek just after sunrise made them jump up. Making their way to the square, they saw a small group of people surrounding something near the fountain. As soon as they got close enough, they recognized the cloak, now steeped in blood. Conall pushed his way through and saw what he had feared.

"No! This cannot be. Who would do this? Did anyone see what happened?"

Aedan joined his friend and gasped, "Elder Padraig." He squatted to get a closer look, seeing a gaping wound.

An elderly woman wearing a kerchief and carrying a basket of fruit muttered that she had heard what sounded like a shrill cry shortly before sunrise. When Conall pressed her for more, she said the cry sounded… unnatural.

The blacksmith commented, "Judging by the size of the wound, I'd say an axe made it."

Conall pulled Aedan close to him.

"It has to be Cichol. The one Déaglán told us who used to rule the Fomoragh. He carries a double-sided axe that shrieks when he uses it. It has to be him."

"That means the Fomoragh are near." He looked back at Padraig. "What do we do?"

"What *can* we do? We wouldn't even know where to bring his body. The townspeople will take care of it. Let's go to the merchant. We're not safe here."

"But, Conall —"

"Aedan, we have to go. If the Fomoragh get to us, we'll end up just like Elder Padraig. I'm guessing they won't attack during the day, so we have to get moving to get as far away as we can. We don't want anyone else in Rusdare getting hurt," he looked down at the deceased, "or losing his life."

The merchant's shop had stacks of musty books and dust-laden trinkets on ramshackle tables. The walls had shelves floor to ceiling packed with assorted paraphernalia of wood, glass, marble, and elements unknown by their appearance. At the back sat a gnarled old man, his hoary beard extending from his chin like silver ivy, scraggly and unkempt. On his head was a limp, conical hat of faded blue velvet. He was tinkering with a metal object that had more parts than it should have for its size.

"Come in, gentlemen, come in! I've been expecting ye." He waved them over.

"You have?" Conall cocked his head.

"Indeed. When you dabble in the otherworldly, sometimes they share things." He chuckled. "That, and the tavern-keeper mentioned it this morning."

"Eoghan was here?"

"Aye, Aedan." The man nodded, grinning. "You come highly recommended. It takes a lot to ensnare that boy's heart, and you had just the right trap, my boy." He snickered again. "He said something about you two needing a map?"

The shopkeeper went into the backroom, flailing his hands for the boys to follow. Conall shrugged at his friend. Through the curtains that flanked the doorway, they entered another room brimming with oddities and baubles. The man stopped at a round table and invited the two to sit.

"You seem to know *us*, but you are?"

He made a dismissive gesture. "Everyone just calls me Shanar, the old man. I'm so old I don't even remember my own name." He roared a laugh that shook the dust in the room. "I am indeed ancient, so the name fits!"

The boys sat on either side of him, watching his head bob back and forth while he hummed. He then firmly put his palms on the table.

"So, what kind of map were ye looking for? Treasure? Lost cities? Pow —"

Aedan reached out and touched the table in front of the old man.

"Actually, we just need a map to the north through the Twisted Trees. We're on a quest. Eoghan said you could help."

"Perhaps I can, perhaps I can indeed. Can you tell me the purpose of this quest, or does it break some sort of rule. Quests always have rules, and they're always so blasted confus —"

"Do you actually need to know the purpose to help us? It's just that the more people who know, the less safe we are." Conall lowered his eyes. "Elder Padraig paid with his life."

Shanar's face grew more solemn, and he put his wrinkled hand over Conall's.

"Lad, the Fomoragh seek to stop you both. That much I know. That's all I *need* to know. It's a shame about the druid, truly. We had crossed paths once or thrice over the years." He smiled. "I think I have what you need, but there *is* a price."

"What is it? We don't have a lot of money.' Conall fiddled in his sack.

"I can't take money from you for this. The map has an enchantment. Nothing ensorcelled by the Sídhe can ever be bought."

Aedan leaned forward, his clipped tone. "Then, what?"

"I need something of value… for a placeholder. Something of great value to you. It must be tied to your heart."

The boys exchanged silent looks and shrugged, and Conall went back to rummaging in his pack.

"I'm not quite sure what I have that's tied to my heart, but I must have *something* in here. What about —"

Aedan extended an open palm. "Will this do?"

Conall looked up and gasped.

"No, Aedan! You can't."

"Will this do?" Aedan asked again. "Hush, Conall."

Shanar picked up the circular brooch, turning it around close to his face. He put on a pair of wiry spectacles and squinted.

"This is tied to your heart, is it?" The old man rubbed it on his sleeve and examined it once more.

In a soft voice, Aedan said it belonged to his mother. She always wore it on her cloak.

"I am of the Fonn." The words emerged like a puff of smoke, indistinct, but they lingered in the room.

The shopkeeper took a small box from the folds of his robe and placed the pin inside it. He rubbed his index finger on the lid, and a thread of light wound itself around the box.

"You have given me what I asked for, and in turn, I will give you what you seek. Your pin will remain in this box until you return the map." He put the box back in his robe. "No magic in the whole world can break the bond of a mother's love for her child, Aedan. That is what the thread binds the box with."

He pulled a narrow wooden box, carved with icovellavna, and the knot designs almost seemed alive, as if a mystical cord had woven itself around the box. Shanar removed a scroll of time-worn parchment and handed it to Conall.

"It's… It's empty." Conall handed it to Aedan. "What kind of trick is this?"

Examining the scroll, Aedan laughed. "Calm down. This is an enchanted map. It probably won't appear unless it's needed. Am I right?"

Laughing, the old man held his belly and rocked. "Of course! My boy, if you jump at everything you don't comprehend, you'll end up in trouble. Mark my words. With this map, you'll see the path you need as well as the path you're on. The Trees understand your journey, and they will place you where you need to start."

The boys thanked the old man, and he followed them to the front of the shop. Just before they exited, Aedan turned back.

"You'll make sure nothing happens to that pin? It's the only thing of my mum's that I have, aside from memories."

Shanar put a hand on Aedan's shoulder and squeezed.

"Of course, my boy. You have my word." His eyes danced.

By the time the boys reached the square, the crowd had dispersed, and they had taken Elder Padraig's body with them. Aedan and Conall said nothing as the approached the arboreal portal. Through it, they saw paths ever-changing, some into forests, others into valleys or even by the sea. The map would put them at the start of their journey as they walked through. They nodded to each other and took steps forward when they heard a voice.

"You weren't going to leave without saying goodbye, were ye?"

Turning, Aedan's eyes widened, and he smiled. Eoghan was leaning against a merchant's cart, arms folded, a wry smile on his own face. Conall stepped over to a fruit merchant to give them some privacy.

Aedan sheepishly replied, "It's been such a strange morning. After Elder Padraig's death, Conall and I just wanted to, you know, get on the road. I do want to thank you for helping us out with Shanar."

Eoghan nodded, smiling. "Just giving you a hard time. You'll be back, though, yes?"

"Of course. I have *two* reasons to return to Rusdare." He shuffled his feet. "When we come back through, we'll make sure to stay longer."

"Be safe, Aedan." Eoghan caressed Aedan's cheek before leaning over to kiss it. As he moved back, Aedan leaned forward and kissed Eoghan's lips, lingering for an eternal few seconds.

"May Brigid guide you, and may Epona watch over your journey."

Conall walked over, crunching an apple. "We should get a move on. Thanks, Eoghan, for all your help."

The taverner nodded, and they gripped forearms. The entwined trunks of the portal rose above them, the corky, furrowed bark of the elder contrasting to the smooth, silvery bark of the oak. The opening itself shimmered like a watery barrier. With the map in hand, Conall took a deep breath and walked through. Aedan turned one more time to see Eoghan, but Conall reached back and yanked him through. Eoghan sighed, a forlorn smile fading as he returned to the tavern.

9 | SILVER TORCS

nce through, Aedan and Conall stared upward at a set of dew-laden stones that looked like giants had set stairs in the earth, grasses growing around them and pale moss blanketing them with the passage of time. One could also think they had grown like mushrooms under a tapestry, a canopy of branches with the occasional gap to let in errant sunbeams. The steps led up to a stone structure with large, flat rocks functioning as a roof. Ivy embraced the megaliths, its verdant tendrils cinching the walls together. By the doorway, an opening that led into darkness, a flat stone sat, a place for an offering. Field mushrooms grew from anywhere they could, and fronds of bracken splayed open as if in prayer. With quivering steps, the boys ascended, taking shallow breaths. Only a few steps from the entry, an owl hooted, making them both jump. Conall reached into his pack and pulled out some small apples he had bought in Rusdare. He was about to place them on the altar by the doorway when he saw something move. Out of the shadows, a small serpent reared its head, tongue flicking. Aedan caught this out of the corner of his eye and stepped back, but Conall didn't seem alarmed.

He placed the apples on the altar, and the serpent surrounded them as if to claim them. "This is a shrine to Cernunnos. Remove your boots."

"How do you know?" Aedan glanced over his shoulder and back.

"There's a similar shrine deep within the Glen. Now, remove your boots."

Upon crossing the threshold, a chill air surrounded them that smelled of moss and moisture. Stone beneath their feet, with darkness all around, they took small steps. Up ahead, a lighter haze had settled. Conall opened his palm and recited the dríocht. A small flickering flame hovered over his hand giving off just enough light to see a few feet ahead. It was as if the flames dared not go farther than they needed to. A soft voice traveled toward them.

"Extinguish the fyre and let your faith guide you."

Closing his hand, Conall quivered a bit. He had been a follower of Cernunnos ever since he was a boy, and to think that the Horned One would speak to him made his eyes water.

"What're you doing? We can't see."

"I was told to extinguish the flame, Aedan. You don't disrespect Cernunnos."

"I didn't hear anything. Perhaps it was your mind playing tricks on you."

"Light your own flame and see what happens." Conall quickened his steps.

Aedan opened his palm, hesitated, and then closed it.

"It's-It's all right. If you say you heard something, I believe you. Let's just keep moving."

About fifty paces later, the earthen tunnel opened to a larger chamber with a hole in the ceiling through which a wide shaft of sunlight fell before a mighty oak, its leaves stretching across the expanse like opened arms. On the dirt floor, scatterings of acorns lay, some of which had sprouted and beheld tiny saplings, like offspring looking up toward its parent. On various branches, birds perched, some chirping. Where the sun had touched, a patch of wildflowers burst forth with butterflies keeping court with the blossoms. Conall dropped to his knees and hung his head. Where his tears dropped, small flowers popped up.

"What's wrong?" Aedan crouched next to his friend. "Why are you crying?"

Conall wiped his tears, looking up at the oak and sunbeam.

"Wh-When I first found Lann, he was an eyas, a tiny hawk, and he was injured. I tended to him, and I prayed to Cernunnos that he would get better. The day Lann was well enough to fly, he flew right out of my window, and even though I was sad to lose him, I was also glad that I could help him heal. Thankfully, Lann returned. It felt like Cernunnos had answered my prayers."

"I remember you mentioning that." Aedan lowered his head. "I understand now."

Making his way around the space, Conall noticed all the tiny details, from the curls of every branch to the sway of the leaves from the mild breezes. He crouched to touch the grasses and reached to feel the bark. As he came around to the patch of flowers, he sat cross-legged before it, his eyes flitting from flower to flower, taking in the bursts of color and texture. He took a deep breath, inhaling the honey-sweet perfume, exhaling slowly to not disturb the butterflies. A few fluttered onto his arm, shoulders, and head, slowly opening and closing their iridescent wings. Aedan grinned, and his eyes watered.

"This is… so incredible. I feel at peace here," he said, seeing his friend at one with nature in this place.

"That is the gift of Cernunnos." A resonant voice filled the shrine. "Peace of spirit. You both honor the Horned One with your pure hearts."

Aedan turned in all directions. "Who are you? Are you Cernunnos?"

The voice laughed. "No, I am not he. I am but a humble caretaker."

From behind the oak came a stocky man bearing stag antlers atop hair of moss. On his face rested a mask of two oak leaves, one green, the other a bronze-like orange. In his beard were woven small flowers. Around his upper arms were bands of gold, and on his neck sat a twisted golden torc. A serpent, its head resting on the man's shoulder, coiled on his left arm. The man wore pants, cinched with a leather cord, that gave him the appearance of furry goat legs. His sleeveless brown robe lay open to show a bare chest with markings.

"Fear not. I bid you welcome."

The druid went over to Conall who had his arms stretched out, his face to the sky, and his eyes closed. Dozens of butterflies had landed on him.

"It seems your friend has lost himself in himself."

"Why did we end up here?" Aedan put his pack down and sat.

"I know not. The Trees put you on the path, *your* path, but they never give a reason. Nor should they have to."

"Who *are* you?" Aedan was entertained by a bright orange butterfly that had landed on his finger.

"Names have little value here. Only your spirit matters. But if it makes you feel better, I am Elder Daithi."

For a while, both Aedan and Conall sat, focusing only on what surrounded them. The whistling of the threshes and goldfinches provided the melody that blended with the lyrics of crickets chirping, creating a harmony only nature could provide. Breezes made swirls of leaves pirouette while making the flowers sway. In the distance, the low bass tone of thunder rippled across the sky beyond the shrine. The druid took his cue from that to begin a dance. At first, he moved slowly, his arms lifting and falling, and then he turned round, bending at the knee, and reaching for the heavens. The serpent on his arm moved to his waist, and then his leg, as if performing its own version of the dance. As the man's choreography quickened, from nowhere seemed to appear two golden torcs in his hands, their twisted metal reminiscent of the twirling of the leaves in the wynd. Conall opened his eyes to see Elder Daithi's humble movements, and he tried to mimic them—first, he moved his arms to and fro, and then he made his body sway to the rhythm. He kept his eyes on every maneuver and mannerism the druid did, until he, too, did the dance of the Horned One. At first, Aedan watched both of them, and he witnessed the butterflies and the birds flying in arcs above. A smile spread on his face, and he joined them. With all three in motion, the thunder grew in intensity, the peals adding their percussion. Around the bed of wildflowers they went, all three in unison. One crack of thunder brought a flash of lightning through the hole in the ceiling, and then the rain. It traveled down the leaves of the oak, one to another, until it ran down the thick trunk, along the roots, and into the wildflowers. The storm, in its climax, split the skies with sound and light, inviting itself to the dance.

Once the rains subsided, so did the choreography, with Aedan and Conall sitting back down. Elder Daithi brought them each a small copper bowl of water.

"I don't know what came over me, but that was so much fun." Conall wiped his lips. "Sitting there, with the butterflies, touched my spirit, but when I saw you dance, something made me. I *had* to join. I'm surprised you did as well, Aedan. I didn't take you for the dancing sort."

Aedan smirked, nodding. "I didn't, either, truth be told. But yes, it was fun."

The druid sipped his water, smiling. He had taken a seat at the base of the oak tree.

"Nourishment comes in all forms. The body requires food and water. The spirit requires peace. Sometimes, if you simply listen to your inner selves, you learn just what you need. You honor Cernunnos this day. To echo *your* sentiments, I did enjoy myself as well."

"Do you dance often?" Aedan leaned back on his hands.

The druid held a chipmunk in his. "Almost daily. Other times, I find myself thinking of the world and how I can bring love and wisdom to it. The shrine gets visitors like yourselves every so often, but it has been a while since any have danced. At least not as enthusiastically as you."

"Do you... speak with Cernunnos? Does he visit this place?"

The elder lowered his hands and let the chipmunk scamper away. "Aedan, what makes you think he isn't here now?"

"Well, growing up, my mother used to tell me stories of the Horned One, who looked... well, like you."

The druid chuckled. "At times. He also takes different forms. He is of life, and he is of death. He is also of the restorative power of the world. A seed is planted. It grows. It flourishes. It offers more seeds. It dies. Such is the way of the universe. Such is the Horned One."

A shadow fell on Conall's face.

"What is it?"

The boy looked at the druid, but he didn't reply. He turned toward the oak tree, then the flowers.

"Elder… I understand that there is life and death. But why is there evil? What purpose does it serve?"

"What brought that thought to mind?"

Aedan chimed in. "The Fomoragh. He's talking about them."

The druid nodded. "I see." — he hesitated a moment before replying — "Aedan. Conall. Our world is complex. We enter it with innocence, we travel many paths to gain experience, and then we leave it with wisdom. We hope that others will travel *their* paths learning from our experiences and our wisdom. That is one aspect of our world. Growth. Every tree grows a branch. Every branch grows leaves and flowers. Every flower brings forth fruit. Every fruit bears seeds. Even when the flower shrivels away, the tree still lives, ready to bring forth new ones the next spring. The branch grows even more branches from itself, and so on. This oak represents who we are. It knows only growth. We achieve a form of immortality this way."

"But what does this have to do with evil?"

'I'm getting to that, Conall. Patience. Everything in our world has two sides. The opposite of growth is destruction. This path is willful and selfish. Its sole purpose is to tear things down. Nothing in nature seeks to destroy. When the wolf hunts the hare, he does so out of survival, not to see the hare suffer. When the river floods the valley after a storm, its purpose is not to drown the animals. It is a natural product of the rains. The waters recede, and new life takes over."

"I guess that makes sense. What we think of as destruction isn't intentional. Death is a part of life."

"Correct, Aedan. But when one's spirit is driven to take that which others have, to strip away one's life, to cause pain, to enjoy suffering, to revel in destruction… *that* is evil. You asked me what purpose it serves. That is its purpose. We who protect the natural world must stand firm, defending others from this. The Fomoragh do not know humility. Their way is to push others down so they look taller. That is their path. Evil, like good, cannot be destroyed. It can be contained for a while, even thousands of years, but eventually, like the spring, it grows once again."

"Seems like weeds in a garden."

"Aedan, weeds are plants like any other. They just grow where people don't want them to. This patch of wildflowers would be considered weeds if growing in a vegetable patch. They're not evil, just misplaced. We can transplant them elsewhere to thrive, to provide beauty. Evil, however, like the Fomoragh, isn't simply misplaced. It will never provide beauty."

From the cavelike entry into the shrine, two pairs of glowing eyes appeared. Conall and Aedan leaped up and drew their staffs.

"Be at peace. They are not here to harm you. Enter, brothers." The druid rose to join them. Once the newcomers came into the light, the boys saw two gray wolves enter, each with something in its mouth. One approached Conall, and the other, Aedan, dropping what they held at the boys' feet. The objects were silver torcs of twisted metal, similar to the one that the druid had.

"I know you must be on your way before sundown, but the Horned One is nothing if he is not generous. These are gifts. Wear them knowing that Cernunnos watches over you both. You have honored him and the natural world, and he now honors you."

Conall gasped and put the torc around his neck with the opening facing forward. Aedan followed his friend.

"I-I don't know what to say." Conall rubbed his fingers against the silver. "Thank you."

He smiled at Aedan and then at the druid.

"You know, Conall, in the ancient tongues, your name means 'strong wolf'." Elder Daithi laughed and pointed to the wolves. "Perhaps you three are related?"

All three of them laughed out loud and the wolves howled.

"Conrí and Cuán here will escort you to the main road where you will continue your journey. Our paths shall cross again, my friends."

The wolves headed back to the shrine entrance with the boys following closely behind. Outside, the rocks were slick from the earlier rains, and they glistened from whatever sunlight shone through the canopy. At the base of the steps, the barely trodden path moved through a forest for about twenty paces until they reached the main road.

"Funny," Aedan looked both ways down the dirt road, "This isn't where we came through the portal. I don't even see the Twisted Trees anywhere."

"We must have needed to stop by the shrine first." Conall nodded at Conrí and Cuán before the gray wolves returned to the woods.

Pulling out the map, Aedan unfurled it for the first time. In the center, two small stick figures stood, and the road went northwest and southeast, with the forest to the east. Farther to the east was a pair of antlers.

"This must be the shrine." He pointed. "Which way should we go now?"

Conall saw rolling hills to the west. Feathery clouds drifted by, covering and uncovering the sun, revealing midday. He headed north, and when Aedan asked why, he simply replied they had to choose one way to go, and this way seemed as good as the other. The landscape shifted from what they had seen closer to home, and Conall commented on how the air felt different, too. Heavier. They had walked less than an hour when Aedan checked the map again. The two stick figures remained in the middle, but the roads had shifted. Plus, lakes and a river were now visible along with groupings of trees, and some had symbols over them. Conall looked over at the map and smiled.

"You know what I want to do?" His voice became lighter.

"What?"

"Follow me!" Conall ran west, off the path.

"Hey, wait for me!"

They jumped over small shrubs and rocks, winded through clusters of trees, and ran faster as they saw what awaited them. Through a veil of low branches and thin birch, they emerged before a crystal-clear pond. A willow sat by an overlook just a few feet above the water, and Conall began disrobing before he even got to the tree. He piled his clothes together and put his pack atop them, covering them with loose branches. The only thing he kept on was his torc. Aedan was less careful about his belongings and threw them in a pile next to Conall's things. Without hesitating, Conall jumped from the rock into the water below. Right after he landed, Aedan did, holding his knees in tight so when he hit the water, an upsurge disturbed the entire pond. They both surfaced, laughing.

"I've wanted to do this for so long. I don't think we've bathed in over a week, maybe more." Conall cupped his hands and poured water over his head.

Like a fish, Aedan swam, surfacing and submerging, his laughter muffled as his head descended. Conall lay back, with arms outstretched, gently kicking to keep himself afloat. The water calmed once more, but that was disrupted when Aedan jumped in again right next to Conall, sending a wave over his head. He shot up, coughing, with his friend's laughter in the background.

"Are you a child? I could have drowned." He spat forth some water, but then he, too, laughed.

Aedan swam over. "Do you remember swimming in the lake by your cottage when we were wee ones? Your da and mine would be fishing on the far side, and they'd yell at us across the lake because they said we were scaring the fish?"

"Ha! Yes, I remember. We tried to catch fish with our hands, too, but they were too fast for us."

"Then, our mothers would have a blanket with baskets of bread and cheese. We'd come out of the water naked, and your mum would say, 'Conall, you're going to catch a chill if you don't put your pants on!'"

Conall guffawed. "That was right before your family left."

Going under once more, Aedan emerged near the edge of the pond and climbed onto the rocks. He combed his short brown hair back with his fingers and lay back on his elbows in the sun. Conall stayed in the water a while longer, splashing and swimming about. When he reached

Aedan, he saw his friend had fallen asleep. He sat down next to him and nudged him with his knee.

"Huh? What?" Aedan squinted under his hand.

Conall's face was toward the sky, and he had the same expression he'd had in the shrine. He'd pulled his knees up and wrapped his arms around them.

"You'll get yourself a nasty burn if you fall asleep in the sun. We should probably keep moving. We have a few hours before sunset, and we don't have much food left."

They resumed their travels north, Aedan's eyes bouncing between the map and the road. Conall hadn't said much since they'd started traveling, and he kept looking at Aedan. Whenever he'd try to make eye contact, it seemed as if Aedan would look down the road or somewhere else. He pulled a piece of brown bread from his pack and handed a piece to his friend. Aedan took it, nodded his thanks, and continued his scouting. Finally, Conall moved alongside him.

"Have I done something? You haven't said anything since we were at the pond. I mentioned something about leaving the Glen, and you left me in the water."

Aedan took small bites of his bread but said nothing back.

"Have it your way." Conall tightened his pack straps and quickened his pace. He could follow the road without a map until he had reason not to. He kept looking back at Aedan.

As they approached late afternoon, Conall had gone so far ahead that when he looked back, he couldn't see his friend. A bit farther, he saw what appeared to be a broken cart with two men trying to repair the wheel. The axle had cracked, and the cart lay lopsided, baskets of produce strewn across the road. When he was close enough, he could see one man putting vegetables back in baskets while the other one tried to lift the cart.

"Do you need some help?" Conall examined the scene.

About five feet tall and scraggy, the man refilling the baskets smiled. "That'd be grand. We're trying to make it to town before sunset. Seems like that'll be more of a challenge now."

Conall brushed off the vegetables as he put them in baskets. The other man was trying to lift the cart from the edge of the road.

"What town is up ahead where you're bringing your wares? Doesn't seem to be much around here."

The traveler at the cart, a husky man with short brown hair and beard, glanced over at him, but said nothing. Then, he saw the man look at his companion. Conall filled one more basket before moving himself to where he could see both travelers. He continued to help, but he picked up one vegetable at a time. A few feet behind the baskets, he saw an axe lying in the brush, half-hidden. Had it not been for the afternoon sun glinting off the blade, he wouldn't have noticed it.

"We really appreciate your help." The man leaned to move a basket, and his shirt lifted to reveal a dagger with a gem-encrusted handle. Part of the blade showed from its scabbard, and Conall noticed dark crimson, what could have been rust or dried blood.

Conall brushed his hands together. "Anything else I can do?" He quickly looked back the way he had come to find Aedan, but he was no-where in sight.

"As a matter of fact, there is." The man who had been tinkering with the cart had his hands on his hips. "That piece of silver around your neck. My friend and I would like it." His toothy grin showed a few pieces of gold where teeth used to be.

"It's not for sale." Conall instinctively touched it, pushing it under his shirt collar.

The other man was behind and to the left. "Oh, we didn't say we wanted to *buy* it. We just said we wanted it."

While they laughed with each other, Conall shook his right arm down, releasing the short wooden rod into his hand. The men hadn't noticed. The burly man pulled a length of chain from his waist, gripped the other end, and pulled it tight. His companion drew his dagger.

"I told you we'd find ourselves some entertainment, Tadgh." He flipped the blade from hand to hand, shuffling across the road.

"And you were right, Griff." He swung the chain in figure eight in front of him. "Now, how about you just surrender that there piece o' silver, and we'll be on our way."

Conall examined how the men stood, which foot they leaned on, and their body language. Tadgh stepped toward him, blade forward, so Conall shook the rod in his hand, extending the staff. Using both hands in the middle, he spun it around, knocking the dagger from the man's hand. Griff, seeing an opportunity, swirled the chain back and forth, and then pulled it back to strike Conall from behind. Pivoting, though, Conall caught the chain, wrapping it around the staff. Giving a stiff tug, he pulled the chain free of Griff's grip and sent it a few feet behind the cart.

"We have ourselves a would-be fighter, Tadgh. This boy thinks he can take both of us."

Griff leaped forward, arms outstretched, ready to grab Conall, but Co-nall rammed his staff into the dirt and swung around, planting both boots on Griff's torso. The impact took the wynd out of the man, and he fell to the road clutching his chest. On all fours, Griff made for the chain.

"Just give us what we want, and we'll leave you be!" Tadgh huffed, bouncing around the road to try to catch Conall off guard.

Conall spun his staff around, tucking it under his arm, reassessing the situation. He could now see Griff behind the cart and Tadgh to his right. Keeping both men in view would be difficult once Griff retrieved his chain. With such an open landscape on both sides of the road, he had no place to go.

"If I come for that torc, boy, I take your head with it. Two trophies instead of one."

"Tadgh, is it? I'm quite happy keeping my head and my torc."

Griff grunted. "You can't take both of us on forever. You'll get tired, and we'll get what we want." He pulled the chain taut a few times as he rounded the cart.

A whistling sound caught Conall's ear, and he turned just in time to position his staff to block the dagger. It couldn't penetrate the wood, so it bounced off and landed at Conall's feet. He crouched without taking his eyes off them and flung it with all his strength over Tadgh's head into the brush over thirty feet away. The man growled and lunged for him, so Conall stooped and swung the staff, taking out Tadgh's legs. He flipped over, landing on his back, crying out.

"My back! He's broken my back!"

Conall saw him writhing on the ground, reaching behind him.

"If your back were broken, you wouldn't be able to move. Stay down!"

Griff jumped up, chain in both hands, coming down on Conall who had placed the staff in front to block it. Unfortunately, he lost his balance and fell backward. Griff pressed the chain down against the wood, using his body weight to push the staff against Conall's throat. He gasped as Griff's knee pressed down, and he pushed hard to keep from having his throat crushed. Griff gripped the staff with one hand and reached for the torc with the other. In the background, Conall heard Tadgh mutter something about having the last laugh, and he hobbled over, axe in hand. As Griff's hand was within inches of Conall's neck, Conall saw the man's head fly backward taking his body with it.

"You bastard! You killed Griff! I'll—"

A few thuds later, and in a flurry of action, Tadgh flew into the baskets, sending the vegetables everywhere. When Conall could breathe again, he looked up and saw Aedan, sweaty and out of breath, an axe in one hand and his staff in the other.

"Conall! You okay?" He knelt down.

Nodding and coughing, Conall slowly sat up. He took a few deep breaths and saw the unmoving body of Griff and a groaning Tadgh not far from him. Aedan dropped everything and hugged his friend.

"I thought he was going to kill you. Praise Brigid you're okay."

"Ow. You big lummox, you're crushing me." Conall coughed and laughed. "I'm fine. Help me up."

Brushing himself off, he had a better view of what happened. Hobbling over to Griff, he checked for a pulse.

"He's alive, just passed out."

Aedan growled at Griff and kicked his leg.

"Aedan, enough. It's done."

"What happened?"

Conall explained everything while they picked through the produce strewn about.

"You should have just given them the torc." He put some plums in his sack.

Conall stopped. "No. This was a gift from Cernunnos. Yours, too."

Aedan cleaned off some onions. "It's not worth your life."

"Actually, it is. My father told me stories of the Horned One ever since I was old enough to understand who he was. My faith got me through many difficult times." He paused. "It helped me find peace during rough days."

As earlier, Aedan didn't respond. He continued to find worthy vegetables to take with them. Rolling his eyes, Conall did the same.

"Look, I'm still sore from my recent fight, so I'm not sure I can handle another one, but what's happening with you? Every time I bring up you leaving, you go quiet. Have I done something wrong?"

The silence clung to them both. When Conall had as much produce as he could shove into his pack, he sighed and took steps to head north. Aedan's hand on his arm stopped him.

"I'm sorry. It's not you. Not really." He closed his pack, and they both walked on. "When my da told me we had to leave, I didn't want to go. If you remember, I didn't have many friends, just you and Seamus, really. Our clan was the only place where we lived together, in peace. When my parents said we needed to move to Oak Mountain, I didn't know my mum was ill then. Once we had moved, she sat me down and explained that she had wanted to die near the place she was born. I didn't know she had been born by the mountain. I was so angry. Angry at the world. Angry at her, at my da. Even at you."

"Me? Why?"

"Seamus had moved back with us, you know, to help out. You were the only one who wasn't there. I felt abandoned, although I didn't really know the word for it back then. Part of me knew you had done nothing wrong. But…"

Conall smiled. "I understand. The sad part is, the longer we were apart, we forgot about each other."

They walked more in silence, but this time, it was a comfortable one. The road and landscape grew together, the gray limestone karst spreading out, and tufts of grass and mosses brought a touch of green to an otherwise barren milieu. Far ahead, gradual hills rippled, and the flora took on a pale orange hue of the sun as it descended. Cairns marked the path when dirt grew scarce to show the way. At the top of a hill, they spied a small structure, and at a precise moment, the sun fell behind it, illuminating it from behind.

"A dolmen, up ahead."

Conall and Aedan reached it just as the sun was halfway absorbed by the horizon. The capstone was large enough for the two of them to rest under, but Conall hesitated.

"We can't. This is a holy ground."

"We're not going to desecrate it, just sleep in it. We'll leave at sunrise. I'll do a protection circle."

They placed their packs between them and leaned against opposite megaliths. The space was large enough for them to stretch out under, and as soon as the sun vanished, they stared out at the star-speckled sky. A crescent moon hung, like a silver hook, and it cast a haze over the limestone.

"Cerridwen, Mistress of the Waning Moon, watch over my parents and Aedan's father," Conall whispered, more out of reverence, since he knew Aedan wasn't asleep. "And over Lann..."

He could see the outline of Aedan's face as he, too, watched the skies.

"You also need to keep both eyes on Aedan. I mean, he does get himself into trouble." He chuckled.

Aedan kicked him playfully.

"Ha!" Conall chortled.

"Did you know that the waning moon is supposed to be her cauldron?" Aedan pointed up at the moon and made a curved gesture.

"I did. My mother showed me that. Oh. Sorry."

"Conall, just because my mother died doesn't mean you can't talk about yours. I miss your mum. She was always so kind to me."

"Except when she scolded us for getting into trouble. If we weren't playing in the mud, we were trying to pull the cat's tail. Thistle really did get her share of pokes and prods."

Their laughs melted away, and the slumber of Cire Ivermeth, the goddess of dreams, pulled them into her embrace. The night breezes were brisk, and wove their way through the dolmen, bringing the musk of the landscape. For the first time in a long while, they slept peacefully. Morning emerged over the horizon, and Conall awoke to the sensation of hot air over him, coming in waves. It smelled of burned wood and a pungency his mind couldn't name, but it did smell familiar. The gusts made the sound of a horse snorting. He wrinkled his nose and turned toward Aedan. A wide grin blossomed on his face, and his eyes teared up.

"Aedan, Aedan, wake up. We have a visitor."

"Huh, what? What do you mean a visitor?" He rolled his head to the right, and a hot gust blasted him in the face. His eyes popped open. "Fiachra!"

He jumped out from the dolmen and took three steps. The dragon, fast asleep, had its head on the ground. Aedan leaned over and hugged his scaly friend.

"I've missed you so much. Is this even real?"

The red and gold dragon lifted its head, looked back at Aedan, and leaned into his chest. His head was almost the size of Aedan's body. Fiachra made a sound that could only be described as purring if dragons could purr. Aedan took a step back.

"By Danu, you have grown so much! You're almost as big as the cottage. How did you find us?"

Conall stood next to the dolmen, arms crossed, grinning from ear to ear. He, too, had missed Fiachra. His grin shrank to a smile, presumably because he missed Lann, but then a sound came from behind him, and he spun around.

"Lann! Praise the moon goddess!" He held up his arm, and the hawk perched on it, flapping its wings, squawking his delight. Conall kissed his head, and the hawk rubbed his head against Conall's cheek.

Conall went over to a distracted Aedan.

"Look." His voice shook.

Aedan's eyes widened. "Yahoo!"

He kept trying to wrap his arms around Fiachra, and the dragon stretched closer to Conall. Squawking, Lann flew over and sat on Fiachra's scaly head. The boys burst into laughter, jumping up and down.

"I can't remember the last time I was so happy." Conall patted Fiachra's shoulder. "All of us in the same place. I wonder how they found us."

"Does it matter? They're here now. That's what matters!" Aedan grabbed his pack. "We should get going, no?"

Conall couldn't take his eyes of the hawk. It was as if Cerridwen knew exactly what was his heart's desire. Lann had grown so much in his time away, as had Fiachra. He was no longer that eyas that Conall had saved years ago.

"What? Yes, we should get going." Conall help up his arm. "Come on."

Lann settled on his friend's leather bracer, and the dragon took off, keeping close by.

"Don't go wandering off!" Aedan looked up at his winged friend. In reply, Fiachra roared. "According to the map, we're heading toward some heavily wooded areas."

Following Fiachra, Lann took to the skies, squawking repeatedly at the dragon. The boys watched them fly off ahead.

"That is just so amazing that they found us. I can't imagine they went through the Trees. I could just see the faces of the people in Rusdare." Aedan guffawed.

Chuckling, Conall shook his head. "Could Fiachra even fit in the portal?"

As their laughter died down, they continued across the limestone karst toward the hills. Jutting from the top of one was a small, conical shape, in silhouette. The rising and falling of the path took them around the barkless remnants of trees, weatherworn and stark. Nothing at all grew on them, and they stood as reminders of a storm's power unchecked. It leaned to one side, and the splintered end housed a finch nest, the mother feeding her hatchlings. Conall smiled.

"Life living with death," he muttered. He touched the torc on his neck.

Two specks in the sky ahead, Fiachra and Lann played, with the boys just telling stories to one another to pass the time. They had missed much from each other's lives, being separated, and this time together filled that void. Tales of Aedan and Seamus getting into mischief were followed by Conall playing tricks on his parents. Being an only child meant he received all of the love and attention, but it also meant he received whatever consequences as well. He wasn't friends with many of the village children, preferring to spend his time with his parents and Lann. The subject changed to the day they were reunited, with the Elders, and how it felt to know they had so much riding on their success.

"Do you ever think about what happens if we're not successful? What would happen if the Ársa and the Fonn did actually battle here, in our world?" Conall had both his hands on the pack straps over his shoulders.

"Every day." Aedan took a few more steps. "If you could go back right now, would you?"

"I don't know. I miss my parents and my room. I miss the Glen. I even miss my chores." He chuckled. "But something is tugging at me inside, and it's something I know is important."

Aedan nodded. "I understand. Even though I left my da on bad terms, I wish I could see him again."

The undulations of the ground led them toward the top of a hill, the one with the conical shape. Their breathing became labored as the incline steepened, with it becoming more challenging to walk over the smooth rock covered in lichen. As they rounded a corner, the path switched back, and then again, until they found a place where it leveled off. The air seemed thinner, and a chill clung to them. Way off, Fiachra's roar and Lann's squawks echoed in the valley below.

Conall smirked. "They seem to be having a good time, eh?"

"Indeed." Aedan huffed and puffed. "To know what goes on in the mind of a dragon or a hawk."

To the right, a deeper valley spread, with darker patches in the distance. Feathery clouds flitted past, and the morning sun sent shafts of light over everything. They headed west along the path, so the sun was behind them. A pocket of silence enveloped them, and all that could be heard was their own deeper breaths and the sound of leather boots on limestone. Aedan was a few steps ahead, and he stopped.

"By Brigid's fyre…" His eyes had locked on the conical shape that was now fully in view.

Conall caught up to him, and he gasped.

"A cairn. But like none I've ever seen."

The pile of smoothed, multicolored stones stood just taller than they were, and vines grew around them. One slow step after another brought them within breathing distance.

"These stones. They're carved with glyphs. Ogham, right?"

Leaning in, Conall was close enough that his exhales made the vines quiver.

"Yes, that's Ogham. I can't figure out what they say, though. Take out the map."

Aedan unfurled the parchment and found the two stick figures representing them.

"It says we're at Syed Epona."

"Epona's Arrow?" Conall put his arms up. "What does that mean?"

Aedan rolled his head around, stretching his neck. "How am I supposed to know? Yet another riddle. And look, the valley is full of mist, so now we can't even see where to go."

"Let me see the map."

Falling into a cross-legged position, Conall saw the same thing that Aedan had seen. The path north stopped where they were.

"It's as if the map doesn't want us to see something."

"Perfect." Aedan kicked a pebble. "We've come all this way to see a pile of rocks, and now we can't even see how to leave." He whistled into the sky, but Fiachra didn't respond or appear. He sighed. "Even better."

"Lann!" Conall held up his arm, but the hawk didn't come.

For hours, they sat or lay back and watched the clouds scurry by, and they even sparred to devour the boredom that attempted to do the same to them. They tried to move in what they perceived was the northerly route, but the mists gathered as gatekeepers, rising up to create a wall. They were being held without knowing how to free themselves.

"Do you think this is a trick of the Fomoragh? Maybe we're being held here until one of them arrives to kill us?" Aedan leaned against one side of the vine-entwined cairn.

"You're a fountain of positivity, aren't you?" Conall sighed. "But, yes, I had thought that, too."

Like an ethereal warden, time kept them prisoner, and the day edged toward the afternoon. The mists swirled and undulated, like the ocean agitated by a squall. From within the haze, the sound of neighing pierced through, sometimes muffled, and other times, blaring, like a monstrous beast.

Conall jumped up. "What was that?"

"Sounds like a horse. But it's coming from everywhere." Aedan extended his staff.

"Do you think a horse got lost from the valley and found its way up here through the mists?"

Again, the raucous horse call rang out.

"It's hurt, Conall. Somewhere out there. What do we do?"

The son of Rinn put his staff away. "We go find it." He started to walk toward the sound in the fog, but Aedan yanked him back.

"What're you doing? This could be a Fomoragh trick? Or—"

"Or, it's a horse that's in danger! Didn't you hear it? It sounded like it was in pain." He shook free of Aedan's grip. "If you don't want to help me, then just wait here."

Conall pushed against the mists, but they wouldn't let him through. He dug his hands into the spongy air and, anchoring himself, leaned into it. He growled, tightened his legs, and pushed, but nothing. Aedan grunted his disapproval before seeing his friend next to him, pushing with his palms against the whiteness. More and more, the horse's squeals rang out, its sounds almost human.

"Come on... let us... in!" Aedan tightened his fingers around the mist.

Without warning, the air softened, and the boys fell forward into the obscurity. Checking to make sure each other was all right, they scoured for the source of the pitiful cries. The percussive sound of hooves approaching brought the boys back-to-back. Like a drumbeat, they continued, getting closer, until the mists gave way and a white horse reared before them. It did this two more times before Conall put his hands up.

"It's all right. You're okay now. Easy, girl." He edged closer, avoiding the front hooves that flew in front of him.

He slid his foot across the ground, repeating his soft plea. The horse's rearing continued, and Conall saw Aedan coming from the side. He held out his hand to his friend and shook his head.

"Easy, girl. You're okay. We're not here to hurt you. I promise."

After a few more minutes, the rearing stopped, and the horse snorted, nodding its head up and down. Conall slid closer, placing his hands on the side of the horse's neck. The beast was much taller than he was. Through the mists, he could see the tail swishing.

"See? It's all right. You're safe now."

Aedan came up next to his friend and tentatively touched the horse's side, patting softly.

He whispered, "I'm impressed. You did it, Conall."

Conall soothed the horse, rubbing under its neck until the mare was breathing normally.

A voice as faint as the mist, a woman's voice, came through the ambiguity.

"You have honored my mare with your compassion, Wyndracer, and by doing so, you have honored me. Thank you."

As if dismissed by a royal gesture, the fog dispersed, revealing the valley once more. Sunlight stretched over the land, and the white mare's coat gleamed. Aedan fed her an apple from his pack. From behind the cairn, a woman emerged, her long, red hair braided with white apple blossoms. Over her shoulders and covering her torso was draped a grass green cloth, cinched at the shoulders with moonstone beads. From her waist to the ground flowed a skirt of pale blue, embroidered with silver icovellavna depicting horses and flowers. In her left arm sat a cornucopia overflowing with fruits, vegetables, and flowers.

Aedan and Conall bowed as she approached.

"I should have known that those who have been blessed by the Horned One should be so kind." She nodded toward their torcs. Her smile made them blush. "Let me see your eyes."

They looked up, faces still reddened, and she touched first Conall's face, then Aedan's.

"Yes. The prophecy has spoken of you both. The Wyndracer and the Fyrehunter."

The mare neighed.

Epona laughed. "She thanks you. You have shown her kindness, risking unknown peril, and I am in your debt. How may I repay that?"

Conall patted the mare. "My Lady, you don't have to. We were just trying to help."

The mare rubbed her head against his hand.

"Humble, as befits a hero." She turned toward Aedan. "And you, noble one, following your friend took great courage. Ask of me, and you shall receive."

He blushed again. "I agree with my friend, My Lady."

Epona reached into her cornucopia and gave them each a silver key.

"Place this on your torc. When you need it most, it will guide you. I know your quest is fraught with danger and the unknown. The ancient gods cannot be allowed to bring their battle here, to this wondrous land. May your path unfold before you like an arrow from its bow."

With that, she mounted her mare and rode off, vanishing into the wynd. The boys did as she instructed, joining the gift of the Stag with that of the Mare. Alone on the hill, they took in the valley to decide which way to go. In all directions, paths moved away from the cairn, each one as viable as the other. Aedan took a step back and folded his arms in thought. His eyes moved all around, and then, as if a puzzle piece fell into its designated place, he smiled.

"Look." He pointed at the cairn. "See where the shadow falls? See how it forms a point on the ground, like an arrow? I think *that* is our path."

Conall patted him on the shoulder. "I think you're right. Let's see if we can make up some time before nightfall."

They hadn't reached the bottom of the hill when two familiar sounds reached across the skies. A red and gold dragon and hawk came from the clouds and circled above them. The boys waved as they walked, their pace noticeably faster than usual. Smaller cairns marked the way, and once in the valley, what was obscured by mist earlier became obvious. Gradually, the limestone gave way to grasses which, in turn, became fields of heather that formed a purple and green blanket for miles. At the edges of the path, dragonflies, like sentries, flew along, alighting on the occasional flower or stalk of grass. Striated with the same purples of the heather mixed with orange and pink, the skies darkened slightly with the encroaching evening. Down and down the path took them, deeper into the vale, and in the distance, the boys saw something that made them stop.

"Whoa. What is that?" Aedan rubbed his arms. "I just got a strange chill."

Conall's eyes widened. "I have never seen anything like that. Check the map."

"It says it's the *Forisha na Fírinne*." The Forest of Truth.

Winding its way down into the valley, the dusty path entered a dense pine forest that seemed more like a dark green island that spread as far as they could see. It stretched so far north that they couldn't see beyond it.

"Then, I guess that is where we go."

Their legs felt the decline with each step, causing them to grunt as they walked. As the sun dipped lower, the forest lay like a regal lioness. With their own distinct calls, Fiachra and Lann communicated that they would await their companions on the other side of the forest. Fifty paces from the entry, Conall and Aedan stopped. Two pines created an arch, reminiscent of the Twisted Trees, only smaller, through which they would have to walk to enter. Shadows embraced them until they disappeared within.

10 | FOREST OF TRUTH

ll around them, beneath the pine branches, slivers of light poked through, just enough to show the presence of sky, but not enough to light one's way. Hovering, faint balls of airy luminescence lingered throughout the forest, like lanterns. Conall put his hand toward one, but it retreated just out of reach. Otherwise, they didn't move. In the darkness, pairs of glowing eyes, some yellow and some orange, peeked from behind trees. Those up above, in the branches, had rounder eyes, like owls. Tiny, winged creatures flitted about, and when they got close enough to see, the boys realized what they were.

"Faeries…" Aedan followed one with his eyes until it vanished into the darkness. "I've never actually seen any before."

They walked on with deliberate footfalls, the crunching of pine needles under their boots. Aedan opened the map but put it back just as quickly.

"Blank. Of *course* it is. The time we could really use a map, and it says nothing."

"There *is* only one path. Let's just see where it goes." Conall let his compact staff slide into his grip. "Just be vigilant."

Pairs of eyes stepped from behind trees to see the newcomers. No matter where the boys looked, they couldn't see outside the forest, even though they weren't that far from the edge. As if it had a mind of its own, the earthen path meandered around trees, up and around rocks, and switching back occasionally. The invigorating scent of pine mixed with fresh rain was a stark contrast to the musty smell of limestone and grasses. At some point in their walk, an odd sound in the distance caught their ear.

Conall turned. "Is that a waterfall I hear? Or are my ears playing tricks?"

"It does sound like it, doesn't it? I'm not even sure which direction it would be in. I've been paying attention to the sound of my stomach more than anything. Maybe we can stop and eat somewhere, but where…"

They rounded a pine whose trunk was six feet across, and on the side of the path was a flat rock. Aedan crunched into an apple from his pack. Conall, however, leaned forward and took deep breaths.

"You okay?" Aedan asked while chewing.

"I'm fine. Just tired. What I wouldn't give for a comfortable place to sleep."

"Well," he munched on, "we'll look for an open place to lie down once we can't go any farther. This forest goes on and on."

With each curve, the path rose around clusters of trees or went in a straight line through more open areas. They couldn't tell how much time had elapsed from the sun, but they both stopped at the same time. The path diverged around a pool at the far side of which was a waterfall. Along the periphery of the water, moss softened the edge while ferns and bladderwort burst in patches. Clusters of powder-blue forget-me-nots interrupted the green, and golden fringed water lilies freckled the pond.

"I knew I had heard a waterfall. Look at the top of it."

Conall pointed to a rough stone statue of a woman whose carved long tresses were accentuated by moss, tendrils of ivy that bore white flowers, reminiscent of Epona. The woman's outstretched hands bore birds who had stopped to rest. Around the statue's waist was carved a belt, and in its center was a triskelion, a symbol of land, sea, and sky. The waters flowed from where her feet touched the rock above the pond. Both boys instantly bowed their heads.

"This is a sacred place, Conall. I hope we have not offended her."

"I-I don't know." He raised his head a little to get another look. "She doesn't seem upset."

Aedan lifted his head and snarled. "It's not actually *her*, you know. Just her likeness. We've done nothing wrong."

When they looked up at her again, they saw a stag standing behind her. Its eyes shimmered in the ambient light. Conall got onto his knees and pressed his hands to his chest, rocking.

"Goddess, we come on a quest. We bring no malice." His voice shook. "Merciful, Danu…"

"Would you get up." Aedan pulled him. "You don't think she can tell if we're good or not? She's the mother of the Tuatha Dé Danann, you know."

Conall yanked his arm free. "Just trying to be safe."

While they talked, they didn't notice the stag coming down from its perch and nearing them. It wasn't until he was a few feet away that Conall realized. The animal was a few heads higher than them.

"N-Nice s-stag. We're not here to hurt you. I don't even eat ven –"

"Conall, stop. You'll annoy him so much that he'll eat *us*."

Even in the dimmer light, the stag's greyish-brown coat shimmered, and his eyes reflected more than what was there. His antlers bore sixteen points which he wore like a crown, and that majesty made the boys look down in deference. The great beast bowed, an unexpected gesture. With caution, they took hold of an antler each. Conall and Aedan's eyes glazed over, and confusion of images poured into them, one colliding with the next. Seconds later, it stopped, and they released the stag.

"What... was that?" Conall shook his head and rubbed his temples. "I saw things, but I don't understand them."

Aedan groaned. "I don't know, either. Maybe he's trying to communicate with us?"

They took steps back before the stag returned to his perch behind the statue of Danu, paused, and then vanished into the forest. Shaking their heads, the boys sat at the edge of the pool, staring out at the rippling water. Fringing the edge, water lilies had blossomed in pale yellows and pinks, their leaves providing a green backdrop. A dragonfly moved from flower to flower, like a gardener taking care of its charges. The serenity shifted when the waterfall slowly stopped falling and the pond stopped moving. Once it had achieved a mirror-like sheen, a voice rose from the water.

"Attend me, son of Odhran, son of Rinn..." The voice had liquid tendencies, soft and calm.

Both boys jumped to their feet, brushing themselves off. They lowered their heads just enough so that if they lifted their eyes, they could see the pond.

"You have traveled far to reach this place, and it is not without cost. Yet, you are the only ones who can complete this task."

Conall opened his mouth. "Goddess... why's that? Surely, the gods-"

"Purity of heart, my child. Those you speak of no longer have purity of heart. You both do."

Conall muttered, "I don't understand..."

"The Tuatha Dé Danann have been tested for thousands of years, and they have been found wanting, my child. Son of Rinn, you are of the Ársa, the Ancient Elements, but you are most connected to air. Of all the Gaoth Clan, only you will have mastery over the winds, and that will grow as you do. The temperate breezes to the harshest gales will be yours to command."

As if on cue, the air swirled around Conall, playing with his hair.

"Of the Keen Ones, you are, son of Odhran. The Fonn align themselves with fire, and that is why you are of the Tine Clan. From the kindled embers to the raging flames that consume all things, you will grow to command such. The prophecy has been released, that of the DragonHawk, and it shall come to pass."

Conall stared at the edge of the pond, shuffling his feet and rubbing his hands.

"Goddess… How did the Ársa and the Fonn come to be at odds? Why fight at all?"

From high above, a gust of wynd swept through the trees, the pine branches swaying and undulating, like an arboreal dance. It subsided as quickly as it came.

"Such is their nature, child. That is all you need to know for now."

"We-We have a map. We're just not sure how to find our first wand." Aedan's voice dropped as he spoke.

After a short pause, Danu replied. "Each of you, take hold of the map, and ask."

Taken aback, Aedan fumbled for the parchment, unrolled it, and saw just the two stick figures that represented him and Conall. Both took the corners.

"Show me where the wands are. Please?" Aedan took a deep breath.

From the two stick figures at the center of the map, sparks traveled, zigzagging all around like an agitated ant hill. In their wake, brown lines revealed roads, bodies of water, mountains, and forests. Along the edges of the paper, icovellavna formed a border of triskelions, circular designs, and shield knots for protection. In the northwest corner, a hawk appeared, and in the northeast, a dragon.

Conall gasped. "What? How is this possible?"

The last image to take shape on the map was the compass before the sparks faded. As the map moved, the compass reflected true north.

Danu's voice reverberated throughout the forest.

"The Forisha na Fírinne has given you what it can. As you quest, be wary of where you are. Beyond this forest, I cannot protect you. The druid has shown you dríochta to keep you safe and guide your way. The hero has taught you how to protect yourself." She paused. "The Fomoragh will test you. Should you fail…"

Thunder pealed above them, a celestial warning.

"One more question, if I can… my friend and I are just boys. Yes, Déaglán and Fionn have taught us things, but we're not warriors or druids. How can two staffs and a few dríochta really help us?" Conall immediately lowered his head, putting his hands on top of it.

"The only way one becomes a warrior or a druid is through experience, child. I do not know whether you will succeed in your quest or not. That knowledge is beyond even me. Stay true to each other, to yourselves, and you can accomplish anything."

Aedan huffed through his nose, shrugging at his friend.

Danu continued, "The guardians of the wands will not simply give them to you. You must prove your worth and bravery."

Aedan nodded at Conall.

"Beyond the pond, the path begins. Remember, follow the map." Danu's voice faded on the last word. The pond grew still.

—ɱ—

By the other side of the pond, the pine-strewn path led them through two pines that had grown together, forming an arch. Open landscape rippled ahead, marked with patches of heather and clover. Their way lay clear for a few hours until an opening in the heather came into view. It wasn't as if the path truly diverged, since the one they were on was well-worn, but this deviation did show it had been used by at least a few travelers. They stared into the purple blanket before them, and then Aedan remembered what Danu had told them. *Follow the map*. The parchment did indeed show this smaller passage, but it gave no indication as to whether it was where they needed to go.

"My gut tells me to keep moving." Conall put his hand to his brow to shade the morning sun from his eyes. "Something isn't right."

They moved on. At a small orchard by a trickling stream, they filled their pouches and picked some apples. Conall always said a silent prayer to give thanks. The map showed a patch of trees on the west side of the path with a vertical line with three horizontal lines to the right: the Ogham for alder.

"I guess the Fearnslat is first." Aedan pointed to the cluster of trees up ahead.

A dozen alder trees grew randomly around a wide one, about three feet in diameter, with an opening in the split bark, like a small cave. Glossy green leaves moved in the breeze. Among the trees, a blanket of grass dispersed, dotted with bunches of clover. Bees hovered over the blossoms, touching down to collect nectar. As the boys peered into the opening in the tree, two beady eyes stared back. Then, a muzzle, white hair along the bottom, poked through. The boys took a step back. A head popped through, and the face of a red fox greeted them. It cocked its head one way, then the other before stepping its front legs through.

"What do we do?" Aedan whispered.

Conall shrugged and waved a little at the fox.

The fox ran around the tree and sat in front of them, its bushy tail swishing, tilting its head again.

Slowly, Aedan pulled out an apple and extended his hand. The fox leaned in carefully, its nose wrinkling as it sniffed the offering. In a quick move, it snatched the apple with its mouth and entered the tree only to return a moment later, seated once again, its tail swishing. Conall's eyes widened and in a soft voice, he told Aedan to follow his lead. Conall got on his knees and lowered his head, not making eye contact with the fox. Aedan, at first confused, did the same. Nothing happened right away, but then the fox stepped up to Conall, put its head beneath the boy's chin, and gently pushed his head up. The fox did the same for Aedan before returning to its seated position. Aedan raised an eyebrow at his friend.

"By lowering our head and eyes, we communicated that we are subordinate to him. This is his den. He's the social superior."

The fox thumped his red tail back and forth. The boys moved to a cross-legged seated position. Conall took out some apples from his pack, offering another one to the fox who eagerly put it in his den. The boys crunched their fruit while the fox watched, moving its head back and forth. It took a while before something happened. Another fox poked its head through the tree opening, a vixen or female. The tod or male stood by the entry and then licked the side of her muzzle. She did the same thing to him before retreating into the den. The boys smiled and giggled. A few minutes later, one by one, three smaller heads appeared in the tree opening, kits. The tod wagged his tail, and the little ones sat by their father, just behind him. Conall bit a piece of apple and held it out in his open palm close to the ground. One of the kits, moved closer one step, then another. Its nose wrinkled, and keeping low, it touched its nose to the apple before using its tongue to snatch it. Aedan had done the same thing, and another kit took the piece. The third kit hid behind its father more, and the father's tail swished over its head as if to signal that it was okay. The massive tail stopped mid-stroke, resting on the kit's head, looking like a furry hat. Conall and Aedan laughed, making the kit back up. Then, both kits pricked their ears up, as did the father, and all three little ones scurried back into the den. The tod growled, taking a defensive posture by the opening, and it took the boys a moment to realize that he wasn't growling at them. A coldness brushed over them, and a shadow fell on the copse of alder trees.

Jumping up, Conall and Aedan took a defensive posture by the fox's tree. Coming down the path was a child, around six years old in dirty rags. His brown, stringy hair hung from his head like dead vines. He held a small, stained burlap sack.

"I'm hungry." His voice quavered.

Aedan looked back at the fox, who was showing his teeth. "It's okay. It's just a wee lad."

Rummaging through his pack, Conall pulled out a piece of bread and an apple. He took a few steps forward, and the fox barked. Aedan tried to hush him, but he kept barking. Conall took another step. The fox leaped in front of him, bared his teeth again, and growled. The child cringed, his eyes watering. The barking grew more insistent, the fox's tail low to the ground.

"I really don't know what's gotten into him. He was fine a few moments ago." Aedan reached to move the fox, but it turned and growled.

"Aedan, animals act this way out of protection for their den. Maybe the fox feels threatened. I don't know why a little one like this would scare him, though."

The child came closer. Taking hold of the boy's ankle, the fox tried to pull him away from the tree, but the boy kicked, sending the fox flying into a tree. The tod yelped on impact and then shook off the blow, charging back. Conall expanded his staff.

"Did you see that? A child shouldn't be that strong."

Aedan shook his arm down, gaining control of his staff hidden in his sleeve. "I know."

"Didn't Déaglán tell us about someone who takes a child's shape?"

Nodding, Aedan narrowed his eyes. "Yes. Dubh."

"This isn't the one who has the evil eye, is he?" Conall closed one eye.

"Nah. That's Balor. Stay keen. Not sure what this boy can do. Fox, if I were you, I'd go back to your den."

Still growling, the fox jumped into the tree. Conall spun his staff around, sizing up his adversary. The child blanched as the boys positioned themselves with their staffs. He shook the sack again, and his lower lip quivered.

"Can I have some food?" Tears welled, and when he blinked, they trickled down his cheeks, washing away some dirt on his face.

Conall and Aedan circled him, unaffected.

"You have bread and apples." His voice trembled. "I'm so hungry." He put a hand to his belly.

Pairs of eyes twinkled inside the tree, and a low growl came from it. Conall and Aedan kept the boy in their sights as they positioned themselves. The lad, however, just stood there, his lower lip quivering. His arms pressed against his midsection.

More tears came, and the innocent cries of a child bubbled forth.

"Why... Why can't I have something to eat?" He shuffled a step forward.

Softened by the plaintive sobs, Conall lifted one hand from this staff and moved it toward his sack. Aedan shouted something, but it was too late. The lad lunged for Conall's staff. Aedan tripped him before he could touch it, and Conall stepped back. The little boy stumbled and fell toward the ground, but before he hit, he stopped, floating just above the dirt. Righting himself, the boy landed on his feet. The air grew brisk, and their breath misted as it left their mouths. The little one touched one of the alder trees.

"I am hungry... so I must feeeeeed." His voice had grown deep, as if a cave could speak. Where his fingers touched, a darkness spread, a blight that withered the bark as it moved toward the branches.

"He burns the wood with a touch!" Aedan positioned himself between the boy and the fox's den.

When the branches became consumed by the darkness, the entirety of the tree fell in a mound of ash.

Conall growled. "Dubh, what do you want?"

"To feeeed." He exhaled and touched another tree, bringing the same result.

"Stop!" Aedan squeezed his staff. "You'll destroy this whole forest."

After the fourth tree crumbled, Conall howled and charged Dubh. The son of the witch Carman grabbed the staff with his free hand, and the wood started to blacken. Conall managed to wrest it free, and the decay stopped, but where Dubh had touched it, the darkened wood remained. The staff retracted on its own back to a small rod, but now with a scorched end. The tod darted from his den and scampered to the farthest alder tree, gnawing on its bark. Neither Conall not Aedan understood what he was doing, but whatever it was, it had gotten Dubh's attention. The fox's behavior attracted Conall who noticed a red sap oozing from the tree at the gnawed area. Then, the tod snatched the staff from him. It took Conall a moment to figure it out, but he pressed the burned end into the sap. The blackened part became whole once again.

"The alder can heal!" He spoke to the fox as if he could understand.

Extending the staff, Conall saw residue of the sap on it. His eyebrow popped up with an idea.

"Conall, look out!"

Dubh was steps away from the tree. The fox returned to its den. Conall spread sap on his hands. He caught a glimpse of Dubh, reached back, and pulled the arm that reached for him. He fell back and used Dubh's own movement to launch him away from the alder, about ten feet. It wasn't much, but it bought him enough time to bound back to Aedan.

"What's all over your hands?"

"Alder sap. It healed my burned staff, so I guess it would protect my hands when I touched Dubh.

The boy shook off the impact, reaching for the tree, but stopped when he noticed the sap oozing down the trunk. Conall saw this and held out his own palms.

"You want to feed? You want power? The alder sap will give you all you need. It made me feel stronger! Maybe then you can defeat us."

Narrowing his brows, Dubh did just as Conall suggested, spreading the sap on his hands. Within seconds, he started screaming.

"What did you doooooo to me? My hands, they buuuurn!" He tried to rub the sap off, but it had already adhered and was using its healing abilities.

His screaming echoed through the forest, frightening off birds and smaller animals. His hands smoldered, a green smoke emanating from them. Dubh tried to draw power from the alder itself, to render it to ash and absorb its energy, but nothing happened.

Eyes widened, he turned toward Conall. "What did you do to me?"

Chest puffed out, Conall laughed. "The alder sap prevents your power from working. Your hands can't hurt anyone or anything now!"

Huffing with rage, Dubh growled and resumed his full form. Even as a grown man, his wailing didn't cease. He tried to scrape the sap from his hands on the bark of another alder, but it wouldn't come off. His frustration growing, Dubh grunted and growled as he tried to wipe the sap away. He was about to jump at Aedan, but the pain in his hands stopped him, and he doubled over.

"M-Máthair, cabhrú liom!" *Mother, help me!* The words were barely out of his mouth when he vanished in a plume of black smoke.

"We did it! We stopped Dubh!" Aedan punched the air.

Conall got serious again. "It can't be that easy. He may be gone, but it's just for now." He started to laugh. "But he had to call his mum to help him too." Conall lowered himself to the ground and rubbed, but his hands became covered in sap, dirt, sticks, and leaves. "How do I get this stuff off?"

"We need to find a stream or pond. I am sure it'll wash off eventually." Aedan giggled. "You look like a forest creature. Raawwrr…" He held up his hands and flexed his fingers.

They laughed a little bit, sighing. From the large alder, the foxes emerged, one at a time. The vixen scampered over to Conall, sniffed his hand, and licked some of the sap. The three kits frolicked around, in between Aedan's legs, while the tod strutted around the trees to ensure the threat had passed.

"I really can't believe we held our own, Aedan. I'm not daft enough to believe we're ready to take on all of the Fomoragh, but I wonder why Dubh didn't come after us harder."

"It was a test. I'm sure he wanted to see just what we can do. When we didn't back down from a fight—"

"What I'd like to know is, why here? He could have caught us on the road somewhere, especially out in the open. He never even tried to get the wand."

As if Conall's words could summon, the tod came up to Aedan with an alder stick in his mouth. About a foot long, it had no distinctive markings or glyphs.

"It's a branch. This is the Fearnslat?" Aedan looked it over, running it through his fingers. "A stick like this has some kind of power? I-I can't believe that. We're traveling from one end of this island to another for ordinary sticks?" Aedan tossed it back toward the den. The tod returned it to Aedan, growling.

"Okay, okay. I'll take it." He saw the scorched marks where the alder trees that Dubh destroyed used to be. "I can't believe a tree as massive as this can be destroyed, but this tiny branch can be used to stop a battle." He rolled his eyes.

"Aedan, the tree is a part of the world around us, and it has a magic all its own. If the sap of the tree can heal, why is it so hard to believe that a branch has any power?"

Standing next to a scorched spot, Aedan pointed with the wand.

"Can it bring this tree back? What would I have to do to make that happen?" He swished the wand around. "What good is magic if it can't be used?"

"Calm down. If everything destroyed by evil could be brought back, that would be a boon indeed. But you and I both know that magic doesn't work like that. Besides, we're not druids. There's no way we could ever use that much power to bring back the dead."

With those last four words, Aedan's eyes widened. He stared down at the wand.

"Mum…" He murmured, and his hands shook.

Conall got right next to his face.

"No. We don't *do* things like that. Even if we could, it's wrong. Bringing back the dead… Aedan, it's unnatural."

"It's not *your* mother who's dead, now is it!" He stomped away behind a tree.

Following him, Conall kept some distance, and when he did respond, he hung his head.

"You're right. Mine isn't. I can't understand your loss."

Through gritted teeth, Aedan replied, "They *took* her from me. They ripped her from this world." No matter how much he tried to control his voice, it shook like a leaf in the wind.

"And they will pay for that, I promise you. You have my word that I will do everything in my power to make sure they do." Conall remained on the other side of the tree.

"Why… Why can't I just wave this wand and bring her back?" Aedan kicked the dirt and grunted.

"When I was younger, my da talked with me about life and death. I don't remember why exactly, but I do remember what he told me. Life and death are part of the same path. When we finish our earthly journey, we continue it in **Tir na nÓg**. In that place, we are free of all illness and pain." He moved next to his friend. "Aedan, if you could pull your mother from the Otherworld, from peace, she would then be vulnerable to the everyday pains and suffering in the mortal world. She died of an illness, and now she knows no pain. Would you be bringing her back for her… or for you?"

Glaring, Aedan bore into his friend with red, teary eyes that had narrowed slightly. But then, his expression loosened, and he pulled Conall into a tight embrace, sobbing.

"I'm so close, so close." He squeezed his eyes shut and rocked in his friend's arms. "I miss her so much, Conall."

"I know. I know." He uttered, with heavy breath, crying, leaning his head against Aedan's.

It was the first time in a while where Saoirse's death had weighed so heavily on Aedan's heart. The two held each other until the kits rubbed against their legs, barking. The boys chuckled and squatted down, petting the little foxes. One of the wee ones had a tuft of fur that had a lighter, almost orange tinge. Aedan stared at it for a moment, then rose quickly.

"I want to try something. Come with me." He stood by where the closest destroyed tree was to the den, its sooty residue staining the ground, and Conall followed.

He held out the wand toward the earth and gestured for Conall to take hold as well.

"What are —"

Aedan shushed him. "Just repeat after me. Three times. *Saol nua ó theine. Saol nua ón aer.*"

After the third time, both voices overlapping into one, the ground itself rumbled a little. Black ash vanished into the ground, replaced by a tiny sprout. It grew into a sapling, about five feet tall, before Aedan exhaled sharply, lowering the wand.

"What did we just do?" He rubbed his arms. "My whole body aches."

"New life from fire. New life from air. I can't bring my mother back, but the alder needed one of its own returned. It was the least we could do." Aedan let his fingers graze the buds on the new tree.

"But, how did you know what words to say? You invoked *both* our elements."

"It's actually funny. The orange tuft of fur on that kit made me think of fire. And you need air to make fire grow. You need fire to make air move." He yawned. "The rest, I guessed." Aedan shrugged.

Grinning, Conall patted his friend's back. They both agreed they needed to rest before they would move on. Using dríocht drained them since they were new to it, but they put a protection charm around the large alder that served as the foxes' den. Aedan commented that he now understood why one of the four symbols of the protection charm was an alder, a *fearn*, for strength. Conall and Aedan leaned up against the bark between roots, and the tod and vixen sat vigil near their human companions. The kits crawled over the boys, finding places to sleep in their laps. For this night, they would be safe.

—ɷ—

Moonrise brought cool breezes that wove their way through the trees, picking up neighboring heather and jasmine. Conall cracked open his eyes long enough to see the silhouette of the foxes guarding them, the starlight reflected in their beady eyes. Sleep returned to him. By sunrise, the kits had already started their play near the tree while the vixen had gone off to find food. The tod moved from Conall to Aedan, licking each one's nose. When Aedan opened his eyes, the fox's cocked head was inches from his face.

"Good morning to you too."

Conall groaned himself awake, stretching. The kits, hearing the boys, scurried over. From the field beyond the forest, the vixen returned, dropping a branch of tayberries near the boys. She disappeared and came back with a small hare hanging limply in her mouth. While the boys enjoyed their berries, they watched as the kits snuffle up small pieces of meat torn by their mother. The tod patrolled the area, moving from tree to tree, its nose to the wind. Aedan and Conall adjusted their packs after breakfast, refilling their water pouches in a nearby stream. They crouched near the den where the tod and vixen played with their offspring.

"Thank you." Conall scratched their noses. "We won't forget your hospitality."

The tod and vixen barked in reply, their tails wagging. Back at the path, Conall turned to see the tod sitting in front of the den, watching them leave. He swished his tail once and then joined his family. The boys' journey continued north, past more heather patches, the morning mists floating just over them, and the sun giving the dew-drenched flowers a vibrant purple hue. The winding road took them by and through more small forests until they reached a hamlet. On a stone, just before they entered, was carved a name: Neadúlcaban.

11 | NEST OF OWLS

Unlike the complexity of Rusdare, Neadúlcaban was a gathering of cottages on both sides of the road. To the west, a dozen stone cottages with thatched roofs had rounded doors, each door flanked by a window with a flower box just under it. Stone chimneys jutted forth with wisps of musky peat smoke curling into the air. To the east, aside from more cottages, were the blacksmith's smithy, a small tavern, a stable, and a market. Hamlet folk moved about, and a few children had gathered around the open smithy to watch a burly, bearded man wearing a leather apron. As his hammer came down on a glowing piece of metal, sparks jumped, making the boys and girls both wince and laugh.

It was into this sleepy place that Conall and Aedan headed directly for the market. Awnings stretched out over tables laden with baskets of fruits and vegetables, wool and woven fabrics, as well as flowers and herbs hanging all around. The boys replenished their provisions, including acquiring wool blankets. A butcher offered them a sample of dried beef, saying it would travel well, so they each purchased a parcel. Aedan suggested they have an actual, proper meal since they needed to keep traveling before nightfall. The tavern had a table in the back, away from most of the patrons so the boys could hear each other over the morning din.

"I'd say we did well." Aedan patted his pack. "This should keep us going a week or so."

A serving girl brought over two flagons of spiced honey water and two bowls of barley porridge.

"Miss, we didn't ask—" Conall pointed to the food.

The girl smiled. "Blessings, good sir." She nodded. "We always give newcomers a meal when they come in. It's our way of saying, 'Welcome to Neadúlcaban.'"

Conall smiled. "Blessings to you. That is kind of you. My friend and I appreciate it."

They scraped every last pearl of barley from their bowl, followed by downing the entirety of their honey water. Aedan sat back against the wall and put his legs up on the bench, exhaling.

"You all right?" Conall belched sideways.

"Yeah. Just thinking about our recent skirmish." He crossed his arms and looked out across the tavern.

"Me too. I keep wondering why Dubh didn't take the wand."

Aedan tapped his lips with his finger. "We don't need the whole town knowing."

"Oh, right." Conall lowered his voice, putting a finger to his mouth.

"I don't think he was there for the wand. I mean, had he beaten us, he would have taken it, but like I said earlier, it was a test."

"Maybe. Makes me think what his brothers'll do." Conall eyed the crowd.

As they left, they handed the serving girl a few coins, but she shook her head and smiled. The boys nodded their thanks as they re-entered the morning. When they passed the market, they stopped at a fabric vendor who was so chatty that it would have been easier for a fly to get free from a spider's web. He asked about their journey, and when they said they were just leaving, he informed them that he hoped they could hunt, because it would be a while before the next hamlet. Their provisions might last a few days or a week, but after that, they'd need to get themselves a hare or even a deer. He suggested they purchase a bow and quiver from his brother, the bowyer. Conall patted his dagger and winked. He did have a question for the man, however.

"I've been wondering why this hamlet is called The Owl's Nest. 'Tis an intriguing name."

The merchant nodded and smiled. "Indeed. Long ago, a young woman stopped here during a heavy rain, but no hamlet existed, only one rundown cottage by an ash tree." He pointed across the road to what used to be a vibrant tree, but all that remained was barkless and weathered. "In the tree, a barn owl had a nest. The woman had traveled quite far and needed to sleep, so she lay on the floor of the cottage to escape the storm. The barn owl who lived in the nest kept vigil over her, preventing mice and other animals from disturbing her slumber. At sunrise, the owl screamed, waking her up, but instead of being afraid, she thanked the owl for keeping her safe. She lived in that cottage for ten years by herself, gathering berries and fruit to live on. One morning, a man and his wee son came by and, like the woman all those years ago, he needed a place to sleep. She let the father and his son sleep in the cottage. He hunted for food for them, and she made a simple home.

"As the years crept on, passersby would sometimes need a place to rest, so the man, who had taken the woman as his wife, kept vigil over his guests, like the owl. In time, some of those travelers built cottages next to the first one, and they later called this hamlet Neadúlcaban, The Owl's Nest. The man, his wife, and the boy lived out there years in the original cottage. The man and the boy lay buried beyond on a hill. Legend says their spirits keep vigil over this place as the owl had so long ago. No one knows what became of the woman, although whispers tell of how she wandered off, never to be seen again."

Conall turned back toward the bleak tree. "I wonder what happened to it."

The man adjusted some of the folded fabric. "A bolt of lightning during a severe storm. The early folk tried to chop it down for fyrewood, but no axe can even make a dent in it. So, there it sits."

"And the owl?" Conall examined a skein of thread.

"Gone. No one knows where." The man made a crooked smile and shrugged.

"Well, thank you, good sir." Aedan tugged Conall's sleeve. "We really should be on our way."

As they headed north toward the main road, the man watched them go, and—just for a moment—his eyes darkened, like those of a barn owl.

Just over the crest of a hill, the road dipped, and the boys grinned at what sat by the path. A red and gold dragon nestled in for a nap, with a hawk seated on his head. Lann squawked a few times and perched on Conall's outstretched arm. Fiachra slept soundly, wisps of gray smoke puffing out when he exhaled. Aedan heard a low purring once he was close enough, and when the dragon opened his eyes, he lifted his head up and breathed a puff of smoke.

"Hey, boy. Hope you and Lann had a good adventure on your own. You up for some flying? We could really use a break from walking."

On all fours, Fiachra stood twice as tall as Aedan. He crouched down to let the boys climb on, and Aedan held onto the dragon's thick neck. Conall held Aedan's sides. With a powerful leap, Fiachra was airborne, flapping higher over the land. Lann joined them, always staying near but away from the powerful red and gold wings. Conall unfurled the map, gripping it tightly lest it fly away. Its edges flapped, and the image showed a stick figure of Fiachra carrying the boys. For most of the morning, they soared, seeing the world from an entirely new vantage. Lakes, like scattered mirrors, reflected the sky and clouds. Tufts of trees looked as if one could run a hand over them. Speckled across the land, gray limestone karst gave the impression of timeworn scars, countering the vibrancy of heather and wildflower patches. By late afternoon, Fiachra needed to rest, and set down near the road by a circle of megaliths from ancient days. As soon as the boys hopped off, they hobbled over to it.

"I love Fiachra, but sitting on that dragon's back isn't the most comfortable ride." Conall laughed, rubbing his backside.

"I must be used it." Aedan entered the circle, his head bowed ever so slightly. "I've never seen such a massive stone circle."

"Hey, this is a sacred place." Conall remained just outside the circle. "We don't want to upset the druids who use it."

Aedan lay back on the grass, his arms behind his head. "Stop being such a worrier. I just need to stretch my back a bit."

"This place reminds me of Dún Ancróga. I miss Déaglán and Fionn. I hope they're all right." Conall grazed one of the stones with his fingertips.

A deep voice replied, "You will see them soon enough, in Tir na nÓg."

Aedan jumped up and stood with his staff ready. Conall went back-to-back with him, in a defensive stance.

In the background, Lann screeched his alarm, soaring above. Fiachra stood up on back legs and spread his massive wings, roaring in response. He huffed, staring down at Conall and Aedan.

The voice moved from one part of the circle to the other.

"They were easily distracted, the druid and the so-called hero. Once you left Dún Ancróga, I had no trouble separating their spirits from their flesh."

The boys looked everywhere, but no one was there. A whistling sound moved closer, and Conall instinctively ducked, pulling Aedan down. A metallic thud above them showed a double-sided axe embedded in one of the stones, stone shrapnel spraying. They moved to hide behind another stone, and when Conall looked back at the axe, it was gone. The towering megalith exploded around them as the axe struck, and they barely had time to cover their heads with their arms.

"You're bleeding!" Aedan saw a small gash on Conall's arm.

"I'm all right. We need to get out of here."

The man's words echoed around them. "The only place you're going is to your demise."

Fiachra spied their attacker and pulled his head back. The center of his chest glowed as he prepared to breath fire, and the red and gold scales made his chest look like a giant forge.

Aedan reached up to him, "No! Don't! No, Fiachra!"

The dragon roared, exhaling his fiery breath into the skies above.

Puzzled, Conall leaned into his friend. "What not? If he can take down whoever's attacking us —"

"No! This is sacred ground. We're not destroying a druid's circle."

"Tell *him* that!" Conall pointed at the rubble. "Whoever this is doesn't care."

The boys scrambled for another megalith, but that, too, shattered. Rubble lay around them, making it a challenge to flee. An inner stone was nearest, and as they pressed their backs against it, a thick length of chain came around, binding them to it. The blood-stained links were the size of their hand.

Conall struggled in vain. "What are we going to do?" Who *is* this?"

Trying to lean forward, they screamed as the chains tightened around him. Conall coughed up blood, and it trickled down his chin.

"My brother was a fool. He underestimated you, but I will not. Your lifeless bodies will adorn my hall, and your blood with quench my thirst. As for who I am? He who shall destroy you."

Hanging limp over the chains, the boys made guttural sounds since they couldn't speak, only able to take shallow breaths. The grass beneath them was speckled with blood. From behind a stone emerged a son of Carman. Clad in black leather armor with dark, spiked metal gauntlets, he wielded his axe over his shoulder. His face, pock-marked and scarred, was angular, with eyes whose pupils were black as pitch. He walked around the boys chained to the stone, laughing to himself. Wherever he stepped, the grass rotted. He lifted Aedan's face with a finger, blood oozing from the side of the boy's mouth. He wasn't unconscious, but close. The man leaned into Aedan's ear, and the fetid breath made the boy cringe when he heard the one word uttered.

"Dian."

He picked up Conall's head with his hand and let it fall.

"Children. Children are to be our so-called deliverers to prevent the Coah na Shirah. My mother's divinations say that you are to gather the Wands of Danu. She must be in error. How can two whelps charged with stopping such a glorious battle do so if they can't stop *me*?" The bass tone of his laughter shook the megaliths.

Dian rummaged through the boys' packs until he found the wand.

"*This*? This is supposed to stop gods?" He gripped the branch, trying to snap it with his thumb, but to his surprise, it wouldn't break. "Gah! No matter. One wand cannot help you when you are dead." He threw it to the ground.

He circled the boys, asking himself aloud whether it would just be easier to let them die chained to the stone or whether he should behead them. Either, he said, would bring him joy. As he walked around them, he spoke of the glory the Fomoragh would share once the gods had waged their meaningless battle. With humanity begging for aid, he and his brethren, along with Carman, Balor, Bres, and the others, would be their salvation, but the cost would be servitude. Dian stopped both his walking and his rant. He lifted the axe, ready to swing. Aedan had lifted his head just enough to see his fate while Conall's hung, unconscious.

"Say your farewells," Dian grunted, pulling his arm back.

Through bloody lips, Aedan spoke. "*Ó aer… Déanaim… iarracht tine.*"

Before Dian could swing, his hair burst into flame, his entire head on fyre in a matter of seconds. Crying out, Dian dropped the axe, running his hands across his head to put it out. In his attempt, his gauntlets scraped his head and face, and his leather armor began to burn as well. His pained howling reverberated among the stones. As he flailed, he tripped over the axe, cutting a gash in his leg. Consumed by fyre and wounded, he called for Carman's aid. Moments later, a dark mass approached, an unkindness of ravens, and they swarmed upon Dian, bearing him into the skies. The chains loosened and fell to the ground with a clang, the boys crumbling. Aedan pulled himself up, holding his sides. Using what was left of his strength, he dragged Conall by the arms to the central circle of stones. He hobbled around the outside, inscribing a protection circle with the alder wand. His injuries slowed him down, but he didn't give up until it was done. He fell to his knees inside the circle, managing to get out three times the dríocht he needed before collapsing.

"With Brigid's fyre and Danu's grace, we invoke their power to protect this place."

Upon the third inciting, the ground etchings glowed bright white before dimming to a pale yellow. The enchantment would hold for a while.

Aedan's eyes fluttered open, and he found himself on a straw mattress in a cottage, his body bandaged and his wounds tended to. He turned his head to look for Conall, but the pain was too much for him. His groans caught the attention of an old woman shrouded in white and gray, standing by a rickety wooden table. Candles twinkled in his foggy eyes, and the woman limp over to him. He tried to ask where he was, but she shushed him, pressing a bony finger to his lips.

"S'all right. You're safe." Her raspy voice had a lilt. "Rest, boy."

Aedan's lips quaked as he replied. "Wh-Where's Conall?"

"Your friend? He's over there on another cot." A bony finger pointed somewhere he couldn't turn his head to see. "Worry not." She smiled. "*Codail.*"

The command was gentle, yet magical. Aedan drifted asleep.

Two days passed. This time, when he awoke, he could sit up. The haggard woman tended to Conall. Her movements were deliberate and ritualistic. Aedan heard her mumbling something as he staggered over. Conall's face had grown pallid, and his breathing was shallow.

"Is-Is he all right?" He reached toward his friend, but the woman gently pushed his hand away.

"Aye. He needs more tendin' to than you." She brushed Conall's cheek with the back of her fingers. "Sleep will be his balm. Come, I made you something to eat."

"I'm not really —"

She turned with a faint smile. "Hospitality should not be refused, my boy."

Aedan craned his neck to look at Conall, but she urged him to the table. His chair wobbled and creaked as he sat, and he noticed the austere setting while she prepared his meal. A clay vase of heather brought its fragrance and vibrant color to the table, along with one of dandelions. Bunches of dried herbs lay strewn about as well.

"Here you are." She placed a bowl of broth in front of him.

Taking care, he lifted a spoon of liquid to his nose first and then swallowed its contents. Satisfied by its flavor, he finished the bowl without stopping. The woman put a basket of fresh bread before him, and he devoured that as well.

"You have a good appetite. That bodes well." She placed another large ladle of steaming broth in his bowl.

"What is this? It's delicious."

"Oh, it's an old family recipe made of hawthorne, mint, and all good things to help you heal." She cackled a laugh.

"Will my friend be all right?"

She puttered by the stove. "Aye. He has some broken ribs, scrapes and bruises, but all in all, he'll recover."

"Thank you for helping us. May I ask who you are? How did you find us?" Aedan slurped down the rest of his broth.

The woman told him the people of the hamlet called her Líadan, The Grey Lady, but she had forgotten her birth name. It had been far too long for her to recall. She went on to tell him that she had found them in the druid's stone circle protected by a dríocht when she was searching for herbs and mushrooms. Before Aedan could ask, she said that those charms only work on those of ill intentions. He opened his mouth to ask something else.

"How I got you here is of no matter." She cackled. "I have my ways. You are just outside **Neadúlcaban**."

His eyes narrowed. "Oh... We had traveled a long way from Neadúlcaban by the time we had reached the circle."

The Grey Lady fiddled about with her vials and bowls, paying him no heed. Looking defeated, he sat at Conall's side. The sleeping boy's chest rose and fell, his torso wrapped in strips of cloth. Aedan didn't see his friend's torc around his neck and gasped, but when he moved Conall's collar, there it was. He instinctively reached up to find his own.

"You have been given great gifts." The Grey Lady still worked at her table. "They will serve you well down the path."

He took Conall's hand in his own and squeezed.

"Come back. Wherever you are, Conall, come back," he whispered.

Again, he heard the woman's voice.

"He'll return when he's ready. Patience, child. Now, come, I could use your help."

Aedan hesitated, staring at Conall's face. He met the woman just outside her cottage. She had taken a seat in a rocking chair. He took the other one. She pulled a long pipe from a satchel, put it to her lips, and took a puff. She exhaled through her nose, and white smoke twisted and turned before dissipating.

"What do you need my help with?"

She took another puff. "Why was Dian after you?"

He lowered his head and turned away. "How did you know?"

"He left his axe. You have this crone wonderin' how you rid yourselves of Carman's boy."

Without turning back, he replied that he'd used a fyre dríocht.

The Grey Lady leaned forward. "Aye? Those are simple spells. You must have done something else."

"That was it." He jumped up, his voice clipped. "I said the words, he caught on fyre, and… well, was taken away."

"Sit." She said it mildly, but it was a command, nonetheless.

She explained that dríocht were simple spells, commonly used by those who appreciated magic but who had no aptitude for it. They required no lengthy training or apprenticeship. By a novice, they could be used to conjure enough fyre to light one's way or enough air to extinguish a candle. To do what Aedan had done would require a connection to larger magic.

"Would being connected to the Fonn help?"

She nodded. "Possibly. But you're not a druid or a mage. You're also too young to have mastered complex charms or spells. Even with Elder Déaglán's help."

He asked how she knew to mention him, and her response was cryptic: she had more knowledge of the druids than the druids themselves. The conversation took many turns, and every so often, Aedan would glance toward the door, toward Conall.

—⁂—

Conall's eyes fluttered open, and the mists around him only gave him a foot or two to see in front of him. No longer on the cot, he was standing on dirt. He extended his arms out to guide his movement and tried to navigate his way around the obscurity. The air itself was brisk and moist, laden with a sweetness that had no discernable name. A chorus of sounds floated around him, indistinguishable voices singing a tune that he had never heard before yet he knew it in his soul. Every so often, in the white haze, faces would coalesce then vanish. He didn't shy away or cringe from them. Then, a hawk's cry sliced through this opaque dreamlike state, and the mists parted, revealing a landscape he had never seen before. At the horizon, streaks of orange, pink, and a pearlescent white layered. Closer, mountains rested, and for as far as he could see, hills of lavender unfolded. Tears trickled from the outer corners of his eyes, and peace appeared on his face. He had never been to this place before, but yet he knew it.

"By Brigid's fyre… this is Tir na nÓg, the Otherworld."

His tears came stronger, and he fell to his knees. Conall lifted his glossy eyes to the skies.

"I must be dead."

The chorus of voices rose, and he heard his name. A kaleidoscope of butterflies swirled around him, landing on his shoulders and head. Opening his palms, they set down, taking spots on his hands. Pungent perfume of the lavender filled the air. Again, he heard his name, far off, in the fields. Making his way down a stony path, he brushed his hands over the grasses. An oak came into view, majestic and sprawling, and beneath it sat a woman in a green dress. Her brown hair was spun around the top of her head, wispy curls framing her face. Something was familiar about her.

"It is good to see you again, Conall. Come. Sit with me."

He took a long look at her, as if he could almost place her.

"Do you remember me?"

The longer he took in her features, especially her green eyes, the more he smiled.

"I-I do. You are Aedan's mother, Saoirse. But how —"

"Conall, you aren't dead. You are dreaming. Dreams and death share consciousness."

He sighed. "He misses you so much."

Saoirse smiled. "I know. I can feel it. I have tried to see him in his dreams, but something keeps me from him."

"He's conflicted. He knows the Fomoragh caused your sickness, and he wants revenge. But he also knows we have a task. I can see it in his face just how tortured he is."

Saoirse's smile shrank. She took Conall's hands in hers.

"Promise me that you will keep him on his path. Revenge will darken his soul."

He nodded.

"I am glad he has you to watch over him." She kissed both his hands. "From the first time I met your mother, I knew our sons would be friends. You were such a wee one."

"Siobhan isn't my mum. Not really." He pulled his hands back and laid them in his lap. "I was brought to their doorstep by Aer Mór of the Ársa. I don't know if she is my mother, but I do know Siobhan isn't."

"She is your mother in the ways that matter." **Saoirse** sat up. "I have never seen a woman love her child as much as she loved you."

"Oh, I know. I love her and my da as much as any son could." He smiled. "I know Aedan loves you that much."

"Listen, I don't have much time with you. I need you to give my son a message. He needs to focus on this journey with you. Tell him... tell him that I love him and that I am always with him."

"He won't believe that you said that to me. It'll sound like I'm just trying to make him feel better."

Smiling widely, **Saoirse** touched Conall's hand. "This is what you should tell him."

—⚹—

"He's coming out of it, Líadan! Come quickly!" Aedan squeezed his friend's hand.

The Grey Lady cradled Conall's head as his eyes blinked open. She patted his forehead with a moist cloth. He squinted and blinked as his eyes became used to the light of day.

Aedan rubbed his thumb on Conall's hand. "Hey, you okay? You had us worried."

It took Conall a little while to push slumber from his foggy mind, but he smiled when he saw Aedan.

"You look terrible." His voice croaked.

The Grey Lady checked Conall's bandages. "Your friend hasn't left your side. He wanted to be there when you woke up. How do you feel?"

"Hungry." He wrapped his arm around his midsection and groaned.

She touched certain spots on his chest. "Your ribs will need time to heal. I made some porridge so you can eat something. Aedan, come help me."

When they were both at the fyre with the pot of bubbling porridge, she handed him a bowl and ladled cereal into it.

"Keep an eye on him. He has an adventurous spirit, and he'll want to leave before he's fully healed. He needs rest."

Since Conall couldn't sit up, Aedan fed him. After he finished eating, Conall wanted to know more about The Grey Lady. Aedan didn't have much to say about her except that she was a skilled healer, and she knew dríocht as well as Déaglán. While they spoke, she knitted in the corner in her rocking chair. It could have been the light from the window or something else, but Aedan noticed that some of the threads of yarn illuminated as she used her knitting needles. Her white hair cascaded over her shoulders in waves, and her nubbly fingers twirled the needles with such motion that it was almost hard to follow. One foot rocked her chair as she hummed.

"Well, it looks like we'll be here for a bit." Aedan adjusted Conall's pillow. "Don't get any crazy ideas about wanting to leave too soon, either."

"Help me sit up."

"You sure? Your ribs—"

Conall used one arm to push himself up. "I just want to sit up a little."

"All right, all right. Let me help."

Once Aedan had Conall settled, they talked about what happened with Dian. Once the chain had pinned them to the stone, Conall said he didn't remember much since he was trying to breathe. Aedan's explanation helped distract him from his pain, and he only winced once or twice in the retelling. The story ended with Aedan waking up in this cottage.

"I don't remember setting the protection circle, but I do remember dragging you toward the center of the stones."

Conall stretched his head from side to side.

"I'm afraid this sets us back a bit. It'll take some time for my ribs to heal. I think that's the worst of it."

"It'll take as long as it takes." Aedan put a cup of honeyed water to Conall's lips. "You need to keep your strength up."

Conall stared at his friend. The Grey Lady called for Aedan, so that gave Conall a moment to close his eyes. He was more alert having eaten, and he could hear them both talking, but he couldn't make out their words.

"I have to go to town for some herbs and food. Let no one in, no matter what. There's a ward around the cottage to keep out black-hearted ones and mischief-makers."

The Grey Lady took up her walking stick and a basket before leaving.

"There's more porridge by the fyre." The door closed behind her.

Aedan took a chair by Conall's bed and watched as his friend rested. He was about to let his eyes close when he heard Conall groan.

"What is it?" Aedan checked the bandages. "Something wrong?"

Conall shook his head. "My legs are sore from lying down so long."

"Líadan said to rest. Do you want more porridge?"

"Did I say I was hungry?" Conall snapped. "I said my legs were sore."

Jumping up, Aedan headed toward the fyre and took up The Grey Lady's knitting. The piece was the size of a small blanket. He uncovered

Conall's legs and put the wool on them. As before, the yarn glowed in spots, moving along the stitches. Tension drained from Conall's face.

"Better?"

Conall nodded. "Aedan, how did you know?"

"A hunch, I suppose."

"The same kind of hunch you had when you used that dríocht against Dian?"

Aedan leaned forward on his thighs, his hands interlaced. They sat together, their quietude filling the void, and Conall rested. Outside, birds chirped, but then one sound pierced that softness like a blade. Conall smiled before opening his eyes.

"He's back."

At the window, a familiar face landed on the sill. Sunlight brought out the shades of orange on his chest and the bluish-grey on his back and wings, and made his yellow eyes twinkle. He cocked his head when he saw Conall. Lann found his perch on the boy's arm and chirped a few times before squawking.

"He's happy to see you." Aedan grinned. "Lann, is Fiachra with you?"

Lann made a few more successive sounds that prompted a dull roar from outside. Leaning out the window, Aedan saw his friend curled up, taking advantage of the shade beneath an ancient oak.

"Good to see you too."

Fiachra snorted and puffs of smoke rose from this nostrils. Conall brought his arm in front of his face so he could see Lann up close. The hawk's eyes glowed from the daylight, and his head moved in small, quick starts.

"You've been keeping watch, eh? Good boy. At the first sign of trouble—"

Lann screeched, and Conall laughed, holding his arm toward the window. The hawk flew out, finding the branch above Fiachra. Conall lay back, content. Aedan napped and only moved when The Grey Lady returned, her basket brimming with herbs and vegetables. She checked on Conall, who had fallen back asleep with a gentle smile, his face toward the window. Putting a shawl on Aedan, she spied the wool blanket she had been knitting draped over Conall's legs. With a knowing smirk at Aedan, she patted Conall's shoulder before returning to her table. Preparing herbs was a ritual she did every time she returned from the market. Twisting bundles of basil, bay, and mugwort, she hung them on nails in the rafters to dry, but they had other purposes as well—protection, mostly.

Busily, she did her work, and then came the time to cleanse the cottage. With the newcomers bringing in their own energy, she needed to bring harmony. With a candle beneath the white sage smudge stick, she lightly blew to get the leaves to glow. The Grey Lady wafted the smoke into the corners and over the boys, whispering her cleansing chant. Aedan woke up after she returned to the table.

"What was that you were saying?" He squinted through the haze. "I don't recognize the words."

The Grey Lady tapped the smudge stick out and left it in a dish by the window.

"Older than the gods, it is." She pulled a mortar and pestle off a shelf and sprinkled various herbs and vegetables into it. As she smashed them, an aroma rose from the bowl and pierced the sage.

"It's sweet, like perfume." Aedan wrinkled his nose. "But, also earthy."

He peered over her shoulder. The mixture in the pestle was brown, speckled with purple, orange, and green. She continued her work, ignoring him while he watched. With each ingredient, his curiosity grew, and he inhaled sharply, his eyes widening.

"What are you making? A poultice? A charm? Something to ward off the Fomoragh?"

She pulled a clay pot from a shelf, threw together some cut vegetables into it, and poured some watcher from a jug over them. Then, she spooned the herbal mixture over everything.

"Dinner." She cackled before placing the covered pot on the fyre.

He sat in her rocking chair by the table while she worked. There was much he wanted to know, like how she knew to bring them to her cottage. While he talked, she wrapped her right arm with fabric and stepped over to the kitchen window. No sooner had she extended her arm did Lann perch on it. Aedan's mouth fell open. He had never seen Lann do that with anyone else. The Grey Lady explained that the hawk flew to her cottage right after he and Conall were attacked by Dian. Instructed with keeping both boys safe, the hawk and the dragon stayed close while she went to Neadúlcaban and spoke with an old friend who had been keeping an eye out for certain travelers. The man told her about two boys who had stopped by his shop on their way out of town.

"Why don't you live in Neadúlcaban?"

"There is some knowledge meant for a rare few, Aedan. Sometimes, knowing too much can be a hindrance. If you feel well enough, perhaps you wouldn't mind collecting some peat for the fyre? There's a stack behind the cottage."

Once he was outside, she nudged Lann onto the sill while she pulled over the mortar, adding one more ingredient before pulverizing it with the pestle.

The Grey Lady glanced over at the hawk. "He's a smart one, he is." She scraped the remaining contents of the mortar into a piece of cheesecloth. Tightening it around the mixture, liquid leached out and dripped into a waiting bowl. Keeping an ear out for Aedan, she sat by Conall and touched some of the liquid to his lips. Instinctively, he licked them. She did it twice more, muttering unintelligible words. By the time Aedan returned with the peat, she was wiping off a few pears on a plate. He stacked the peat by the other pieces, putting a few pieces on the fyre and then wiping his hands on his pants. Lifting the lid off the pot, she stirred the stew with what looked like an ordinary branch.

"I've never smelled anything like it. I can't wait to eat it." He reached to taste it with his finger, but she swatted his hand with the branch.

"Patience, child. It's not quite done yet. Go tend to Conall, and I will let you know when it's ready."

Walking past Conall's cot, he observed his friend breathing deeply, fast asleep. He pulled up a stool, staring out the window where Lann had made his appearance earlier. The afternoon sun had darkened the sky to reds and oranges, with a hint of dark purple. He turned his ear and heard Fiachra snoring still beneath the oak.

"So much has happened to us since we started this journey. We both had just started our Nascah, and now look at us. Two lads in search of ancient magic. How is this even possible? It feels like it was only yesterday when I had that fight with my da and left. Will I ever see him again? To lose both parents would... would —"

He felt something on his arm, and it was Conall's hand.

"I have to tell you something," Conall grumbled, blinking himself awake.

"Huh? Weren't you just sleeping?" Aedan chuckled.

Smiling, Conall patted his friend's arm. "Until you started talking, I was. But listen, I want you to know something. Earlier today, I was —"

The Grey Lady brought a small wooden table next to the cot, and then a stool for herself. She returned with three bowls of vegetable stew. Conall felt well enough to feed himself, something that made Aedan happy, and The Grey Lady asked them to share what their most memorable meal was. For Aedan, it had been his da's freshly baked oaten bread. Conall regaled them about the berry pies his mother made for Lughnasadh, the beginning of the harvest season. He remembered taking one of the bilberry pies and eating it until he got sick of them, but he didn't care. The Grey Lady pointed to the stew they were eating, sharing the story of how her mother used to make it on special occasions. She went on to say there was no specific recipe; whatever vegetables were in season worked equally as well, but potatoes and turnips gave it a sweetness that she enjoyed. The ambient candlelight from all around the room gave her cheeks a rosy glow.

Having scraped the last stew remnants from his bowl, Conall exhaled sharply, commenting on how stuffed he was. The Grey Lady returned to her table to scour the bowls with water and a bunch of sticks, leaving them to dry on the table. She put a pot of water on the fyre to prepare some tea.

"It's good to see you feeling a little better." Aedan patted his own belly. "A hearty meal tends to do that for me."

"I slept well. Better than I have in a while." He looked toward the window. "Aedan, I need to tell you something. Earlier today, while I was sleeping, I had the strangest dream, or at least I think it was a dream. I opened my eyes, but I was in a foggy place. At some point, that haze cleared. I could see the most beautiful place I had ever laid eyes on. I believe I was in Tir na nÓg."

Aedan laughed. "You couldn't have been. Only spirits of the dead go there. Must have been some dream, though."

"That's just it. I don't think it was one. Seated under an oak tree was a woman. She knew me."

"Oooh, how strange." Aedan shook his hands and chuckled. "Did you ever find out who she was? Some Sídhe or fairy?"

Conall nodded. "I did. It was your mother."

The words turned Aedan's smiles to a glare so strong that, had he been a cockatrice, Conall would have turned to stone.

"What are you saying? How could it have been my mother?" He stood so fast that his stool fell over. "You're mistaken. It couldn't have been her."

"Aedan—"

"No! It wasn't her. You couldn't have seen her. How-How can you be so cruel?" He stormed out onto the porch, the door slamming behind him.

The Grey Lady hobbled to see if Conall was all right, and he had clamped his eyes shut to keep the tears in. She pulled a stool to his bedside.

"What's wrong with Aedan?"

After a few deep breaths, Conall explained his dream to her, except what Saoirse had told him to say to Aedan. Her expression grew solemn, the rosiness fading from her cheeks. She pressed a hand on his. He went to move away, but then relented, allowing her to console him.

"Why would he think I would hurt him? I *did* see his mother. She even told me to tell him something that only the two of them would know. I was about to tell him when he ran out."

Her smile returned the glow to her cheeks.

"What was it?"

"She told me to…" He paused to take a breath, and then opened his mouth to sing.

"'Let the moon sing you to sleep, dear child. Let the moon bring you sweet slumber. And the stars will sing in harmony, a joyous tune, one only a mother knows. Moon and stars, moon and stars, their voices sing of dreams aplenty.'"

The Grey Lady put a knuckle to her eye and wiped away a tear. "Oh, that was lovely. Surely, a mother's love for her little lad."

A low voice came from near the fyre. "My mum used to sing that to me when I was a baby. Every time I was scared, she would hum it while she held me."

In silhouette, Aedan stood, and as he went closer to The Grey Lady and Conall, the candlelight twinkled in the tears that had run down his face. He knelt by Conall's bedside, unable to look his friend in the face, and took his hand.

"I'm sorry I lashed out. I know you would never joke with me about something as important to me as my mum. Forgive me."

Conall put his hand around Aedan's. "Nothing to forgive."

"Did she say anything else?"

"She wanted me to tell you that she's tried to reach you through your dreams. That's how I was able to see her. Dreams and death share a consciousness. She wasn't sure why she couldn't see you. That was why she reached out to me." He lifted his friend's chin. "Her exact words were, 'Tell my son I love him more than the stars love the moon, because it's their light that makes the moon shine so brightly. He makes me shine, even here. I will keep trying to reach him, as long as it takes.'"

Throwing his arms around Conall, he cried into his friend's shoulder, such heaving sobs that the cot shook. Conall patted him on the back, cringing from the pain, but he didn't stop Aedan.

"It's all right. Let it out. Let it out."

Two weeks passed, and one morning, sunrise burst forth, hindered by clouds, with just enough light poking through to show that morning had indeed arrived. Conall woke up, getting his bearings, and looked over the side of the bed to see Aedan, in a fetal position on the floor, wrapped in the shawl, his head resting on his arm. Yawning, Conall stretched as far as his arms would let him, his ribs a little tender still.

"Time to rise, little ones." The Grey Lady nudged Aedan with her stick. "I don't know why you insist on sleeping on the floor when there's a perfectly good mattress."

Breakfast came and went, and Conall felt strong enough to take a walk. He hadn't been out of the bed since he arrived, except to heed nature's call, and even then, Aedan had to assist him. This time, he wanted to go out on his own. At first, Aedan insisted he go with him, but The Grey Lady said she needed his help gathering mushrooms and herbs.

It took Conall a little bit to sit up since he hadn't used those muscles in a while without help. Next to his cot was a walking stick, no doubt left by The Grey Lady. He went onto the porch and heard the birds singing louder than he was used to. The path from the cottage split, one path heading toward Neadúlcaban, the other, toward the forest and, beyond, a lake. Cool breezes toyed with the branches, rustling the leaves, and he inhaled the brisk air. He had been so used to the peat-warmed air from the cottage that he took a few more deep breaths to feel the chill touch his insides. Conall examined both paths a few times before choosing the one lakebound. The stick sank into the soft earth a bit as he walked. The Grey Lady had said she wasn't far from Neadúlcaban, but this road didn't seem familiar. How far *were* they from town, he wondered. It didn't take him long to find the lake, smaller than the ones he had seen. Mirror-like, the water reflected the sky above, and the pattern of clouds and rising sunlight was unlike anything he had experienced. In the center of the lake was a small island, no bigger than the cottage, and it had some objects on it, but the island was far enough away from him that he couldn't tell. The path turned north around the lake, and as he progressed, the island kept catching in his peripheral vision. From a different vantage, he made out a barkless tree, similar to the one he had seen in the hamlet, albeit a bit shorter. Fifty feet down the path, an old, weathered raft was propped up on a rock. Unlike the view from when he began his travels around the lake, this one afforded him a place to see the cottage to the left in the woods, its peat smoke wisping from the chimney, the shoreline that continued south, and the island to his right. In the distance, he made out more smoke, presumably from the hamlet itself.

The raft was made from logs tied together, each one stripped of its bark and made smooth. Instead of rope, leather straps were interwoven around each one, attached with nails—not a typical raft by his standards. Something moved on the island, perhaps an animal or even something attached to the tree, and that was all he needed to see. Without a paddle, he lay on the raft, chest down—surprised that his chest wasn't sore anymore—and used his arms to paddle his way to the island. He had to stop after about a dozen strokes, letting his arms rest and allowing the raft to glide across the smooth waters. It took him half an hour to reach the island, which seemed even smaller once he stepped onto it. Sure enough, a storm-battered tree jutted forth, one lone silver branch extending out with a forked end. A few feet from the tree was a cairn of smooth stones waist-high to him, stacked in a unique pattern. Conall walked around it, his mouth agape at the intricacies of how each stone had been placed. He leaned in to get a closer look, and a screech made him jump. At the center of the tree was a hole where a barn owl perched just inside.

Conall bowed his head, not sure what else to do. He hadn't brought anything to make an offering, assuming this was otherworldly.

"My apologies, great owl. I didn't mean to disturb you."

The owl took off around the lake. Its screeching echo rippled outward, making the hair stand up on Conall's arms. It continued to soar along the shoreline, shrieking its cry. Standing in the center of this tiny isle, he turned around, taking in the entire lake. With smoothness like he had never seen, the water showed the landscape and sky in reverse. Up and down, left and right. A perfect balance of sky, earth, air, and water.

"I think I understand." He whispered, as if speaking to a greater being or sacred presence.

Upon its return, the owl landed on the far end of the forked branch. Something about the way it sat proudly made Conall smile. He walked under the branch.

"Not sure what you're trying to tell me, ulcabán, but I will think on it."

—⚜—

He walked into the cottage to the confounded looks of Aedan and The Grey Lady who had been untangling skeins of yarn. Conall's distant expression and faint smile remained on him the rest of the day. When either one asked him where he had gone, he didn't say a word. He nodded. During supper, Conall put spoon after spoon of stew into his mouth, staring off. Every time Aedan tried to engage him, The Grey Lady shook her head. Finally, when she could see how frustrated he was, she leaned into his ear.

"He's had an awakening. When he's ready, he'll tell us. Patience."

A full moon hung in the night sky. Aedan stepped onto the porch for some fresh air and looked out at the stars, taking in a deep breath through his nose holding it, and exhaling slowly through his mouth. After the third breath, he sat on the steps.

"Magical, isn't it?" came a voice on the porch. It was Conall in one of the rocking chairs.

Aedan gasped. "Brigid's fyre, Conall! I didn't see you there." He gazed back skyward. "'Tis indeed that. Magical."

"I've been making sense of what I saw today. That's why I've been aloof."

Taking another rocking chair, Aedan moved the chair with his foot.

"What did you see?"

Conall told the story of the island and the owl. He explained everything in minute detail, down to the ruffling leaves on the trees along the shore to the echoes of the barn owl.

"The Grey Lady said you'd had some sort of awakening."

Nodding toward the moon, Conall replied that he had.

"We have been so focused on getting the wands and finishing our task that we haven't tried to understand the bigger picture. You and I were told by the Elder Circle that it's been foretold that we are to fulfill the Drag-onHawk prophecy. Have you stopped to ask why? Do we even know why the Ársa and the Fonn want to bring about the Coah na Shirah?"

Aedan's foot stopped moving.

"Líadan, could you join us for a moment?"

Aedan gave her his chair while he sat on the porch. She had her pipe and took a few puffs in succession.

"Something on your mind, lads? She leaned back and moved her foot to rock the chair.

Conall turned his chair toward her.

"We were curious about something and wondered if you could help us."

She puffed again on her pipe. "If I can."

"You know all about our quest. But Aedan and I don't understand why these two groups of ancient gods would bring the war to our world. What would happen if they did? Why should we be stopping it?"

The Grey Lady puffed three times, exhaling in one controlled plume. The boys watched her rock a little while before she stopped her foot.

"I suppose you wouldn't take as your answer, because of the proph-ecy?"

They shook their heads. She laughed and puffed again.

"No. It's not time for you to know."

"What?" Aedan rose and clenched his fists. "It's not time? After all that—"

"Sit." She pointed her pipe toward the porch, and her grey eyes bore into him.

Glaring, he complied in a huff.

She puffed three times. "In the grand scheme, you are but wee ones, children playing a game of the gods. Dian and Dubh were testing you. Carman's sons would not be so easily defeated. What they did learn is that you won't back down. That concerns them more than what you can do. The Fomoragh see you as two boys who've dabbled in warrior training and magic, neither skill of which would protect you if the Dark Ones brought their full force upon you."

She reached over and touched Conall on the arm.

"However, it is that very warrior training and magic that will keep you alive. If you're smart. They're best known for their ability to deceive and manipulate. Keep a clear head about you, and you may just fulfill that prophecy. Now, I may not be able to tell you *why* the Ársa and Fonn want to wage war, but what I *can* tell you is much more important."

A few more puffs on her pipe brought a white cloud above her head. In that, shapes formed, of people and objects, as she prepared to tell them a story.

"Before I begin, I have to ask. Conall, what did you think of your journey this morning?"

He went to the edge of the porch and looked out at the stars.

"When we passed through Neadúlcaban, the merchant's story about how the hamlet got its name, 'The Owl's Nest,' seemed interesting. It made sense to me. But this morning," he turned toward them, "I walked to the lake and traveled out to another owl's nest, and that one..."

The Grey Lady chuckled. "Gave you insight."

"It did. The polished lake reflected the sky, the land, and the air all around, and I could take it all in. I saw the world before me, with time to make sense of it. Everything became clear to me."

"It felt like you had all the answers you needed, didn't it?" She exhaled more white smoke.

"In that one brief moment, I did have all the answers. But when I left the island..."

"Those thoughts melted away, like the fading echo of the owl's cry. Don't worry. You'll remember when you need to. So, here's what I want to tell you."

12 | WANDS OF DANU

After the Ársa and Fonn, the First Ones, had laid out the world, and the gods grew in number, power was split among more and more. By the time the Tuatha Dé Danann rose to prominence, a safeguard was needed to keep the gods in check, should they become too powerful. Such an object would hold the key to containing the energies of immortals—a binding charm. Gathered together were the greatest blacksmiths of all the known world, mortal and Sídhe alike, called into service by the First Ones, who put out a challenge to create this safeguard. Artisans renowned for their craft turned to the Ársa and Fonn for any guidance, and it came by means of one sentence:

"Let the year be your guide, to shape that which will protect the world."

First from this came the idea that one object should be made, to represent the year as a whole. Blacksmiths and masons had a moon cycle to come up with something. Furious fyres raged and stone fell to the hammer and chisel. When the final day arrived, the artisans had come to a consensus and each group brought one gift before the First Ones. From the smithy came a circular shield, carved with runes and glyphs, locking in the great magic—an enchantment to use in dire need. Carved with icovellavna, intricate woven line work to bind it to the world, the shield was a masterpiece. Then, the masons came, bringing with them a wheel made of different stones, also adorned with icovellavna for binding. Around the side edge, symbols of power made this an item worth much to the gods and humanity.

The First Ones deliberated for another month, and they brought their decision to the assembly of mortal and Sídhe. The eagle, Eagna, spoke for the Fonn.

"With great care and deliberation, along with craft, these objects have been made, with attention to detail and purpose." She paused. "However, who would take care of either a shield or a wheel? How could one be its sole caretaker? Should that one fall to temptation, as magic knows neither goodness nor evil, who could stand against him or her?"

Mhór Cré, speaking for the Ársa, agreed with her.

This caused turmoil among the mortals and Sídhe, and they deliberated once more. Looking back at that which was supposed to guide them, they saw the year as comprised of thirteen pieces, months in the calendar. Back to the blacksmiths and masons the task went. Metalworkers took inspiration from the natural world and ultimately forged their unanimous idea with combinations of metals to bring out the beauty needed for such an object. The stoneworkers, observant as they were, came to another agreement, and their work took shape over the next cycle of the moon.

Before the First Ones the artisans came again, and the smithy presented thirteen metal rods, each the length of a forearm, and each a piece of art in itself. From the masons came thirteen stones, similar in shape to the metal rods, and each was of a different type of rock. Some bore jewels, others had streaks of color found within the rocks themselves. For yet another month, the First Ones convened.

Grá, the horse, spoke for the Fonn, and he voiced his reply:

"As before, these came from a place of inspiration and love, with attention to detail. That there are thirteen brought us joy, but metal rods or stone would be hard to contain."

For the Ársa, Mhór Aer agreed.

A third time, these artisans brought together their ideas, and they looked back at the guiding premise of their task. Since the tool must safeguard the world, it must come from the world, one that lives and grows, because that is what a world must do. The blacksmiths and masons abandoned their smithies and workshops, stepping into nature. Where can we find balance, they asked one another, and how can we draw from that example? For most of the month, they wandered the land, until one day a storm ravaged everything. Finding shelter under a broad oak to sleep and take shelter from the rain, the blacksmiths and masons pondered their dilemma. They had a short time before they had to speak to the First Ones.

At sunrise, they awoke, and they thanked the mighty tree for its protection. A wynd blew through the leaves, and then the idea was born. When next they gathered before the Ársa and Fonn, the blacksmiths and masons brought forth a cloth bundle. With all eyes on their creation, Giobniu, the god of the smithy, unfurled the cloth to reveal branches, each the length of a forearm, from thirteen different trees.

"We bring to you, O First Ones, that which will protect our world. Not of metal or of stone, they are of the trees, symbols of life everlasting."

The First Ones examined the wands, and the lion, Ciall, of the Fonn, addressed him.

"We accept this offering. It is of the earth, and for the earth."

Mor Tine of the Ársa agreed.

The question then arose into whose care would these wands be delivered, to keep them from evil. Mhór Uiscí rose from his seat.

"She who has been the guardian of all, the nurturer and earth mother, Danu."

Danu, eyes wide, accepted the offer, but she had a plan and asked Cernunnos for his bow.

"First Ones and gods, mortals and Sídhe, cover your eyes." Danu lifted the bow to the heavens.

Once they complied, she ensured none could see, and shot each branch to the farthest reaches of the world. As she returned the bow to Cernunnos, she kissed his brow.

The god of love, Aengus, songbirds on his shoulders, asked why she wanted all to be blind. Surely, he said, the vision of the gods could not be prevented by a hand over one's eyes. In all her grace, she touched him on the cheek.

"'Tis an act of trust."

He nodded and took his place among the other gods and Sídhe.

"Henceforth," said she, "these thirteen wands shall be called the Slata Danann, the Wands of Danu. In time of dire necessity, one of Ársa and one of the Fonn together must collect them. Only then, can their power be used. So it shall be."

All bowed their agreement, and the First Ones smiled, receding into the mists.

—⚏—

With her story complete, The Grey Lady made a casual gesture with her bony finger and a breeze dispersed the cloud of smoke. Entering the cottage, she commented that it was time for tea. Conall and Aedan stared at one another for a bit before they heard her call their names.

"Well, that explains why you and I have to do this." Conall scratched his head.

Aedan grumbled.

The tea smelled of lavender and honey. The Grey Lady puttered about and brought three pieces of honeycake to the table, humming. Conall asked her why she seemed so happy, she just kept humming, even when she put a piece of cake in her mouth. The boys had questions about the wands, but she shook her head, enjoying her cake. When they finished, she asked Aedan to fetch some peat. As soon as they were alone, she tugged Conall's sleeve. When he turned, she kissed him on the cheek, patting it with her gnarled hand. Aedan saw a weird smile on his friend's face when he returned.

"What happened?" He stacked the peat in the corner.

"I'm not sure." Conall blushed.

The boys retired a short time later, and The Grey Lady sat in her chair knitting, still humming. When the sun rose, they found themselves alone in the cottage with parcels of food on the table along with two woolen blankets. Pinned to one was a note.

"Trust your instincts and each other. - Líadan"

They searched for her outside, but she was nowhere, and she didn't respond to their calls. Finally, they secured all their parcels to their packs and went on their way, taking the path away from Neadúlcaban. Conall felt his ribs, and they didn't hurt. They ached the night before, but then The Grey Lady kissed him on the cheek. Could that kiss have healed him completely, he wondered.

Beyond the trees, Fiachra and Lann joined them, soaring above. Conall looked back and saw the lake through the forest. As if knowing he was looking, the owl screeched. Aedan had the map out. The dragon and the hawk played in the skies. Everything seemed to be back to normal for the moment. Conall bit into a pear, glancing at the map as he walked. Dark patches of forests showed up on the parchment as the road meandered. Even Fiachra and Lann appeared in stick figure form next to him and Aedan.

"Any idea where we're headed?" He finished the pear, wiping his mouth with his hand.

Aedan put the map away. "Not a clue."

Reaching behind his shoulder, Conall pulled the Fearnslat from a pocket in his pack. He thought back to the feeling he had the day before when he was on that tiny island. Blue, cloudless skies stretched out before them as the path gradually shifted from dirt to the limestone karst once more. In through his nose he took air, and out through his mouth. He had to block out the noises of the dragon and hawk. The only sound he allowed himself to hear was his own footsteps. Aedan was a little bit ahead of him. In Conall's hands, the alder wood felt brittle, as if with one snap, he could break it. He even tried to bend it ever so slightly, to see if it would give. It would. Why would the wands be so fragile? That didn't make sense to him. It looked like any other branch from a tree. Then, recalled that Dian had tried to snap it, and it didn't. He asked himself if the wand had the power of the old wizards and witches he had heard about as a child. His mother used to tell him about the hoary crones whose wands could shoot bolts of energy or manipulate others. Even the wizards of old could stop mighty beasts in their path with the wave of a staff. Conall pictured himself in a flowing cloak, waving the Fearnslat at an oncoming horde of creatures, bringing them to a standstill or turning them into stone. In his dreams over the next days, he imagined himself a great druid, like Déaglán, whose magic was unmatched. When he'd wake up, always around sunrise, he would feel well-rested. Something was different about him, something he couldn't pinpoint. When Aedan awoke, Conall had already prepared their morning meal of brown bread, butter, and bilberry jam that The Grey Lady had tucked into one of her parcels.

"Good morning," Conall spoke through a mouth filled with bread.

"Yeah, yeah. A morning it is." He cracked his neck and stretched his arms. "You're awfully chipper."

"Just in a good mood. Here." Conall handed him a sandwich.

"We've covered quite a bit of ground." Aedan fit half of it in his mouth. "So, what's with the smiling? You've been doing it for days."

"Ever since we left Líadan, things are different. Maybe it's because I feel like myself again. I was in that bed for so long. My ribs are fully healed too." He patted his chest and polished off his sandwich.

Eating with one hand and holding the map with the other, Aedan used his finger to follow the road. An Ogham glyph showed up.

"Would you look at that? I know where the next wand is. Let's get a move on."

Over a hill, a copse of holly trees grew, about a dozen. Their spiky, glossy leaves seemed light green in the morning light, and the berries a rich red. Each tree stood about ten feet tall, and the leaves grew down to the ground. Fiachra set down in a field nearby to eat, and Lann perched on Conall's arm.

"Careful, my friend. These berries are poisonous." Conall wagged his finger at the hawk.

The wynd carried with it a smell, one that they each recognized. Toward the grazing dragon they went and made out a string of nearby horses, also enjoying the intermittent grasses that grew between the limestone. Aedan patted Fiachra, who seemed uninterested in the horses, on the back.

"You must be hungry if you're not paying attention to them." He laughed. "Good boy."

Conall had moved a bit closer to the horses, his mouth open in awe, but then he joined Aedan.

"Wild horses. It's been so long since I've seen any. According to the song of the druids, the Tineslat would be from a stallion in the holly."

Aedan moved his head around, examining the horses.

"What're you doing?" Conall patted Fiachra.

"Looking for the stallions. You just have to look for — "

"I know how to determine a stallion from a mare, you dolt." Conall chuckled. "Question is, even if we find any stallions, how would we know which one is *the* one?"

Aedan furrowed his brow. "We need to find the dominant one. I think I know which one it is."

Among the string, one horse stood a bit taller than the others when his head was raised. A chestnut brown, he had a white blaze down his nose, and his tail was entirely white. He paid no attention to the boys' or dragon's presence. Conall decided to head to the trees. In the background, the horses whinnied and carried on, but he was more intrigued by the perfectly shaped conical trees. Not a branch poked through to blemish the line of the foliage. Each tree grew through the limestone, something he scratched his head about. Aedan seemed less interested as he approached.

"What're you looking at? They're trees. We just need to figure out how to get the stallion to give us the Tineslat. You don't suppose it's just one of these branches?" He reached toward a tree.

The sound of the earth rumbling came next, and before they knew it, the horses were circling them, moving their heads and snorting. Aedan withdrew his hand, but it was too late. The dominant stallion stepped closer and neighed, rearing up. The boys backed away slowly. As soon as they were outside the copse, the horses calmed down. They didn't leave the trees, though.

"Gah! Now what do we do?" Aedan clenched his fists. "The horses won't let us near the trees."

Conall tried offering an apple to one of the mares, but she backed up and snorted. The stallion stepped between her and the boy, making no noises. Conall tried to offer the apple to the stallion instead, but the horse knocked it away. Every time one of the boys tried to get closer to the trees, that one horse was there. Finally, they returned to Fiachra, who had fallen asleep, and sat up against his scaly body.

"So frustrating." Chunk of bread in hand, Conall tore off pieces and shoved them in his mouth. "Any ideas?"

Arms behind his head, Aedan had his eyes closed.

"Aedan, how can you sleep at a time like this?"

"It's easy. I need a nap. You should try it."

Conall grunted. He watched the horses, who had left the trees but remained close to them. The stallion was off to the side, grazing, and he seemed to be watching the boys. Eventually, Conall fell asleep. Midday, a crack of thunder from an approaching thunderstorm woke the boys with a start. Storm clouds rolled closer from the west, and they lit up from the inside. Intermittent lightning struck the earth in the distance. Westward wynds accelerated their approach.

"What should we do?" Aedan peered over the dragon's body. "Our tent won't withstand that kind of storm."

"Maybe Fiachra could fly us somewhere?"

Aedan patted his dragon. "Possibly. I checked the map, though, and it didn't show anywhere with caves or even a small town. We can stay ahead of the storm, at least. We'll come back here after it passes."

"What about the horses? They have no stable or shelter?"

"If they're smart, they'll move. Wild horses know how to take care of themselves."

Conall sent Lann flying, and the boys mounted Fiachra. They circled around, the blackening sky rolling in like a dark tide. Each lightning strike came closer together, and the air vibrated with the subsequent thunder. Flapping his massive red and gold wings, the dragon headed east, but Conall looked west at the copse of holly and the horses, who had moved back to the field to graze. Higher the dragon flew, and Aedan turned him to see the storm. North and south of it, the grey stretched, with no glimmer of a reprieve. They were far enough away to safely see the holly copse in the distance, and the storm was almost upon it. Aedan turned Fiachra eastward again. The rippling effect of the thunder shook the air so much that the great beast roared. You can do this, boy, Aedan thought. Then, they heard Lann's shrieks nearby. He circled about Fiachra and the boys, his cries rivaling the thunder. Conall saw the hawk turn back toward the copse.

He leaned into Aedan. "Follow him!"

"Conall, we —"

"Do it! He's heading back toward the horses. Please!"

Grunting, Aedan used his right knee to signal Fiachra to turn, and they saw Lann ahead. Directly over the trees, a grey blanket sat, its electric tendrils striking more frequently. The wynds made it a challenge for the dragon to stay on course, and rain pelted them. One bolt of lightning irradiated the skies, and in its wake, some of the holly were on fyre. Lann squawked even louder. Two knees from Aedan into Fiachra prodded the dragon faster. Water ran down the boys' faces, with Aedan trying to steer with one hand while clearing his eyes. Another blinding flash made the dragon rear back, but he then pressed on. Once they passed through the curtain of rain, Conall pointed.

"The trees! They're burning!"

Fiachra flew closer and banked around the copse.

"Some of the horses are trapped!"

Despite the torrent, the fyre had spread from tree to tree. Most of the horses had fled to find cover, but three were surrounded by flames. Neighing, they kept close to each other. Fiachra landed, and Conall jumped down. He got as close as the fyre would let him, trying to assess the situation. At one point, he heard neighing near him, and the stallion reared up by one of the flaming trees. Through the sheets of rain, he looked for an opening. Aedan made his way over.

"If we could let the trees burn, they would eventually die out." He had to shout. "But the horses might die before that happens."

The stallion moved toward the trees, and the fyre burned his flank. His neighing rose above the thunder. Neither of the boys could get close enough to check the horse for severe injury, but the singed hair was obvious. Conall paced, his hands flailing. With the storm raging and the trees consumed, there wasn't anything they could do. Wynds had picked up as well, making things more precarious. As if struck by lightning himself, Conall's eyes widened and fumbled in Aedan's pack. Before his friend could ask what he was doing, Conall removed the Fearnslat.

He gripped it in both hands in front of him and closed his eyes.

"*Ó tine, Déanaim iarracht aer.*"

Nothing happened. He shook his head, grunting, and clenched his eyes shut.

"*Ó tine, Déanaim iarracht aer. Ó tine, Déanaim iarracht aer!*" At the third try, he was shouting.

Air circled around the holly tree on fyre nearest to him, spinning faster and faster, until the flames were extinguished. Aedan, seeing the opportunity, ran toward the trapped horses, waving his arms to get them to leave the fiery circle. Conall fell to one knee, drained. The three horses escaped, but he didn't see his friend exit as well. Before he could go in after him, the stallion charged ahead, and after a few moments, galloped with Aedan lying over his back. Conall put him on the ground clumsily since he was worn out from the dríocht. Aedan's face and clothes were singed, and he was coughing. A shadow covered them suddenly, and the rain stopped pouring down. It was Fiachra, stretching out one of his wings.

"Are you all right?" Conall assessed Aedan's face.

Nodding, Aedan tried to sit up. His coughing had diminished.

"The burn doesn't look too bad. You're going to need some new clothes, though."

While Aedan caught his breath, Conall stepped out into the rain to check on the horses who had huddled together. He took slow steps toward the stallion who, despite his injury, stood tall. Eventually, the horse allowed Conall to get close enough to see his flank. The burned area had singed hair, but it was too hard to tell about the skin beneath it. With nothing he could do in the rain, Conall returned to Aedan under Fiachra's wing to wait out the storm.

By the time the worst of it had passed, and as the grey clouds dissipated, the sun was close to the horizon with streaks of purple and red in the west. The fyre was out, and the holly copse had been destroyed. Only burnt remnants of each tree jutted forth, still smoldering. One by one, the wisps of smoke ceased. Conall walked among the cinders, his lip quivering. He couldn't blame this on Dian or Dubh or Carman. This was simply an act of nature. Aedan pulled some lavender oil from this pack.

"Conall, come help me. We need to treat the stallion's burn."

Conall lingered for a moment. He comforted the horse while Aedan poured some oil on a cloth and lightly touched the wound. At first, the horse resisted, but the scent of the oil calmed him. Smiling, Aedan retrieved one of the blankets that The Grey Lady had made and put it over the horse's back. Small wisps of light, like burning embers, appeared and disappeared all over the wool.

"I saw what the blanket did for you, so I figured I would try this."

"Well done, my friend." Conall patted the stallion's shoulder. "You'll be just fine, boy."

Songbirds sang their tunes as the golden disc sank. The boys dined on dried meat and bread under the stars. Aedan had applied some of the lavender oil to his own burns, and the scent helped him fall asleep leaning against Fiachra. In the distance, Lann squawked to let them know he was around, and smiling, Conall succumbed to slumber.

Aedan awoke to a nudge on his shoulder, and when he swatted, his hand met a horse's nose. The stallion snorted. Yawning, Aedan checked on the horse's burn and found it was almost healed. The blanket had done its work. In the early morning light, the stumps of holly were in silhouette, a stark reminder of nature's fury. The horses scampered nearby, but the stallion remained with the boys. Lann landed on Conall's arm, greeting them with chirps and screeches.

"It's sad about the holly. I don't know how long it will take to grow back, if it will." Aedan crouched by one of the scorched stumps.

Conall nodded. "I wonder if we'll ever see the Tineslat now."

They prepared to move on, adjusting their packs. They had mounted Fiachra when the stallion approached, a stick in its mouth. Conall took it.

"It-It's a holly branch. And it's not burned." He looked at the horse. "Is this…"

The stallion struck the ground with one hoof and snorted.

"Thank you. May your holly grow back stronger than ever."

Back in the skies, they headed north for a while until a town came into view built around a river. The stone bridge had wooden platforms built on either side to support what seemed to be cottages or perhaps merchants. To the north of the river, a gathering of armed men and women engaged in sparring, and there also sat a stable. To the south, the square with an elder tree whose trunk was so thick and whose roots were so gnarled that it looked like a sleeping giant, one that children were playing on. After making a few passes around the town, Fiachra set down near the stables under an oak.

"He can stay here while we explore the town. I need to find some new clothes." Aedan looked down at his burned tunic and boots.

As they walked past the sparring grounds, they saw swordplay, staffs, and archery practice. Conall commented on how it seemed odd to have the warriors out in the open with no wall or barrier to contain their training. Aedan was more smitten with a meat merchant near the bridge whose market had various fowl clucking in a pen behind him. Roasting venison over glowing embers sat next to this table. As soon as the boys walked up, the jolly man roared laughter, his rosy cheeks plump.

"G'day, lads. You're not from here, it seems. Well, step on up. You look hungry, too."

"G'day, merchant. My friend and I were wondering where we might be. Our map doesn't show a name for this town." Conall couldn't help but smile back at the man.

Meanwhile, Aedan seemed much more intrigued by the meat. He inhaled deeply and closed his eyes.

"I think I'll like it here." He muttered, licking his lips.

The merchant sliced a little piece of venison off for Aedan who all but inhaled it.

"My boys, you're in Arvador. Now, what can I get you? Did you like that meat? I roasted it with rosemary and thyme."

Aedan gasped and pulled his friend back.

"The legend of Arvador!"

13 | ARVADOR AND THE TWO KINGDOMS

The legend of Arvador?" Conall's face contorted.

Aedan leaned in even closer. "My da told me. It's a story about two princes who fell in love, but their families didn't allow it. They stretched across the river and became that stone bridge."

Conall threw his hands up. "And? There has to be more to the story."

Laughing, Aedan lightly jabbed him with his elbow. "Of course, but that's all I remember."

Laughter from the merchant got the boys' attention.

"So, y'know some of the story, eh? Every Beltaine at midnight, Sionainn and Uaine stand on the bridge and finally get to hold each other's hands. We gather at the river to await their arrival and celebrate their moment." The merchant wiped a tear. "A shame Beltane won't be around for a few weeks. It's truly a sight to behold."

"How beautiful." Conall picked up a burlap bag of dried venison. "How much for this?"

"Twopence, my boy."

Arvador wasn't like Neadúlcaban or Rusdare, both of which paled in size by comparison. Outward from the main road on either side were groupings of cottages. Both kingdoms had fallen to time, but each side of the river retained distinct aspects. Conall wanted to explore the market, and Aedan was drawn to the sparring grounds, so they agreed to meet up later in the day.

Nestled between a baker and a farm stand was a small cottage with the word LEABHAIR carved above the door. Conall pushed the door open, poked his head in, and couldn't believe his eyes. Stacks of books and scrolls towered against the walls. Tables placed haphazardly looked like islands in a literary sea. Intermingled with the books were glass paper-weights that kept stacks of parchment in place. Light that managed to find its way inside from the dusty windows made these spheres sparkle. He brushed his fingers across books of all sizes, ranging from great tomes to smaller books the size of the palm of one's hand. When he lifted one up, swirls of dust remained in its wake. Some covers were etched and gilded, while others had the rough craftsmanship of jagged boards and weak binding. Curled parchment bore inked manuscripts with icovellavna around the edges or simply glyphs in Ogham or other languages. From the ceiling hung oil lamps, their threadlike black smoke having darkened the wood above. The scent of musty paper blended with peat from a nearby fyre, tinged with the sweetness of white sage. Toward the back, Conall saw a ladder that led to a second level with heaps and piles of more books. It was from that loft that an old voice cracked.

"Something I can help you with?" Emerging from the shadows, an elderly woman placed her bony hand on the ladder.

"You have some incredible discoveries." Conall turned in circles. "I'm actually just looking around if that's all right."

"Of course, dear. There's no rhyme or reason for the piles. You never know when you'll find a treasure." She cackled as she stepped down the ladder, waiting until both feet were on a rung before she descended to the next.

Conall turned a thick book around in his hands, examining the binding. "Are some of these from the royal library?"

The woman smiled. "You know of that, do you? Aye. The kingdom may be gone, but its legacy remains." She pulled a cloth from her sleeve and slapped the books with it, making clouds of dust.

"Are books from both kingdoms here?"

She blew on a stack of books, contributing to the haze all around. "Mostly from the southern kingdom, I'm afraid. If you're keen, you'll find a few from the northern kingdom strewn about."

He continued to forage through the landscape of literature, browsing through some texts, gasping when he found a particularly unique one. The woman brought a pot of tea from the back of the shop and poured a cup, offering him some. Conall approached and extended his hand, but when he saw her face, he gasped before taking the steaming cup.

"I-I'm sorry. I didn't mean—"

"Tut, tut, my child. It's not the first time, and it won't be the last."

Her eyes were an opaque white, like two smooth pearls.

He sipped his tea. "How did it happen?"

"Born this way, I'm afraid." As she sat in a wobbly wooden chair, she made almost the same creaking sounds as the chair did.

"So, you've never read any of this?" He waved his arm around.

She laughed. "Smart boy."

Conall, his face red, walked around the shop, his cup in hand. Meandering his way around the tables, he kept glancing back at the woman who just sat there, sipping her tea. Sunlight created a warmth all around, like the feathers lining a bird's nest. He eventually found a few books and sat in the corner close to the window so he could see better. Books creaked open, presumably having not been touched in more time than Conall could imagine. One of the books had hand-scrawled notes and recipes, probably someone's journal. He flipped the pages, stopping at a recipe for bilberry lemon jam before putting it aside.

"You're at peace. I can tell." The woman's voice sounded like it was right next to him.

All he did was look up and raise an eyebrow.

"It's your breathing. Plus, your heartbeat."

He lifted both brows and opened his mouth as soon as she said that.

"I don't get as many visitors as I used to, deary, so stay as long as you like." She climbed the ladder and retreated to the back of the shop.

Conall pulled a few more books down from the table, building his own small towers, settling in for a while.

Just past the bridge, the fields opened to the west, and more than two dozen leather-clad men and women trained in archery, quarterstaffs, and swords. Aedan heard the familiar clacking of staffs and followed it to the source. Stretching across the trodden land were a dozen warriors, some on their own, while others sparred together. He shook the staff from his sleeve, extended it to full length, and spun it around. It had been a while since he had practiced with his staff. He slowly worked with it until he felt the rhythm return to his hands, and soon he was like the other solo warriors. A young man and a woman who were practicing stopped when they saw him. Aedan was concentrating on his own footwork and motion so much that he didn't see them move closer and watch. As he turned to finish a maneuver, he realized he had an audience.

"Oh, hey… I didn't see you there." He brushed his hair back.

"Nice work, friend." The man clapped a few times. "You seem to know your way around a staff, or a few things anyway." He extended his arm. "I'm Cuinn, and this is Falon."

Aedan and Cuinn gripped forearms. Falon nodded, the faintest smile as her greeting. Cuinn asked how old Aedan was and asked under whom he had trained. Rather than tell them he had worked with Fionn Mac Cool, since he didn't know the hero's reputation in these parts, he simply said a warrior from the south. Cuinn gestured with his staff that he wanted to spar with Aedan. Before they began, Cuinn had a playful smile and said he would go easy on Aedan. Having learned a little about humility in his travels, Aedan replied that he hoped he could learn from such a well-trained warrior.

As the session began, Cuinn spun his staff around, showing off a bit, as he and Aedan moved in a circle facing each other, and the latter's facial expressions showed he was impressed. He even said he'd need to remember that particular move. Soon, though, they launched into their play, with Cuinn blocking Aedan's strikes. The Arvadoran's footwork gave him an advantage twice, hitting Aedan in the thigh, but then he crouched to sweep Aedan's legs out from under him. Doing a backflip, Aedan avoided the move. Cuinn grunted as he passed the staff behind his back, twirled it around, and prepared to strike from above, but Aedan remembered his training. He dropped to one knee to brace himself and pushed up with his staff, meeting Cuinn's. As his adversary recovered, Aedan used his position to catch Cuinn's ankle, making him fall backward.

Falon chuckled. "Seems this one might actually know a thing or two, eh, Cuinn?"

Aedan extended his hand to help the young man up. They began the second round, and this time, Cuinn didn't hold back. His own warrior background kicked in, and soon they were tied. A small crowd had gathered around, with Falon leading the cheering. Aedan won the fourth round, so they were tied once more, but he needed a break. One of the warriors tossed him a waterskin, and then he passed it along to Cuinn.

"I am impressed, friend." Cuinn poured some water over his head and then shook it off. "Rest up, and then we'll see what you can do with Falon."

Aedan spun around to see the woman wink at him, exhaling a deep breath. This is going to be a long afternoon, he thought. While he recovered, he looked out to the tree where he knew Fiachra would be, and a tap on his shoulder by Falon's staff summoned him to another round. Her movements had a smoothness and fluidity to them, unlike Cuinn's occasional abruptness. She watched Aedan step and move, tracking his feet as they did the warrior dance around each other. He saw an opening and lunged. Falon spun around, but she didn't strike back. Again, Aedan found an opening, and again she slid out of the way. Cuinn sat on a tree stump grinning, muttering his enthusiasm from time to time. Neither combatant had made contact with the other, and the continuous motion resembled more a sacred dance than a sparring session, although some would say that to be a great warrior, one must know this specific dance well.

Falon knew just where to hit Aedan to get him to lower his guard or make him stumble. She hadn't caused him to fall yet, like a predator toying with its prey. He would parry her strikes, his eyes bouncing around to take everything in. Unlike Cuinn, who enjoyed playful banter while he fought, Falon kept that wry smile, preferring to let her skill speak for her instead. Like earlier, a crowd gathered, but this one followed her example and observed without comment. Paying close attention to her face, Aedan swung around, but gestured as if he were going to strike low, but went high instead, causing her to shift her focus. He hit her hand, forcing her to release her grip, and then he spun around. She leaned a bit too far to parry his shot, and she fell to one knee.

"Clever." Falon giggled.

Aedan shrugged, with a knowing smile. She lunged, and he jumped back. As he moved the staff to deflect her strike, she swept in with her leg, using the grittiness of the dirt to aid her. His foot slid sideways, and he landed on his hip, his staff rolling from his hands. Cuinn got to his feet to see if Aedan was all right, but Falon blocked him with her staff.

"He can do this on his own."

Walking off the fall, Aedan rocked his head back and forth, cracking his neck. Taking his stance, he motioned with his hand, "Come on."

"He sure is a glutton for punishment," muttered Cuinn, sitting back on the stump.

Aedan's expression had shifted from jaunty to stern. This time, when they engaged with each other, a stoic gaze replaced his playfulness. He met her blow for blow, jumping her sweeps and blocking her strikes. Then, she did something he had never seen her do: she crouched down low, holding the staff tight against her. He cocked his head and took a small step toward her, thinking she might be wounded, and that's when she jumped up and somersaulted over his head. Falon's foot had barely made contact with the ground behind him when she brought her staff across his throat. The crowd gasped. Aedan had to drop his staff to clutch hers. The moment it landed on the ground, she released her hold. Instinctively, he reached for his throat, although she hadn't hurt him.

"Nice move." Aedan shrank his staff, putting it back in its sheath. "Reminds me of a friend. She's Banféinní."

Falon was adjusting her bracers when she heard that word and stopped.

"Everything okay?"

"Yes." She fixed one of her boots. "Aedan, when did you come across Banféinní? I trained with some a few years back."

"Conall and I met one earlier in our travels. Her name is Daimhain."

Falon shook her head. "It's not a familiar name to me. Did she teach you some of those maneuvers?"

"A few." He laughed. "I suffered some bruises with her as well. I'm going to see if I can find my friend, Conall. I'll see if I can get him to match skills with you both."

—m—

By the time Conall had finished exploring the books, he had constructed a wall of towers, organizing them by those he liked, those he wanted to read more of, and those that didn't have anything of interest. He was just about to start putting some books back when he noticed a brown leather-bound book under the table. Blowing on the dust, he recognized some of the glyphs, and one word in particular: slata. Wands. With his sleeve, he wiped off most of the dust, uncovering cracked gilded lettering: *Slata, Dríochta, agus Ceardaíocht an Draoi.*

"Wands, Magic, and the Druid's Craft." His heartbeat was almost audible outside his chest. As he turned the book in his hands, his expression soured. A locking mechanism kept the book sealed, and it was like no lock he had ever seen.

He went as close as he dared to the back of the shop and shouted for the old woman.

"I don't suppose you have a key for this lock?"

No answer. Closer to the sunlight, he brought the lock to his face. The keyhole was an awkward shape, a sort of wavy opening with spots for what looked like thorns. In vain, he tried to pull the lock open by hand. As old as it was, it was secure. He then attempted to pull the covers open, but the mechanism was a part of it.

"Hello? Are you still here?" He raised his voice again, but it was absorbed by the stacks of parchment and books.

Conall had been sitting for quite a while, and his back was stiff from being hunched over. Rolling his head around to loosen his neck muscles, he heard a tinkle. He removed the torc given to him by Elder Daithi and dangling on it was an oddly-shaped key, the one given to him by Epona.

"Oh, Cernunnos, I pray this works."

After fumbling with it, he inserted the object into the lock. It fit. He tried to turn it. A click! The mechanism popped open. He returned to his literary hideaway and slowly open the book, the cover creaking. A thin piece of vellum covered the title page, upon which was a phrase.

'Féadfaidh na daoine is fiú a fháil amach cad a lorg siad.'

He whispered the words. "'Those who are worthy may find what they seek.' Well, let's hope I'm worthy."

Page after page of knowledge sat in front of him, but there was one problem.

"I can't understand a word of this. It's not Ogham. Blast!" He slammed the cover shut and pushed the book off his lap.

The woman's voice made him jump.

"It's older than Ogham, my boy. It's written in the druid's tongue. Bring it here."

She was back at her table again, knitting.

"I called for you earlier. Did you just return from somewhere?" He put the book in front of her.

She cackled. "I've been here. Just not where I could be found. Now, let me see..." She pulled the book over to her and held out her hand.

Conall wasn't sure what she wanted, but then he remembered the key. He touched the torc, raising an eyebrow.

"I can't help you if you don't give me the key. Come, now. It's all right." She extended her withered palm, the creases in it resembling the parchment.

He placed it in her hand, never taking his eyes off it. Once the book was open, she returned it to him. She turned to the same page as the phrase, moving her finger across the ink.

"Now, tell me. What makes you worthy?" Her face took on a smugness he hadn't seen before.

"Is this some sort of riddle?"

"Merely a question. What makes you worthy?"

Conall twisted his face around, pursing his lips. After a few minutes, he sighed, lowering his head. He shrugged.

"I-I don't know. I wish I knew what to tell you. I am no more worthy than anyone else."

He headed for the door, slouching.

"Where are you going?"

"To find my friend. We said we would meet up, and he must be worried. Thank you for letting me look through your books."

Conall's hand had just touched the door when the woman called him back.

"*That* is why you're worthy, child."

"What? What do you mean?"

"Well, the answer is twofold. You didn't try to tell me why you were, in fact, worthy of the book, but you also showed concern for your friend. Only one with a compassionate spirit and humility can truly be worthy."

As he walked back to the table, she turned the book around and pushed it toward him. He looked at her and then turned the page. At first, the symbols were the same as earlier, but then Conall's eyes widened.

"I can understand this. I don't know what language it is, but I can read it! Thank you!"

The woman laughed. "My boy, I didn't do anything. This was *your* doing. Have a seat."

He turned to see a chair behind him that wasn't there earlier. Now, sitting across from the woman, he pored over the pages, taking in every word, every syllable. Hours later, he had finished the book. Conall sat back, exhaling, his eyes glazed over, and he yawned. The woman had fallen asleep in her chair, snoring a little, her head bobbing with each breath. When he closed the book, her eyes fluttered open. He patted the cover, his mind elsewhere. The crone reminded him he was to find his friend, and he broke free from his reverie, sitting up. Thanking her, he was just about to leave when she asked if he would like to keep the book. Bouncing on the balls of his feet, he thanked her, clutched the book to his chest, and grinned. He hadn't taken three steps outside when he saw a familiar face.

"Conall!" Aedan waved. "I've been trying to find you everywhere. Have you been in the shop all day?"

"I have! I need to tell you what—"

"Not now. I want you to meet some people. Besides, after sitting so long, I'll bet you could use some moving around."

"Um, okay. But we need to talk later. And, I'm so hungry."

"Sure, sure. Let's find food first, then." He hadn't even noticed the book in Conall's hands.

—⁂—

Leaning against the slumbering Fiachra, Aedan pushed handfuls of dried venison into his mouth, while Conall told him about the book. Words poured from him, sometimes cutting himself off to talk about something else until he finally stopped and took a breath. One of the most important things he had learned was that the more wands a person has, the stronger the bearer's connection to magic grows. Not all wands conjure openly, like the ones they have. However, a person has to have a natural connection to magic. To the average person, a wand is a stick. Having a wand that actually weaves spells was rare. Even a novice could use one, although not well, and using it without proper training could bring about devastating consequences. Aedan commented that that was why he must have been able to attack Dian, because of his elemental connection to fyre in close proximity to the alder wand. Conall agreed, adding that he was able to conjure wynd from fyre in the holly copse for the same reason. His natural affinity for the power of air was heightened.

"That scares me a little," Aedan spoke through a mouth full of food. "The more wands we find, the stronger we grow, too. Without someone like Elder Déaglán to guide us, we could really hurt someone."

"Exactly. That's why the ancient magicians created a protection to prevent that." Conall opened the book to a page with a drawing of what looked like a leather quiver, but with a cover. "See the icovellavna on it? When wands or other magical objects are put inside, the symbols bind the power, preventing it from affecting those connected to magic. The wizards thought of the danger as well."

While Conall thumbed through some pages, Aedan continued to eat, his cheeks puffed out. As soon as he was finished, he put his hands behind his head and closed his eyes. A few minutes later, Conall noticed he was asleep, so he went back to his reading. He mumbled to himself that there was so much to learn. At some point, he heard Aedan's name. It was Cuinn. Conall kicked Aedan's foot.

"Hey, your new friend you told me about is calling you. Maybe he wants a rematch?"

"I told him *you* might spar with them," Aedan yawned. "I've been bruised enough for one day."

Again, Cuinn underestimated his adversary. Conall had an advantage because Aedan told him about Cuinn's weak points. The Arvadoran commented that he was surprised that these two weren't aligned to a warrior clan considering their expertise. Their mock fighting ended with one win apiece. Falon tapped Conall's staff with her own, an invitation to engage. This time, she started off knowing she had a worthy adversary and went into it without restraint. Aedan and Cuinn engaged in their own side conversation when they saw Falon react to something Conall said, fumbling her own staff. Conall took his opening, caught her behind the knee, putting her flat on her back. He held the tip of his staff over her. Falon, at first, narrowed her eyes and glared, but then her expression softened and she pulled on Conall's staff to help her up. They shook forearms.

"What happened?" Cuinn tossed a water pouch to Falon as she approached.

She gulped down some water. "He knows that his staff isn't his only weapon. A well-placed verbal jab can be equally effective."

Aedan leaned into Conall's ear. "What did you say to her?"

"It's not important." She wiped her mouth with the back of her hand, smiling at Conall.

Aedan rolled his eyes.

"Hey, any tactic that brings victory, as long as it doesn't dishonor either combatant, is fair game. So, two on two?"

This kind of staff play was new to the boys, and they reveled in it. At times, different pairs would focus on one combatant, so no one had any allegiance to another. Late day sunlight was fading, and the other warriors had returned home for supper. Conall took a swig of water and spied Cuinn looking at him. When Cuinn saw he'd been caught, he flashed a smile, and Conall broke the contact, blushing. Aedan said he was going to check on Fiachra, and Conall hustled to catch up.

"I have never known any creature that sleeps as much as he does." Aedan chuckled, his arms crossed. "Seems you have an admirer, by the way." He chuckled.

Conall's face reddened again. He admitted that he was curious about Cuinn as well, especially when the young man flashed a wry smile.

"Do you think you'll ever fall in love? You know, like Sionnain and Uaine?" He patted Fiachra.

Conall pushed out his lower lip and shrugged.

"You should talk to him. Hey, think of it as a way to learn more about Arvador."

"True."

Falon found them and invited them to sup with her and some of her friends. She looked at Conall and commented that Cuinn would be there too. It seemed Aedan wasn't the only one who noticed.

They could hear the warriors carousing before they entered her cottage. As they walked in, the others cheered them, raising their flagons. The table easily sat a dozen, with Aedan and Conall finding seats toward one end. Falon made introductions, with each raising his or her flagon to the boys, and then Cuinn arrived with the same fanfare. Some even pounded the table with their fists. He put a hand on Aedan and Conall's shoulder, saying how glad he was that they could join, before taking a seat across from them.

Supper lasted for hours, with platters of roasted venison, bread, and assorted other victuals. Falon had provided a feast, and they all partook, grabbing food from various platters and pouring flagon after flagon of ale. Conversation consisted largely of stories the warriors told of their exploits, especially the times each of them had been brought down by an adversary. They took magnificent pleasure in embarrassing one another, all in jest. Conall looked across the table and, again, saw Cuinn eyeing him, the young man's eyes buoyant and sparkling in the lamplight. When he turned to respond to a comment, Conall lingered on his face, his dark, rough stubble outlining his jaw, and his hair brushed back into a short ponytail. Falon walked passed, whispering to Conall that Cuinn actually combed his hair, something he rarely did. She added that it must be a special occasion. Conall blushed.

The hour grew late, and one by one, the warriors said their farewells. Cuinn commented to those who remained that he was going to take a walk by the river before he headed home, making sure Conall heard him. Aedan wiped his mouth, using his eyes to gesture that Conall should follow. Conall smiled and looked down. Aedan kicked him from under the table, and a moment later, he excused himself, saying he'd like to enjoy the night air.

Cuinn sat on the bridge, tossing pebbles into the river. When Conall arrived at the beginning of the bridge, Cuinn commented that he wasn't sure Conall would come to which Conall replied that he wasn't sure he would, either. Cuinn patted next to him, and Conall sat, but leaving some room between them.

"The moonlight, if I may say, makes your eyes come alive."

Conall turned away.

"So... tell me more about you." Cuinn stared up at the moon.

Without getting into too much about their journey, Conall opened up a bit. He started with his family and where he was from, hesitating, and having a hard time keeping eye contact with Cuinn. Their conversation gradually became a bit easier, with Cuinn explaining his own past in Arvador, his adventures in his childhood, and how he became a warrior. His ancestry could be traced back to the northern kingdom, with his great-grandfather one of the finest warriors the monarchy had ever seen. He had wanted to be a warrior ever since he was little, but he also took pleasure in music and poetry. Story after story unfolded from both, and their laughter echoed, occasionally having to lower their voices before they would wake up the town. Cuinn slid his hand so that it just barely touched Conall's. They stayed that way while they wove tale after tale. The subject of the quest came up. Conall skirted the issue. Cuinn said he understood Conall's shyness. Revealing too much could be problematic. Instead, he directed the conversation toward Conall's friendship with Aedan, and that opened up the floodgates. He regaled Cuinn with childhood mischief, how Aedan moved away, and how they only recently came back into each other's life.

Cuinn raised his head toward the night sky, pointing at a cluster of stars. He put his other hand on the bridge behind Conall's back, close enough that if Conall moved, he'd know. Cuinn explained that the constellation was called An Faireoir, The Watcher. Conall said it reminded him of a hawk, and Cuinn was surprised that he could discern that from just the stars. Conall smiled awkwardly, and then, Cuinn nudged himself a little closer. At first, Conall didn't react, but then he scratched his nose, putting his hand back down lightly touching Cuinn's leg. In the silver of the night, they examined each other's faces. Stars mirrored in each other's eyes. His breathing quickening, Conall changed the subject by asking about other stars, so Cuinn pointed out other constellations and their origins. An awkward silence came between them. Every time Conall made eye contact, he turned away and smiled. Cuinn leaned back on the bridge with his arms behind his head and admitted he'd had a dream recently where he was on the bridge at sunrise, and he heard a hawk screech. When he looked toward the horizon, the hawk flapped its way past him, calling out to him. He said he reached out, but the hawk flew off. Conall remarked that it sounded like Sionnain and Uaine. Conall lay back, eyeing the sky, but keeping Cuinn in his periphery. At one point, they had turned toward each other, and they just stayed like that for a few minutes. Cuinn's eyes glanced at Conall's lips, and that made Conall stammer that he needed some sleep, but perhaps they could meet again on the bridge the next night. Cuinn grinned. He said that a banshee couldn't keep him away. They walked close enough that their hands brushed against one another and found Aedan and Falon engaged in laughter.

"Well, well, nice of you two to return." Aedan laughed. "Thanks for dinner, Falon. Hey, Conall, Falon was nice enough to arrange a room at the inn for us since her cousin runs it."

Conall kept glancing back at Cuinn. "That's great. Thanks, Falon. Cuinn, tomorrow. Same place."

In the room, Aedan noted that straw mattresses were better than none and groaned as he lay back. Conall was on his side, facing his friend.

"We don't need a lamp with your smile. It could light a room. It was a good night?" Aedan pushed the mattress in places to get comfortable.

"Mhhmm," he sighed.

Laughing to himself, Aedan rolled his eyes. "We're not going to sleep now, are we."

—⁂—

For a week, the boys lingered in Arvador, and each night, Conall and Cuinn met by the bridge. Aedan told his friend he hadn't seen him this happy since they got reacquainted. He joked about Seamus back home. Conall replied that Seamus hadn't even paid him any attention, spending more time on his poetry. He knew that they wouldn't be staying in this town much longer, and he would have to say goodbye to Cuinn, at least for a while. Aedan sympathized, saying he wished he could have spent as much time with Eoghan as they had spent together. They both agreed that, when the quest was over, should circumstances allow it, they would see what the future held with their respective interests.

One morning, after they had been training with the warriors, Conall went into town. He had told Cuinn that it felt a little like home, just bigger. Walking through the market was a pleasant distraction, and the meat merchant would always offer him a sample of that day's dried meat special. A new merchant had set up a tent, one who had bird cages hanging from the awning. Interestingly, the cages remained open, and birds flew in and out, singing. It seemed strange to him, yet it reminded him of Lann. He hadn't seen his feathered friend in a couple of days, but he knew that the hawk spent time with Fiachra as well as doing what hawks do. Making sure he wasn't near the bird cages, Conall whistled and held up his arm. It didn't take long for Lann to perch, squawking away. The townsfolk stopped, and then they did something Conall didn't expect—they bowed their heads. From that point on, as Conall walked past merchants, they regarded him with more intentional respect. Children pointed, and a few walked right up to him, asking about his hawk. One wanted to know if she could pet Lann. Instructing the girl to be gentle, he let her fingertips graze the top of Lann's head. She giggled and pulled her hand back. The hawk chirped.

"You're doing all right?" Conall fed him a piece of dried meat. Lann cocked his head. "Everything fine with Fiachra, I take it?" The hawk's head jerked all around, and he made softer squawks. "Don't be a stranger, okay?" He kissed Lann on the head and held up his arm.

The next day, Conall woke up confused, his brow moist. Aedan asked if he was ill, but he said no. He'd had a strange dream he couldn't understand. In this dream, he saw a hawk on a tree branch. When he extended his arm, expecting the hawk to perch, the bird flew toward a dragon seated beside a rock. He said that he thought it was Lann and Fiachra, and that he was frustrated that the hawk wouldn't go to him. Aedan shrugged it off as just a dream. Conall wasn't so sure. He went outside and whistled. As usual, Lann arrived. Conall didn't understand. Aedan found him with the hawk, saying things looked normal to him. He was going to meet Falon and the others for some sparring. Conall said he'd join him later. He wanted to head into town for some more healing herbs since their supply had been running low and perhaps go back to the book merchant.

The healer's shop was near the river, and Conall enjoyed talking with the apothecary, a healer herself, and seeing what worked for different ailments and injuries. Out of the corner of his eye, he noticed children playing with some ducks. He turned his attention back to the woman, but then a shriek made him spin around. The children were pointing toward the river. He sprinted over and asked what happened, and a boy said his friend was chasing a duck onto the bridge, slipped, and fell in. Without a second thought, he ran to the edge of the bridge, saw the girl flailing, and dove into the water. Using the current to his advantage, he swam toward her, eventually grabbing onto her arm and pulling her close. He looked around for a branch or rock to hold onto, but when he couldn't find one, he tried to whistle, water getting in his mouth. He then just shouted for Lann as loud as he could. Clutching the girl, he instructed the hawk to get Fiachra. It didn't take long for the dragon to arrive. Conall told her to wrap her arms around his neck and hold on as they continued downriver. He had managed to extend his staff and held on tightly. One of Fiachra's taloned feet grabbed hold and lifted them to safety.

Sodden and dripping, he carried her back to town and found the girl's parents. The crowd cheered for Conall. Cuinn ran up and pulled him close.

"Are you hurt?" He cradled Conall's face and kissed him hard.

Conall's eyes widened. "Um, I'm fine." He giggled. "Just wet."

Cuinn brushed the hair off Conall's forehead as Aedan and Falon ran over. Conall explained what happened. Fiachra soared above the town, roaring, and at first, the crowd gasped, but then they cheered again. Cuinn wouldn't let Conall go and held his hand until they arrived at the inn where he had to say goodbye for the moment. They agreed to meet at their spot later that evening. Aedan, his expression flat, shouted up to the window at Conall that he wanted to join Falon and the others.

Clothes hanging on the chairs in the room, Conall sat on the bed. He pulled over some scrolls about druids he had borrowed from the old woman in the book shop, skimming for other knowledge that might help them on their quest. His thoughts kept returning to Cuinn. Finally, unable to concentrate, he lay back on the bed, arms behind his head, and wondered what his life could be like with love in it. He reflected on what he knew: Cuinn was a year older, a seasoned warrior who loved stargazing and poetry, ruggedly handsome, and completely smitten with him. Having spent the fleeting time in Arvador, he had begun to think of these people as friends, a welcomed addition since his journey with Aedan had been so filled with quietness and introspection. When he prayed to Aengus, he confided that he was falling for this Arvadoran. He shivered with the thought that he and Aedan would eventually leave this place, and he didn't know when he would see Cuinn again, if at all. He lit a candle on the table with a dríocht, and while it flickered, Conall stared into the fyre.

"O god of love, if it's within your power, look out for Cuinn. May it be your will..."

Rolling up the scrolls, he pulled the blanket over him and stared at the flickering candle. Aedan came in just after sunset. He pulled a feather from his pack and tickled Conall's nose. He awoke swatting near his face.

"Hey, the sun's down. I'm going to get supper. Are you meeting Cuinn later?"

Grumbling his reply, he sat up, stretched, and yawned. He noticed a change in tone with Aedan's voice with a lifted eyebrow and replied that he must have needed that nap after what happened earlier. Aedan told him to meet at Falon's and left. After getting dressed, Conall used his fingernail to etch the Ogham glyph for 'love' in the candle which had burned out. Kissing the symbol, he made a silent prayer before heading to meet Cuinn.

A few days later, the father of the little girl, holding two burlap-wrapped parcels, arrived at the training field. He told one of the men preparing for practice that he needed to speak with Aedan and Conall. They sprinted over.

"Is your daughter all right?" Conall was out of breath.

"Of course, of course. She's with her mother right now, but I wanted to thank you properly for what you've done. Both of you. I am Liam."

Conall touched the man's shoulder. "There's no need. I'm just glad I was there."

Liam put a parcel in each of their hands. "It's a small token of my thankfulness. My wife and I are eternally grateful. Grainne is our only child. I-I... well, I just wanted you to know that you are always welcome in my home. Please. Stop by for a meal before you head out of town, whenever that is."

Aedan held out his parcel. "Liam, I didn't do anything to help —"

"It was *your* dragon that pulled them from the river. As far as I'm concerned, you should share in our gratitude."

"Of course." Aedan, smiling, wrapped his arms around the burlap. "Thank you."

Liam returned to town. That evening, before supper, Aedan and Conall were in their room and unwrapped their gifts. Conall gasped.

"Aedan, look." Folded, there was a rust-colored sleeveless tunic and a brown leather vest. The embroidery around the buttonholes, of gilded thread, resembled feathers. "This is incredible." He looked over at Aedan, whose mouth was also agape.

His tunic was dark green, and his vest was made of leather died crimson, with gold piping across the chest and torso, making it resemble dragon scales. Embedded in the leather were golden studs. He held up the tunic.

"What is this?" His voice shook.

At the base of the tunic, in the front, was more embroidery — a large beast, like something one might see on a coat of arms. He turned it toward Conall who stared at it, holding up his own with the same design.

"Do you know what this is?" Aedan asked, but in a tone where he knew the answer. "The body is a mix of Lann and Fiachra's bodies, with dragon's wings combined with a hawk's. One foot has a dragon's talons, the other, a hawk's." He ran his fingers over the craftsmanship.

"I have never seen anything like it. It-It's a... dragonhawk."

In addition, both boys had a new pair of hide pants and boots. Conall's were of green leather, laced up the front. Aedan's were brown, with a crown of dark gold leather pockets around the top of each. Conall wanted to bathe before he wore his clothes and suggested Aedan do the same. Upriver, according to Falon, a small lake that used to be connected to the river sat, but time had dried up the tributary, and foliage had kept it hidden. They had time before their friends would be supping. Heading west along the river, they saw the weathered wooden sign that pointed toward the lake. Aedan was the first to strip down and dive in, tossing his head back as he rose above the surface, with Conall diving in right after. Once he had washed as fully as he could, he floated on his back.

"So, Conall, we should move on from Arvador soon. For as much as we like it here, we can't stay a lot longer." Aedan started putting his clothes back on.

Conall exhaled, letting himself slowly descend, his air bubbles popping on the surface. Aedan, realizing he had probably upset his friend, took a walk around the lake. As he surfaced by the shore, Conall shook his hair and put on his clothes. By the time Aedan came back, Conall had drawn lines and shapes in the dirt.

"What's wrong? I know how much you want to stay, because of Cuinn."

He continued making random shapes with the stick. "No. You're right. We've been here longer than I expected we would." He continued scratching out symbols. "Aedan, do you think we'll come back to Arvador?"

"I'm sure we will. I don't think anything could keep you from coming back. Look, we don't have to leave today, but in the next few days, we should. Let's head back and put on our new clothes."

Conall looked up at Aedan, and when he saw his friend's sullen face, his goofy grin diminished. When they walked into Falon's cottage, the usual carousing and laughing surrounded them, and then came the gasps and silence. Cuinn walked right up to Conall, eyeing his new look.

"I have never seen a more dashing spectacle." He gave Conall a peck on the lips. "I need to take this all in." He walked around Conall, scrutinizing every inch.

Aedan rolled his eyes, but then followed that with a smile. Falon rubbed the leather of Aedan's vest between her thumb and fingers, nodding with her lower lip puffed out.

"Well, well. Liam sure does beautiful work. You two look like royalty." She giggled, her eyes catching a glimpse of the dragonhawk. "By Brigid's fyre…"

"What is it? Is something wrong?" Aedan examined his clothes.

Falon lowered her voice. "It all makes sense now."

"What does?" Conall looked down at his own tunic.

She examined both images. Taking them by the hands, she presented them to the rest of the warriors assembled.

"My friends, who knew that these two were actually royalty?"

Everyone was able to see the dragonhawk imagery and lowered their heads. The boys shrugged at each other. What once was the noise of friends telling stories and teasing one another had been replaced by stillness.

"What's happening, Falon?" Conall giggled. "We're *not* royalty."

"But you wear the crest of the dragon, the guardian of the northern kingdom, and the hawk, the guardian of the south."

Aedan chuckled. "We're not from there. I'm from Oak Mountain, and Conall's from Silver Birch Glen. We had never even heard of Arvador before we arrived. It's just a coincidence."

One of the men stood. "But... we saw Conall tame the hawk. And the dragon that saved—"

"I found Fiachra as a hatchling when I was a child. He's been my companion ever since. When Conall was younger, he nursed Lann back to health and the two have always been inseparable. Falon, what is this about?"

She poured herself a flagon of honey ale and leaned against a support post.

"I guess I have to start at the beginning. Sionnain and Uiane are only a part of the story. This region was once two kingdoms, Lacedae to the north of the river, and Aithnea to the south. Both kingdoms shared fishing rights, but each had to stay on his own side of the river. The Lacedae flag had a dragon holding a sword, and the Aithnean, a hawk holding a torch. I'd say were about equally split in here as to whose family is Lacedaean and whose is Aithnean."

Conall chimed in, "And both kingdoms didn't get along, right?"

"Aye. No one really knows why, either. The problem, though, was with the queens, not the kings. Both regions were matriarchies. Both kings had been friends since childhood, but they had no luck in easing the tensions."

Everyone except Conall and Aedan knew the full story, yet each one sat forward as Falon wove the tale.

"Prince Sionnain of Aithnea grew up surrounded by scribes, artisans, and craftspeople, and his talent in the arts was known throughout the kingdoms. On the contrary, Prince Uiane of Lacedae had gained renown for his warrior skill. When the princes each reached his eighteenth year, Uiane joined the royal army while Sionnain became the head of the royal arts guild. These young men couldn't be more different." She sipped her flagon. "Then, whispers came across the river that Lacedae was planning to invade Aithnea."

"And no one knew why? Sounds a bit daft to me," Aedan muttered.

"Then," Falon continued, "the unexpected happened. One sunrise, Sionnain stood at the riverbank, staring across into the kingdom that would soon wage war against his. While he pondered what the future might bring, Uiane appeared on the other side of the river. This was the first time they had ever seen one another. For reasons passing understanding, the two young men opened a dialogue and became friends, but their mothers forbade it. Sionnain and Uiane would not be stopped, however, and found ways to meet in secret at various points along the river, usually around midnight."

Conall's eyes widened. A quick look at Cuinn, who caught him sneaking it, made Conall drink the rest of his flagon.

"Ultimately, Aengus smiled upon them, and they fell in love!"

The whole room cheered. Conall smiled to himself, looking down at the wax still left on his fingernail.

Falon walked around the cottage. "They worked out plan after plan to bring peace between the kingdoms, but then they would realize that the rivalry was too hard to undo. At least, they thought, they had each other, and perhaps someday they would find a way. As fate would have it, they were found out by a Lacedaean spy who overheard the princes arrange their next meeting. Cuinn, can you finish the story while I fill my flagon?"

Cuinn lifted his flagon to her, then turned his attention to the boys.

"Even with their differences, both Aithnea and Lacedae celebrated Beltaine, and while the peoples of both rejoiced, the princes met by the river. They had no sooner begun to speak when warriors from both sides arrived." —Cuinn got animated with his expressions and gestured dramatically— "The Lacedaean queen had sent word to her Aithnean counterpart, despite their feud, that their sons had planned this rendezvous, and both agreed to stop it. As the warriors got closer, the princes reached across the river to each other, praying to Aengus to let them be together. Each prince became half of a stone bridge, and it grew together over the river."

All in the cottage leaned forward, wide-eyed, anticipating the rest of the story.

"Once it connected both realms, the royals arrived and met halfway across the bridge. Each queen dropped to her knees, trying to embrace the stone. In their shared grief, they consoled each other. From that time on, they agreed to put aside their differences and work together to create a unified kingdom. That was how Arvador came to be."

Falon stepped forward, wiping her mouth with the back of her hand. "Every Beltaine, at midnight, the spirits of Sionnain and Uaine meet on the bridge, finally able to hold hands. The druids later said that when a hawk and dragon would come together, it would augur great things for the people of the town."

Tipping back her flagon, Falon finished her ale. Both Aedan and Conall sat in silence, absorbing what they had just heard.

"That certainly explains *that*, doesn't it?" Conall smirked. "I can assure you, though, that neither Aedan nor I is royalty. We just both happen to have a hawk and a dragon." He sighed.

Cuinn took Conall's hand. "Everyone, why don't we eat?" They sat together at the corner of the table.

Another evening meal went by. Aedan could tell from body language and conversation that some of those gathered did, in fact, think differently of him and Conall. A few wouldn't look him in the eye, and others seemed to fawn over them. With things winding down, the overall atmosphere moved from raucous laughter to low chatter, especially after so much food and drink. Cuinn and Conall started to rise to take their walk by the bridge, but Aedan popped up.

"Excuse me, everyone. I'd like to say something."

Conall reached out toward Aedan.

"No, this has to be said. Ever since we came in here with these new clothes, you've been looking at us differently. Look... Conall and I are the same people we were yesterday. I can't deny the similarities in the hawk and dragon from the two kingdoms. Who knows what the gods have planned? Maybe there *is* some sort of connection, but I don't know what that is, and neither do you. Conall and I have come to think of you all as friends. Why should that change? Even if we were royalty, it doesn't change a thing. Not for me. Not for Conall."

Smiling, Conall nodded. He turned to Cuinn, who then stood up as well.

"Friends, Aedan is right. I admit, I, too, started to look at them a little differently. These two have sparred with us, shared meals with us. Forget clothing. Forget stories. Remember who they are to us."

Most were convinced by Aedan and Cuinn, but a few still held onto their apprehension. Conall and Cuinn left and headed toward the bridge, but then Conall turned back to his friend.

"Hey, Aedan. Come take a walk with us."

Aedan hesitated, but then followed. He hadn't seen the river at night. Catching up with them, he put his arm around Cuinn's shoulder and pulled him away from Conall.

"Come with me."

Conall stood there, mouth open, while his best friend and his boy-friend walked on.

"Listen, Cuinn. I've watched you both get closer, and I just wanted to say this. If you ever hurt him…" He stopped, putting his hands on Cuinn's shoulders, having to look up just a little. "You will answer to *me*." Aedan locked his eyes on Cuinn's.

At the bridge, they watched the rushing water, the spilled silver of the moonlight giving it luminescence. Aedan grilled Cuinn about growing up in Arvador, his family and friends, and even his prior relationships. Conall glared at his friend, and Cuinn noticed. Out loud, Cuinn told him that he knew why Aedan was asking so many questions.

"Aedan is looking out for you. You're friends, and he's worried that I might do something to hurt you." He turned toward Aedan. "That about sum it up?"

"Pretty much." Aedan gave a cockeyed smile to Conall. "Lighten up." When no one was looking, he again rolled his eyes.

As the night progressed, Cuinn had his chance to ask Aedan questions, and before long, all three were joking and teasing. Conall collapsed on his bed back at the inn. Aedan was taking off his boots, and then he stopped.

"Conall, I'm —"

With half-closed eyes and a sleepy smile, Conall turned toward Aedan.

"Don't apologize for being my friend. Now, go to sleep."

Under his breath, Aedan said that wasn't what he was going to say, but then he voiced a "g'night" before climbing into bed.

14 | ELEMENTS COLLIDE

When the sun peeked over the horizon, a rooster crowed the morning alive, shaking Conall from his heavy slumber. Barely awake, he stumbled around the room while getting dressed. By the time he'd put his boots on, he glanced over at Aedan's bed to find he wasn't in it. They had both been spending late nights with their friends in Arvador, with Conall and Cuinn by each other's side almost the entire time. Conall splashed water from a bowl onto his face and ran his hands through his hair. He pressed a piece of torn cloth to his face and placed it back over the chair where it normally hung. Reaching his hand for the door, it swung open, and a bedraggled Aedan stepped into the room, his hair a mess and smelling of a peat fyre. He grunted at Conall before collapsing in his bed.

Conall sat back on his bed. "You're just getting in? Should I even ask what mischief you were getting into?"

Aedan rolled onto his back and put his arm over his eyes.

"Does the sun have to be this bright?"

Conall chuckled. Turning his head toward Conall, Aedan's arm lay flopped over his head.

"You and *Cuinn* have a good time?"

"What's that supposed to mean? I was with you and the others as much as I was with him."

"But you were clinging to him like a mushroom to a log. I mean, we all know you like him." Aedan rolled over and huffed.

Conall glared at Aedan, and without a word, he left.

It was midday when he returned only to find Aedan asleep, his mouth open, and a string of drool down his cheek to his pillow. Conall rummaged through his pack for his druid book. He was just about to leave when Aedan grunted at him.

"What?" Conall snapped, turning around.

Grimacing, Aedan propped himself on an elbow.

"What's wrong with *you*?"

"Nothing. Go back to sleep." Conall shut the door harder than usual.

A short while later, Aedan found Conall reading by the oak tree where Fiachra liked to nap, but the dragon was elsewhere. Conall's attention was firmly planted in the pages, and he didn't hear his friend approach. Aedan stood in front of Conall, his arms crossed. Conall glanced up.

"Can I help you?" He returned his eyes to the book.

"What did I do to you? Are you going to ignore me by sticking your head in that book?"

Conall kept reading. Aedan growled.

"Fine. Be that way."

Unable to concentrate, Conall wandered through the merchants in town. Having been an only child, he spent a lot of time alone, so this was normal for him. Every so often, someone he knew would wave at him, and he waved back, but he kept walking. He found himself by the book merchant and popped inside. A few others browsed as well, saying nothing as they shuffled on the wooden floor, kicking up swirls of dust. Mindlessly opening books or grazing covers with his fingers, he wound up by the table where the merchant was the last time he had been in. Like his first visit, she was nowhere to be found, so he slumped into a chair. He was lost in thought when he heard a sound on the table and saw a steaming cup of tea. When he looked around for the merchant, he saw no one. He peered at it a few times before picking it up to take a sip. Following his swallow, he closed his eyes and smiled. After he put the empty cup on the table, he put a coin on the table and left. The little bell that hung above the door jingled as he walked out, and as it shut, he heard another jingle. Reaching into his pocket was the coin. With a puzzled expression, he turned toward the shop, then shrugged before continuing through town.

Beyond the bridge lay the fields that functioned as sparring grounds, and the familiar clacking of staffs and clanging of swords brought Conall from his reverie. He kept himself out of view by veering off the road and walking behind trees. The forest that bordered the road had more shadow, and he hopped over the roots until he was farther from the fields. He sat at the base of a pine tree, leaning his head against it, and looking up through the canopy to where the blue skies showed. Occasionally, the faintest of clouds would brush by. When he looked down a little later, he saw he had been pulling apart a cluster of pine needles from a fallen branch. It was then he heard his name. Peeking around the tree, Falon was there asking some of their friends if they had seen him. He turned back and pulled his knees up to his chest, resting his chin on them.

The sun was nearing the horizon when he awoke. Warriors still sparred, but they were not all the same ones as earlier. Among them was Aedan. He and Falon laughed by a tree stump that doubled as a makeshift table where some weapons lay. Making his way from the forest toward the road, he again tried to stay out of view, but his feet crunched on a stick, betraying his position. Falon strode over.

"There you are! We've been looking for you all day. You doing okay?"

He saw Aedan over her shoulder glance at him, then look away to tie his boot.

"Aye, I'm fine. I just needed some time for myself. No need to worry." He started to walk toward town.

"You know, Cuinn was asking about you earlier. He thinks you're mad at him."

Conall perked up. "What? Mad? Why would he think that?"

"I don't know." She shrugged. "I just know that he said he'd tried to find you at all your usual haunts, and you were nowhere to be found. He's at the blacksmith right now."

Sighing, Conall said he would find Cuinn. He walked backward for a few steps, noticing that Aedan was talking with some of their friends before swinging around and taking determined strides toward the smithy. All he had to do was follow the thick, black plume of smoke in the center of town. Unlike most merchants, the blacksmith kept his door open, largely because of the smoke, but also because he liked it when passersby would peek in when he was hammering. Conall stopped at the entry. Cuinn had his back to the door, watching the burly man with the hammer put an edge back on a few swords. A few raps on the door frame got Cuinn's attention, but the blacksmith was so enrapt in his work that he didn't stop.

"Conall! I was so worried about you." Cuinn pulled Conall into a tight embrace.

Laughing, Conall squeezed back. "I'm fine. I just needed some time to myself. Sorry to have worried you."

"I'm just glad you're all right. I thought you might have left without saying goodbye." Cuinn's cheeks behind his scruff reddened.

"Don't be silly. Of course I wouldn't do that. So, what's Old Lorcan making for you?"

"He's repairing some swords. Seems we really spar hard, and the swords lose their edge. Even though we don't strike with the blade, it's safer for the blade to be smooth." He leaned over to see the work and then leaned back. "Did you work out whatever you needed to?"

Conall scrutinized Lorcan striking the swords, and the sparks flew in all directions. After a few strikes, he snapped out of his musing.

"What? Oh, yes, I did. It's… complicated."

Guiding Conall outside by the arm, Cuinn leaned toward his ear.

"I understand. I've been sensing something odd about Aedan lately. I take it he's not as keen on..." — Cuinn pointed at Conall and then himself. Conall didn't say anything, but Cuinn smiled. "It'll be all right."

Dinner with Falon and the others was smaller than usual, eight, including Conall and Aedan. While Falon filled flagons of ale, another Arvadoran, Donal, was telling them all about his latest hunt. Every detail was the biggest or tallest or fastest he had ever seen. Laughter filled the cottage. Once in a while, Conall and Aedan made eye contact, but just as quickly, they averted their eyes. Donal's voice would rise and get everyone's attention once more as he jumped from his chair and galumphed around the room like a wild beast, sharing the stag's final moment in dramatic detail. Donal conveniently forgot the details of what happened *after* he slew the deer, but it didn't matter — his story brought smiles and camaraderie to those assembled. Conall excused himself, giving the reason he was tired and headed back to his room. Aedan returned much later, and Conall was sound asleep, lightly snoring. Instead of going to bed, Aedan sat slumped in the chair, staring out the window at the moon. The sound of snoring would get him to look at his sleeping friend, but then he would go right back to the moon. When he awoke just after sunrise, Conall wasn't in the room.

The squawking of Lann guided Aedan to Conall in a meadow where the latter was tossing a small leather ball in the air, and Lann would bring it back. The crunching of twigs made Lann shriek louder. Aedan stomped through the meadow, and Lann, at first, flew down to greet him, but Aedan waved him off and got within a foot of Conall.

"So, are you?" He hadn't raised his voice like that since they became reacquainted.

Conall took a step back. "What in Brigid's fyre are you talking about? Am I what?"

"Staying in Arvador." He huffed through his nose.

Wide-eyed, Conall crossed his arms. "Why would you think that?"

"I overheard Cuinn talking to Falon. He said he was going to ask you to stay in Arvador for a while longer. Well?"

"I-I didn't know that." He dropped his arms. "When did he say that?"

"Does it matter? Last night, after dinner." — He got closer to Conall — "You left, and I thought he was going to follow you, as he usually does. He and Falon started talking. I was walking over to say good night when I heard him say that he wanted you to stay." Aedan's breathing grew heavier, and he was clenching his fists. "So, are you?"

"I suppose I hadn't really thought about that. I mean, I *do* want to stay —"

"I knew it! I knew you'd just abandon me. The first chance you had." He stormed off.

"Aedan! I didn't say I was going to. I said I *wanted* to." Conall hurried up to Aedan, putting his hand on the boy's shoulder. "Hey!"

Aedan spun around and pushed Conall back hard enough that he fell. Without hesitation, Conall launched himself up and pushed Aedan back. Aedan extended his staff, his breath heavy. Conall took a defensive posture with his. They side-stepped in a circle a bit before Aedan began his attack, and the crashing blow shook Conall harder than he expected. He returned the blow, swinging his staff low, trying to take out Aedan's legs. Breathing became almost feral, with grunts as they made contact. Aedan pushed against Conall's staff, trying to use his foot to trip him, but Conall spun around, making Aedan fall forward a bit. Conall kicked his backside, and Aedan fell onto his chest. With a howl, Aedan lurched at Conall, and the once mild clacking of staffs during other sparring sessions sounded like Lorcan's hammer against steel. Neither said a word.

From the forest ran Falon, Donal, and Cuinn, stopping short once they saw the source of the commotion. Cuinn wanted to stop it, but Falon held him back, saying they needed to work this out for themselves. This had gone beyond the playfighting of warriors learning how to use their tools and their craft: this was a battle.

"I-I've never seen these two go at each other like this." Donal looked over at Falon. "You sure we shouldn't stop it?"

Cuinn straightened up. "No. This has been building for a while. They need to get it out."

Nodding, Falon said she could tell there was a tension between them, she hated to say, since Cuinn and Conall had started spending time together. She was about to say something else when they heard shouting.

"This isn't about Cuinn, is it?" Conall crashed his staff against Aedan's. "This is about Eoghan."

A large grunt came from Aedan as he parried the attack. They spun around each other, each moving with intent.

"I never said we had to leave Rusdare when we did. If I had known-"

Aedan poked Conall in the knee, forcing down to the ground. "What? If you had known what? You don't know anything!"

Conall took a few steps back, his breathing heavy. "This *is* about Eoghan. If you had said you wanted to stay in Rusdare longer, I would have been fine with that. You just had —"

"You know nothing!" Aedan screamed. "*You* know nothing."

Looking into Aedan's eyes, bloodshot and teary, Conall cocked his head and narrowed his brows.

"Nothing." — he paused — "I know what this is about. I understand."

"You —"

Conall held up his hand. "I *do* have Cuinn. I also have *two* parents. And you left Oak Mountain angry at your da. So, you feel like you have nothing. And you think *I* have everything."

Lunging, Aedan swung his staff. Conall stopped it, pressing back.

"Aedan, your da loves you, no matter what. I spoke to your mum. *She* loves you. She contacted me from Tir na nÓg to tell me so, remember? We'll go back to Rusdare."

Aedan continued to push against Conall's staff, grunting and crying.

"I promise, Aedan."

Then, Conall stepped back and dropped his staff. He held his arms out with open palms.

"Come then. Attack me. I'll not stop you."

Heaving, his eyes red, and his knuckles white as he held the staff, he stared at Conall. He exhaled hard a few times, staring off. Clamping his eyes shut, he took deep, heavy breaths, striking the ground with his staff. Clods of dirt flew everywhere. Aedan dropped to his knees, tilting his head back, tears streaming down. Using the staff to help him stand up, he focused on Conall. Then, he dropped his staff. In a few staggering steps, huffing heavy breaths, he stood face to face with Conall who remained silent and unmoving. In a swift move, Aedan threw his arms around his friend, crying into his shoulder.

"I-I'm sorry. I'm so sorry." He bawled, squeezing tighter. "Don't leave me."

"You've nothing to be sorry about." Conall whispered in Aedan's ear. "This was a long time coming. And I told you, I'm not going anywhere."

A few minutes passed, and Aedan turned toward Cuinn, waving him over.

"I owe *you* an apology too. I'm not angry at you. If Conall wants to stay—"

"Aedan." Conall put his hand on Aedan's shoulder. "I'm not staying. *We* have a quest to finish."

Conall and Aedan walked shoulder to shoulder back to town with the others just behind. Their first stop was to the apothecary to tend to their wounds. When Conall removed his shirt, he had bruises all over his arms and chest. Aedan cringed, apologizing again. Chuckling, Conall poked Aedan with a finger on his chest, causing a yelp. Once the woman covered the salves and ointments with cloth, the boys returned to their room. Later that afternoon, Cuinn and Falon brought a basket of food for them. Aedan invited them into the room, and all four ate together on the floor. This would be their last meal together before the boys would depart Arvador, and he wanted it to be with their friends.

15 | BEALORAGAN

The boys hobbled with their packs to the river at sunrise, as per Falon's request. Even with a night's rest, their bodies needed more time to heal after their mutual bludgeoning the day before. Those they had come to know wanted to say goodbye. Blankets laid out had baskets of food, some for their travels and some for this time. Seated were Cuinn and the close-knit group of Arvadorans they had come to care about. Falon said it was customary to see people off with a morning meal just as the sun rose to bring good fortune. Moon-painted dark skies gave way to the brighter sunlight on the horizon. With the imminent departure came questions about where the boys were headed, with a few offering up their knowledge of the area to guide the journey. Aedan said he and Conall would be at Falon's looking over the map. Cuinn said he would make sure they had provisions. Once the sun had freed itself from its earthly bond, the group dispersed. Before they would meet up, Conall told Aedan he needed to talk with him before they went to Falon's cottage.

Back at the inn, Aedan arranged what went into his pack while Conall, who had already prepared much earlier, unfurled the map on a small table in their room.

"We're going to look at that at Falon's. What are you doing now?" Aedan tied the cords around the pockets of his pack.

"I need you to see something before we show the others." He stared at the parchment.

On the map, Aedan saw their little stick figures, the thin line depicting the main road, one for the river, and boxes for the town. Far north of the river, a line meandered across the road, a boundary or border, but no name or other symbols. In fact, beyond the wavy line, nothing showed up.

"This is no different than we've seen before. What did you want to show me?"

Removing the Fearnslat and Tineslat, he placed one on the table at the top of the map and the other at the bottom.

"Just watch."

In just seconds, the depictions on the map evolved into much more detailed versions. Their stick figures, although small, became almost life-like, down to the new clothing they were wearing. The road, town, and bridge looked as if drawn from above. Even depictions of Fiachra sleeping beneath a tree and Lann flying overhead.

"Look at the river." Aedan reached out to touch it. "It's actually moving."

"That isn't the best part. Look north of Arvador."

That meandering line that cut across the road had become a wall of black fog, and as it moved about, crags showed through. Bursts of light, like lightning in a cloud, appeared sporadically, and renderings of creatures, although obscured, became illuminated for a moment before fading.

"Remember how I said that the magic of the wands can increase our power? It seems it can do that to magical objects, like this map."

"That is amazing." Eyes narrowed, Aedan got down close to the craggy darkness.

"No, Aedan." He pulled his friend up to look at him. "It also means that anyone else who has access to magic will also be strengthened."

Aedan clenched his jaw. "The Fomoragh."

"Exactly. And look here." Conall pointed to a small Ogham symbol that came into view as the fog moved around. "See that? It's Ogham for 'ash.' I think that's where we'll find the Nionslat."

Conall rolled up the map and put the wands away. As they left the inn for the last time, Aedan asked who guarded the Nionslat.

Sighing, Conall answered, "An adder."

A handful of their new friends greeted them at Falon's cottage. Conall pulled out the map, explaining it was different from others they might have seen. One of the men, Fergus, asked half-heartedly if it were magical, and when Conall said it was, the man's face paled. Falon noted that enchanted maps weren't all that uncommon anymore, and she unrolled it. The stick figures of Aedan and Conall showed up in a slightly different location in town. Conall explained that they always showed up in the center, and the landscape symbols changed as they traveled. Another man, Riordan, explained places he'd seen farther east and west of the town if they were to follow the river in either direction, but he became silent when Aedan asked if he knew what lay beyond that wavy line to the north. The others averted their eyes from him. He pressed the issue, informing them that that's where they were headed. Finally, one of the women, Bevan, stepped up to the map and pointed.

"That's Bealdrágan. The Dragon's Mouth."

"Not a place we should go for fun, I take it?" Aedan laughed.

Falon put a hand on his shoulder. "Aedan... Aithnea and Lacedae had always been able to take care of themselves, and Arvador, too, but when the kingdoms became one, curiosity beyond our borders led some to wonder who else lived in the lands around us. The elders formerly of Lacedae told the queens and their spouses that a few mysterious enclaves lay due north, but beyond them, a place no one dared go. They wouldn't even speak its name, and they vehemently criticized anyone whose foolish curiosity arose about it. To the west of it was the sea, and to the east, no one knew. About twenty years earlier, a scouting party headed north to explore. Only one returned. When she met with the elders, she just kept mumbling something about a dragon's mouth, and that's the name that stuck. She couldn't even describe what she had seen."

Conall nudged to Aedan to speak with him away from the others.

"Excuse us."

They moved into a corner and spoke in a whisper.

"Do we say anything about... well, you know."

"Conall, the fewer people who know about the wands and what they can do the better. Remember that the Fomoragh are all about deception."

"You don't think..." Conall blanched.

Aedan put a hand on his shoulder. "No, I don't know Cuinn is. Or Falon, for that matter. Call it a feeling. But the others? There are five people here who volunteered to help us, and how well do we really know them? I mean, we've sparred with them and eaten meals. A few conversations, even." He glanced over at the others. "I'm just saying be careful. I'll support whatever you decide."

Back at the table, Conall put the map away, thanking them all for their hospitality. Cuinn came in with a few items he'd obtained, saying he'd run into Liam who wanted to see them off. Aedan and Conall said their farewells to the others while Cuinn waited by the door. He walked with them across the bridge to the tree where Fiachra lay asleep. Liam sat on the grass nearby.

"I wanted to make sure I saw you before you left. I have something to show you." He walked behind Fiachra, and they followed.

Lying on the ground was what appeared to be an enormous saddle with two seats, one behind the other.

Aedan gasped. "What... is this?" He ran his hand along the tooled leather. "Did you make this for Fiachra?"

Liam nodded and grinned.

"I can never fully repay you for what you did for my daughter. Had it not been for you both… well, I don't want to dwell on that. But I know you have a long journey, and I can't imagine these scales are all that comfortable."

Fiachra groaned, snorting smoke.

"Sorry." Liam giggled.

"I-I don't know what to say. It's up to Fiachra, though. He has to be comfortable with it." Aedan patted the dragon.

Liam helped them buckled it around Fiachra's girth and a harness went across his chest. Aedan asked the beast if he was comfortable. The dragon backed away from the tree and launched himself into the skies, soaring and diving, and then returned. Standing tall, he raised his head and snorted.

"I'll take that as a yes." Aedan smiled. "If he didn't want it on, we'd know."

"I added a few saddlebags on each side to carry supplies. This way, you won't have to wear such heavy packs yourselves." Liam showed them some of the compartments. "And look." He pointed to the front of the chest harness. "The dragonhawk I made for your tunics. I put one here as well."

Hugs of gratitude followed, and while Liam explained more about the harness to Aedan, Cuinn led Conall by the hand to the other side of the tree. He just stared at Conall's green eyes, and his smile grew and faded with what was to come soon enough. Opening his mouth a little as if to speak, he closed it. Cuinn did that a few times before Conall took hold of his hands. Before Conall could say anything, Cuinn managed to speak.

"I've lived in Arvador my whole life, falling in and out of what I thought was love over the past few years. We haven't known each other a long time, but I have grown to care about you. Every day, I've gone to that field to play at fighting, putting all my frustrations into making myself the best warrior I could be. It wasn't until I met you that I realized that I was really fighting against my own heart. I've been my own adversary."

Conall opened his mouth to respond, but Cuinn put his finger on Conall's lips.

"Let me finish. With each night sitting by the river, I feel like our hearts have always been together." He put his hands on the sides of Conall's face. "Conall Mac Rinne, I will miss you more than I can say. No matter how far you are from me, know that I am always with you."

He kissed Conall, who responded by putting his arms around Cuinn, pulling him close. Aedan and Liam turned their heads away, smirking. With the farewells completed, the boys mounted Fiachra and headed north.

Once they were airborne, Fergus, who had been hiding behind another tree, watched them fly off. A dark-clad figure cast a shadow behind him, and Fergus acknowledged that by looking to the side.

"It's like I told you. They're headed toward Bealdrágan. I've kept my word, now you keep yours and give me my payment."

Fergus turned, his hand out. As the sword pushed through his chest and exited his back, his face contorted. Blood gurgled from his mouth. His body crumpled, unsheathing the gory blade, and the figure laughed to himself.

"Your payment is passage to the Otherworld."

Fergus' limp body blackened and turned to ashes, swept away by the wynd, and the dark-clad one, still laughing, melted into mist.

—ɷ—

Over the vast expanse Fiachra flew, his outstretched reddish-gold wings glimmering in the morning sun. Conall's hands gripped the horn of the saddle behind Aedan, his feet in the stirrups Liam had so carefully crafted. Puffs of sparse trees passed beneath them. The landscape gradually shifted to limestone karst once more with tufts of grasses like green fringe. From that height, a patchwork of bluish-grey stone was offset with shades of green and brown. Farmland stretched for miles, with piles of cut peat drying along the edges of the road. Judging from the map, when they had gone about halfway, they landed to give the dragon a break and to let them stretch their legs. Cuinn had packed smaller parcels for their midday meal, and Conall was more than happy to share some of it with Lann who had been following along.

"You know," Aedan spoke with a mouth full of food, "from this point forward, there's no turning back. We've come this far."

"I know." Conall took a swig from his goatskin. "Next stop, the Dragon's Mouth."

"Let's hope it's not quite as hot as this one's." Aedan nodded toward Fiachra who had found some patches of dandelions to munch on.

"We never did send Lann with a message for home when we were at the Twisted Trees. I'm afraid it would be too far for him to fly now." Using his teeth, Conall tore a piece of dried venison, giving a piece to Lann and eating the rest. "I miss my parents."

Aedan checked the harness for tightness. "Yeah. My da too." He took a deep breath. "You about ready?"

Nodding, Conall sent Lann off before they hopped onto Fiachra. While they were in flight, it was hard to hear anyone speak, so the boys didn't say much. Every so often, one or the other would point out some interesting sight below. Neither one could see each other's sadness, however. This would be the most challenging obstacle they had overcome since leaving Dún Ancróga. A swath of solemn gray clouds appeared on the horizon, undulating and swirling, stretching far to the east and west. It rose like a thunderhead with flashes of light illuminating the clouds. Monstrous shapes moved inside them. Severe and forsaken, the ground withered the closer they got to Bealdrágan. Conall rubbed his arms as the air temperature dropped. Even Fiachra grunted.

Aedan leaned forward. "Easy, boy. You won't be flying much longer."

Within a few hours, a crossroads appeared: one road heading west, one east, and one north, right toward the clouds. Aedan pressed his knees into the dragon, signaling the time to land. They donned their packs and checked each other for preparedness. Lann perched on Conall's arm.

"Listen, boy, you might not see us for a while. Find your way around this place. If... *When* we get through, I'll look for you." Lann squawked a few times before flying off.

Aedan told Fiachra to keep an eye on the hawk before thwapping his flank to get him to go. Roaring his discontent, the dragon then turned his head toward Aedan, snorting. The boys approached a conical cairn made of rock and bones in the center of the crossroads, and wintry breezes picked up. Half a mile ahead, the clouds towered above them, and where the road ended, an arch of three stone megaliths sat. As if there were an invisible barrier to keep it contained, the blackness didn't go beyond the portal. Carved into the rocks were glyphs. Aedan touched the stone, feeling the grooves of each symbol. Conall followed the etchings up the left side, over the top, and down the right.

"Any idea what it says?"

Conall shook his head. "None. Very carefully, touch the fog."

"It's soft. And sticky." He pulled his fingertip back, and it clung to the skin before releasing. "It's like a spider's web."

"If you and I can't read this, and we can't walk through..." Aedan's voice trailed off, and then his eyes grew wide. "Conall, show me the map!"

The opened parchment displayed their stick figures right in front of the wavy line. Aedan growled. Conall took the wands from his pack and brought them closer to the map. Like before, images became more detailed. A symbol showed the portal from above with the darkness beyond.

"Nothing. How are we supposed to —"

"Aedan, wait. Let me try something." Conall pulled out the book the old woman had given him, thumbing through a few pages. "There. I knew I'd seen this."

Rows of different handwritten glyphs spread over two pages, like a glossary. Conall held the open book in his left hand, pointing to the first symbol on the lower left of the portal. As he saw what each one meant, he pointed at each other carving, identifying it in the book. When he had finished with all of them, he handed the book to Aedan.

"If I'm right, this reads, *'The pain of your heart is the key.'*"

Aedan put the book, map, and wands away.

"I don't know if I want to feel more pain."

With a hand on his friend's shoulder, Conall looked at the portal.

"I know. But we need to move forward. Here's to seeing what's on the other side."

Both put their hands on the spongy fog, nodded to each other, and stepped forward, pushing their way in. The substance gave way, almost sucking them in, and they inhaled before moving into it entirely. Then, the fog closed behind them.

Conall's eyes darted around, seeing nothing at first. Then, images came into focus, a man and a woman in a cottage. His pulse raced and his gut twisted. Seeing Rinn and Siobhan close enough to touch made a harshness of sounds grow in his chest. The realization of just how long it had been since he had seen his parents set in, like an iron anvil on his heart, pressing down. The image seemed so real. Even the familiar smells of the peat fyre and his mother's skin, softened with lavender oil, were as if he were in the same room. He tried to reach out to them, but his arms wouldn't reach. He had had dreams about them since he left Silver Birch Glen, but none as vivid as this. Conall opened his mouth to speak, but his voice was absorbed by the fog. Calls to his mother and father grew to panicked shouts, his arms stretching to their limit but touching nothing. Voices broke through the thick barrier, and the lilt of his mother and the gruffness of his father pierced his ears, making him cry out. Then, as if they could hear him, they turned toward where he was, their eyes narrowing as if taking in an apparition. When it looked as if his mother's eyes met his, he screamed for her. That iron anvil pressed down harder.

Like his friend, Aedan was disoriented, his eyes glossy and his breaths shallow. A scene opened before him with a woman in a chair holding an infant. He tightened his jaw when he realized it was his mother, and she was holding him. She sang a soft lullaby to him:

"'Let the moon sing you to sleep, dear child. Let the moon bring you sweet slumber. And the stars will sing in harmony, a joyous tune, one only a mother knows. Moon and stars, moon and stars, their voices sing of dreams aplenty.'"

A man stepped onto the porch where she was sitting. It was his father. Saoirse smiled at her husband, but she never stopped singing. Odhran looked down at his sleeping child and nodded, kissing his wife on her head. The image faded to grey, and a new one emerged. This time, his mother was tending their garden, watching a two-year-old Aedan scamper about, chasing butterflies. His tiny legs buckled, and he dropped to his backside, laughing. Saoirse smiled at him, but then her face hardened. She could see something in the grasses, lurking. She called to the boy, but he was so enrapt with the butterflies that he didn't hear her. The threat moved closer. With one eye on the grasses and one on her son, she picked up her rake. What loomed moved, barely visible, but Saoirse could see it. She jumped in front of her son, rake held high, and the wolf ran off. Scooping up her son, she went into the cottage, checking out the window. She could still see the wolf's ears perked above the grasses, but then it turned and ran. Darkness prevailed once more, obscuring the image. Aedan clenched his fists, heaving as he held his emotions in check, but the tears didn't need his permission to flow.

Willing himself to move forward, Conall pushed one foot in front of the other, the sticky fog clinging to him. That anvil pressed down with each thought of his parents until he thought his heart would burst. The ethereal substance around him thinned, and he could see shapes. In a few more steps, he had cleared the gate, collapsing to his knees. Finally able to breathe, he inhaled deeply and exhaled his sorrow in loud sobs. As he pulled himself together, he looked back toward the gate, but all he saw was darkness. Aedan hadn't come through yet.

Swirling like smoke over a fyre, Aedan's thoughts moved, until finally another memory surfaced. On her bed, Saoirse lay with half-closed eyes, weak hands holding her son's hand and her husband's. The illness had spread to where no remedies could prevent its advance. All that was left was time. Young Aedan pressed his mother's hand to his cheek, and she mustered a faint smile. She asked him to sing that lullaby with her that she used to sing to him as a baby. In a soft voice, she began it, and the little boy joined in, his voice cracking. By the third line — "...*Moon and stars, moon and stars, their voices sing of dreams aplenty.*" — she was gone. Odhran put his hand on his son's shoulder while the boy still held her hand. Young Aedan turned and embraced his father, wailing into him. The man picked up his son and left the bedroom. Blown away as if by wynd, the image vanished, and Aedan fell forward, out of the gate. He saw Conall. His friend pulled him into a tight embrace.

"Are-Are you okay?" Conall whispered into Aedan's ear.

Nodding a little, Aedan collected himself, wiping his teary face with his sleeve. "Let's keep moving."

Beyond the gate, the realm before them extended outward with toothy rocks jutting forth around the serpentine road and into the valley below. Light grey clouds blanketed the skies, with flashes of light from within.

"This looks nothing like where we just were. At all. Where does the map tell us to go?"

Aedan saw they would pass a cluster of rocks called The Crags not far from their position. Around the bend, sharp, curved stones extended in all directions. He commented that they resembled talons of a hawk or owl. To continue, they would have to walk right into the middle of that area, but the map showed nothing else. Rising and falling, the road narrowed in places so that only one person could move through at a time. With their packs, it was a tight squeeze. Fortunately, the rocks had a polished sheen, so it wasn't terribly challenging to pass through them. Much of the road curved, so there was no way to see too far ahead, and danger could be lurking around any bend. A half-mile into The Crags, they saw the shadow of a flickering fyre. Off to the side of the path was a small cave, and outside of that was a bronze cauldron with a greenish patina. The fyre burning in it was small as if it hadn't been tended to in a while, but as they got closer, it grew in intensity.

"Am I the only one getting a weird feeling about this?" Conall craned his neck to see what he could.

"No. But unless you want to know who lives in that cave, we should keep going."

Conall extended his palms over the flames and then rubbed them together before walking away. He hadn't gone two steps before an old woman's voice stopped him.

"Blindness comes not from lack of sight, but from lack of vision."

When he turned back to the cauldron, three crones sat on varying heights of stone, each with long, straight white hair that fell over their shoulders. Their faces and arms had icovellavna that glowed a bluish-white in the fyrelight.

"What does that even mean?" Aedan stepped closer to Conall. "Let's go."

Conall hesitated. They walked ten steps when the voice repeated the statement. Conall stopped, but Aedan continued to walk, and then he went back toward the women. Aedan called for him, but he didn't respond. The cauldron fyre rose once more with his presence.

"What did you mean? About blindness?"

A woman, her eyes covered with a white cloth, replied, and as she spoke, her bone necklace rattled.

"Sight and vision. They are not the same, dear boy." She cackled. "One requires eyes. The other, inner understanding. Which do you seek?"

At this point, Aedan joined him.

"I'm not sure. My friend and I are on a quest. One that requires both sight *and* vision, I suppose. Are you able to help us, with one or both?"

All three women sniggered. A woman with one blue and one green eye replied.

"Our ability is only limited by your desire. The more you wish, the more we can help."

Aedan smirked and muttered, "For a price."

"Little, if anything, comes for free. Even life itself has a price." As she spoke, her different eyes reflected the fyre.

"I'm Conall, and this is my friend, Aedan. We —"

The blindfolded woman rattled her necklace.

"Word of your travels, Wyndracer and Fyrehunter, has reached us even here." She played with the bones in her fingers. "I am Mórga. The quiet one…" She gestured toward one who had white eyes. "…is Thano. She does not speak. My colorful sister here is Cerro. Some refer to us as the Cosantóirí."

The boys bowed their heads.

"The Protectors."

"Aye, Conall Mac Rinne, that we are." Mórga grinned. "But who we protect depends on much. Which do you seek, sight or vision?"

The boys conferred for a moment.

"Sight. Our map doesn't tell us much about what lies in wait for us here, and we'd like to prepare ourselves a little." Conall shifted from one foot to the other.

Aedan raised an eyebrow. "What's the price?"

The cauldron quenched itself of the fyre, and then it filled with water to the brim. From the center, a bronze dagger rose, its polished blade reflecting the water.

"No more than a drop of your blood." Mórga smiled sheepishly. "No more, no less."

Exchanging glances, their silence signaled agreement. First, Conall touched the point, wincing as the metal pierced his finger. The ruby substance oozed down the metal. Then, Aedan did the same. Their blood mingled as it diffused into the water. All three women descended their stony perches and placed their aged hands on the edge of the cauldron. In the mirror-like sheen of the water, sparks swam, like lightning bugs, brightening and diminishing.

"Wh-What would be the price of seeing our parents?"

"Aedan, son of Odhran, for that the price is more. Much more." Mórga extended a hand over the cauldron.

"No, wait. I just want to know the price."

Laughing, Mórga lowered her hand. "A year. A year from the end of your life."

Both boys gasped.

"Conall, we'll see them again," Aedan blurted.

"But," Conall began, "But, we don't know when we'll die, so —"

"Hence, why the price is so steep, my child," Cerro chimed in. "You have paid with blood. What do you wish to *see*?" She smirked, and her eyes shimmered like water.

"We want to see what lies before us here, in the Dragon's Mouth."

Mórga raised her voice. "You have spoken your desire. Take hold of the cauldron, and watch…"

Varieties of forest life bloomed in the water beneath the surface, animal and otherworldly. A cave opening, its maw black with shining eyes inside. A forest path. Individual trees. A mixture of serpents. Fyre.

The water receded from the cauldron, and the fyre returned, flickering as if nothing had happened.

Cerro returned to her crag, then Mórga, then Thano. Before the boys could ask questions, Cerro held up her finger.

"Of all in this place, you will encounter the Sídhe most of all. Fickle they are, and playful as well. Be wary where you step, and never leave the path. Ever. Upon the Uaimh na Brónna you will arrive, the Cave of Sorrows. Mischievous Sídhe will try to lure you into the darkness, into perpetual madness. For everyone, the darkness holds different sorrows. Assuming you can break the spell, you cannot be lured again."

"Then, the marshy lair of Caorthanach will you enter." Mórga continued. "You must pass her to continue. The Mother of Demons is swift and shows no mercy, and neither does her venom. There is a way to stay safe. If you touch a sacred tree, a billee, Caorthanach cannot harm you."

Conall help up his hand. "Excuse me." His voice shook. "H-How do we know which trees are sacred?"

Both Mórga and Cerro laughed while Thano merely smiled.

"Moss. Where grows moss on the roots, a billee grows." Mórga played with her necklace. "Rivers and streams you will cross, but their water is not safe. Only water with air on both sides should you drink." Her giggle mixed with the rattle of the bones.

Cerro added, "To leave the Dragon's Mouth, you must succumb to its fyre. Walk through and let the fyre burn. It reveals truth. Like the way into Bealdrágan, you must have the key to leave. Deceive, and you remain here, burning for all time."

Aedan and Conall stared at the flaming cauldron, the crackling and popping the only sound. Mórga told them to travel during the day as the Sídhe that lurked at night had a playful side and might not let them sleep. They could rest by the cauldron until morning as its fyre never went out. Contemplating what they were told, the boys ate in silence. Leaning back against a boulder across from the cauldron, they would share a look from time to time. The dimmer fyre cast the Cosantóirí in shadow, Mórga and Cerro whispering to each other. Thano gnawed on a bone with remnants of meat. When she finished, she threw the bone into the cauldron, causing sparks to fly up. She hobbled down from her perch, limping her way to the boys. Only a white cloth surrounded her, a shroud of a sort. The boys sat up when she approached, but she held up her hand. Thano touched her collarbone and pointed to the torcs around their neck, her bony hand shaking.

"This? They're gifts from Cernunnos." Conall took his off to show her.

She brushed her fingers against the metal, exhaling sharply. Aedan's eyes narrowed. Thano nudged the torc back to Conall. The crone took a small stick and drew in the dirt.

Aedan leaned forward. "What is she doing?"

"She's drawing us. And here..." Conall pointed at a circle with glyphs between the drawing of them. "This is a shield with a protection dríocht."

She pointed to their torcs and then at the shield.

"I think she's telling us that we can use the torcs for protection." Aedan then saw her nod. "I'm not sure how, but these can keep us safe."

Thano nodded. She drew a line connecting Aedan's hand to Conall's.

"Together. We can use the torcs for protection only when we're together. Right?"

Again, Thano nodded.

"But, how?"

Conall's question would go unanswered. She returned to her crag in shadow.

"Let's just try to get some sleep." Aedan pulled his blanket up to his chin.

Coupled with a starless, cloud-shrouded sky above, the nighttime sounds of Bealdrágan—shrieks, whistles, and cries of unknown creatures—kept Conall awake a little longer.

"Cernunnos, please. Keep us safe." Conall whispered, touching the twisted torc.

16 | THE SHIMMERING PATH

Unlike in the commonplace world, where sunrise and birdsong marked the onset of day, in Bealdrágan, the sound of three crones cackling broke the boys' slumber. Faces contorted from hard sleep returned to normal as they stretched and reclaimed their bearings. Like carrion, the women gnawed on bones of unknown origin. As soon as the boys had collected themselves, they thanked the women again and set off, glancing back toward a now-abandoned craggy space, as if the Cosantóirí had performed their task and returned from whence they came. A barely trodden path through rocky terrain showed a forsaken place, one that hadn't known the colors of the world beyond the boundaries of fog and fyre.

Clouds of grey fleece fringed with wisps of black crawled across the sky with the occasional fleeting glimpse of sunlight brave enough to poke its way through. Paths through boulders taller than most trees kept the air cold and still. Breezes rarely blew through, and when they did, they conjured goosebumps. Eventually, the stone gave way to dirt, becoming wetlands with each step. On either side of the path, marshland spread, with tree roots descending into murky bogs like vulture's talons. Around one turn, an offshoot path meandered to a mound with roughly-hewn rocks by its feet. Between the rocks lay a darkness. Conall and Aedan hadn't said anything to each other since they left The Crags. Only their breathing and footsteps sat in their ears. They passed a massive willow at the edge of the marsh, and a human voice stopped each of them.

"It's been a while, hasn't it, Aedan." A young man in brown pants and a sleeveless green vest leaned against the tree on one of the roots, his arms crossed. His curly blond hair stopped at his shoulders. "It's good to see you again. I've missed you."

"Niall? Is that you? What're you doing here?" He moved closer to the tree. "Why—"

Niall hopped onto the path. "I'm here to see *you*." He smiled.

"How did you even know I was here?"

"Aedan, you know you were never good at keeping secrets." Niall laughed. "Come, sit with me. Tell me what you've been up to." He patted the tree root.

—⁓—

The voice Conall heard came from a different source—a young man seated on a rock across the path from the tree.

"I'm so glad I found you. I was worried."

Conall's face lit up, and he blinked away a few tears.

"Cuinn? I-I didn't... How?"

"I followed you. I didn't know when we'd see each other again."

"But, how?" He moved closer to Cuinn. "Is this a dream?"

Cuinn laughed and grinned. "It's always a dream when I'm with you. Sit here and tell me about your journey."

—⁓—

Niall had pulled his legs in, wrapped his arms around them, and rested his head on his knees, hanging on to every word of Aedan's.

"—got to a fort where we met up with Fionn and Déaglán. It's taken me a little while, but I appreciate all they taught us."

"Sounds like you've been on some great adventures." Niall touched Aedan's arm. "Then what did you do? I'm so glad we have this chance to talk again. It's been far too long." He blew strands of hair from his face.

Aedan grinned. "I remember you doing that all the time. Your hair would always fall forward." He reached out and pushed some hair from Niall's forehead. "There. Now, I can see your face."

Picking up from where he had left off, Aedan continued recounting his adventures.

—⁓—

Cuinn had laced his fingers with Conall's as they leaned against the boulder.

"—then we freed ourselves from the fog. Seeing my parents again, well, it brought a lot back. What did you see in the fog? You had to have passed through the gate as well."

"It's not important." He gently squeezed Conall's hand. "I'm proud of you for getting so far along in your quest. I feel like we have so much more to learn about each other."

They locked eyes, and Cuinn leaned forward, lightly touching his lips to Conall's.

"It looks like it's about to rain soon. Let's get somewhere where we won't get wet."

He led Conall toward the side path that led to the cave.

"See? I have a tent ready. Then, I want to know more about you. About your family."

—⚹—

A breeze blew the fronds of the willow, making Niall shiver.

"—then we left Arvador. After... Hey, are you all right?" Aedan moved closer to him.

"Just a chill." He looked at the sky. "I think it'll rain soon. We should probably go somewhere dry. I've set up a tent."

"You were always so resourceful." Aedan helped him up. "I miss our riverside talks."

Niall put his arm around Aedan. "Me too."

"I remember how you'd bring some of your mum's apple tart for us to share. How *is* your mum? I know your da wasn't too keen on me back then."

"They're fine." Niall smiled, guiding him toward the side path.

—⚹—

Cuinn, his face aglow with joy, walked backward, holding both of Conall's hands.

"We're almost there. It'll be so nice to have more time together."

Giggling, Conall followed, his eyes crinkled from smiling.

"I never knew I'd ever feel the way I do right now. I'm hoping we can head back to Silver Birch Glen once this quest is over."

Just smiling, Cuinn didn't respond, moving toward the tent. Occasionally, he'd laugh a little.

Conall continued. "You know, when you told me how you felt about me back in Arvador, I was just speechless. I don't want you to think I don't feel the same. I do. Cuinn, I—"

Having kept his eyes on Cuinn the whole time, he wasn't watching where he walked and stepped on a rock, twisting his ankle. Pain shot through his foot, and then he gasped. Instinctively, he looked down. As he looked up, he saw a small creature in front of him, about half his height, its arms extended like Cuinn's. Conall narrowed his eyes.

"A Sídhe..." He clenched his fists and growled.

Behind the imp, he caught a quick glance of another one leading Aedan toward the cave.

"Aedan! Stop!" He tried to go toward his friend, but the creature stopped him, its eyes turning red. "Aedan!"

His friend was nearing the cave. Again, Conall tried to go forward, but the imp wouldn't allow it. Looking for another way around, he remembered the warning about staying on the path. He stepped down on his injured foot, and then popped up straight.

"Of course! The spell broke because of the pain. Physical pain." He glared at the imp. "If you don't let me pass... *Ó aer, Déanaim iarracht tine.*" A flame formed in his palm. "I'll burn down a tree. You protect them, don't you. What'll it be?"

Unruffled, the imp stood its ground. Conall pulled his hand back to throw the flame at the closest tree, and the imp vanished and appeared by the tree. Aedan was a few steps from the cave. Extending his staff, Conall aimed it at his friend. The imp reappeared, grabbing Conall's leg, forcing him to drop the staff. Aedan was now one step inside the cave. Scrambling for his weapon, Conall swung it at the imp at his feet, causing it to disperse, and then he hurled it toward the cave. As Aedan lifted his right foot to step into the darkness completely, the staff struck him behind the knee. A cry of pain from inside the darkness made Conall bound toward it. He reached into the cave opening and latched onto Aedan's foot, pulling as hard as he could, but the darkness of madness had its hold. Muffled screams pierced the barrier, making Conall pull harder. Then, tendrils of darkness like serpents twisted around Conall's hands, working to envelop him as well. His hands and Aedan's foot disappeared in the obscurity.

Conall's eyes turned bright blue, and he grunted as he tugged with all his strength. More of the darkness wound itself up his arms, tightening and nearing his shoulders. Just before it reached his face, he screamed, his eyes blazing white.

"Aer mór, tabhair neart dom!"

From his arms came gusts of wind pushing back the blackness until he could see his hands and Aedan's foot once more. Bracing his legs, he leaned back, gritted his teeth, and strained every muscle in his arms. Winds pushed against the cave opening, weakening the hold the darkness had, and with one giant tug, Aedan came free. Both fell backward, crashing against the ground. Conall pressed his hand to his chest and caught his breath. He rolled Aedan onto his back, checking for wounds and broken bones.

"Aedan... Aedan!" His eyes scanned all over his friend. "Aedan, wake up!"

Gasping in one large breath, Aedan shot up, his head turning in every direction until he saw Conall.

"Are you all right?" Conall brushed dirt and leaves off his friend.

Nodding, he clenched his eyes closed for a moment.

"Can you stand?"

Aedan gripped onto Conall's shoulder while his friend helped him up. He staggered as he got his bearings, not letting go. Shaking his head, he blinked from the light.

"I'm… I'm all right. The madness in there. It's worse than the fog at the gate. My head… it's better now."

The imp, growling, jumped out from the cave opening, its eyes fiery. Aedan's back was to the cave, but when he heard the sound, before the imp could even take another step, Aedan spun around.

"*Dóim.*" Burn.

Flames consumed the imp in a flash, and it howled before vanishing.

Conall, wide-eyed, said nothing. He leaned on Aedan to get him back to the path. A little way past the cave, they found a place to sit. Conall removed his boot and noticed a purple bruise on his ankle.

"When I was in the cave, I heard you scream something… in an ancient tongue, like a dríocht. You asked the air to give you strength."

Checking his foot, Conall shook dirt from his boot before putting it back on.

"I'm not sure. I was pulling to get you free, and suddenly something inside me told me what to say. I'd never felt that connection before. And now I have a headache."

Swallowing mouthful after mouthful from his water skin, Aedan passed it to his friend.

"I don't know about you," —he wiped his mouth with the back of his hand—"but I'm tired of having my heart used against me. Who knew I was so weak?"

"You're not weak at all. It's our heart" —he tapped his chest with his fist—"that keeps us strong. Seeing my parents, seeing Cuinn… I wouldn't trade those thoughts for anything." He took another drink. "Who did you see?"

Staring off, Aedan didn't answer. Conall started to stand up.

"Niall. I saw Niall. Of all the people in the world, it had to be him." Aedan shook his head.

"Why's that?"

"He broke my heart, that's why. His father, Turlough, thought I was no better than a rogue. Niall and I would meet by the river, sort of like you and Cuinn, but Niall and I had to sneak around. Turlough was the blacksmith. I don't think I've ever seen such a large man before. His arm was bigger than I was. The way he wielded that hammer… but, Niall had this way of making me feel like everything would be just fine. I truly thought I was in love."

"So, what happened?"

"I went to our place by the river, the patch of grass where we'd left a small pile of pebbles. I waited. We'd meet at night. I'd always tell my da that I was going to visit Seamus. I sat by the river for hours, watching the moon rise. If I heard a rustle, I'd think it was Niall, but it turned out to be a fawn or a fox. I woke up at sunrise. Alone. When I got back home, I managed to sneak back into the cottage before my da woke up. Later, he went to the market, and when he returned, he commented that Turlough had sent Niall to live with his aunt in Ashbarra, a town a few hours north. I never saw him again. To this day, every time I pass by the smithy, I can see that smug look on Turlough's face." Aedan snarled.

"That's a shame. It was Turlough, though, and not Niall. He didn't have a say."

Aedan popped up, ready to go. "He could have fought harder, that's all I'm saying. We should go if you're able."

Shadow and mist hung around them, making it hard to get a clear view too far ahead. Strange noises and chattering kept them looking about. Some sounds stopped them in their tracks. At one point, Aedan knelt by a stream to refill his waterskin, but Conall reminded him that water with air on both sides was safe. They passed spider webs as large as blankets, some of which bearing silk-shrouded prey caught by the eight-legged monstrosities sitting at the center. A few had multicolored bodies, like the motley of jesters. Others, black as night, speckled with yellow or red. They ranged in size from a human head to an arm's span. Yew trees grew along the path, some with trunks as wide as the boys were tall. Branches formed a sinister canopy, forks of arboreal lightning stretching in all directions. One, a foot wide in girth, formed an arch over the path. Mists hung like ethereal skeletons, waving in the breezes. As if the heavens could roar, thunder resounded in the distance, an ominous reminder of the mysteries of Bealdrágan.

Where the mists thickened, pairs of glowing eyes watched. They would vanish and reappear in random places. Just past a gnarled dead oak, a mud pit gurgled and bubbled, like the cauldron of the Cosantóirí. Beneath the surface, streamlined creatures swam, their bodies kept hidden by the muck. A white unicorn with its pearlescent twisted horn bounded past them, and Conall mused that it could be a good sign, but Aedan simply groaned in reply. He said that things of beauty in this place were more likely púka, shapechangers that interacted with people for their own amusement. Farther down the path, a hare jumped into their way. Aedan grumbled, pulling back his foot to kick it. It reverted to its regular form — a dark-furred feline body and head, with bat's ears, a tail, and tiny wings — before jumping back into the muck. Conall warned him that, from what he knew, púka could be either mischievous or helpful, and it wasn't wise to upset them. He also said finding a place to camp should be their first job. The encounter at the Cave of Sorrows had drained him. Aedan agreed, and they kept their eyes open for a safe place, although that would be a challenge. Both agreed that caves didn't seem like a good option, but sleeping out in the open would make them easier prey for the inhabitants of the Dragon's Mouth. Despite their misgivings, however, they settled on a small opening under a rock ledge. Conall remembered that Thano told them how they could protect themselves. Creating a protection charm outside the opening, Conall told Aedan they should use their torcs to strengthen it, but Aedan didn't know what that meant.

"Well, four trees make up the charm. If we were going to strengthen two of them, I'd think it would be rowan, for protection, and alder, for strength. What do you think?"

Shrugging, Aedan put his on the alder Ogham sign, making sure the opening of the torc faced inward. Conall did the same for the rowan.

"I guess it can't hurt right?"

The markings they scribed into the dirt flashed once, much to the surprise of the boys. Even though it would be hours until nightfall, they both agreed that rest would help them clear their heads. They would have to trust that the torc-enhanced protection circle would do its job. Beyond the shelter, storms rumbled. Conall leaned against his pack, staring into the marsh until his eyelids fell. For Aedan, he chose to watch the surroundings.

When Conall opened his eyes, what was once a dank wetland had become rocky hills, like the limestone karsts to the south. Purplish-blue skies sparkled with only a few stars near a sliver of moon. As he lowered his eyes toward the horizon, a figure sat near. Wisps of white smoke rose from it, and when it turned its head toward him, white icovellavna surrounded the eyes. Whatever it was, it was opaque, its body outlined in a faded light. Conall thought about moving closer, and instantly he was within an arm's reach. The figure turned its head again, and the proximity revealed a wolf sitting with its back to Conall. He felt himself reach out to touch the shimmering animal, and the wolf opened its mouth. As soon as Conall's hand was inside, the wolf bit down. A blinding light exploded in front of Conall, and then, he woke up.

He shot up, panting, checking his hand, relieved to see it undamaged.

"You all right?" Aedan still looked out at the marsh. "Bad dream?"

"Not sure." — he looked at his hand — "Still trying to make sense of it. How long was I asleep?"

"A few hours. I'm not that tired. Just been thinking."

"The protection circle works. No púka attacks or Sídhe?" Conall chuckled.

Aedan laughed. "Actually, I fought off a half dozen rabid chipmunks. Too bad you missed it."

Conall joined his friend with a pouch of dried venison, handing Aedan a chunk.

"Seen anything?"

Aedan ripped a piece with his teeth. "Nah, just things moving around in the mists and shadows. More of the same, I'd imagine."

"We *are* going to make it through this."

"The question is, in what condition. Something's out there, Conall. Something... dark."

"Well, we *are* in the Dragon's Mouth. That's to be expected." He chewed another piece of meat.

"I mean beyond what should be here. Every once in a while, the hairs on my arms stand on end. I thought it was the púka, but those things don't scare me." Aedan shuffled to the back of the opening. "I need to close my eyes for a bit. You good to be on watch?"

Conall agreed to trade places. Staring out, he would occasionally check his hand, opening and closing it. It bore no marks, but he remembered the pressure of the wolf's jaws, just no pain. Rather than concern himself with what lay beyond the protection circle, he distracted himself by drawing in the dirt with a stick. At first, he made a pair of eyes. He then drew designs that matched the icovellavna on the wolf's face. Using his finger, he traced the grooves, expanding the symbols. He erased it with his hand and did it again. This went on for several hours.

By the time Aedan woke up, Conall was eager to get going. From what they could tell, it was morning, although the cloud cover did make it a challenge. Both agreed they needed to find more water, but they didn't understand what Mórga had told them about air being on both sides. The path took them through areas that were ankle-deep in muddy water, and the boots that Liam had made for them had lost much of their newness, but they kept the water out. With the new day came different sights, especially when Aedan spotted billee — the sacred trees. Even in this nightmarish place, they stood out with their green moss along the roots. In some spots, feathery ferns fringed the base as well. Occasionally, they came across deeper stagnant pools where the moss was a verdant carpet, with water skippers leaving ripples where the surface was clear. The acrid smell of decomposing plants lay in pockets as they made their way through the thickest part of the marsh. In this area of Bealdrágan, clouds of gnats and other flies, attracted by the odor, replaced the mists. As the water level rose over the path, rocks became the best means of travel, so the boys had to hop from one to another without slipping off. It was then they heard the snoring of what had to be a large beast.

Without much visual clarity, they turned in all directions each time they heard the rumbling exhale. Aedan muttered it might be a dragon; Conall, a monstrous frog — they wanted to meet neither. They swatted their way along the stones. Aedan slipped as he landed, but Conall caught him from behind, submerging his foot in the process. Each stone became its own small obstacle, causing them to pay more attention to their next foothold than the slumbering creature nearby. Two dozen stones later, the snoring grew louder, and with each exhale also came the fetid smell of rotting flesh. Conall passed through a cloud of gnats to find the cause.

"By Brigid's fyre…" He gasped, putting his hand out to stop Aedan. "That has to be Caorthanach."

Out in the still water lay a small island from which grew an ash tree, although all that remained was its bottom half, worn free of its bark. Coiled around it was a serpent with green and black scales. Scattered along the body, gold scales illuminated randomly.

Conall lowered his voice. "It-Its body must be two feet thick. How are we going to get past it?"

"Your guess is as good as mine. Carefully?" Aedan combed his hair back with his fingers.

"With the rocks as slimy as they are, even if we're careful…"

Nodding, Aedan jumped to another stone. Caorthanach remained asleep. Conall also jumped.

"Just one at a time. She's not even twitched, so maybe she's a sound sleeper." Aedan shrugged.

After two more stones, the path emerged more clearly. Conall gasped. Their path would take them directly toward the island, and they would have to pass right by her to go beyond.

Conall pressed his hand to his chest, taking a deep breath.

"I'm scared. I don't know if I can do this. Maybe there's another way around."

Aedan put a hand on his friend's shoulder. "I'm scared too." He looked over at Caorthanach. "Whatever you want to do, I'll follow. Do we risk getting off the path?"

Lowering his head, Conall shook as he exhaled.

"I-I don't want to die. And we've come too far to turn back." He lifted his head. "Let's just take a moment to think."

Aedan spotted a sacred tree close to the path and gestured for them to sit at its base.

"We'll be safe. For now. I don't know how these trees work, but if they're sacred, I don't think she can touch us."

"*That issss true. I cannot. But… you can't ssstay there forever.*"

Caorthanach had lifted her head, her tongue flicking. The swaying of her body, with its hypnotic effect, was an attempt to lure them off the tree, but since they were touching it, her power had no effect.

"*Come closer. Let me sssee you.*" The golden scales lit up randomly, adding to the mesmeric quality of her movements.

Her head rose higher, and her underbelly had horizontal scales that pulsed their illumination down her body. Aedan shifted his body weight to get a firmer stance on the tree root, and his foot slipped out from under him on the moss. He landed on the rock at the base of the billee tree.

"Take my hand! Hurry!" Conall stooped and extended his arm.

Aedan's eyes glazed over, and he began to sway like Caorthanach, caught like a fish on a line. He didn't look back as he moved from one rock to another. The serpent used her allure, like a dance, to keep Aedan in her thrall. All Conall could do was stare wide-eyed.

"Come to me, boy. Let me embracccce you."

Conall extended his staff, but after looking it over, he put it back. He then turned his attention to the tree. All living trees were homes to Sídhe, he thought. He placed his palms on the trunk.

"Please, tree spirit, help me. My friend is in danger, and I don't know what to do."

Nothing happened. Conall shivered and hunched over at the thought of losing his friend. He saw Aedan moving closer toward Caorthanach. Soon, he'd be within striking range.

"Aedan! Stop! Please!"

Leaves rustled, and when Conall looked up, branches from the tree stretched out and wrapped themselves around Aedan, pulling him back to the safety of the tree. Still entranced by the serpent, the boy reached out, squirming in the arboreal grip. A ghostly shape of a girl sat on an upper branch above him. She had dew drops for her headpiece and leaves covered her. On her back were opaque wings, and she fluttered down to Conall and touched his chest with a slender finger. She rose back to Aedan and touched his chest as well, a small spark disappearing inside him. In a moment, he was back to himself. The tree fairy became one with the tree, and the branches released Aedan.

Conall waved his hand in front of Aedan's eyes. "Are you back?"

"What did that fairy do? When she touched me, I felt a warmth enter me, and my mind cleared."

"I'm not sure, but we have to get past Caorthanach." He turned his attention to her. "Caorthanach! What do we have to do to get past you? What can we offer you?"

"Let me embracccce you, child. Just one moment of pain, and then… peace." She pushed her head forward and flicked her tongue.

They pressed their backs against the tree, gripping the trunk, turning ashen at her words. Unable to leave their safe haven, they sat on the roots on the other side. Conall suggested maybe one of them could distract her while the other got past, but then he realized that the one left behind wouldn't be able to leave. Aedan wished he could summon Fiachra. If nothing else, the dragon could fly them to safety. Remembering when Lann saved him from a bear, Conall laughed a little but knew that the hawk wouldn't stand a chance against Caorthanach. A night-time departure would be unlikely since she would have the element of surprise along the path. Plus, they knew snakes had an extraordinary sense of smell through their tongue. If they strayed off the path, who knew what other dangers they would happen upon. Caorthanach wasn't the only peril to avoid. They thought using the wands would help, but they had limited knowledge of dríochta. If the most they could do was summon wynd and fyre, they wouldn't be able to do much in a wetland. Conall wondered if their torcs might offer some protection, but other than enhancing the protection circle earlier, they didn't know how else to use them.

Conall checked to see what Caorthanach was doing, and she had coiled herself around her tree again, giving the appearance of sleeping. He didn't trust that, though. It would only be a matter of time when she would try again. He and Aedan both knew they couldn't stay where they were for a lot longer. While they contemplated what to do, Conall felt it was a suitable time to share his dream with Aedan.

"Maybe it was a sign from Brigid? Wolves are sacred to her."

Conall shrugged. "Or Cerridwen. All I saw was the wolf."

"Did it say anything or do anything?"

"Other than bite my hand?" — Conall chuckled — "No. As soon as its mouth closed on my hand, I woke up."

"You know, we are in a sort of otherworldly place. That could have affected your dreams. Or, maybe it was the Cosantóirí."

"But what could it mean? The only wolves we've seen were — "

"With Elder Daithi, at Cernunnos' shrine." Aedan wagged his finger. "You think it has something to do with Cernunnos? Or maybe… your caomhnóir?"

Conall rested his head against the tree. "I don't know. So much has happened to us so fast, it's almost hard to keep up with it all. I wish we could just find a way past this she-serpent."

Aedan scanned beyond where the path moved past their position. He sat back down in a huff.

"If only these sacred trees were close enough together, we could just hop from one to another. The only safe place is when we're touching one." He sighed. "You don't think that tree fairy could fly us away, do you?" The way he twisted his mouth denoted sarcasm.

Conall raised an eyebrow. "Hmm."

"What's 'hmm'?"

"I'm thinking. Give me a moment."

Aedan laced his fingers behind his head and leaned against the tree and tapped his foot on the root. He noticed Conall looking all around the trunk and branches. He knew from experience to let his friend work through his thoughts.

"I... think I have an idea. We know that the sacred trees prevent us from being harmed. What if we could bring one with us?"

"Brilliant. Let's chop this one down and carry it with us. I'm sure the Sídhe would love that."

Conall smirked. He pressed his palms to the tree and closed his eyes. After a few minutes, he opened them and smiled.

"What? What's happening?"

"I know how we can get out of here." After scraping moss from the bark, he rubbed it on his arms and face.

"Now I know you've lost what's left of your mind."

"I asked the tree fairy if we could take some of the moss. That's what makes this billee. The tree becomes sacred because of the moss. If we put it on us, we're protected."

"Mhmm."

"Fine, don't believe me. You want to leave, don't you?"

Grimacing, Aedan rubbed the moss all over any exposed skin. Conall stepped onto the rock, keeping his eye on Caorthanach. He managed to get a few rocks down the path but stopped where the rocks curved toward the sleeping creature. After he turned back to make sure Aedan was right behind him, he took another step and was face-to-face with two yellow eyes and a thwipping tongue. Caorthanach's head was close enough to touch. Her golden scales illuminated, and she swayed, attempting to lure them again.

"*Embraccce me.*" Her tongue came close to touching them both. "*You think that moss will protect you? I am the mother of all demonsss.*"

She reared back to strike, and the boys took that as a cue to leap to the next rock. Conall landed on his backside because the surface was slick, and Aedan latched onto him when he made it over. Her head reappeared in front of them once more, her body undulating and shimmering. In an attempt to ward her off, Conall ignited a fyre in his palm. It did make her hesitant to move closer, but with one breath from her, the flame extinguished.

"*Neither druidsss nor wizardsss you are. I have filled my belly with many.*"

Retracting her body, another strike was imminent. Aedan stood tall, preparing for her. Conall, however, wasn't convinced.

"What are you doing? We need to move."

Grinning, Aedan winked at him and clenched his fists. As she sprung her head forward, she had to stop just shy of him because of the moss. Instinctively, he stepped back a bit, but he was closer to the rock's edge.

"See? What did I tell you?" He turned to gloat, but she came at him again, and this time he fell off the rock into the water.

Conall reached for him. "Are you daft? The moss will wash off. You won't be protected!"

Up to his chest in muck, Aedan couldn't get a foothold in the mud below. Conall, on his knees, gripped his friend's forearm and tried to pull him up on the stone. Out of the corner of his eye, he saw Caorthanach rearing back.

"I can't pull you up. Get to the tree! Hurry!"

Aedan scrambled to reach the roots. He screamed for Conall to get back to the tree, but his friend bowed his back and clenched his fists. Like a whip, the serpent lashed out. Conall crossed his arms in front of his face and turned his head just as she reached him. Aedan couldn't watch. He then heard laughter — hers.

"Clever boy. The magic of the tree mossss did indeed protect you from me. But… the moment you ssslip into the marsh, I claim you. Your friend, however…"

Striking like a thunderbolt, she snatched Aedan from the water. Conall screamed his name. When she pulled back, Aedan was holding onto one of her fangs, trying to avoid the tip. His pack fell into the water. She shook her head to dislodge him, but he held on, his legs flailing. Her forked tongue stabbed at the air while her body wriggled. In an attempt to remove him, she turned her head up before crashing down into the water. She recoiled to her tree, crouching tightly together, always vigilant. Aedan scampered for the closest billee, throwing himself on the roots, his breathing erratic. Since he had washed off most of the moss, he quickly reapplied it but also put some inside his boots. Conall had used a branch to retrieve Aedan's pack, now sodden. Thankfully, he had secured it well to keep things inside, but water would make his food unfit to eat.

"This way, if I fall in the water again" — he muttered to himself — "I'm still touching the moss, you scaly witch."

He caught his breath and made sure Conall was all right before joining him. Both watched Caorthanach for any sign she would strike again. They moved onto a few more rocks, realizing that they were even closer to her. Conall said he had an idea for a distraction, but it would take both of them. He whispered what he was thinking, but Aedan's contorted expression conveyed uncertainty. They were out in the open, clearly an easy target if Caorthanach wanted to try something. Her body movements quickened, and her tongue flicked faster. Her underbelly shimmered along with her golden scales. Even though her hypnotic charms had no effect while the boys were protected, it was her nature to use the tactics she had always used. Aedan and Conall held hands, extending their other hands toward her.

In unison, they repeated the fire dríocht. Aedan hesitated, but nonetheless, he continued.

Caorthanach laughed. *"Fyre doesss not affect me, little onesss."*

They kept saying it, with Aedan putting more enthusiasm into it, countered by her rising laughter. They, however, were not focused on her.

Caorthanach writhed and wriggled in her contentment. That came to a stop, however, when the top of the dead tree to which she had clung burst into flames, illuminating the marsh. Hissing at the fyre, she unfurled her massive body into the waters, using her tail to douse the burning wood. Conall and Aedan used this opportunity to jump from stone to stone until they reached a billee. Caorthanach did, in fact, put out the fyre, but not before the boys were well out of her reach. The mother of demons coiled around her tree once more, the shadows of the marsh concealing her. Gradually, her illuminations diminished. The worst, for the moment, was over.

17 | CONFRONTING DARKNESS

Zigzagging their way through the marsh, Aedan and Conall reached a tiny barren island surrounded by ferns and lily pads. Jutting from the water, white lilies looked like sentries guarding the space. The boys fell to the ground, winded. Laughter from unreleased frustration burst forth until they fell silent, staring at each other. They both inspected their packs. Aedan shook the last drops he had from his waterskin into his mouth. Without wasting any time, they did a protection circle around the island which was barely large enough to fit them both. Considering their last encounter, they knew it would give them peace of mind. Aedan really wanted a nap, but Conall wasn't sure that was a good idea just yet, especially since they didn't have any water left. None of the water in the marsh was fit to drink, nor did it have air on both sides, a puzzle neither of them could solve. A brief respite would be best until they could find safer ground, however.

The island itself was not much larger than ten feet in any direction, but it served a purpose. No caves of madness, no púka, and no monstrous serpent. Eventually, what seemed like insects hovered around them, but upon closer inspection, they were fairies. Curiosity had lured them, and they simply lingered above. Each fairy had a distinct color—some pale blue, others pink or orange. Conall held up his finger. A bright green fairy alighted on him, slowly opening and closing its translucent wings. No bigger than a grasshopper, once it had satisfied its curiosity, it flitted away. For a little while, they lingered until, one by one, they vanished into the marsh.

"It's strange. Of everything we've seen in Bealdrágan, we haven't seen much to make us smile." Conall watched the last fairy disappear.

"We should go soon. If we don't find water, we're not going to make it out of here." Aedan smacked his lips.

"Just a little longer."

While they sat in silence, Conall looked down at his hand, the one the wolf bit in his dream, and wiggled his fingers. At that moment, he clenched his stomach, then it moved to his chest, and his face contorted. Tears streamed down. He leaned over and wailed. Aedan, who had been paying attention to his surroundings, turned at the sound. Conall's body heaved, and he squeezed the dirt. Aedan put an arm around his friend, and then Conall cried harder.

After a little while, Conall sat up, using the back of his hand to wipe his face.

"I'm all right." —he choked out, patting Aedan's arm—"Thanks. So many feelings at once. I think it's this place. Leaving Cuinn. Seeing my parents in that fog. Caorthanach. My dream. I..."

Conall's expression prompted Aedan to squeeze.

"I'm fine now. We should go." Conall brushed himself off and hopped to the next rock in the path.

Before he followed, Aedan said in a whisper, "Cernunnos, watch over him. He's my family."

—⚌—

The marsh waters deepened, covering the rocks on the path, which left the only other way to travel—the trees. In the wetlands, roots grew above the water, some gnarled and twisted while others were smooth as polished stone. The boys jumped from one to another, glancing over to where they assumed the path was so they could keep moving in the right direction, but muddy water, especially with moss, obscured their view beneath the surface. Once in a while, they'd find a billee. Above, the canopy stretched all around them, with gaps to see the grey clouds moving and swirling. Lightning from distant storms flashed brighter than it had when they were deeper in the marsh; thunder cut into the breezes as if announcing its imminent arrival.

They lost track of time since they couldn't see the sun, and it seemed they had gone deeper into a part of the Dragon's Mouth than they had intended. The path remained unknown to them, but they pressed on. Disturbing the moss on the water's surface were more swimming creatures, ones the boys hoped they wouldn't have to deal with. Púka could take any form, and some had mischievous temperaments. Whatever they were, they never broke the surface to reveal their appearance. Conall stopped.

"Look. Those vines growing from that water oak. How odd."

"Maybe it's a curtain of snakes." Aedan chuckled, wiggling his fingers.

Conall glared. "Not. Funny."

On the other side was a sound like pouring rain, but it wasn't raining where they were. Upon closer inspection, Conall exhaled when the vines were, in fact, vines. Vigilant just the same, since snakes did live in trees and could use the vines as camouflage, he scrutinized each one until they passed through the hanging barrier. A grassy mound, twice as tall as they were, lay before them, and water poured over the top into the marsh.

"Must be a spring that flows through the rock and comes out at the top. It's almost like a waterfall."

Where the water fell into the marsh, it disturbed the moss and water skippers. Aedan put his hand out to touch it, but Conall snatched it back.

"It's probably not safe." — he pointed into the waters below — "No fish."

"Have you seen any fish since we've been here?" Aedan reached again, sticking his hand into the cascade. "I think it's okay to drink."

"But —"

Smirking, Aedan pointed. "What did Mórga say? Only water with air on both sides. See? This little waterfall has air in front of it and behind it. It's safe." He cupped his hands underneath and put it to his lips.

Conall cringed. Aedan took a sip.

"Hmm. Tastes clean." He gulped down a few handfuls. He spread his arms wide. "See? It's fine. I'm fine."

With caution, Conall did the same. They then filled their water skins. Running their heads under the cascade, they also washed their faces and arms since it would probably be a while before they could bathe to remove all the moss and mud. That alone invigorated them enough to press on. The skies darkened, and they agreed to stop to make camp once their visibility diminished more. At a small island, they found a tree, its trunk about two feet wide, and decided that it was as good a place as any to rest. Roots had moss, so it was a sacred tree. Aedan nestled between two large roots, like the arms of a great chair, while Conall leaned against another nearby. Exhaustion claimed them soon enough.

Aedan yawned as he awoke the next morning, and an odd sensation made him look at his lap. His sleepy eyes widened. A visitor slept — a snake. Without moving his mouth, he voiced Conall's name a few times, trying not to move. As soon as Conall saw it, his mouth fell open.

"Well, we've found the ash tree."

Aedan kept perfectly still. "How do you know?"

"Aside from the fact that I know what an ash tree looks like? That snake in your lap? It's an adder. Stay still."

Every time Aedan moved an arm even slightly or flexed a leg muscle, the adder moved its head. It seemed perfectly content to sleep in the warmth of his lap, and as long as it wasn't agitated, Aedan didn't try to move.

"Looks like you've made a new friend." Conall grinned.

"You're hilarious. What do we do?"

"Hmm. Good question. Wait until it moves?" Conall leaned around to get a closer look.

"You do realize that I had a lot of water. At some point, well, you know…"

Conall chuckled but stopped himself. "Sorry. I don't mean to laugh. It's just the idea of you having to –"

Aedan grumbled. He added that adders were known to strike if provoked. Conall's response was, aptly, not to provoke it. Despite being poisonous, adders weren't known for killing people, just causing severe and distressing symptoms. They had just escaped Caorthanach, a serpent considerably larger, but a regular-sized snake could easily affect their quest. Leaning back against the tree, Aedan's eyes darted around as he thought of a way out of his predicament. Unable to move, he eventually fell back asleep. Conall couldn't help but stare at the snake, but he, too, succumbed. When he opened his eyes, his head leaning against the thick root, he was face-to-face with the adder. His heart immediately raced and sweat trickled down his brow. The adder, sensing Conall's fear, moved back, looking as if it might strike. Aedan moved to get more comfortable, but he remembered the adder and checked his lap. Sighing at the adder's absence, he moved his eyes to Conall, his face drained of color and sweat-laden.

"Don't move. I'll try to distract it." Aedan looked around for something to coax the snake away.

Conall raised his hand from his side.

"Conall, are you daft? Put your hand down. Slowly."

Aedan couldn't have expected what happened next. Conall reached out for the snake. At first, it didn't react, just flicking its tongue, but then it hissed and struck. Conall retracted his hand and cried out, but he checked; the spots where the wolf's teeth had bitten him glowed white for just a moment. The adder retreated to a niche within the tree between the two roots where Aedan had sat.

Aedan jumped over to his friend. "What is wrong with you? Did it bite you?" He grabbed Conall's hand.

"Relax. It did bite me, but it didn't break the skin." He pulled his hand back and sat up. "Where did it go?"

"Into the tree. That's why it was on my lap. I was sitting near where it lives." He shivered.

"I think this is where the Nionslat is. An adder in an ash tree. Makes sense, eh?"

Nodding, Aedan stepped closer to a small opening at the base of the tree but avoided getting too close. He questioned how they could even check the tree for the wand and suggested they should probably wait for the adder to leave its home to feed before looking for it. Morning moved forward.

"Maybe it won't come out because we're here?" Aedan rocked back and forth on a root.

"Could be. How long do you want to wait?"

"Where are we going?" — he smirked — "If this is the right tree, we need to find the wand."

Aedan shrugged. "It's not like we're going to stick our hand in the tree."

Conall grinned in response.

"You really are daft. That's a poisonous snake! You got lucky last time, but there's no telling what will happen if you shove your hand in there. There has to be another way."

Moving toward the opening in the bark, Conall knelt slowly. "I don't think so. Trust me."

"Let me use a little fyre. Maybe scare it from the tree?" Aedan opened his palm.

"And burn down the tree?" Conall touched his torc, making a silent prayer.

He extended his hand, holding it steady. Little by little, he put it inside the opening.

Aedan tapped his foot on the ground. "Anything?"

"Shhh," Conall said softly, staring at the blackness.

He had extended half his forearm into the tree. Gasping, he held up his other hand to stop Aedan from approaching. He mumbled that something touched his hand, probably the snake's tongue. The beads of sweat that had formed on his forehead merged and dropped down his temples and his nose. The snake moved along his hand, the glossy slickness of the scales sliding over his skin. As he pushed his hand in more, he made the slightest smile. A loose stick was within the touch of his fingertips. He flicked the stick once and waited to see what the snake would do. When nothing happened, he nudged it closer to his hand, eventually hooking it with two fingers. Still, the snake moved around his hand and wrist, gliding over them without stopping. Once he was able to close his hand around the wand, he slowly retracted his elbow. His forearm came out, but it had a passenger. The adder had wrapped itself around his arm, its head near the inside of his elbow, the rest coiled around his wrist and hand. The light touch of the flicking tongue tickled the tender skin of his arm, but he kept himself from laughing. Once he had removed his entire hand, the adder raised its head, moving it closer to Conall's face.

Speaking softly, Conall lowered his head a little. "Adder of the Ash, we mean you no harm. You have guarded the Nionslat, and now our quest has need of it. We will take good care of it, as you have. I swear it."

All around them, a sound like the blending of leaves rustling and breathing grew. Aedan jumped a little at a sensation near his feet, and he froze as he looked down. Slithering past him, a few dozen adders moved, heading for Conall. He opened his mouth to say something, but he kept clipping his own words.

In a low voice, Aedan stammered, "Brigid protect us... C-Conall. We're not alone. *Don't* move."

Turning his head as far as it would go, Conall blanched. When he turned back to the adder on his arm, the snake's head was still at eye level. Its tongue flicked, and it didn't budge. The other adders climbed his legs, moving around his torso. When they stopped, Conall's legs and other arm were hidden beneath scaly serpent bodies. Out of the corner of his eye, movement of flicking tongues and undulating snakes kept him from moving. Aedan froze. He would try to say something, but then he would stop himself.

"J-Just so you know, *all* of the snakes are now on you. They're not doing much, but they're there."

Conall closed his eyes and slowed his breathing, a bit challenging with his body surrounded by adders. The single adder on his other arm moved closer to his face until its nose touched Conall's. The boy's eyes opened and widened — he whimpered. Then, the adder rubbed the back of its head on Conall's nose and returned to the tree. Nothing else happened for what must have seemed like an eternity to him, but one by one, the adders unfurled their bodies and returned to their homes. As soon as he was liberated, Conall dropped to his knees and took a deep breath.

"Are you...?" Aedan crouched next to him.

All Conall could do was nod a few times, taking deep breaths and exhaling slowly.

"I'll be fine. I just need a moment."

Before he stood up, he caught a glimpse of something carved into the bark above the opening. It was an Ogham symbol.

"Would you look at that?" Conall ran his thumb across the nubbly etching. "Mishna." Courage.

"What is it?" Aedan edged closer, watching for the adder.

"A test of courage. This marking on the tree." He laughed to himself. "*You* get to go for the next wand."

Conall examined the Nionslat before putting it with the others in his pack. Before they left the island, he drew the Ogham for gratitude in the dirt. Aedan playfully scolded his friend, saying that his luck would run out if he weren't careful. He made Conall promise he wouldn't stick his hand inside any trees anymore. Laughing, Conall agreed. When Aedan asked what gave him the courage to do it, his friend replied that he wasn't sure, but it had something to do with his dream.

—⚏—

The stones in the water emerged as they moved from tree to tree. Despite the danger of being away from sacred trees, the stone path offered more stable footholds. A storm raged ahead, with the beginnings of cooler wynds making the hair stand up on their arms. The trees became sparser as well, meaning they'd have to walk unprotected through the torrent. If the water rose enough, it would obscure the path again, and they'd have no safe places to travel. Wetland stretched as far as they could see, and only broken, dead trees remained as reminders of what once thrived in this part of Bealdrágan. It was hard for them to believe, Aedan commented, that anything could flourish in such a forsaken place. Conall reminded him of what Elder Daithi had said about growth and destruction. Everything had a purpose. For some reason, these rotted trees must be a part of a larger cycle. Unconvinced, Aedan scowled at the idea of having to be surrounded by death and said under his breath that he had grown tired of the darkness. He felt it beneath his skin, crawling like insects just waiting to chew their way through. With the drop in temperature, mists rose over the moss-laden water with lightning from the distant storm showing shapes in silhouette. With the haziness making it a challenge to see the stones until they near, Conall growled to himself, until he remembered a dríocht from the druid's book and informed Aedan he wanted to try it. Using the map might be easier, Aedan replied, especially since they had three wands.

Conall held the wands in one hand near the map while Aedan held it open. An animated manuscript showed the haze over the path with the downpour ahead. Beyond the storm, images returned to their more primitive sketchiness, meaning the magic of the wands wasn't strong enough. What they could see, though, was a patch of black like spilled ink. Conall said they would have to try the dríocht. As a precaution, they inspected one another's packs to be sure they were secure. Using magic had unforeseen consequences. Holding his palms together, he opened them, keeping his fingers interlocked.

"*Aeir, soiléir mo chosán.*" After asking the air to clear his path, he blew into his palms. Nothing happened.

"Maybe you have to say it three times?"

"That's not what the book said, Aedan. Just give me a moment." He took a cleansing breath, positioned his hands, and tried again.

From behind them, a gust forced its way past, opening a tunnel into the mist. Before it dissipated, Conall saw something in the path. He leaned over, dropping his hands to his knees. Magic certainly took its toll. He composed himself and told Aedan an object blocked their way about four stones ahead. When the mists resumed, they thickened, so in order to see their next stone, they had to stand at the edge of the one they were on. Fortunately, the distance between the stones wasn't that big, but the obstacle in their path made Aedan grumble. A dead tree had fallen, its bark worn away with time. Even with both sets of their hands pushing, they only moved it a hair at a time. About two feet wide, the log was slippery, but Conall climbed onto it to see what was blocking it from the other side. The next stone lay a few feet away. If they stood on the log and jumped, they might not get a firm enough footing and slip into the water. Their best bet, Aedan surmised, was to move the log. If they could get it into the water between the stones, they could ride it until they reached land. Putting his hands to his face, Conall groaned. They took hold of what they could on the tree and rocked it back and forth to get the leverage they needed. It would barely budge. Using their growing frustration, they kept at it until a crack of thunder split the skies, followed by a blinding flash. The rains had arrived.

The cold cloudburst pelted them like little arrows. It didn't take long for the water around them to rise. Soon the stones would be covered, and they wouldn't be able to find their way. They decided to mount the log and wait out the rains. Aedan used his staff to push against the rock below, growling as he did it, muttering how a little leverage would move them. Conall tried as well. Nothing helped. The storm continued to thrash them for almost an hour before the log began to move. The water had risen just enough. Pushing with all their might, they succeeded in loosening the log from the stone and began floating alongside the path they couldn't use. With boots almost submerged, they coordinated their efforts to make the log glide. Lightning overlapped thunderclaps — the worst was directly overhead. Sheets of rain coupled with the mists made it even hard for Aedan to see Conall, who was sitting only a few feet in front of him. Moss no longer concealed what swam beneath, and the sight of red-scaled water serpents made the boys lift their feet up as much as they could. The creatures made no attempt to attack but merely moved alongside the floating tree. Blinded, the boys did what they could to keep the log from hitting the stones or rolling over. The downpour diminished to a drizzle, and the mist lightened, giving them a sight they had longed for — land. Pushing hard, they launched the log onto the muddy bank. Before they moved on, the red water serpents broke the water and dove into the murk, making the boys shriek and jump back. Aedan joked that, had they fallen in, those red-scaled swimmers would have cleaned all the flesh from their bones. Unamused, Conall smacked him on the back of the head.

The landscape returned to what it had when they had arrived, barren with toothy crags. They had managed to get through the wetlands with bruises, scrapes, and much emotional battering, but they had survived the best they could. With no sacred trees in sight, no trees at all in fact, they both agreed to push forward until they absolutely needed to stop. Checking the map, they had a clearer view ahead, including a final barrier to cross. That inky patch, though, would be another unknown they would have to deal with before they could leave Bealdrágan.

—ϫϫ—

With each nook and niche, Aedan remarked how he expected to see the three Cosantóirí appear, with their bronze cauldron and appetite for bones. The question as to how they were "protectors" had yet to be answered, especially after everything the boys had endured. They rounded a mound of boulders, and a bronze cauldron was there, nestled in the curve. Spinning their heads around, they scoured the path for the three women. The pot lay empty except for wispy cobwebs. Shrugging, they took a few steps forward, but a rustling made them turn, and on various rocks sat Mórga, Thano, and Cerro.

"How funny that we just asked ourselves whether we'd see you again, and there you are."

Mórga cackled. "Son of Odhrain, names have power. Invoking them touches the magic in the world. You have fared well, we see. Either you have luck or skill."

"Or both." Conall leaned forward, his chest puffed out.

"Perhaps, perhaps," Cerro squeaked. "You asked for sight when last we met. Is it vision you seek now?" She had a strange smile, alluring and odd.

Aedan asked what the price would be to answer a question. It depended, Cerro replied, on what answer they wanted. Pulling him aside, Conall needed to know what his friend was thinking, and Aedan whispered back. The concern on Conall's face made Aedan roll his eyes and try to convince his friend that this could change everything. Then, it's worth a lot, Conall retorted, and they didn't have anything to give, except more blood, and he didn't want to part with more than what he had already given. Mórga, combing her long, white hair with a comb of bone, added that there were no such things as questions without price. Even the most basic of questions had a cost, gaining knowledge meant losing innocence. Ask the question, she added, and they would learn the price.

"Well... we want to know, how will gathering the thirteen wands of Danu prevent the Coah na Shirah?"

At the same time, all three women cackled. Thano sprinkled something into the cauldron, it coughed fyre, and then the flames receded. As earlier, water rose to the brim, getting a mirror-like sheen. Mórga stepped down to the path, hobbling over to the boys. She leaned in close.

"What you ask has great value. Are you prepared to pay the price?"

"W-Well, what *is* the price?" Conall tapped his palms together.

Aedan crossed his arms, and his wide eyes bounced from the crone to Conall. Mórga took Conall's hands in her own.

"Child, I see purpose and valor within you. But I also see shadows. You are tied to great power, like your friend. I must ask *you*… why do you want to know? Will that change your fate? If we give you the answer, will you be bolder in pursuit or will it weaken your resolve? Knowledge for knowledge's sake holds little value."

Aedan leaned closer to Mórga. "How can we know what we'll do with the knowledge before we know it?"

"That, my dear boy, is the question you must first answer for yourselves." She doddered back to her stony perch.

The boys stepped away from the women to confer. Aedan's opinion was that they'd figure it out, so why pay a price for the knowledge now. While Conall did see his point, he argued that peace of mind would be a good thing, and it could help them make better choices on their journey. The cost could be great, like losing a limb or an eye, Aedan put forth. Trying to make a joke, Conall said he could hobble around and started jumping up and down on one leg. They *had* to agree, Aedan said, since the cost could affect them both. Another idea came to Conall, and they joined the women.

"What could we get, with the same question, with another drop of our blood?"

Cerro's mouth widened into a grin, wider than one would think a mouth could go. She put her bony hands on the edges of the cauldron, the icovellavna on her arms glowing white. The same thing happened to Thano and Mórga's symbols.

"Clever though you think you be, you cannot trick the sisters three." All three women spoke as one. "Your question's price would have been each one tooth, but a drop of blood each gives you lesser sooth."

Conall put a hand up to his mouth and narrowed his brows, shaking his head. Moving his tongue around his mouth, Aedan expressed his disapproval. He told the Cosantóirí that he and his friend would be keeping their teeth. A muffled giggle came from the women, and Thano held out her gnarled palm over the water. A bronze dagger rose, its point piercing the surface until it hovered over the cauldron. One by one, the boys touched it, and their blood was absorbed into the blade. Once the dagger descended into the water, the liquid turned crimson. Tiny sparks, like tadpoles, swam around, until they faded.

"Pay heed, young ones, to these things three, as they regard your destiny: to fulfill your task, all thirteen wands you will need. Of them all, *two* are the key. And last, by those matched to you will you strengthened be."

The skies above darkened to grey, clouds swarming, until lightning flashed. A fork of electricity struck the cauldron, and when the light subsided, there sat the bronze pot, again filled with cobwebs as if the Cosantóirí had never been there. Stunned to silence, the boys called for the women, but only the wynd replied, and it had nothing to say. Where grey skies once were, filled with churning clouds, a pale blue returned, attended by wisps of white clouds.

"I guess they really didn't want us asking more questions." Conall shrugged. "Did you understand the last part?"

Aedan exhaled hard. "I'm not sure. So, was that worth more of our blood?"

Conall stared at the cauldron. "I hope so. I'm not giving up any more to anyone in exchange for answers, that's for sure."

Along the meandering path they continued, trying to work out the last piece of information from the women, but since they had no answer, they fell into quietude. Their shoulders slumped as they walked, and occasionally Aedan threw pebbles to keep himself occupied while Conall lost himself in thought. At one point, Aedan tossed a pebble at Conall's leg, and the latter swiped it away as if it were a bug. By the third pebble, Conall caught on and started throwing them back. Laughter filled the void of their journey.

—⁂—

A clear patch of dirt surrounded by rocks on the west side of the path became a place to stop and dry out since their layers were still damp. Conall gathered withered branches from the few blasted trees, those split by lightning, and made a fyre while Aedan did the torc-enhanced protection circle. Despite the cooler temperature, they stripped down to their undergarments so their clothes could dry. Aedan, cringing, used one of the twigs to scrape the moss from his feet which had pruned from so much exposure to water. The rain had done little to cleanse them, only wash off the surface dirt. Cold ashes from the fyre rubbed onto the skin helped minimize the stench of being in the mud. By the time their clothes had dried, all they had to do was shake everything out and the dirt fell away. They wondered if Liam had somehow enchanted their clothes or it was something he treated the material and leather with. All of the perishable foods they had from Arvador had been destroyed by the water. Only dried meat remained, but it had a gamey taste according to Aedan. Conall, once he chewed it a bit, said it tasted fine, but he grimaced while eating it.

"I miss my bed. I could wrap myself in the wool blanket my mum made and sleep for a week." Conall tore some meat with his teeth.

"Well, I'd give anything for a bath. The ashes aren't doing much to hide the stench." Aedan waved his hand by his face.

Conall chuckled. "I know. What good are clean clothes if we both stink like pigs in a sty. I guess it's better than nothing, right?"

The crackling fyre sent up sparks that tumbled and swirled. Aedan held his palms to the fyre, staring into it. He stood up, stretching his arms. Without a word, with his gaze locked on the swaying flames, he began moving his body in a slow dance. Conall laughed, but then he recognized the movements from when they were with Elder Daithi. Amused by his friend's whimsical decision, he joined him. Before long, their dancing complemented each other, their arms going in arcs while their legs bent and kicked. Aedan took his movements around the fyre, using the music in his mind to inspire him. Even though Conall didn't hear that music, he followed his friend's example until they had made many revolutions. As if they had rehearsed it, both bowed toward the fyre, finishing their dance. The boys erupted in laughter that echoed throughout the crags until their outburst dwindled to just smiles.

"You know something? I needed that." Aedan checked his clothes. "With all we've seen, we need to take the time to dance more."

Conall got dressed. "I couldn't agree more." He made a flourish with his hands. "Dancing like we just did made me realize how much our quest really is like one long, drawn out dance."

"Maybe life is like that, too." Aedan smirked.

"Look at you, getting all thoughtful. But you're right. Life *is* like that, isn't it? Some parts smooth, others ragged. Some slow. Some quick."

"How are we going to dance our way out of here?" Aedan waved his hands.

Conall stamped out the fyre. "Like we just did. Together."

Smiling for the first time in a while, and with newfound energy from the dance, the boys continued north.

—⟶⟵—

Crags diminished until the boys reached a hill of dead grasses over which the land became cracked limestone similar to the karst they had seen to the south. At the base of the hill, a regular dirt path began again. It was hard for them to believe they were still in the Dragon's Mouth. In the distance, a bright light flickered, like stone on fyre. On either side, a rock wall spread. Before they would reach the way out, they had to pass a dolmen to the east, just a little way off the road. Something about the tomb seemed off to them. Aedan checked the map. That was the source of the inky spot. By the time they reached the path that split toward the dolmen, someone was sitting against it. Aedan stopped Conall, telling him he didn't feel right leaving the main road, but Conall insisted, saying whoever it was could be hurt. Reluctantly, Aedan followed but slowed his pace when he got a closer look. The figure wore black leather armor and Aedan said whoever it was had a similar bearing to someone they had seen before. However, something was different. He took hold of Conall's arm.

"We've come across men in black leather armor before."

Conall scrutinized the man more and pulled out his staff. "It must be Dother, then. I was so willing to help someone in need that I would have blindly walked right up to him. What do we do?"

"We get back on the path. That portal up ahead is the way out. The dragon's fyre."

They had resumed their travels when a heavy, raspy voice called out to them.

"I am who you think I am."

Aedan and Conall kept going.

"I am not here to harm you." Raising his voice, the man grunted as he adjusted his position.

Conall spun around and took a few steps. "Why should we believe you? Isn't it in your nature to trick people?"

Dother nodded. "Aye. I did come into Bealdrágan to look for you, to stop you. But—"

"See, Conall? I *told* you. Let's go."

"In my haste to find you, I met up with that she-serpent." —his voice dropped—"She took my leg."

Both stopped in their tracks.

"Then you got what you deserved." Aedan spat. "Conall, we have to go."

Holding up his hand to Aedan, Conall took steps toward Dother. He stared at the remaining part of the man's leg oozing blood, darker than one would see.

"Why can't you just disappear or get Carman to whisk you away?"

Dother lowered his head. "She abandons those who fail her."

Aedan rolled his eyes and sighed. "Conall…"

Conall continued. "So, she just left you here… to die?"

"Aye." He wouldn't make eye contact with Conall.

"You don't believe him, do you?" Aedan threw up his hands.

"I-I don't know. It's possible, isn't it?" Conall stared at the man's leg.

"This could all be a deception! A dríocht to make us think he lost his leg."

Dother, his voice labored, turned to Aedan. "Assuming that is true, why go to all this trouble to deceive you? I could have stopped you without an illusion, if I were whole—"

"Ah! See, he admits he was going to—"

"If you had not interrupted me, I would have said that I could have stopped you without an illusion if I were whole, *but* I chose not to. I could have lain in wait until you arrived and attacked you."

"So, what, you had a change of heart?" Aedan put his hand to his chest. "We're supposed to believe you're no longer evil? That you just changed?"

Aedan tried to convince Conall they should just go before it got too late in the day. He appealed to Conall's gentler nature and asked him why he hesitated. There was no reason to believe that Dother was telling the truth. With Dian and Dubh, their actions came from a place of darkness. As a son of Carman, Dother would be the same. Aedan's voice grew louder and gruffer when Conall said nothing, which prompted Aedan to call his friend naive. All Conall would say was that what Aedan saw as being naive, he saw as optimism. It's not that he trusted Dother; on the contrary, he was quite skeptical of the man's motives. But he didn't feel right leaving him in Bealdrágan injured to where he could die. That is not how he was raised, he told Aedan. His mother had taught him to be compassionate, even to those who didn't seem to deserve it.

Dother told them that, if he could have healed himself, he would have. Caorthanach's poison prevented him. He didn't have the means to walk, otherwise he would have tried to leave The Dragon's Mouth and searched for a healer who would be sympathetic enough to help him. Since the man was incapacitated and seemingly unable to do anything, Conall bowed his back and stepped closer.

"We've done nothing to hurt you. Why are you so determined to stop us? Do you really want the Ársa and the Fonn to bring the Coah na Shirah?"

No response came from Dother. Instead, he focused on Conall's face and the emotion it conveyed.

Conall leaned closer. "Are you not going to answer me? The world as we know it could end." He threw his hands up.

Aedan got close to Conall's ear. "We need to go. Now. Leave him to rot."

Glaring at Dother, Conall tightened his fists.

"No. He's done nothing to us. We should at least get him out of Bealdrágan. He can't die here."

"And after that?"

Conall exhaled, "I don't know." He turned to Dother. "If we agree to help you get through the dragon's fyre, will you let us bind you?"

Dother hesitated, but then he nodded. He extended his arms, expecting them to be tied together. Before he knew what was happening, Dother had Conall's torc around his neck, and the boy spoke a dríocht.

"I call upon the Horned One to bind you to our purpose, that you bring no harm." — he touched the torc — "By the moon and stars, by the sky above, and the earth upon which we stand. So shall it be. So shall it be. So shall it be."

Aedan asked where Conall got that piece of magic from, but then Aedan figured it out and smiled, asking how long it would last.

"Until sundown, unfortunately. So, we need to move. Help me with him."

Conall and Aedan wore their packs over their chest so that Dother could put his arms over their shoulders. The boys turned their heads and wrinkled their noses at the smell of sweat-soaked leather mixed with Caorthanach's poison that lingered at the severed leg. The son of Carman stood a head taller than they were, but he had to hunch over when he hopped. He grunted with each footstep, bearing his full weight on the single foot. All three had to stop to rest every ten or fifteen paces due to the weight of the man's brawn and armor. At the rate they were able to move, it would take them at least two hours to get to the gate. Dother grumbled every chance he got to the point where Aedan threatened to drop him in the middle of the road if he didn't stop. Conall parted his lips slightly as if he wanted to say something, but no words came out. At the halfway point, the boys had Dother lean against a tree stump so they could stretch. Conall offered Dother some water from his water skin. Aedan cringed when Conall put the same skin to his lips to drink. Despite how his brothers had acted, Dother avoided eye contact with the boys and said nothing.

Much to their surprise, they come across no obstacles to reach the portal out of Bealdrágan. The path climbed inclines and descended steep switchbacks which made moving with Dother a challenge, but they didn't have to get past any serpents or creatures that would lure them into caves. About ten feet before the portal, the road changed to what resembled rough cobblestones. The fyre raged before them, darkening the arch with soot. The wall stretching from both sides disappeared far in the distance. They would most assuredly have to endure this last task if they wanted to leave The Dragon's Mouth. At the top of the arch, pointing downward, were spikes that were meant to resemble dragon's teeth.

With no rocks around, the boys lowered Dother to the ground so they could assess what they needed to do before pressing on. Conall wanted to know what Aedan thought they should do about Dother once they passed through. They couldn't carry him on their journey. Aedan suggested they leave him at a crossroads. At least then he would have a chance to find a healer. Conall wasn't entirely convinced of that, but he didn't have a better option. Dother wasn't looking particularly good either, even with his traditional pallor and harsh features. Caorthanach's poison must have worked its way into his body from the wound, Aedan surmised. Conall inspected the portal for what had to be an inscription, much like on the other archway when they entered. He removed some dirt from symbols along the outer edge of the stone and did, in fact, reveal something.

"Gaze upon Belenus' crown ere you see your truth." Conall scratched his head. "Nothing is ever easy, is it?"

While the boys pondered the inscription, Dother broke his silence.

"Sunrise," he grumbled.

"Ah. Thanks." Aedan scowled at him. "We're camping here, then."

With the sun nearing the horizon, Conall handed a blanket to Dother who took it without a word. When Conall went over to Aedan, Dother reached up and tugged at the torc, but it wouldn't come loose. Aedan volunteered to find something for a fyre but advised Conall to let him know if he needed any help, glancing over at their new traveler. As soon as Aedan was gone, Conall checked the sun's position. Once it dipped below the horizon a little, he went up behind Dother, touched the torc, and repeated the dríocht. It would last until the next sunset. Dother asked if it was entirely necessary to keep him bound since he wasn't a threat while he was missing half a leg. Conall reminded him that they had met his brothers and didn't trust him. Night had set upon them when Aedan returned, handing Conall a bundle wrapped in cloth. He had fyrewood under one arm and a rabbit he'd caught in his other hand. Conall unraveled the parcel, recognizing the contents, and found a few rocks near where Aedan was setting up the fyre. He pounded what Aedan brought him until it was a pulp. Unfortunately, Aedan couldn't use the fyre from the portal to ignite the campfyre—it didn't work the same as regular fyre; he'd have to use his dríocht. In a small metal cup, he heated water into which went Conall's mash. As soon as the water reached the right temperature, Conall took the cup off the flames with a cloth and let the contents steep. He tasted the liquid with his finger, passing the cup to Dother.

"Here. Drink."

"What is it?" Dother took the cup.

"Burdock tea. It'll help you get rid of the poison in your blood. Drink the entire cup."

Dother sniffed the liquid, giving Conall a strange expression. Conall took a sip to show him it wasn't poison.

"Happy now? I couldn't harm you even if I wanted to. The enchantment that binds you from hurting us also keeps us from hurting you. Trust me. Be thankful for that. Aedan wouldn't hesitate to bring you pain."

Dother drank the tea. "And you?" He returned the cup.

"As I said earlier, I was raised to be merciful, even to those who might hurt me."

"Mercy shows weakness. Why should you care if I live or die?"

Conall leaned into Dother's face. "Having compassion doesn't mean I have to like you. All life has purpose, though, I guess. Even yours."

He sat next to Aedan who had put skewers of rabbit over the fyre. The skin had been scraped clean and wrapped in cloth until they could find a way to use it. It showed disrespect to the animal, as well as the gods, to discard any useful part.

"How is he?" Aedan poked the embers.

"He'll be all right for now. The burdock won't clear all the poison, but it'll help."

"Look, I'm not happy he's here, but I understand your reason. All life has purpose. Isn't that what Elder Daithi said? Once we get him through the portal, we'll deal with our next step. I *will* be keeping my eye on him."

"Oh, don't worry. So will I."

The fyre popped and crackled, the smoke carrying with it the aroma of dinner. Conall brought Dother a skewer and the three quietly tore bits of rabbit off with their teeth. Aedan wrapped the bones in another cloth to dispose of later. The portal's fyre looked blue at night as opposed to the brighter orange during the day, perhaps a warning not to enter. Dother slid his way over to the glowing embers of the smaller campfyre to keep warm. In the ambient glow of both, Dother took on a more sinister appearance, largely because of the blue fyre coupled with his black leather armor, and his eyes shimmered. He said nothing while the boys talked among themselves, paying little attention to them at all. Rather, he stared into the embers. An occasional branch tossed in ignited to keep the fyre going at least as long as they were awake. Conall knelt next to him and asked how his wound felt. The pain had dulled to a low ache, he said. Being careful, Conall removed the leather around the severed limb to reveal the skin. He had made more burdock tea and dabbed a tea-soaked cloth on the wound. Dother sucked air through his teeth as Conall made contact, grunting with each touch. Once he had cleaned the wound as much as was possible, Conall poured the remaining tea over it. He had torn one of the blankets into strips and wrapped the stump loosely, tying it with a leather cord just enough to keep the cloth in place. While Conall tended to Dother, Aedan observed the man's every move and expression.

"You know that my brothers were testing you. The sons of Carman wouldn't be turned way by simple dríocht. Dubh and Dian will strike again, and next time, your child's magic won't save you." Dother inspected Conall's handiwork.

"Why didn't they just kill us when they had the chance?" Aedan took a few steps closer.

Dother roared with laughter. "Where's the fun in that? Playing with your prey is half the amusement. Rest assured, lads, when they come for you, they'll leave nothing behind but your bones, if you're lucky. That you got past Caorthanach says you're clever, though."

Aedan leaned over into Dother's face. "Well, we got past *her* with our child's magic."

Dother lay with his back to them so he could be on his good leg. "Lucky, then," he muttered.

Since he wasn't tired, Aedan said he would take the first watch. From the moment Conall's head touched the ground, he was asleep. Aedan couldn't tell if Dother was asleep, though.

The Dragon's Mouth had no birds who sang, so silence that pressed against them filled the night. Embers glowed bright red and orange through an ashy skin, giving off the slightest illumination. Aedan, with the faintest slip of a smile, rested his eyes on Conall. As he moved to Dother, that smile flattened. His eyes bore into the man as if to look inside him and see his intentions. He turned his attention to a starless sky. Being inside this otherworldly place, it wasn't entirely a surprise that stars didn't shine. What else would shine its light in the mouth of a great beast except that of the storm and the fiery breath? Aedan remained locked in his own mind until morning. At the faint glow in the sky before sunrise, he nudged Conall with his foot.

"Why didn't you wake me to take over? You haven't slept all night." He yawned and glanced back at Dother who was sitting, his one good leg pulled up. "Did you sleep well?"

"Yes." Dother tightened the straps on his bracers and adjusted his armor. Strands of his black hair hung over his eyes, the rest sat like a shoulder-length shroud.

"We'll see Belenus' crown soon, so we should be ready." Aedan stamped out the remaining embers, sending sparks fleeing.

Conall straightened his tunic, swinging his arms to stretch. "Once in the fyre, we must accept the truths about ourselves. Otherwise, we're stuck in the fyre until we do."

"Then, I guess we won't see *him* on the other side, will we?" Aedan chortled, nodding at Dother.

Offering his hands, Conall helped the man stand. Dother put his arm over their shoulders, and they moved closer to the portal whose flames had turned from blue to pale orange. Sunrise edged closer. Once the fyre glowed brightly, they all moved into it until it consumed them. It flared around the edges of the stone and then died down a bit. They would have to see if they could handle their truths — all of them.

18 | FIRES OF TRUTH

iving in to the fyres within is what it means to be in a dragon's mouth. In a *real* dragon, this amounts to being incinerated. In Bealdrágan, however, one must confront the harshest truths inside his heart and mind.

Unlike the entry point to this realm where the heart's pain is the key, truth doesn't have to hurt. Seeing a part of who someone is, and ultimately accepting it, can be a positive experience, almost life-affirming. On the other hand, accepting a hard truth might leave someone emotionally scarred. Anyone who passed through the portal could never really say how long he or she was within the flames. Some thought it was hours; others said days. Regardless, they all came through it at some point, in whatever condition the truth saw fit.

Stumbling out of the stone arch first, Aedan fell to his knees, his body still smoldering from the fyre that didn't burn. He gasped, extending his arms to find his balance. Getting his bearings took a moment since the land beyond Bealdrágan looked nothing like the land before it. As soon as he realized he was safe, he fell on his back, his arms wide. His breathing slowed to normal. A pale blue morning sky empty of any clouds left him with nothing to focus on. Unlike the night before, where no sounds of birdsong interrupted the silence, different tunes created melodies and harmonies all around. Aedan sat up. Reddish-orange flames poured forth from the gate, with no sign of Conall or Dother inside.

The next one to exit the fyre was the one Aedan had no interest in seeing. Dother fell forward, whimpering like a scared child as he clawed his way from the portal. He lay on his stomach, arms splayed out, sobbing. Aedan turned his attention toward the flames. Whatever truths you had to deal with, Aedan muttered, I hope they brought you torment.

Dother pushed his arms up to see where he was, dirt clinging to his face. When his eyes landed on Aedan, he snarled.

"This-This was *your* doing!"—he growled, throwing dirt toward Aedan—"*You* made me do this!" He made a guttural noise and flipped himself over on his back.

"You know, for a big, burly son of a witch, you're acting like a child. You didn't have to come with us."

Dother, grunting, tried to crawl over to Aedan, but his one foot couldn't move him more than a few inches. His stringy hair fell over his face. In the daylight, his grayish skin went with his black leather armor which, in the brighter hues of morning, revealed stains of crimson and gouges from prior battles. Metallic studs ornamented the chest plate and shoulders, with more prominent spikes on the bracers. It was then that Aedan's eyes widened when he saw the scabbard strapped to Dother's thigh with the black diamond-encrusted handle of a dagger. Rocking his body, Dother managed to sit up. He pulled his fists to his head and cringed.

Aedan smirked. "What's wrong?"

"Nothing!" The man rocked as much as he could having only one and a half legs.

"Fine. Don't tell me."

Grabbing the torc with both hands, Dother pulled hard enough to make himself yowl. He shook his hands, looking at the palms that now had the grooves from the metal. Trying again, he made noises like a beast.

"Get this damn thing off me! Now!"

Chuckling, Aedan stood in front of him and crossed his arms.

"I can't. First, Conall put it on you. Second, the dríocht ends at sundown. Why are you so agitated all of a sudden? Did the truth hurt?"

Dother glared and reached up to grab him, but he ended up on his back due to the momentum. He pounded his fists into the ground repeatedly. A different sound made Aedan turn around; Conall lurched from the fyre, and Aedan caught him as he fell forward. He lowered his friend to the ground.

"Conall! You all right?"

Aedan poured some water on his face, and Conall sat up, disoriented. As soon as he locked eyes on Aedan, he pulled him into a tight hug. Dother laughed to himself.

"Weren't you just shrieking like a crazed dog a minute ago?" Aedan helped Conall stand.

"We made it?" Conall looked back at the fiery arch. "I can't believe we're finally out of that place."

Dother, who had been grumbling to himself, stopped when Conall approached and got down on one knee.

"How's your leg?" He reached to check it, but the man turned away. "I need to check the wound."

"Leave me be! You and your friend have done enough."

Aedan pulled Conall out of Dother's earshot.

"Tell me what happened in the fyre."

Conall explained that, at first, he felt like he was drowning in a flaming sea, but when he adjusted, thoughts ran through his head. Memories crashed into him, like charging animals, forcing him to relive moments of his life. He remembered random times like when his father wanted him to use the plow for the first time. Or, when he was teased and didn't want to sit with the other children for morning lessons. All his insecurities came back to him, wearing him down. But he accepted that as part of who he was. Every time he ran off to chase animals or put himself into harm's way made him see his impulsiveness in times that frightened him, even when he would try to deny it to himself. Other visions surrounded his loving nature, loyalty, and compassion — truths that he wholly embraced. He stopped talking, and his expression grew dour. Aedan leaned closer.

"One of the truths that I never really wanted to admit to myself, but now I have to… Aedan, I love Rinn and Siobhan so much, is that… I want to know who my birth parents are."

Aedan put a hand on Conall's shoulder, nodding.

"I-I think Rinn and Siobhan, your *parents*, would understand. I do."

They checked to see what Dother was doing, and he sat muttering to himself like a senile old man. Conall redirected the inquiry back to his friend. All the past moments where Aedan had been protective and strong, or sensitive, were truths that he accepted without question. He felt those parts of who he was made him bold. Both Odhran and Saoirse had raised him to express himself and take responsibility for his emotions. Buried feelings would unearth themselves in ugly ways. He told Conall that he hadn't fully accepted his mother's death, even though he knew it was real. He *had* grieved. A memory that surfaced was the day of her burial, with the members of the clan. He remembered leaning against his father, taking what strength he could from that man. Aedan recalled feeling his father's hand on his shoulder, gently squeezing. But when he looked up and saw Odhran's scruffy face, his eyes red from hours of tears, Aedan realized something, a truth he had hidden for a long time.

"Conall, I shouldn't feel this way, but I do. I know that my mother was sick. I even know that the Fomoragh had a hand in it. But the truth is… I-I've been blaming my father for her death. I think that's why we left things the way we did, or I should say that *I* did."

"You didn't know about the Fomoragh until after you left home, Aedan. We'll figure it out. I promise." Conall smiled. "Let's get going. I know what I said about trying to help Dother, but the sooner we find him a healer, the better."

At first, Dother wouldn't let the boys help him up so they could travel. Something about his experience in the dragon's fyre unsettled him to where he seemed delusional. They were about to depart without him when he became apologetic and emotional, begging them to take him with them. This time when they supported him on their shoulders, all he would do was mutter to himself in unintelligible words. His own thoughts had distracted him. The boys would catch a glance with each other and exchange that high-eyebrowed look of disbelief. It wasn't long before Aedan was kicking himself for not having checked the map before they set out down the road. At least there *was* a road, Conall added, hoping to give them reason enough not to have to stop. If they had to put Dother on the ground again, they might have to deal with his mood swings.

A crossroads came upon them, and signs pointed to different towns to the west, north, and northeast. Without having seen the map, they wouldn't know where they should go. They each agreed that they just wanted a place with an inn where they could get some good rest, replenish their food, and hopefully find someone to look after Dother. Aedan commented that at least the man's gibberish meant they didn't have to argue with him. Looking down both roads as far as they could, they chose the northeasterly one for no other reason than they saw what they perceived to be smoke in the distance, and that was more than likely a town. Without provisions, they would need to either find an inhabited place or seek out somewhere to hunt. A quaint village in due course appeared. The most they could find were a few farms to get some produce, assuming the farmers were generous because the boys had no more money, and water from nearby streams. At least they could find places for Dother to sit. One man offered them a hefty quantity of fruit if they were willing to help him till his land. They figured it would take a few days to do all that work, and stopping too long with Dother would raise suspicions. It was bad enough that women and children avoided contact when they saw the scraggly-haired, grouchy leather-clad man accompanying the boys.

Conall wondered to Aedan if the poison had worked its way to Dother's mind despite the healing efforts. Aedan thought it had more to do with what the man had seen in the fyre. Truth could change someone if it were something they hadn't expected to see, and with Carman's kin who followed a darker path, those truths could be quite sinister indeed. On their way out of town with just a small amount of fruits and vegetables, they saw a broken cart and decided that would be as good a place as any to set Dother down so they could check the map. They left him munching on an apple while they spread out the parchment, carefully pulling out the wands. The magic of ash, alder, and holly would attract anyone touched with the mystical, and putting them close together near Dother might spark a clearer mind. Coming into focus, the map's pictures showed the road, the prior crossroad, with mountains to the northeast. To the west of their position, they saw lakes, some dolmens, but no Ogham symbols denoting wands. Before the mountains, a forest, and then the paper had a crinkled spot with red markings as if from moisture, but that didn't seem right to them since the rest of the map was dry. Perhaps the red was from ink that had bled, Aedan wondered aloud. The parchment had been wrapped tightly in many skins and tied with strips of leather, so this created a puzzle. Something had disturbed the land itself, Conall guessed, but he couldn't figure out the red, saying it looked like blood. Picking up their travels, they said nothing to Dother who was more amused with his apple core than anything else.

By the time they reached the forest, they sighed and smiled seeing the road well-worn, unlike the watery path they had taken in Bealdrágan. Aedan suggested they find a place to make camp, and he would hunt for dinner since Conall had a much better rapport with Dother. Not many open spaces offered themselves up, but one clearing, strewn with pine needles, was large enough to accommodate all three of them. Aedan waited until Conall did the protection circle before he left them. Dother seemed more than content to sit after all that walking, grumbling how his one leg ached. Conall remembered to enchant the binding spell again, much to Dother's reluctance. Even if he didn't want to be bound, the spell prevented him from doing anything about it. Without his torc, Conall hoped the protection around the clearing would be strong enough. Aedan would have to place his on the circle when he returned to intensify the enchantment. Due to the proximity to the pine needles and the neighboring trees, they couldn't build a fyre. It wouldn't matter, however, since Aedan returned empty-handed, saying he saw no small animals around which seemed odd. He did find bilberries, wild carrots, and dandelions. Their stomachs would barely be satisfied with this and the little they had managed from the village. This time, Conall sat vigil. Forest creatures scurried about under the darkening sky while Aedan slept. Dother plagued by what he saw in his mind, grunted and whispered, rocking back and forth. Under the silver moon, Conall lowered his head, mouthing a silent prayer.

A roar a few hours later made Conall jump up and shocked the other two awake. Aedan assumed a defensive posture with his staff while Conall saw to Dother who had barely shaken the slumber from his eyes. Early morning sounds of the forest continued as if nothing had happened, and Conall suggested that maybe the sound was a dream. Aedan countered with the thought that three people don't usually share dreams. Dother looked more clear-headed, his peculiar expressions and behavior no longer as obvious. While they prepared to leave, even though it was before sunrise, Conall whispered to his friend that he'd prayed to Cerridwen that Dother find some peace of mind, adding that perhaps his prayer had been answered. Aedan thought it had more to do with the sleep than the prayer, but he was thankful not to have to deal with the man's ramblings.

Since they had to support Dother as they walked, the boys couldn't talk to one another as openly, and it was obvious to Conall that Aedan had something on his mind. Conall, too, looked as if he wanted to share. He kept glancing at Dother, signaling to Aedan that what he had to say shouldn't be said in front of the man. As the morning moonbeams cascaded through the forest canopy, they gave the forest an otherworldly glow. Dother perked up a bit when they could see the exit of the forest in the distance. He stared ahead as if he knew what was out there, giving a fleeting look at both boys before turning his attention to the road. A warmer luminescence of new sunlight replaced that of the moon as if the two traded places. By the time they were footsteps from the exit of the trees, snow-capped mountains lay in the distance, larger mountains than the boys had ever seen. The road curved to the left behind a grassy mound. Dother paid more attention to the boys but said nothing. Strange sounds came from around the corner, and then a familiar noise made the boys smile—it was a dragon's roar.

Hobbling as quickly as they could with Dother's arms on their shoulders, they almost lifted him off the ground as their glee increased. Once around the bend, they gasped. It was indeed the dragon they had hoped to see, but he was netted to the ground. On a nearby tree hung an iron cage with another familiar creature, one that Conall knew well. What prevented them from rushing toward their imprisoned companions was a looming figure, armored in silver. His red cloak hid his face in shadow. As tall as three men, he stood between the boys and their animal companions at the base of a large birch tree. His hands dripped with blood. A pile of bones and torn flesh lay at his feet.

"Balor." Dother's one word, spoken from a sane mind, almost made the boys drop him.

"Carman said you had failed her."—Balor picked up a fleshy bone and began gnawing—"It looks to me that you have exactly what she wanted. You have done the Fomoragh proud."

"Do not touch these boys, Balor. If not for them, I would have perished in Bealdrágan."—he turned toward Conall—"Release the binding."

Aedan's face contorted. "No, don't! We don't know what he'll do."

Dother locked his gaze on Balor but spoke to the boys. "I have trusted you thus far. Now it is your turn to trust me."

Conall and Aedan realized they didn't stand a chance against Balor as well as Dother; they would surely be killed. Balor used a twig to pick the remnants of animal flesh from his teeth, keeping his face hidden.

"Just kill them and be done with it." The giant spit more bits of flesh to the ground.

Using only facial expressions, Aedan and Conall conferred without a word, and then Conall nodded. He put his hand on the torc.

"Horned One, hear my plea, may he who once was bound, now be set free. So shall it be. So shall it be. So shall it be."

As Conall put the torc back on his own neck, he grew pale. Neither he nor Aedan knew what would happen next. Rocking his head around to stretch his neck, Dother hopped away from them, standing on his one good leg. He signaled that they should stay behind him. Under his breath, he said something incoherent. From the rhythm and intonations, Conall said to Aedan that it sounded like a dríocht. From beneath the strip of blanket that Conall had tied to Dother's thigh, black mist swirled, descending to the ground. In its wake, what once was removed by Caorthanach, the Mother of Demons, had now regrown. Bare from the knee down, the new appendage had the same greyish tone as the rest of him.

Conall leaned over to his friend. "Did you know he could do that?"

Shaking his head, his mouth open, Aedan just stood there. Dother put his weight on his new leg and turned back to the boys.

"The she-serpent's poison weakened my power. Because of your aid, Conall, I feel like myself. I owe you."

Balor snickered. "So, now you are their minion, eh?"

At first, Dother said nothing. The next dríocht he spoke fixed his leather pants and boot. He shook his arms out from his sides, and short swords flew from his sleeves into his hands. Crossing them together in front of his torso showed distrust toward one's opponent and a willingness to fight.

"I do no one's bidding but my own, you one-eyed fool. I repay a debt of honor, then the slate is clean. Let the boys pass." He turned slightly toward the one's behind him, not taking his eyes off Balor.

"When next we meet, we do so on different sides." — he put both eyes back on Balor, but his words were meant for Aedan and Conall — "Go. Seek your quarry. This is the birch you seek. Find the Beitheslat."

From the moment Dother finished speaking, Balor roared with laughter, escalating until the distant songbirds abandoned their nests.

"If it is the stag you seek, look at my feet." Balor picked up the severed head of the deer, its antlers still attached, and held it high over his head. His hearty laugh filled the skies.

The boys couldn't move. Seeing the carcass of the animal they sought desecrated birthed a rage in them that, had it not been for Dother, they would have met their death at the hands of the giant. Conall's anger and tears sounded like a feral beast who had been taunted one too many times. Aedan seethed in silence. The arms that had once needed the support of the boys to keep Dother upright now became the barrier behind which these same boys would remain unharmed.

"Do not waste your anger on him. Should you see his dreaded eye, your flesh will fall from your bones before the bones themselves wither into dust."

Conall managed to breathe the words, "The wand..." from his tightened jaw.

"You mean this?" Balor held up the bloody twig he had used to clean his teeth between his fingers.

Flames climbed from his fingertips up the fragile spindle of birch until ashes covered his hand. The Beitheslat was no more, and its guardian as well.

"By Danu's grace... the wand... It's gone." Conall deflated to where Aedan had to support him. "What are we—"

Aedan's lip quivered. He tried to part his lips to speak, but he exhaled hard instead. With Conall's face caught in his eyes, he lowered his head. It was then he noticed the key on the torc around Conall's neck and remembered Epona's words: 'When you need it most, it will guide you.' He held his friend by the shoulders.

"Conall, listen to me. You and I have traveled from our homes to train at Dún Ancróga, gone on to the Twisted Trees, through Arvador, and now Bealdrágan. Both Cernunnos and Epona have given their blessings. This is one of those moments we have trained for. We know what to do. If we don't fight now, when do we?" He picked up the fabric that had once been Dother's bandage, tore into two strips, and handed one to Conall. "We make our stand here. In honor of Lann and Fiachra."

In response, Conall put the strip over Aedan's eyes, tying it behind his head. He then took the other strip and tied it around his own eyes. He put his forehead to his friend's.

"Anam cara. Forever."

They each extended their staffs and turned toward Balor, standing on either side of Dother.

"Foolish children," Balor growled. He drew his silver blade. "Your fate will be like that of the stag. I will consume your flesh and wash it down with your own blood. Who do you think you are?"

Conall Mac Rinne and Aedan Mac Odhrain, in one voice, spoke as if they had prepared their whole lives for this one moment.

"We are the guardians of Wynd and Fyre. We are the DragonHawk!"

ABOUT THE AUTHOR

David Berger fell in love with books when he was 8 years old, and from that point on, his life's journey would never be without a book in his hand. An English teacher since 1993, he continues to share his love of literature with his students. His first novel series, *Task Force: Gaea*, started his writing career in 2012, and he has published numerous pieces of short fiction in anthologies in addition to now bringing the tales of Conall and Aedan into the world. He currently lives in Tampa Bay, FL with his sidekick, his dog, Argos.